C000227187

From Me to You

by
Kelly Marie Thompson
and
Garry Berman

To Liz (AKA Mother Liz)
Thank you for buying
this book, and for being
my awesome friend,
Love from

Kelly
(AKA Miss Alice
Frances)
x

For my Mam, Dad, Kate, Ashleigh, Jessica, Nana, Martin, Brian, and Steven for all their support. And thanks to Becka for the early read-throughs, Anna and Joanne for the encouragement, and Penny for the fab book cover.

Thanks to Garry for making the writing of this book fun.

--Kelly

Thanks to Kelly, for being a ruthless editor when I needed one.

Thanks also Susan Ryan and Noel Stevens for their input. And the good people at Panera Bread in Moorestown and Mt. Laurel, New Jersey--Lexie, Jonathan, Maria, Jayla, Aleta, Marc, Steve, Charlie, Alex, Carlene, and everyone else who make me feel so welcome as I sit with my frozen mocha drinks and lunch--several times a week--to work on my books.

For Karen, and for Beatles fans everywhere, from the first generation onward.

--Garry

Front cover illustration by Penelope Hudson

Dizzy Lizzy enjoy

HHudson. X

Also by Kelly Marie Thompson and Garry Berman:

Barkers Upon Tyne: An Original Sitcom

From Me to You

Chapter 1

Maggie Carter hurried her way atop the cobblestones of Liverpool's Mathew Street as fast as she could. Of all days to get out of work late, it had to be that day. She outsmarted herself by taking the early shift, only to find herself in a hurry anyway. There were Beatles tickets at stake—and not just for any Beatles gig at the Cavern. These were for a Beatles gig that, ironically, she hoped wouldn't happen, but she wanted to be there for it just the same.

She tried to concentrate on that only, even though a good number of random thoughts insisted on that particular moment to fly around inside her head.

Among them:

"Why is the 'Mathew' in 'Mathew Street' spelled with only one 't' ?

And:

"Why does this street always seem to be in the shadows, even in the middle of the day in July?"

And:

"If I trip on these cobblestones with my heels on, I'll probably break my neck."

She also thought about the letter she had begun writing that morning, with the hope of having a great ending for it when she continued that night:

21 July 1963

"Dear Ricky,

So far my summer has been amazing. I love the sunshine, and the warmth. And the freedom from college is dead nice. It gives me more time to pursue the other priorities in my life. It's sort of a sad yet happy time at the moment…

But the only thing she really wanted to think about as she negotiated the uneven street, was securing a good spot in line to get the tickets. Hopefully, Claire would already be there holding a place. Maggie knew she'd have to stand in line even to have a chance at it. There were plenty of other 17-year-old girls vying for the same prize—but even if 299 of them got there first, there would still be one left for Maggie.

As she continued running tip-toe down the street, she raced through a patch of sunlight that had found a gap between two brick warehouses. It shone down on her auburn hair as her white blouse and tartan plaid skirt briefly shimmered in the light before returning to the shadows of her route. The end of the line finally came into view. Countless young people stood along a row of brick buildings, waiting. They had been passing the time talking, eating, and smoking as they occasionally turned their attention to the front of the line, which took an abrupt turn into a narrow doorway and down a flight of stairs, enveloped in darkness.

Maggie reviewed more of her letter in her head as she scanned the line.

"In two weeks, the Beatles will have what we fear might be their last concert at the Cavern. It breaks my heart. They might be back someday, but I doubt it. They've been on the telly a lot, touring the country, moving to London. Why would they come back to a hot, smelly hole in the ground in Liverpool when they're big stars?"

Before she could answer her own rhetorical question, she spotted Claire, and hurried to her.

"What took you so long?" Claire asked, with equal parts relief and annoyance.

"The projector broke during the film, and I had to wait until it was fixed and finished before Mr. Dunhill let me go."

"You were running the projector?"

"No, genius, I was at the snack counter, as usual."

Maggie turned to a boy standing behind them in line. He was clad in a black leather jacket and blue jeans, with the leg cuffs upturned to reveal his black boots. His hair was as black as his boots and greased up enough to catch fire if he stood in the sun too long; quite the opposite of Claire's, whose blonde strands turned golden under the sun's rays.

"Trev," Claire said sweetly, "is it all right if Maggie cuts in here?"

Trevor's eyes shifted from side to side.

"Yeah, go ahead. Don't let the lads know I'm such a gentleman. Bad for my image."

"You don't have an image," Maggie reminded him.

"Aye, but I'm working on it."

"Is that why you're wearing a leather jacket on a hot day?"

"Yeah, it's killing me."

"Well take it off then!" she ordered. He complied.

"Bloody hell, that feels better," he exhaled with relief.

Maggie turned her attention to Claire.

"What if it gets sold out before we get ours? I'll die."

"They only went on sale ten minutes ago, so we're in good shape."

Maggie sighed. "I can't believe it's going to be their last time here."

"You should have gotten used to the idea by now, Mags. They've only been back once since, when, February? Besides, wherever they go, we'll go. Our pact, you remember."

Maggie's attention again returned to her letter.

"I guess this must sound silly to you, Ricky, us girls getting so gushy over a rock group. But you'd have to see them on the stage to appreciate it. Besides, you did say you liked some of their records that I sent you..."

An hour later, the girls emerged triumphant from the bowels of the Cavern, clutching their tickets in their hands and squealing with excitement. They were to be a part of history, or so they were convinced--even though they had seen the Beatles perform there thirty-two times before.

"I can't believe we got them!" Maggie shrieked as they ran down the street.

"Guard them with your life."

"Are you kidding me? I'm not letting mine out of my sight."

> *"I hope this won't be the last time I ever see them again in person. It feels as if they're breaking up with me. That is, me and thousands of other Liverpool girls. Claire and I did get our tickets for their final show here, but decided to be more mature about it than the rest of the girls."*

"Maybe we should hold on to the stubs after it's over, they might be worth money one day."

The suggestion caused Maggie to slow their pace. "Oh yeah and who's going to pay money
 for a used ticket stub?"

"I don't know," Claire shrugged. "People do for Elvis. I read about it."

"Yeah, well, there's no accounting for taste. Besides, mine will be going in my scrap book."

They came upon the local newsagents, a shop of which they knew every square inch.

"Hey, let's stop so I can get the new MM," Maggie suggested. "You know, my possible future employer."

MM was their nickname for *Merseyside Music* magazine, the local publication that served as the Bible of the city's music and entertainment scene for young people. They could have referred to is as "MMM," but decided long ago that it sounded too silly to say aloud in public, or anywhere else.

"Mags, I've told you about my cousin who knows the bloke who works for them. I think he prints it. Let me see if he can get you in."

Maggie stopped at the shop doorway to address the matter once again.

"No, that wouldn't be fair."

"Why not?"

"I need to get my articles printed because they're good, not because I know someone who knows someone who knows someone else. You know?"

"You're too honest, Mags."

"Yeah, well, nobody's perfect."

A middle–aged man in a plaid jacket, cap, and a cigar clenched in his teeth, appeared from behind them and squeezed past Maggie to get into the shop.

"You think that's how the real world works?" Claire continued. "Honesty will prevail, the hero always wins, the underdogs get their day? You will get nowhere in life without making connections."

"Don't worry, I'll make connections, but I've still got to write some good articles first."

She stopped still as she spotted a tall, brunette girl with her hair in perfect curls, stepping out of the shop. She was carrying a paper that looked suspiciously like a copy of *Merseyside Music*. Maggie's blood began to boil.

"Curly Shirley," she muttered through clenched teeth.

"Hi, Maggie, hi Claire," Shirley smiled as she eased past them.

Claire knew what was coming.

"I don't believe it!" Maggie fumed. "She's got MM. I bet it's the last copy."

Normally Maggie was the kind of person who got on with everyone. She treated her elders with respect, she mixed easily with people her own age, and she was a big hit as entertainer to her younger cousins. But Shirley Trotter, or 'Curly Shirley' as Maggie had unaffectionately nicknamed her, was a different story.

It started way back when Maggie and Shirley were eight years old, and in the same class at school. They'd been set the task of making Christmas cards for their parents; paper, glue, crayons, glitter and sequins were provided for decoration. Maggie had her heart set on drawing a Christmas tree on the card cover and decorating it with red and green sequins – very Christmassy, but by the time she'd finished colouring in her tree and added glue for the sequins, Curly Shirley had stolen all of the red and green sequins for her own card, and received praise from the teacher for her artistic flair. From that point on, Maggie felt one step behind her rival, and the worst thing was, they were competing for the same career--as well as for the most nods from the Beatles on stage.

The shop door opened as the man in the plaid jacket, now carrying a newspaper on his way out, once again had to step slowly and gingerly past Maggie in the tight space while avoiding the sort of physical intimacy commonly frowned upon in public, especially between a middle-aged man and teenage girl who had yet to be properly introduced.

"You could leave a wee bit of room, miss," he grumbled. "Could you not have your chin wag off to the side?"

"It would help if you had your cigar off to the side," Maggie grumbled back with a cough, before noticing his newspaper. "Is that *Merseyside Music* magazine?" Are there any left? It's important I get one."

"What's that?"

"I asked, is that *Merseyside Music*?"

"Yes, and I asked, 'What's that?" the puzzled man replied.

"You mean, 'what's that' as in, what did I say?"

"No, 'what's that' as in, "what's *Merseyside Music*?"

"It's a magazine for-- oh, never mind. If you have to ask, I think you're too old to know."

"Good," said the man as he walked off.

The girls finally stepped inside the shop, where Maggie made a bee line for the magazine rack, as Claire scooped up a bag of jelly babies.

"That was a bit brusque of you, Mags."

"I'm sorry. My emotions are in a tizzy at the moment."

"Anyway," Claire continued, "You've got no problem writing. Any one of your articles could get you a job in MM."

Maggie found the current issue of MM on the magazine rack, and with a sigh of relief, grabbed it with an uninterrupted sweep of her arm.

"Yes, but what I really want is my own column."

"Ha! Crawl before you walk, girl!"

"Everyone in the papers is chasing Rory Storm now. I'm going to get the interview of a lifetime with him, if I play my cards right."

"Doesn't he have a bad stutter? I don't know if he gives interviews. Or plays cards."

"Well, Gerry Marsden, then."

They left the shop and continued their meandering way home, with Maggie flicking through the paper without much need to see where she was going, and Claire indulging in her beloved Jelly Babies.

"Want one?"

"I think you have an addiction to those things."

"I think you're right."

"Ooh, look, here's the story about the Beatles gig. Only half a page! I'd have given them a two-page spread. What were they thinking?"

"They were thinking that not all of their readers are crazy for the Beatles like we are."

"Well, they should be," Maggie said conclusively.

"Are you going to send a copy to your American dreamboat?"

"What do you mean, dreamboat?"

"I've seen the pictures he sends you, remember? I like the one of him asleep on the sofa, snoring."

"Oh, that. He told me his little sister slipped that one into the envelope in place of the good one he picked out. He says she drives him mad sometimes."

"That's all right, I've seen the good pictures of him as well."

"Well, you can save the 'dreamboat' stuff, for a start. It's not like that with me and him. We're just friends."

"Have you ever thought about going over to America to meet him?"

"Oh yeah, like I can afford that on my wage."

"Save up."

"Right, so I'll be able to visit him when I'm 73 then."

"He might be worth the wait. Or, when you make your fortune as a famous journalist, you could visit him a lot sooner."

"Journalists don't make fortunes. Besides, I'd settle for a nice local lad. Trouble is, all the lads around here are useless."

"I know what you mean," Claire said. "One day last semester I was flirting with Geoffrey from the art class, but by the time he'd realised I was flirting, I'd gone off him."

"How's it his fault that you're bad at flirting?"

"He should have noticed it sooner."

They approached Claire's house, where she headed up the steps to the front door.

"See you later, Mags. And don't lose that ticket!"

Maggie continued home with a mind full of anticipation, excitement, wistfulness--and Ricky.

Let's see, she thought, trying to remember where she left off in her letter to him...

"I'm not sure when their next record will be out.
Probably next month. I'll send you a copy, as always.
I'm sure it will be great! Sorry about not sending you the
'Please Please Me' album. I just know it would get damaged
on the way. I hope the 45s will do for now.

I received a letter the other day and I thought it was from
you, and then I realised it was missing an airmail stamp.
Turns out it was from my father. He wanted to know how
my final year at school went, and if I'm getting a job. He
offered me a job in his B'n'B, with his new wife, asked
if I wanted to be a maid... err... no thank you. I don't think
he meant it, anyway, and I'm not interested in his job or
his new wife. And I certainly wouldn't leave my mother to
spend time with him. I just feel like he's the one who left us

and only bothers to write once or twice a year. Not even a phone call. Why should I even respond to him?

Sorry for going on a bit. Hope that's okay. Oh and by the way, happy 6-month anniversary! Can you believe we've been writing to each other for six months? It feels like I've known you a lot longer. Wait a minute, that could be taken as an insult! It's meant as the opposite, of course.

Anyway, how are things going for you? Write soon.

Best, from me to you,
Maggie

A week later and an ocean away, in a New Jersey suburb almost within sight of the New York skyline, a 17-year-old Ricky Kramer sat in his bedroom, adorned with photos of baseball players, movie stars, and rock singers. His eyes were fixed on the loopy handwriting running across several lightly scented pages of a letter, which had arrived only moments before, in an envelope affixed with a stamp featuring Queen Elizabeth's profile, and a pre-printed PAR AVION in the opposite corner. As always, he savoured each sentence, reading the letter slowly and carefully, so he wouldn't reach the end too soon. He almost didn't hear when his mother called from downstairs.

"Ricky! Kenny's here!"

"I'll be right down."

He got up and opened his desk drawer, the cozy home to a stack of a dozen or more other airmail envelopes nestled together, and slipped the newest one inside, for the time being.

He joined Kenny as the two jumped into Kenny's car—a hand-me-down convertible from his father--ready to see what their day off from the ice cream shop had in store for them.

"It's hot out," Ricky observed. "That's good."

"Of course it's hot out," Kenny said. "That's why they call it summer."

"I love summer," Ricky sighed happily, tilting his head back against the headrest, feeling the sun directly on his face. "It's summer in Liverpool, too."

"That's... random."

Kenny started the car and headed down the road, through the leafy neighborhood, still growing since its construction in the boom years just after the war.

"Where are we going?" Ricky asked.

"I don't know. I thought I'd just start driving and then think of somewhere to go."

"Let's stop by the shop for a few minutes and mock everyone for having to work on such a
nice day."

"So, when *we're* working tomorrow, they'll come in and mock us?"

"That's the way of the world."

Ricky took in the warm summer air blowing through his hair as they continued through town, but he thought of another stop he'd like them to make.

"I want to go to the record store, too. Do you mind?"

"I wish you'd get your own car already."

"I'm saving every penny I get. I've got my eye on a '56 Chevy for sale a few blocks from my house. Then I can drive myself to the record store in all kinds of weather, and the only moaning I'll hear will be from the car."

The ice cream shop, Never On Sundae, had become both a place of employment and a relaxing hangout (often at the same time) for Ricky, Kenny, and their friends for the past two summers. That particular day had Marie and Dave on duty, plus Dave's father –and owner—Stan.

The guys entered to find Dave cleaning a few empty tables and Marie at the counter, awaiting customers.

"Hey, Dave," Ricky said with a nod.

Dave barely bothered to look up. "You two aren't working today, are you?"

"Nah, we're just here to say hey."

"I thought so. See you later, I'm on dishes." He picked up a tray full of dirty dishes and cups and carried it into the back room. Ricky made himself comfortable in a booth and reclined as Kenny made his latest of several decidedly smarmy attempts to invite Marie on a date.

"So, how about me and you at the movies Friday night?" he murmured. "James Bond?"

"I'm working Friday night," Marie said, long accustomed to swatting away Kenny's clunky advances like a pesky housefly. "You're working, too."

"I am?" he asked Ricky.

Ricky nodded. "Afraid so. Looks like I'm the only one who can go to the movies Friday night."

"Hilarious," Kenny sighed, defeated. He sat down opposite his friend. "Now you just need a date."

Dave returned from the back room, wiping his hands on his apron as he joined them. "The dishes told me they're going to wash themselves," he explained, not wanting to be left out of the conversation.

"Ricky needs a date for Friday night," Kenny announced. "He's not my type," Dave replied.

"I don't need a date," Ricky protested half-heartedly.

"Well, you can't take your girlfriend from England, unless she's in town," Kenny said.

"She's not my girlfriend. We just write to each other."Dave's eyes lit up with amazement. "What? You have an English girlfriend? From England? That's so tough! I can't even get an American one."

With no customers to serve, Marie broke free from the barrier of the counter to join them at the table. "Oh, you mean that girl from the club after school?" she asked.

"Yeah," Ricky confirmed, "the Anglo-American Club."

Marie possessed the ability to find a romantic angle for just about every facet of everyday life. "You kept writing even after the school year was over? That's so sweet."

"Does she have a really great accent?" Dave asked eagerly.

"I guess. We've never talked."

"Then, does she *write* with an English accent?"

Ricky gave Dave a lingering look. "Yes, Dave, she writes with an English accent."

"That's so tough! How old is she?"

"Our age. But over there, they call high school 'college,' or something like that."

"So what do they call college?"

"I don't know. University, I think, sort of like us. We haven't gotten into those kind of details."

Ricky, beginning to feel a tad claustrophobic, by both the questions and the questioners, got up to make himself a treat behind the counter.

"Chocolate cone, Kenny?"

"Yes sir."

Ricky nodded. "And an egg cream for me."

He proceeded to pour some milk and squirt chocolate syrup into a cup as Dave clung to the idea of Ricky conversing with Maggie.

"You should call her sometime, just to listen to her accent."

"Are you kidding?" Ricky said with a chuckle. "A two-minute phone call to England costs about a hundred dollars."

Dave was not dissuaded. "So, make it a one-minute call and talk faster."

"Fine, if you pay for it."

"You should go to England and visit her."

"Oh, yeah, that would be much cheaper than a phone call." Ricky moved to put the finishing touch on his egg cream—which, as they all knew, did not include either an egg or cream among its ingredients. He reached for the soda fountain handle. "Watch out," Dave warned, "That handle isn't working right." "Which one?"

Ricky got his answer when he pulled on the handle and received a powerful stream of soda water in his face and chest.

"That one," Dave specified.

Ricky grabbed a towel and did the best he could to dry himself, and his shirt. "Why didn't you tell me?"

"I was hoping the sentence beginning with 'that one isn't working right' would give you pause."

Ricky, a bit flustered, soldiered on and returned to the table with his drink and Kenny's cone.

"His pen pal sends him pictures of herself, too," Kenny volunteered, fanning the flames just for the hell of it. "I saw one of her."

This piqued Dave's interest even more.

"Really? Does she look English? Let's see!"

"I don't carry them around with me," Ricky said.

"I've seen her picture," Kenny boasted, "and she's very cute." He somehow felt that was a good moment to lean over and offer his latest sweet nothing in Marie's ear. "But not as cute as you, of course."

Neither Marie nor the others bothered to take him seriously "Oh, please," she said, rolling her eyes, shoving Kenny out of her personal space. "But I think that's really neat, Ricky. It's just the kind of thing you would do, writing letters to someone overseas. Very smart, and thoughtful. Sophisticated."

"I write letters, too!" Kenny protested.

Marie wasn't having it. "No, you write fake notes from your mother to get you out of gym class. Not quite as romantic."

She turned her attention back to Ricky. "Besides, you want to be a writer anyway, don't you?"

"That's the plan."

Stan appeared from the back room, none too pleased to see his son taking a break.

"Dave, back to work. Those dishes piling up aren't going to wash themselves."

"They told me they would!" Dave protested.

Stan nodded to Ricky and Kenny. "You bums have nothing better to do than take up space here on your day off?"

"We're off to the record store anyway," Ricky said, as he and Kenny started for the door.

"For ten minutes, but that's all!" Kenny warned. "Then it's back out to the fresh air, sunshine, and Frisbee. See ya later, suckers."

Stan gave them a wave as he reached for the soda dispenser handle.

"Dad," began Dave, "that handle is a little—"

His warning was again both too late and insufficient, as a spray of soda doused his father.

"Yeah, that."   He said, returning to the back room.

Twenty minutes later, Ricky and Kenny approached the window of Sal's Records, a small but popular Main Street shop that usually did a good job keeping up with the latest releases—"usually" being the operative concept. The boys stopped to look over the promotional posters and album covers in the window display case.

"What you looking for, Ricky, anything special?"

"The Beatles. Maggie told me about their new record, but I guess it's not coming out here yet."

Kenny shook his head.   His friend seemed to talk about that Maggie girl more often with each passing week. "You know, when we were in the club to become pen pals with people from England, we didn't have to continue writing after school was over. It's not like we were getting graded or anything."

"I *like* writing to her. Besides, it's really cool receiving mail from overseas. Stamps with Queen Elizabeth on them..."

"The Brits are just like us, only they talk funny."

Ricky cast a disapproving eye. "I don't know why you even bothered to join that club when I did. You were terrible at writing letters. How was your pen pal supposed to answer your question, 'What's it like in England?' You could have been a little more specific."

"Oh, you mean, 'What's it like in *southern* England?' Or wherever she was?"

"She was in northern England, for the record. I bet you stopped writing because she used long words in her letters that you didn't understand."

"Hey, I understood perfectly well. But she was too different from me. Was never going to last.   So who are the Beatles anyway? I've never heard of them."

"Yeah you have, I played them for you, at your birthday party. Maggie sent them to me."

Kenny thought long and hard—never his specialty—and with his mouth open, which always annoyed Ricky. "I can't remember my birthday party," he confessed.

"Who knows, thanks to Maggie's tip, I could be the first American to have their album—maybe the *only* American! It came out in England a few months ago, but it hasn't shown up here, even as an import."

"Who are you talking about again?"

"The Beatles. They're from Liverpool. Keep up! They've got a good beat, and they write their own songs, too."

"That English girl is brainwashing you. Nobody's heard of them."

"They're famous in England, you know, and in Europe, too."

"Doesn't matter. If they're not famous here, it doesn't count."

"That's very xenophobic of you."

"Yeah, I thought you'd see it my way."

"It means a dislike for foreign cultures."

They entered the shop and strolled about, giving the place a quick once-over to see what was new on display that week.

"Oh, hey, now I remember," Kenny said. "The Beatles are the ones with the long hair, right? Do all guys in England have long hair?"

"I doubt it, I but don't listen to them for their hair. They only have one album and a few singles out so far, but they're really good. They play some American stuff, too. Maggie was able to send me the 45s, but she's afraid of the album getting damaged if she tries to mail it."

They approached Sal at the counter.

"How ya doin' boys?" smiled the jovial, if absent-minded man in his late fifties with thinning hair, moustache, and a paunch. He continued reading his newspaper as Bobby Darin's rendition of *Mack The Knife* wafted out of the speakers.

"Do you have the *Please Please Me* album by the Beatles?"

"The who?"

"The Beatles. They're from England."

"Don't think so. Maybe. The distributor just sends me this stuff. I don't know what the hell I'm getting half the time. I asked for an extra box of the Beach Boys' new record, and they sent me something else. Must have been a bad phone connection. Beach Boys, Beatles, Beethoven, who can tell the difference?"

Ricky shrugged. "Well, Beethoven probably could. And he was deaf."

Sal glanced at some paperwork. "How do you spell that?"

"B-E-A-T-L-E-S."

"Nope, no new Beatles listed here. Sorry."

He slid off his stool behind the counter and peered into a 12" x 12" cardboard box on the floor. "Oh, what do you know. *There's* the Beach Boys shipment. Sorry, kid."

"Okay. Thanks for your musical expertise."

The boys left the shop with little sense of accomplishment.

"If you keep spending your money on some English group, you'll never have enough to buy your car," Kenny warned. "I think I want you to get a car even more than you do."

They lingered by the shop entrance, casually looking up and down the street, unsure of their next destination.

"Where to now, Ricky? I'm getting hungry."

Ricky suddenly spotted something on the ground by the curb, about twenty feet away. "No way," he whispered to himself. He walked over to something and put his foot squarely down on top of it.

"What are you doing? Bug hunting?"

Ricky knelt down and discreetly picked up his target from under his foot, and pocketed it. He looked in all directions as he returned to Kenny. "Over here," he mumbled, feeling like some sort of international spy. They moved away from the shop entrance as Ricky reached into his pocket. He pulled out a folded twenty-dollar bill and flashed it to Kenny.

"This was on the ground."

"A twenty!"

Ricky unfolded it and, to their astonishment, found another twenty, and a ten-dollar bill. Fifty dollars, keeping each other close company.

"Wow!" he gasped.

"Are you serious? You just found that? Or is this a gag?"

"I swear, it's no gag. I just saw it by the curb. I've always had a good eye for finding money on the ground. I don't even look for it. I just find it." He tried his best to glance down the street as casually as possible, in case whoever lost the money might be on the way back to search for it.

"Fifty bu--" Kenny began to shriek, before Ricky clasped his hand over Kenny's mouth.

"Shhh! Don't cause a scene!"

"The car gods are smiling on you, all right. You'll be able to buy one in no time. Why don't I ever get that lucky?"

"Lunch is on me."

"You're damn right, it is."

Chapter 2

Maggie enjoyed her stroll down the street, doing her best to appreciate the wave of nice weather that Liverpudlians instinctively know not to take for granted. She smiled at a few kids skipping rope, and a neighbor washing her doorstep.

"All right, Mrs. Beacham?"   "Hello, Maggie love. Fine day. What have you been up to? Seen those Beatle boys around?"

"Not lately, but soon."

"I think I saw them on the telly the other night. They look younger on telly."

Maggie moved on and arrived at her own door at number 28 and opened it. It wasn't locked. Home was simple but comfortable. Mum was usually there, keeping the household running in an orderly way.

Maggie continued into the living room and checked the coffee table for anything of interest in the mail.

"Mum? Are you in?"

Her mother's voice called from upstairs. "I'm upstairs."

"Just checking."

A letter addressed to her on the table caught her eye. She tore open the envelope. Maybe it was a letter from an editor telling her how much he loved her submission. She had sent out quite a few in recent months to smaller magazines and newspapers in the area, without receiving any encouraging responses.

> *"Dear Miss Carter, thank you for your interest*
> *in our newspaper and thank you for your submission.*
> *Unfortunately we are not currently taking on any new*
> *staff. I wish you luck in your endeavours.*
>
> *Yours sincerely,*
> *Edward Thisk, Chief Editor."*

Maggie stuffed the letter back in the envelope, shaking her head. "Tisk, tisk, Mr. Thisk. You should have hired me. You'll be sorry, someday."

The phone rang. She hurried to answer, assuming, as always, that the call would be for her. Nine times out of ten she would be right.

"Hello?...Hi, Mr Dunhill...but I'm not supposed to be working today...Six o' clock? Yeah, I'll be there...No, it's no trouble...Ta."

Maggie's mother came down the stairs carrying a basket of laundry.

"I suppose that was for you again."

"Mr. Dunhill wants me to work later."

"It's your day off! You should have said no."

"It's all right. I could use the money."

"Fancy you'd rather work than skiving off to see those lads with the guitars down Mathew Street again. I was talking to Mrs. Bennett the other day, her sister lives down the road to that lad in that group."

"Which one? Paul?"

Her mother thought a moment. "No..."

"John? George?"

"No. I don't know, the one who wears all the rings."

"Ringo?"

"And what kind of name is that?"

"A pretty good one for someone who wears a lot of rings."

"Skiving off and spending all your time screaming for some lads in a rock and roll group isn't going to help your education or future career you know. You're too smart to waste your life.   Maggie half-retreated into the kitchen to find a sweet roll to munch on.

"Ah, but that's where you're mistaken, Mrs. Carter," she said, with some cheek. "First of all, we don't scream, and it *is* helpful, if I want to write about music. Mum, they've got records out, and have been on the radio and the telly! They're doing really well. They might even go to America. If I can just get an interview with them, I could be offered a job with a top newspaper or magazine, and I wouldn't even need to go to college anymore. Or work at that stupid cinema."

Her bite of the roll got only halfway down when she realized she had gone too far. Her mother's disapproving glare was a dead giveaway.

"You're not dropping out of college, my girl, you'll stay there until you're finished. You'll thank me someday. Not many girls like you have the chance for a good education. College wasn't even an option for me back in the old days."

Maggie half-heartedly finished her bite. Her mother's words were a humbling reminder.

"I know, mum. But I also know what I want to do. Isn't that a good thing?"

"All in good time, dear. Have some milk with that. And don't talk with your mouth full. 'Ere, there's a letter for you came today, but not from your American boyfriend."

"He's not my boy—I already found it on the table."

"From anyone I know?"

"Just another editor turning down one of my articles."

Mrs. Carter's face softened with sympathy. "Sorry, Mags. I know you're trying. You're quite good, even though I don't know anything about those bands you're writing about. Don't you give up."

Maggie appreciated her mum's words of support, but thoughts, plans, and articles to write were coming too fast and furious in her mind to dwell on the latest setback.

Fast and furious was also the pace at which she had to work at the candy counter in the movie theatre that night. The evening crowd, on their way in to see *Cleopatra* starring Elizabeth Taylor and Richard Burton, was eager to purchase their fill of snacks and drinks before sauntering into the theatre. Maggie frantically tried to keep up with the orders for candy bars and soda being shouted at her from all directions.

As she held a cup under the soda dispenser, Mr. Dunhill appeared from the back room to mutter in her ear.

"Maggie, you can take your break when it's convenient."

It was convenient. She let the half-filled cup fall to the floor and retreated to the back room, leaving another wage slave to deal with the mob.

Finding welcome peace in the staff snack room, she sat at the table with a cup of ice cream in one hand and a pencil in the other, writing in her battered notepad with its precious few remaining pages. She felt a compulsion to write about anything as long as it kept her in practice, and might possibly produce a work of great insight and wit—one that Liverpool's editors would be fools to turn down. Might as well have a crack at reviewing the film that was catching the public's fancy at the moment.

She found the inspiration strangely lacking. After a few half-hearted attempts, her notebook page read:

"Cleopatra...is...It stars...People seemed to enjoy it."

She let the pencil drop onto the paper.

"Who am I kidding? I hated the film and I've seen it seven times. It doesn't get better with age."

She crossed out the false start and turned to a fresh, clean page, as if to prevent contamination. A moment passed before she began again, but this time with a sudden sparkle in her eyes.

"I can barely relate to you the anticipation I felt waiting to see the Beatles perform at the Cavern for what might be the last time.
For me, it was a confluence of emotions—sheer joy and heartbreak intertwining, as they probably were never meant to do…"

She didn't know it, but she smiled as she wrote.

A few days later, she and Claire once again visited the news shop and, once again, left with a bag of jelly babies and a copy of *Merseyside Music* magazine. But on this day, they were headed straight to the building housing that very publication's offices.

Stopping outside the main entrance, Maggie took a deep breath and reached for the door.

"You're just going to walk in, unannounced?"

"Oh, I don't need to be announced," Maggie joked. "I'm not that posh. Right, here goes, fingers crossed."

"What are you going to show them?"

"A few articles about some of the local bands, and the one about The Beatles last gig at the Cavern, of course."

"But that hasn't happened yet." Claire silently offered Maggie the bag of Jelly Babies. Maggie poured a few in her hand.

"I know it hasn't happened yet, but I want to get in first before everyone else with a pen
and paper who thinks they can write the review, like Curly Shirley.

"But how can you write the review? It hasn't *happened* yet."

"I know! But I'll tell the editor that once I've actually seen the gig, I'll add that bit to the first part of the article. It begins with how it's sad that it's their last gig, but it's hopefully not really their last Cavern gig forever. I also wrote how they have prospects for America. You know, stuff that leads up to the concert."

"Well, I guess you know what you're doing. And stop worrying about Shirley! Maybe she doesn't even care about it."

"Maybe."

"Well, anyway, good luck in there. Use some big words to impress them."

Maggie considered the suggestion. "Well, let's see…I can use the word 'loquacious' in a sentence."

"You're having me on, aren't you? Go on, then, use it in a sentence, whatever it means."

"Right. 'I told her to loquacious going, but she tripped anyway'."

"You what?"

Maggie smiled. "It's a pun. Never mind. Actually, it means talkative. Maybe I should skip it.
I'm so nervous!"

She started through the entrance.

"Break a leg, or whatever they say to writers looking for jobs. Break *two* legs!"

"I want employment, Claire, not a month on crutches. Well, here goes nothing."

She took a deep breath and knocked on the door marked "Merseyside Music Magazine" and slowly opened it. She looked around and hadn't expected the office to be so small, and with only two or three employees going about their business—and one of those was the receptionist.

"Yes? May I help you?"

Maggie took a few cautious steps towards the reception desk. She suddenly felt her nerves begin to fray. "Is Mr. Harris here?"

"No, he's out for the afternoon. Can I help you?"

Maggie's confidence began to ebb away, at an increasing rate with each syllable she uttered.

"I, uh, I was wondering if I could leave a few articles with you that I've written. I mean, they're not about *you*, of course...they're about some of the Liverpool bands. Perhaps you could consider them for the magazine? My college instructors tell me I'm quite good."

"You can leave them, and if we can use them, we'll let you know. But we can't promise anything."

"Oh, I understand."

"Do you have any writing experience, other than at school?"

"Oh, I've been writing almost all my life. Not just for school, on my own as well. I love to write about music, films--except *Cleopatra*. It's rubbish--and long. Anyway, I see as many of the local bands as I can, especially the Beatles. One of these articles is a review of their final gig at the Cavern."

"But that hasn't happened yet."

"Everyone keeps telling me that."

"It is true, you know."

"I know, but I have a ticket for it. And if I write about the concert afterwards, this could be a sort of *pre*view and *re*view all in one."

"I'll make sure Mr. Harris sees them."

"Thank you," Maggie said as she turned, feeling discouraged instead of excited. She started for the door then quickly spun around to offer one last desperate qualification. "I can use "loquacious" in a sentence!"

"Pardon?"

Maggie nervously cleared her throat. "I, uh, told her to…er…look where she was going, but she tripped anyway…No, that's not right."

"Who tripped? What are you talking about?"

"I'm sorry, I'm not really like this."

"Don't worry, if your articles are well-written and have something interesting for our readers, there's every chance we'll put one of them in an upcoming issue. And we'll pay you."

"Fair enough. Thank you for your time."

She retreated to the door, timidly closing it behind her.

The receptionist continued with her work as she mumbled to herself.

"Loquacious?   That's never a word."

Chapter 3

It was just another working day for Ricky in the ice cream shop, when the one customer he dreaded more than any other entered. The man looked to be in his early thirties and wore glasses, yet still always squinted while looking up at the big menu board to review the list of twenty ice cream flavors. He need not have bothered, as he mostly likely had the menu memorized, but asked for same flavor every time he entered—a flavor that was not on the menu.

Ricky recoiled slightly as the man, known among the staff as "Mr. Mocha Nut," slowly advanced towards the counter, still examining the menu board.

"Oh, here he is again," he muttered to Marie. "Guess which flavor he's gonna ask about for the millionth time."

"I know. I'll let you handle it," she said, quickly finding some busy work at the other end of the counter.

"Thanks."

Ricky clenched his teeth before greeting the customer.

"Can I help you?"

"Do you have mocha nut?"

Bingo, Ricky thought. At least this guy was consistent in his ignorance. "No, sir, we don't. We've never had mocha nut. Ever."

"You're sure? I could have sworn-"

"Nope. No mocha nut. I've never even seen that listed as a flavour anywhere in the world, to be honest. Especially here. And I've worked here for two years."

"Then do you have anything that's similar to mocha nut?"

"Well, philosophically speaking, since mocha nut doesn't exist, I wouldn't really know how anything could be similar to it. Catch my drift?"

"I'm sure I've had it here."

Ricky had begun to wonder if the man was being paid by some

anonymous practical joker to walk in the shop every few weeks and make a nuisance of himself. "I can mix mocha with maple walnut, to make a sort of maple-mocha-walnut combination."

"Nah, I don't like the maple in maple walnut. Or the walnuts in maple walnut."

"Of course you don't," Ricky sighed. "Macadamia nut, perhaps? The nuts are harvested and flown in to our distribution warehouse, directly from Macadamia." Ricky knew he could tell the man almost anything with a straight face and get away with it.

The customer thought long and hard about it. Inspiration finally struck. "How about just a black and white ice cream soda--the white being the vanilla ice cream."

"Yeah, I'm familiar with—"

"I'll do it, Ricky," Marie interjected. "I think Dave needs help in the back."

She smiled sweetly to help keep Ricky's blood pressure in check. He got the hint and sought refuge, joining Dave in the back room.

"It's the mocha nut guy, isn't it!" Dave said.

"Marie just kindly prevented my first-ever strangulation of a customer."

"Whenever he comes in, I usually just mix mocha and maple walnut, and tell him it's mocha nut. He never knows the difference. One time, I mixed chocolate syrup, ketchup, and cottage cheese in a cup and told him it was an experimental new custard we were trying out. He slurped it down and said, 'I think you have a real winner here'."

"I'd better just refill the sprinkles out there and not engage that mocha-nutter in any more conversation."

He grabbed a refill jar of sprinkles and turned in time to catch sight of Marie about to pull the faulty handle on the soda fountain. In what felt like slow motion, he shrieked "Noooooo!" and dashed out to stop her. But his legs moved as if he were slogging waist-deep through a swamp of molasses, and he could only watch helplessly as Marie pulled the handle, unleashing a strong gush of soda water onto her and just about everything else behind her. She grabbed the handle in a panic to stop the torrent. It broke off in her hand as the seltzer continued to spew out uncontrollably. Ricky hurried to her, slipping on the wet floor, and sending his jar of sprinkles airborne in all directions. He continued with a commando-style crawl behind the counter, as if avoiding enemy crossfire, making it to the pipes and reaching for the valve under the fountain and switched off the flow. He and Marie slowly got to their feet, soaking wet and covered with multi-colored sprinkles. They stood facing Mr. Mocha Nut in silent humiliation.

"Maybe just a vanilla cone," the man suggested.

Ricky had the next day off, but Marie had to return to the scene of the disaster for her shift.   He was concerned about the repercussions for her. When he arrived at the shop, he found her sitting glumly on the curb outside.

"Stan didn't fire you, did he?"

"No, but he's docking me a week's pay, so he can replace the stuff that got wet and ruined."

"But that wasn't your fault. He should have had that handle fixed by now. He even got himself sprayed the other day."

"I should have used the other handle."

"I'll talk to him and plead your case."

"No, that's okay."

"Did he say how much it'll cost him?"

"He thinks about fifty dollars, but he'll only take out a week's pay from me, which is about thirty-five."

"That's still too much," Ricky protested. "You need that money."

Marie shrugged, not having the heart to cause a fuss, even if there was a principle at stake.   Ricky stood up and headed for the door.

"I'll take care of it," he said.

"What do you mean? What are you gonna do?"

"Let's just say I'm in a position to help you out this week. And it won't really cost me anything."

"Ricky, don't. Really."

"Too late," he said with a smile, as he pulled open the door.

He continued in, and approached Stan cleaning behind the counter. Easy come, easy go he thought to himself.

"Stan, I have something for you. Here, for the mess we made when the fountain went crazy. It wasn't Marie's fault." He handed a confused Stan several folded bills. "Here's forty bucks, and I owe another ten--thanks to Kenny's voracious appetite."

"Huh? What's this about?"

"So you can still pay Marie next week."

Stan, still unsure of what was going on, cautiously took the money. "Uh, yeah, sure. This is real money, isn't it?"

"Yeah, it's real. I gave up counterfeiting years ago. The ink kept turning my fingers green."

"Okay, Ricky, thanks. I'm having the fountain fixed tomorrow."

"Good!"

"Oh, and hey, keep the last ten bucks. We're square."

As they talked, Marie watched through the shop window. She couldn't read lips, but there was no mistaking what was going on. A warm smile lit up her face.

That night Ricky kept his radio on low volume in his bedroom as he wrote.

July 30th, 1963

"Dear Maggie,

For a short time today, I came a step closer to having enough money to buy the car I've had my eye on. I found fifty dollars on the ground! I don't know how much that is in pounds, but in dollars, it's a lot!

But my good (or foolish) nature stepped in. I helped out Marie, who was in 'a spot of bother' as you might say, with our boss. She owed him some money for a bit of a mishap behind the counter. I didn't want her to be so upset. I read a piece of advice once, from a writer or philosopher, about always helping out a friend when you can, even if they don't seem to appreciate it at the time. They will, someday. That idea always stuck with me, for some reason. So, I would have felt kind of guilty about keeping the money.

So, I'm back where I was in my efforts to save for the car. But I've waited this long, and it was for a good cause. I might have to watch the Mets on TV instead of spending the money to see a game in person, but I can live with that for a while. They're such a bad team, it might be less painful to watch them lose on TV than to see it from the stands."

Maggie and Claire sat on Maggie's bed, listening to the Beatles' *Please Please Me* album on the record player. They had each and every note and syllable memorized, right down to the occasional scratch and audio pops on the well-worn vinyl. Claire clutched a bag of jelly babies as she tossed one in the air and caught it in her mouth.

"Boys are just so annoying," she said. "How am I supposed to find one to settle down with?"

"Well, I guess when you stop calling them annoying, one of them just might ask you out. But it's early days for that sort of settling down talk, isn't it? What's your rush?"

"So Geoffrey, who I liked before but then went off, well, I like him again. He said hello to me today on the street and I swear for a second my heart stopped beating."

She extended a bag of Jelly Babies to Maggie.

"Just from hello? Good thing he didn't say anything more. He might be bad for your health. Really, Claire, you don't know what you want, do you?"

"I guess not."

"One minute you're complaining about blokes, and the next minute you're talking marriage."

"You complain about them as well."

"Fair enough."

"You never complain about Ricky, though," she said with a teasing smile.

Maggie's mother called up from the kitchen.

"Maggie? Is Claire staying for dinner?"

Claire nodded.

"Yes!" Maggie shouted back.

"Right, it's mince and dumplings."

"Fantastic," Claire said happily. "I love mince and dumplings."

"You haven't had my mum's," Maggie said with a frown, throwing cold water on her friend's enthusiasm. "Around here, we usually follow a round of dumplings with a round of antacid. Hey, you reminded me-- about Ricky, I got a letter from him this morning."

"Oh, let's read?"

"Okay." Having no secrets from Claire, Maggie retrieved an envelope from her desk and handed it to her.

"Maybe *I* should write to him," Claire said, opening the envelope. "I feel like I know him as well as you do."

"Well, you would, wouldn't you, as you keep reading my post."

Claire read down the page. "Ooh, he's saving money for a car. Those Americans aren't half posh."

"He's not posh. He's just like us."

"No, he's just like *you.*"

"What does that mean?"

Maggie's mother interrupted their conversation again.

"Does Claire's mum know where she is?"

Maggie turned to Claire.

"Probably," Claire shrugged.

"Prob—I mean, yes," Maggie shouted out the doorway. She shut the door and sat back on the bed. "Does your mum ever know where you are?"

"Nah, now that she's too busy watching our new telly. I think she watches it starting in the morning until all the shows stop in the evening. Her new favourite is *Z-Cars*. I didn't think she was into cars."

"It's a police drama--not really about cars."

"Well *that* was misleading."

Maggie's mother once again shouted from below, her voice beginning to sound a bit hoarse.

"Maggie, some chap is on the telephone for you."

"What does he look like?" she called down, with a hint of a grin.

"Well, he's—how the bloomin' hell should I know? He's on the *phone!* Don't be so cheeky."

Maggie looked at Claire and ran down the stairs. Claire grabbed her bag of sweets and followed close behind. Mother handed Maggie the phone and jumped out of the way.

"What does he look like…" she muttered, shaking her head.

"Hello? Maggie speaking...Oh hi...The Beatles review?...Yes, I know it hasn't happened yet, it's just an example of my work...Oh, that's too bad…Gerry and the Pacemakers?...Yeah?...Oh that's fantastic! Thank you!...Yes, I understand...What? Oh, it means talkative…Yes, all right. Thank you!" She hung up, beaming. "That was an editor at *Merseyside Music*. They don't want to print my Beatles article, but they liked the short piece I wrote about Gerry and the Pacemakers and want to print it in the next issue! Isn't that amazing? I'm going to be published!"

The two shrieked and jumped with excitement, as if on invisible pogo sticks.

"Well done, Maggie!" her mother said, giving her a hug.

"Thanks, mum."

"I'll make the mince and dumplings extra delicious tonight," she said, returning to the kitchen.

"We can only hope," Maggie whispered.

"That's brilliant, Maggie!" Claire gushed. "You're having an article in MM! The Beatles will probably read it!"

"Ahh! I know! It's an article about Gerry and the Pacemakers, so it would be nice if *they* read it as well. And! And! The woman on the phone said my Beatles-at-the-Cavern article was good and that I have a chance to get that in as well. It's not definite, but there's a chance! This is huge!"

Maggie could barely write fast enough in her letter to Ricky that night.

31 July, 1963

"Dear Ricky,

I have big news. One of my articles is going to appear in Merseyside Music magazine! When I found out I don't know how I managed to remain so calm…"

She smirked to herself at the fib.

"This is so exciting, I'm going to be a published reporter. When they phoned to tell me the news, an amateur probably would have screamed in their ear, but I'm glad I kept my composure. I'm a professional after all; I didn't want to make a fool of myself. I'll send you a copy as soon as I can, from me to you!

P.S. --Excited? Yes! Nervous? Yes! But don't tell anyone!"

Chapter 4

Maggie and Claire carefully navigated their way down the steps of the Cavern Club; Claire holding onto Maggie's arm in case she fell off her high heels.

The girls had never seen the Cavern looking so full; it was always a popular place but tonight it looked as though there were three times as many people as usual. There was no chance of getting a seat at a table, but Maggie wasn't interested in sitting down, she was determined to push her way through to the front of the crowd to get the perfect view of her four favourite musicians. Chances were, by the end of the night, Claire will have taken off her shoes in favour of dancing and would have to walk home barefoot.

"I'll get us some drinks," said Claire, "Two Cokes, right?"

"Yeah, I like the hard stuff."

Claire made her way to the little snack and drink bar and it took almost ten minutes for her to get the attention of the man at the counter, not her personal best.

Sipping on their fizzy drinks, careful not to let the people pushing past knock the glasses out of their hands, Maggie started measuring up the best way to get to the front of the crowd.

"Remember last time?" Claire asked. "When you wanted to get to the front of the crowd to see Gerry and the Pacemakers, and you put a mince pie in that girl's hood?"

Maggie looked sheepish. "It's all I had that would make her turn around. My mum made it, so it was no great loss. Anyway, it worked didn't it? I got to the front, got some good material for an article."

"Shame we don't have any right now," Claire said, "or people wearing coats with hoods. We've got nothing to work with."

"I think we're just going to have to maneuver our way to the front. Plain and simple. But stay close to me, don't want to leave you behind. You ready?"

Claire nodded and took hold of Maggie's hand. "Lead the way."

The two girls battled their way past sweaty bodies, avoiding lit cigarette ends, spilling drinks and one fight that almost broke out over some lad eyeing up someone else's girlfriend. Halfway through the journey, Claire and Maggie's hands were separated.

"Go on without me," yelled Claire, "just leave me behind! Save yourself!"

But Maggie would have none of it. She could see the way to base, a few rows away, but she doubled back and grabbed Claire by the wrist, dragging her through the milling crowd.

When the girls stepped out into the front row, a few other girls already waiting by the side of the little stage looked them up and down and glared, but that was the least of their worries. Claire turned to Maggie, who was beaming at her success, despite the fact her hair looked like she'd been through a wind tunnel.

"I've lost a shoe. I have to go back for it."

"Are you crazy? If you go back there I might never see you again, it's a jungle!"

"But it's my shoe!"

"You always lose shoes! They've got a lost property box here filled with your shoes, none of them matching. They'll just add that one to it and you can get it later. Don't go back there, it's not worth it."

Claire took off her other shoe and threw it to the side. "*You* can explain to my mum this time why I need another pair of shoes."

"Then wear a smaller size, so they won't come off so easily."

Looking to the side of the stage, in the direction she'd sent her shoe flying, Claire spotted something that she knew would dampen Maggie's spirits.

"Mags, whatever you do, don't look to the left."

Immediately intrigued, Maggie looked to the left, "Why, what is-? Ugh...Curly Shirley! And she's closer to the stage than we are!"

"Don't worry about it. Fair's fair, Mags. She must have gotten here ages ago."

"I don't care that she's here to support the lads, I care that she's here to write an article. I knew it."

The girls were looking and talking about Shirley so much, the vibes must have caught Shirley's attention. She waved over.

"She's waving, Maggie. It doesn't look like a sarcastic wave."

Maggie smiled and waved back. Claire did the same.

"Was yours a sarcastic wave? Mine wasn't."

"Sorry, but I don't think I know what a sarcastic wave looks like. But I'm willing to learn. I'll just have to hope the article I already sent in to MM is good enough. But it won't be, compared to Shirley's."

Claire shook her head. "You don't know she's going to write something. Just enjoy the Beatles!"

Maggie smiled. "You're right, nothing can spoil tonight!"

The crowd waited with excitement for half an hour before there was any sign that the Beatles were ready to come on stage, but a few false alarms met with a few hundred groans when a random man who was probably hired security, stepped out from behind the door.

Though the buzz throughout the room had been intense, it was nothing compared to when the manager of the club, Bob Wooler, announced the band. John, Paul, George and Ringo took their places on stage as Maggie and Claire both screamed and yelled each of the Beatles' names until they felt their throats go coarse. Their favourite boys were back in their home-town, probably for the last time, and this was going to be the best night ever.

"Thirty-two!" she informed Claire.

"What's thirty-two?"

"That's how many times we've seen them here, including this one."

"You've kept track?"

"Of course!"

There was a real buzz in the air, Maggie couldn't figure out if it was coming from the four musicians on stage and sweeping through the audience, or if the audience were feeding the energy of the band, but either way it was electric. They knew the Beatles were well on their way.

The group began to play their set list of popular covers, among them "Roll Over Beethoven", "Twist and Shout," and even a few of their original songs, mixing in a bit of cheeky comedy, and instantly their legendary magic took over.

"The set list hasn't changed," shouted Maggie, so she could be heard over the music.

"What?" Shouted Claire in response as she twisted around in what she described as dancing.

"The set list! It's the same as usual really." Maggie gave one more "Woooo!" when a song came to an end and John announced the next number.

Maggie didn't want the moment to end, but she knew the Beatles would be done with their set in no time. Soon enough, the boys said their goodbyes to the audience and made a hasty exit. Girls tried to grab them as they went past, but mostly ended up clutching at empty air.

"How amazing was that!" Cheered Maggie, she had the biggest smile on her face. "I'm feeling such mixed emotions."

Claire didn't answer.

Since Claire was never one to go speechless, Maggie turned her attention to discover her friend was no longer standing beside her. Instinctively, she looked down to see Claire lying in a heap on the floor.

"Oh my gosh, Claire!"

Maggie dropped to her knees to check if her friend was okay.

"Claire? Claire?"

She nudged Claire a couple of times until she began to stir.

"Mmm, that was good." Claire mumbled. Then she realised she was on the floor. "What happened? Who moved the floor?"

"Are you okay?" came a voice that wasn't Maggie's. "Did you faint? It is hot in here."

A boy about eighteen years old knelt down and helped Claire to her feet.

"Do I know you?" Claire asked.

"No, I just thought I'd help you," the stranger replied. "Where are your shoes?"

Maggie hadn't said anything because she was too busy staring at this stranger, the stranger with nice dark hair slicked back, and lovely green eyes.

"I'm Jack," he said to Claire, as Maggie reflexively leaned in between them.

"I'm Maggie," she said and quickly grabbed Jack's hand to shake it. "This is my friend Claire. She doesn't faint normally." She turned to Claire. "Although there was that time you thought you saw the Pope riding the number 23 bus."

"Maggie!" Claire admonished, widening her eyes to signify a stern 'shut up!'

"Gig's over, want me to walk you two outside for some fresh air?"

Claire nodded, then straightened her hair. "Air, yes, air is good."

Jack helped Claire make her way through the crowd, Maggie following close behind, marvelling at what a gentleman Jack was.

Outside the Cavern, Claire took a deep breath of fresh air...not bothered by the cigarette smoke drifting over from the group of teenagers huddled by the doorway.

Jack lead the girls into the street. "Are you feeling better now?"

Claire nodded. "Yes, I don't know what came over me. I'm probably the first person to faint at a wink from Ringo. He winked at me you know. Did you see?"

"Yep," Maggie said, "And Paul smiled at me! I think he recognizes us, by now, after 32 gigs. That was so amazing! They're getting so much better! I can't wait to write about it."

The girls jumped up and down for a few moments as the excitement from the best gig they'd ever seen sunk in.

Jack shrugged his shoulders. "They were good. They've improved a lot. Not sure that hairstyle's going to catch on though. My mother would have a fit if I went home with hair like that." He smiled to himself. "Maybe I'll try it. Oh, here comes the man I've been waiting to see."

Jack nodded at a young man heading his way. It was Trevor.

"Alright, Trev? Where you been hiding?"

"Could ask the same of you. You got those records you promised me?"

"Just came in on the boat. I'll bring them 'round yours tomorrow."

"What's this?" asked Maggie.

Trevor grinned. "Jack gets me the latest records from America. He's got contacts."

"Knocked off?" asked Claire.

"My uncle works on a cargo ship, and every time he goes to America he brings back a load of stuff to sell. Rhythm & blues, country…I mean, he offers a bit of stuff when he comes back from the far east as well--but I'm not talking records, if you know what I mean, and I'm not interested."

"Maggie's got contacts in America," offered Claire.

Jack looked Maggie up and down, "Oh aye, who do you know in the States then? A rich man from Wall Street who's going to whisk you away from this decrepit town?"

Maggie blushed. "I wish. No, he's a pen pal, lives in New Jersey.

"New Jersey, eh?"

"Next to New York," said Claire.

Jack nodded. "The Yanks are always stealing names from us and putting 'New' in front, aren't they? So, this bloke's your boyfriend then?"

"No!" she snapped, with such emphasis that she even startled herself. She wasn't entirely sure why she did that. "I mean, no. He's just a friend. We write to each other. I send him Beatles records from here that they haven't gotten in America yet. So, I guess your uncle and I have something in common."

"Aye, but I'll bet you don't have a tattoo and a wooden leg like he does, do you?"

Maggie was a bit taken aback, wondering if Jack was just being cheeky. "Don't be daft.   I wouldn't get a tattoo."

"So I shouldn't be jealous of your Yank friend, then?" Jack gave a wink.

"Um, well, unless you've always wanted to live in New Jersey..." was all Maggie could think to say. It was an odd, flirty question from him, she thought. But maybe he wasn't flirting, maybe he was just being

Jack. After all, she'd only just met him.

"Alright, well, it was nice meeting you girls, might see you both around here again. I have to go get those records from my uncle. Trev, I'll be round yours tomorrow."

Jack nodded his goodbyes and walked off.

Maggie's attention could not be caught until Jack had turned the corner, out of sight.

"Maggie," said Claire for the fifth time."

"What?"

"We heading home then, or what?"

"In a minute. Trev, how do you know Jack?"

"I've known him years, why?"

"No reason," Maggie shrugged, "he seems nice."

Trev laughed, "Yeah, that's what all the girls say about him. I can put in a word for you if you like, though I don't think I need to, I think he fancied you, too."

"Hey, let's not forget he was coming to *my* rescue," said Claire. "But okay, you can have him, he's not my type."

"What do you mean I can 'have' him? I didn't say I want him. I don't even like him that much. He's far too cocky."

Claire and Trevor looked at each other, holding back a laugh.

"Yeah right, you practically drooled all over his painted leathers. And he obviously fancies you."

Claire and Trevor started to head down the street, away from the crowd still mingling outside of the Cavern. Maggie quickly followed. "And besides, I'll probably never see him again anyway."

A week passed. Maggie hurried into the news shop as soon as she knew the magazine would have been delivered.

Claire struggled to keep up with Maggie as she marched quickly toward the newsagents.

"Mags, slow down, he won't have sold out, it's not even 9a.m. yet!"

"It's exciting!"

Claire took a small run to catch up with Maggie and tried to match her pace.

"It's not natural walking at this speed. I should warn anyone who wants to be your friend that they'd better train with a track coach first."

Maggie chuckled. "Well I promise to buy you some Jelly Babies if you make it to the shop without keeling over."

"Make sure he puts more red ones in the bag, and tell him to leave out the green ones, they remind me of vegetables and nobody wants that in their sweets."

"You're very strange, Claire."

Minutes later, Claire stepped out of the newsagents with more sweets in her mouth than in the paper bag. Under her arm she held the latest copy of Merseyside Music. Maggie stepped outside, carrying two copies of the magazine, already hurriedly flicking through the pages of one of them, trying to find her article. She turned the pages furiously and suddenly stopped when she saw her name on the by-line of the article. She turned away and looked again. It was still there. They had kept their word—and, just as important, spelled her name correctly. She was a published writer in her favourite magazine.

"This is so exciting! Here it is! Here it is! Page 14!"

Claire pocketed her sweets and turned to page 14 in her own magazine.

"Oh amazing," Claire said. "It's in my copy as well!"

"Fancy that."

"There's your name, in black and white! You're famous, Mags!"

"This is the best thing ever!"

Claire read through the article as Maggie just stared at it with delight.

"I need a pen so you can sign it, and I'll be the first person with your autograph," Claire said.

"Don't be silly, reporters don't give autographs."

"So, you can start a trend."

"You'll be asking for the newsagent's autograph next." Maggie's smile widened. "Okay, I'll sign it, just for you! When I find a pen."

"Really, well done, Maggie. You're so clever. Look, your story's jammed between Rory Storm and Pete Best's new band."

"Aww, look at that, I fit right in."

The two friends laughed in celebration.

"What did you buy two copies for? In case one of them breaks?"

"I'm sending one to Ricky, but maybe I should buy another spare copy, just to put away."

"Why is it Ricky gets a free copy and I had to pay for mine? Favouritism, that is."

"I paid for your sweets."

Pulling a red jelly from her pocket, Claire nodded. "Oh yeah, ta. My dentist will thank you as well."

"Your dentist will bloody propose to me, more likely."

Maggie couldn't help but take another look at her article.

"I did it, I actually did it!"

"Maybe they'll give you a regular slot?"

"Hopefully. They still haven't gotten back to me about my Beatles article yet, and that had to be the first one on their desk. Maybe I'll drop another article in tomorrow. I could become a regular." Flipping further through the magazine, Maggie came across something that took away her smile. "There's another Beatles article in here."

"Good, they should be in every issue," replied Claire.

"It's by Shirley," said Maggie, her voice sounding as muted as her change of mood.

"Oh. Well that doesn't take away from your article, Mags. Yours is still brilliant," said Claire.

"Yeah," Maggie sighed, unconvinced. "But I really hoped they would print mine. I mean, it's their big Cavern concert, maybe their last, and I worked like a dog on that article--even before it happened! What's so great about Shirley's?"

"I guess they had their reasons, Mags, but they still printed your other one! Why not celebrate that?"

Maggie took an instant to silently ask herself what she'd ever do without Claire as her cheerleader. "I guess you're right. Come on, let's go show this to my mum."

6 August 1963

Dear Ricky,

Guess what? Merseyside Music printed my article! I know I already told you they were going to, but look--they actually have! My words in print, in my favourite magazine! I have enclosed a copy for you to read. And I signed it, Claire encouraged me to. I'm so over the moon about it. There's
another article in there about the Beatles. It's not written by me, it's by another girl I go to college with. Truth be told, she's probably a better writer than I am. But I hope you like my article anyway, even though you probably don't know who Gerry and the Pacemakers are.

Thanks for your letter. I'm sorry you were so upset about the New York Mets. I don't know anything about baseball, but they do seem to be horrendous, by your account. I applaud your loyalty, though, however maddening it must be.

Sounds like you did a very good thing for your friend Marie. Is she just a friend, or…?

Chin up, Ricky, you'll get that car soon.
Warmest regards, from me to you,

--Maggie

Chapter 5

August 12, 1963

Dear Maggie,

*Congratulations on being a published writer! Your
magazine arrived this morning. I'm very impressed!
I've read your article twice already, and I'll be showing
it to my friends, too. Maybe someday I'll see my own
article in print. I think seeing your achievement has
inspired me.*

*I wish I could come to the Cavern club with you
sometime, it sounds like an amazing place. It's really
a club underground? We don't have anything like that
here. You have me very curious. Isn't it a bit
claustrophobic, though?*

*The summer's been okay so far—hot! I spend most of
my time working at the ice-cream store. I'm still saving
up for that Chevy too. I'll have to scoop a lot more ice
cream before I can afford it, though.*

*Kenny is still trying to convince Marie to go on a date
with him, he's having no luck, Marie doesn't like him
that way. I'm sometimes not so sure she likes him at all!
Poor Kenny.*

*Anyway, speaking of them, let me tell you about
yesterday when the three of us took a trip to New York
City...*

As Ricky wrote his letter, the images and sounds of the previous
day, when he and his friends took a trip to the Big Apple, replayed in his
mind. It was perhaps the most memorable of his many visits to
Manhattan. He had known about a record store in Rockefeller Center

that stocked an impressive array of imported records, so his goal was to hunt down whatever elusive Beatles records that had, so far, been only available across the pond.

He managed to persuade Kenny to let him drive Kenny's car into Manhattan. Ricky figured if he, as a fairly new driver, could drive through New York City and return home without any dents or dings on the car, he could drive anywhere. It was a rite of passage of sorts for any new driver in the greater metropolitan area.

Marie sat in the back seat watching the New York skyline with awe. It was a familiar sight, yet one she never took for granted. Crossing the George Washington Bridge meant that the hustle and bustle of Manhattan was only minutes away. She always loved going to the city, and hoped to live there someday.

Ricky confidently navigated the cross streets and avenues of mid-town—not without a close call or two—and, after circling several blocks in search of a parking space, found one and eased the car in. He dropped a few coins into the meter and handed Kenny his keys back.

"See, simple. I did it!" he said proudly.

"Well done, Ricky!" Marie said, with a pat on the back.

Kenny pocketed his keys. "Yeah, well done, but we still have to get out alive yet."

The trio headed in the direction of Rockefeller Center, with Ricky walking with particular purpose, occasionally forcing himself to slow down, lest he leave his companions in the dust.

They crossed 5th Avenue and stepping onto the plaza at Rockefeller Center, with its array of flags, sculptures, gardens, all lorded over by the majestic, golden statue of Prometheus and its surrounding fountains. The trio agreed it was a cool place to see, and be seen.

Ricky practically dragged the others into the record store with him, where he took a quick but intense look around the layout and, upon seeing a small "IMPORTS" sign in the opposite corner, hurried across the shop. His search through the "B" record bin yielded nothing, so the next step was to ask an employee.

The only available staff member at the moment was a fifty-ish man, unshaven and somewhat slovenly compared to his fellow employees in slacks and ties--and especially slovenly for a store in such a prestigious location. But Ricky was determined not to judge a record by its cover. He caught the man's attention.

"Do you happen to have the *Please Please Me* album by the Beatles?"

"The what album by the What-les?"

"It's called *Please Please Me*, by the Beatles."

The salesman thought for a moment, casting his eyes upward as if the answer would appear to him from the heavens above. Ricky offered his only other available morsel of information.

"It came out a few months ago in England. March, I think."

"Kid, I've got an encyclopedic knowledge of every record in this place. I got 'Please Pardon Me' by Leadbelly, the blues singer…"

"No, this is *Please Please Me*. It's a rock & roll album."

"I got 'Please Come Home For Christmas' by Charles Brown…"

"No, I don't usually look for Christmas songs in August. This is called--"

"I got 'Please Please Please' by James Brown. Is that the one you mean?"

"No, not at all. First of all, that's got an extra 'please' in it. And, it's by James Brown."

"You got somethin' against James Brown?"

"No," Ricky said, struggling to retain his composure. "So you haven't heard of the Beatles? They're an English group. I thought this store was known for its imported records."

"Sorry, kid, never heard of them. Try again in a couple of months." The salesman quickly turned his attention to another customer, as if his exchange with Ricky had never even happened.

Ricky came up empty in his search, but he liked the feeling that he might be an early explorer in the search for music's next Big Thing. He wasn't sure what to look for specifically, but he did know that he wanted to immerse himself in new music as often as possible.

The trio felt hungry again, and meandered to the Horn & Hardart automat for a snack. They browsed along the walls of little windowed compartments with everything under the sun. A few coins dropped in a slot would ensure an egg salad sandwich its freedom.

They ate with healthy abandon and joked their way through their opinions of everything, including their mutual friends, mutual enemies, music, TV, and, more reluctantly, the upcoming school year.

"I can't believe summer is almost over," Marie lamented. "I was sort of hoping more would have happened." She eyed Ricky as she said it, hoping he'd pick up on her attempt at a quasi-telepathic message. You know, something memorable."

"Yeah, but it was fun," he said, as he had already included that very day along with the others he had enjoyed most throughout the summer.

Ricky was in his element, doing what he always enjoyed more than anything. Here he was with his friends, taking New York by storm, on that hot, humid August afternoon. Was it his imagination that Marie was shooting looks at him? He couldn't be sure. He also noticed that Kenny's usual heavy-handed flirting with Marie was uncharacteristically muted that day.

Ricky suddenly raised his head like a dog awakened by a high-pitched whistle. "Hey, how long has it been since we parked the car?"

"I don't remember," Marie shrugged.

"The meter will probably run out soon," Ricky said. "We'd better get back and put more coins in it."

They sacrificed a more leisurely conclusion to their meal for a considerably rushed one, and weaved through an obstacle course of slower-moving pedestrians in their race against the clock.

They rounded the corner of 55th Street, and zeroed in on the parking space where they left the car. The space was still there. The car was not.

"Oh, my God!" Kenny shrieked. "It's gone! Are you sure this is where we parked?"

"Of course it is," Marie said. "I made a mental note of it. Right across the street from the Kosher Polynesian Pizzaria. There's not much chance of there being two of those in Manhattan."

Ricky inspected the parking meter. "It ran out. We can't be more than a few minutes late. The tow truck must have been lurking in some dark alley, ready to pounce as soon as the meter ran out."

Marie shrugged. "Unless it was stolen."

"Oh, that's a cheerier possibility!" Kenny snapped, as he began to hyperventilate. "What do we do now? We're stranded!"

"Call someone to pick us up?" Marie suggested.

"Call who? The only people I'd trust to pick us up are you guys. And you're already *here*!"

"I mean our parents," Marie elaborated.

"My parents are gonna kill me as it is," Kenny said. "No way. Call *your* parents."

"Okay, let's keep calm" Ricky said. "I'm sure it was just towed by the traffic cops. We'll have to go over to the impound lot and pay to get it back."

Kenny, slobbering and sweating with panic, had begun pacing in a semi-circle, nearly colliding with several passers-by. "How do we know where the impound lot is?"

"It's on the West Side Highway and 38th Street. Everybody knows that."

"Okay, Mr. Know-it-All, how much will it cost to get the car?"

"I don't know. We'll find out when we get there. Let's take a cab."

They hurried back to the corner where a continuous and robust selection of cabs kept a steady flow down the avenue. They flagged one down and piled into the back seat.Before they could announce their destination, the cabbie, listening to a baseball game on his radio, provided them with a sports update.

"Mets are losin' again, 4 to 2. Throneberry bobbled one that cost them the go-ahead run."

Ricky leaned forward. "Thirty-eighth street and the West Side Highway, please."

"Got your car towed, huh?"

"Yeah. We got back to the meter late."

"Wouldn't have happened if you took a cab."

When the trio discovered they didn't have enough cash among themselves to retrieve the car at the impound lot, crisis saw a happy conclusion thanks to Ricky's credit card. His father had given it to him in exchange for the promise that it be used only in an emergency. To Ricky, being stranded in Manhattan with no way of returning home ever again qualified as an emergency. He had saved the day, but he also knew he would have to pay back his father for the towing fee and parking ticket. Marie and Kenny promised to pitch in, but with their salaries, it would take time.

Kenny was in no condition to take the wheel. "I think you'd better drive it home," he said to Ricky. "My nerves are shot."

The drive back to New Jersey had them feeling a little better, thanks in part to listening to Dan Ingram on WABC and his hilarious remarks in between the top 40 hits of the summer. But Ricky's thoughts were centered on his setback to save enough for a car.

"I'll never be able to save enough for a car at this rate," he whined.

"Every time I get close, something happens."

"I guess you'll have to hope you'll find more money on the ground," Kenny shrugged with a smile.

The remark got Marie's attention. "What do you mean?"

"Oh, it's nothing," Ricky mumbled, hoping to avoid going into detail. "I found some money in the street a few weeks ago."

"Really? How much?"

"I don't remember."

"I do!" Kenny volunteered. "Fifty bucks! Too bad you couldn't find that much today, when we really needed it."

"Wow," Marie said. "You never mentioned it." This new piece of information got her thinking. Reclining in the back seat, she thought back to Ricky's gesture to repay Stan a few weeks earlier for the mess behind the soda counter. Interesting coincidence, she thought. Could he really have paid Stan with the money he found?

Somehow, the phrase "knight in shining armour" passed through her mind, putting a smile on her face as Ricky drove across the George Washington Bridge back to New Jersey.

Chapter 6

The first week of September brought with it the first week of the school year—senior year for Ricky and Kenny, junior year for Marie. They continued their carpool from the previous year—with an occasional guest appearance by whoever needed a ride on a particular morning. Kenny, the only one with a car, became chauffeur by default, but was compensated for gas on a semi-regular basis.

Ricky decided it was a good time to join the school newspaper, *The Searcher*. He could have done so the previous year, but somehow the idea interested him more now that he was a senior—good to have on his academic record as an extra-curricular activity. A good many of the student body didn't take *The Searcher* very seriously, but there were others who appreciated its school news every other week. Ricky took to it with enthusiasm, and managed to talk the editor into letting him write a music column, reviewing albums and predicting which new songs and groups might be on the cusp of success. It was mostly guesswork, but Ricky felt he somehow had a little extra insight when judging new music.

"Are you gonna write about that rock group from England your pen pal is always talking about?" Marie asked at lunch one day.

"The Beatles? I don't know. Nobody's ever heard of them here."

"So, you'll be the first person to tell everyone about them. You'll be a trailblazer. That's what your column is for, isn't it?"

"I don't think anyone would be interested."

"But you've got a source in England to tell you who's popular there. Nobody else here does."

"Yeah, but no English singers have ever hit it big here."

"That's true. Well, what do I know. It's your column. Good luck."

After giving the matter some thought, Ricky saw Marie's point, and began scribbling his first draft of an article about the group with long hair from Liverpool that no one in America had heard.

Maggie's first week back at college made her feel as if she'd never been away from the place, except one thing was different; she was starting her new school year as a published writer. A couple of the girls in her class had asked if that was really her article in the magazine, it made her feel popular that a few people were making a point to come over and talk to her just because of the publication. But the attention didn't last long and Maggie realised if she wanted to keep building her reputation she was going to have to get something else published quickly. Plus, it was rather deflating to think that the magazine had not accepted any of the other five articles she'd sent in and had completely rejected her article about the Beatles Cavern gig, she was so sure getting in first would guarantee her another publishing.   It was a bit more nerve grinding for Maggie to realise that Shirley got the article for the Beatles Cavern gig printed. Maggie kept telling herself it wasn't a competition, and that she was working at her own pace, but it just looked all too easy for Shirley, whilst Maggie seemed to struggle down a slow path.

"Hi, Maggie, I've seen your name in Merseyside Music, pretty brilliant," said a girl as she meandered passed Maggie and to her own class.

"Thanks, Carol," Maggie said with a proud smile.

A distance down the corridor, she overheard the same girl congratulating someone else.

"Shirley! You nabbed a Beatles scoop huh? Nice one. I'm sure they read that magazine, now they'll know your name!"

Right then and there, Maggie resolved to push herself even harder.

She was going to have to up her game, but not a lot was going on that was big news in the city, except of course the Beatles but they weren't scheduled back in Liverpool and there was a rumour that they were heading to America, and she doubted her mother would give her the air fare to go and get the scoop on the lads in the States. Besides, there would probably be a lot of American Shirley's over there she would have to compete with.

Back into a regular routine of studies, chores and evenings of homework, Maggie was also ready to get back into her routine of weekend fun. The best part about being back at college she thought.

The first day of October was a chilly one, but Maggie rarely thought much about the weather. Her mind was usually too preoccupied, especially on this morning. She rang the bell of Claire's front door. Claire's mother answered.

"Oh hello, Maggie."

"All right, Mrs. Barnes?"

"Claire's still upstairs. You do realise it's a Saturday don't you? Early Saturday."

It was 8:00 a.m.

"Yes, I'm sorry, I know it's early, but I need to talk to Claire."

"Is something wrong?"

"No, I just--"

"That's all right. You know the way."

She stepped aside to let Maggie quickly make her way up the stairs to Claire's room. Claire wouldn't mind the intrusion, she figured, as long as Maggie didn't mind waking her up. And Maggie was never shy about such things.

"Claire, wake up, I've got a good idea," she said, as she burst into the bedroom. Claire didn't wake. Most of her face was nestled under a blanket.

"Wake up! Don't ignore me, I know you can hear me. You're being rude."

She bounced on the edge of the bed. Claire didn't open her eyes. "I think the rude person is the one waking me up in the middle of the night," she slurred.

"It's eight o'clock."

"It's Saturday."

"Southport."

"What about it?"

"The Beatles!   They're going to do a concert at Southport. Not in a club or anything, in a big hall! October fifteenth. That's two weeks from now. We've gotta get tickets!"

Claire reluctantly opened her eyes. "Have you been drinking?"

"Yes, coffee.   It's awful. I don't know how the Americans can stand it. But I need a new article, right? Inspiration. And you were saying only the other day that you're sick of doing the same old things over and over again."

"I did?"

"Yes, you said it over and over again. So, we're getting up, jumping on a bus to the train station, and going to get tickets for the Southport concert."

"And us getting tickets to a Beatles show is a brand new thing to do?"

"You know what I mean. But we have to leave now! We have to get to Liverpool Central for the train."

"Come into money have you?"

"I've got enough. You?"

"I don't know, I have some, but how much is it going to cost to go to Southport?"

"How much could it be? It's not that far. Get up and sort yourself out and then we can go on an adventure. You've got twenty minutes—no, make it ten minutes. I'll see you downstairs."

By nine a.m. an energized Maggie and sleepy Claire sat on the top deck of the number 47 bus heading to the train station. They felt a cool draft sneaking in through the windows.

"What if we miss the return train and get stuck there?" asked Claire.

"We won't. But if we do, we'll hitch-hike."

"Hitch-hike? We might end up walking in the wrong direction, and get hopelessly lost on the moors…"

Maggie shook her head. "Claire, we're getting Beatles tickets, not doing a production of *Wuthering Heights*."

"Oh, it's not that I don't want to travel, I do."

"Excellent, so you can start with Southport."

"Hmm…I was thinking more of London, to be honest. Maybe even live there one day."

"So do I. We'll go together. You can open a hairdressers there instead of here. That's what you've wanted to do here, right?"

"I don't really know what I'm planning to do after college. I guess I should plan to start planning."

"You've been talking for ages about how you'll apprentice at a salon, and then maybe open your own shop. Ringo even said he wants to open a string of hairdresser shops someday. Imagine working for him!"

"Oh, well, the hairdressing's not set in stone is it. And anyway, how could I open a shop? That costs money. A lot of money. Where am I going to get that from? I'd have to rob a bank, or a department store. Or a hairdressers—"

"Jack."

"No, it's true."

Maggie shook her head. "No, there's Jack!"

Claire looked up and spotted Jack finding a seat down the front of the bus.

"Should we go over and say hi?" Claire asked.

Maggie shook her head. "You get wrong for standing up on buses…Oi! Jack!" she yelled, getting the whole of the top deck of passengers turning to look at her. She glared back. "Are you all named Jack?"

The others turned their attention back to gazing out the window or reading their newspapers, as Jack waved and made his way to the back of the bus to join the girls.

"Look who it is," Jack said with a grin. "The girl who faints a lot and her friend with the wooden leg. Maggie and Claire, is it? Never seen you two on the 47 before, do you come here often?"

"We're taking the train to Southport to get Beatles concert tickets" Maggie said, trying not to be obvious as she gazed into his eyes.

Jack raised an eyebrow. "Why? You've seen them here in town dozens of times.

"Thirty-two, to be exact," Claire yawned. "Maggie and I made a pact, so she tells me. We're following the Beatles wherever they go in the world…if we can pay the fare."

Jack chuckled. "Right, well, that sounds a bit—"

"Daft?" Maggie suggested, just to test him.

"Expensive. But where there's a will, there's a way, I reckon. Mind if I join you?"

"You want to come with us to Southport to wait in line for tickets?"

"Why not? I've got nothing on for today. I don't fancy getting concert tickets, but I'll go for the ride, if that's all right. I have a mate lives there. Maybe I'll see him."

Maggie bit down hard on her lip, trying not to smile the most obvious smile ever, having seen her day just get a whole lot more interesting. Not so bad having a good-looking chap to keep her and Claire company.

"So, Maggie, I —'ere, your lip is bleeding," he said, pointing.

"It is? Oh, that's nothing. It's the weather. Chaps my lips this time of year."

"Anyway, I read your article in *Merseyside Music*," he continued. She didn't hear much of what he was saying. She was too preoccupied simply observing him, making mental notes of the way he talked, the words he chose, his body language, what made him tick. He seemed so relaxed and comfortable in his own skin that she almost began to resent him for it.

"Oh yeah, did you like the article?"

"Spot on, in my opinion. But why'd you write about Gerry and the Pacemakers? I thought you were into the Beatles? I noticed some other girl wrote about them playing at the Cavern."

Maggie frowned. "Don't remind me. But I like a lot of the local bands. I love Gerry and the Pacemakers, but the Beatles are my faves. Did you see them on *Ready, Steady, Go!* the other night? They were brilliant!"

"They were lip-synching."

"So what? They looked great. But anyway, I guess there's too much competition writing about them these days. I'm a small fish in a big pond."

"Well don't give up, you've already proved you've got the talent. Maybe you could try and 'discover' a new band."

"Got someone in mind?"

"Not really, but there's a lot of good acts out there at the minute, if you know where to look. They don't all play at the Cavern, mind, you have to check out some other places. If you can get in that is. Just don't write about my band, that won't get you anywhere."

Maggie's eyes lit up. "You're in a band?"

"Not a very good one."

"What instrument do you play?" Claire asked. "You look like a drummer. Strong arms."

"Rhythm guitar. But like I said, not very good. I try though. I'm taking lessons, learning a few chords. But I just like being in a band with me mates. It's a laugh, really."

"You should pursue it," Maggie said. "You could make records, become famous, get on the radio and that."

Jack laughed. "I don't see playing guitar looming large in my future. I play because I enjoy playing, but it's not a career choice."

"Well, you're eighteen, what do you do for a living? You're not in college, are you?"

"I dropped out. Wasn't for me, all those posers just marking time until they have to go out into the real world."

"So what do you do?" she asked, finding herself somewhat disappointed by his apparent lack of ambition.

"Thinking about signing up, my uncle can get me on his ship. Merchant Navy. Gonna see the world!"

"But you'll have to leave Liverpool!"

"That's the point. You're leaving as soon as you're done with college, right?"

"I don't know. Eventually. Claire and I were just talking about that."

"Why would anyone want to stay here if they can get out and see a bit of the world?"

Maggie couldn't argue that point. But she didn't hate Liverpool, not the way Jack seemed to. She found it quite exciting at times. He already seemed jaded by it.

"So where do you live, then?" Claire asked him.

"Woolton. One or two of your Beatle boys used to live there as well."

The girls' eyes widened.

"John Lennon's from Woolton! Do you know him?"

"No, but I know where his house is. I used to pass it every day on my way to school, before he was who he is."

"Oh my God," Claire gushed. "If you had made more of an effort to get to know your neighbours, who knows, you could have been in the Beatles!"

Jack tried not to laugh. "Your logic is amusing."

Maggie's giddiness on the train from Liverpool to Southport refused to be tempered by a few minor inconveniences. She didn't care if her leg was in a cramp, or if Claire complained of being thirsty every thirty seconds. Once they had their concert tickets in their hands, it would all be worth it. The fact that Jack wasn't buying any tickets still piqued Maggie's curiosity as to why he really agreed to come along on their little adventure. She was trying to convince herself it was just because he was at a loose end, but Claire's insistent whispers of "he likes you, this proves it, why else would he be here?" caused her mind to race. Yes, Maggie liked him, but did she *like* him?

"So how is your American boyfriend?" he asked.

"Who?"

"That Yank you write to."

"Ricky? He's not my boyfriend," she laughed nervously. "Not at all. How daft." She suddenly questioned why she felt a need to correct Jack and set the record straight that she wasn't spoken for. Did she protest too much?

"Sounds more interesting than 'pen pal' though, doesn't it?"

"If you like," she said, trying to sound way too casual.

Claire re-entered the discussion, with her usual sledgehammer subtlety. "I think Maggie has her eyes on someone more local."

"I haven't got my eyes on anyone," Maggie said, glaring at her friend. "I have no eyes at all! Why the fascination?"

"Just making conversation," Jack shrugged.

A half hour later, the train pulled up in Southport Station. Maggie wasn't sure how to get to Floral Hall, but Jack had enough local knowledge to lead the girls to the hall ticket office, where they weren't surprised to be joining the end of a very long line—one hundred and seventeen people, according to Claire's count. They'd seen worse. But they didn't' know how many people had already been and gone, leaving with tickets.

"No worries," Maggie said with a stiff, if scarred, upper lip. "We're old pros at standing in line."

"Right then, I'll see you two back here in a bit," Jack announced. "I'm off to take a walk. If you get your tickets before I'm back, don't wait for me to get the train back home. I'll get the next one."

Claire looked curious. "Where are you going?"

Jack smiled, then winked and walked away.

"But—"Maggie began, bewildered by his departure. He disappeared around the corner. "Do you think he practices being mysterious in front of a mirror?" she wondered.

Claire shrugged, "He's probably just going to find a pub. Don't get too attached, Mags. He's one of those."

"One of those what?"

"One of those not to wait for when it's time to go home later."

More people, mostly girls, joined the growing queue for tickets.

"There should be an easier way to get tickets, instead of having to queue," Claire protested.

"Like what?"

"I don't know, we could send a letter promising to pay when we arrive, if they send us the tickets first."

Maggie reacted with a sideways glance. "Yeah, I see that happening."

Suddenly, her sixth sense detected a wave of melancholy and disappointment heading down the queue from the head of the line at the box office and coming her way, like a quiet but menacing tsunami rippling along an otherwise smooth ocean surface.

"Uh oh," she said out loud to herself.

"What?"

"Something's wrong."

Indeed, a wave of moans, curses, and yelps of distress made its way down the line of girls, knocking them off-kilter like a string of dominoes.

"Sold out!" was the phrase that cut through the air over and over. Bloody sold out.

A swarm of girls gathered around the box office window to make a desperate plea for a different outcome, but their efforts failed.

Maggie and Claire skulked away as the others from the queue reluctantly began to disperse aimlessly.

"I was looking forward to this so much!" Maggie pouted.

"Me too."

"We would have gotten to see them in a real concert hall, instead of that hole in the ground. And I could have written a story about it, and maybe get it printed.   How many more chances are we going to have?"

She was angry that their pact to follow the Beatles around the country seemed to be unravelling so quickly.

Claire sighed, but left most of the histrionics to her friend. "Where should we go now, stay here and wait for Jack, or go back to the station? I say we leave. He's probably off somewhere with some mates, and forgot all about us already."

Maggie wasn't listening. "They're going to be on the telly more often from now on, going on more tours…They just won't need people like us anymore, Claire, people who saw them before they made it big, and who cheered them on and danced to their music and lost their shoes…"

"Maybe it would help if we told the box office chap that we've seen them thirty-two times at the Cavern?"

"Oh, sure, he'll say, 'In that case, no worries, darlin', I've put two tickets aside just for you!'"

"Well, let's go then. Jack said not to wait for him, right?"

"Yeah, I don't want him to see me like this."

"Oh, so you *do* fancy him."

Claire locked arms with Maggie as a show of moral support, as they began to retrace their route back to the train station.

"Well," said Maggie, "I hope he's laughing it up at the local with his pals. No sense in all of us wasting the day."

They turned the corner and almost collided head-on into Jack.

"Whoa, ladies, if that's how you walk, I'd be afraid to see you drive. Got the tickets then?"

"No," Maggie said, "Sold out."

"Oh, that's too bad. Fancy some chips before we head back?"

"Is that all you can say?" Maggie said, with genuine hurt in her voice. "We're very upset, Jack. We've got no appetite, all right?"

"Well," Claire ventured, "Maybe we have a little appetite."

"Claire!"

"Sorry, Mags, I'm upset too, but I'm hungry as well. Someone made me miss breakfast, remember?"

"I think I can lift your spirits," Jack said.

"With what? Spirits?"

"Something else."

He reached into his jacket pocket and with a dramatic flourish produced two tickets to the Beatles concert at Floral Hall. The girls' eyes bulged with shock.

"Go on!" Maggie said. "What's that then?"

"What do you think? They're for you."

"Ya what?"

"That's what you came here for, isn't it?"

"But...but..."

"How'd you do that?" Claire demanded, examining the tickets as if they were diamonds smuggled out of the Crown Jewels exhibit. "You didn't cut in line ahead of us where we couldn't see you?"

"No, I wouldn't do that. Let's just say I made arrangements in case you got shut out, which you did. Here. Take 'em. No charge."

"You don't want them?" Maggie asked.

"Nah, I'm not bothered to come this far just to see the Beatles."

"What do you mean, no charge? Did you steal them? Mug someone as they were walking away from the box office with them?"

"Oi, what do you think I am, a common hooligan?"

Maggie gave him a lingering look. "I don't know what you are."

"Don't worry. No crimes committed. Shall we get back to the station now?"

And with that, the stunned girls silently followed Jack to the station. Silently, that is, until they suddenly screamed with joy in unison, turning the heads of several fellow pedestrians.

"We're going to see the Beatles concert, Claire!"

"And you can write an article about it!"

They screamed again.

"And Paul's hair might be an inch longer by then!" said Jack, mockingly.

Maggie and Claire screamed again, louder, causing Jack to shield his ears.

"Okay, I think it's time I got you two back to Liverpool, before you pass out from hyperventilating."

Maggie and Claire secured their tickets in their purses, smiled at each other in understanding, and continued on, following their hero to the station, and back home.

Chapter 7

16 October 1963

Dear Ricky,

*I'VE SEEN THE BEATLES IN CONCERT! Now, I
know I've already seen them thirty-two times at the
Cavern, but this was a real concert in a posh, big hall, on
a proper stage, with a very big audience, over a thousand
people. It was magical! I mean, I couldn't hear a word
they were singing because of all the screaming, and I
couldn't see them very well because we were so far
back—that is, compared to being right by the stage at
the Cavern--but the atmosphere was electric! I had
goose bumps.*

*They sang Roll Over Beethoven and Love Me Do. I think
I even saw two or three girls that had fainted and had to
be carried out, not to mention the girls who tried to storm
the stage and got escorted out. But it was so exciting to
see those four lads go from a small underground club to a
huge glamorous stage to play in front of that many people
going crazy over them. We really got caught up in the
excitement, and if I'd have stopped screaming long
enough, it would have brought a tear to my eye. Oh, and
Claire did lose another shoe; long story.*

*The train journey to Southport isn't long, but it seemed to
take forever to get there. On the way back, though, it
went like a flash. We were so hyper we never stopped
talking all the way home. We almost missed our stop. It's
funny, we almost missed out on that night. The tickets we
stood in line for were sold out, but Jack managed to
produce two tickets from his pockets, clever trick that.*

*Did I tell you about Jack? We met him at a Beatles gig
down the Cavern. When Claire fainted he came to my*

rescue, I mean her rescue. Turns out he's mates with our friend Trev. And he's in a band (Jack, not Trev),I'm planning to go see one of his gigs. His band is called "F Off" because none of them can play the F chord yet. Get it? But yeah, Jack is...Jack is nice. And mysterious. And some might say he's cute. And, yes, I'm one of the "some."

How are things on your side of the Atlantic? Did you get your car yet? Did the Mocha Nut guy come back?

I'm looking forward to your response,
Maggie

With his mouth agape, Ricky managed to stammer, "Whoa, who's this guy Jack? And no, Maggie, you haven't told me about him, until now."

An odd rush of jealously overcame him. He almost immediately felt childish for indulging in it, but the feeling clung to him regardless. Even worse, it steadily began to feel more like panic, and ultimately depression. He struggled to remind himself, as he had reminded his friends countless times, that Maggie was just a friend, and one who lived far, far away. He knew she was bound to find a boyfriend in her home town. It was only natural. And yet, he hated reading about it in black and white. Would this "Jack" be taking up most of her free time now? Would they be going on dates and enjoying each other's company in who-knows-what ways?

Over the next few weeks, Ricky kept a promise to himself to write to Maggie as if she hadn't even mentioned Jack, his philosophy being that he shouldn't ask questions he may not want to know the answers to. Just before Thanksgiving, he decided to write her again to tell her of his plans for the upcoming holiday.

But then…

3 December 1963

Dear Ricky:

Thanks so much for your letter. You wrote so soon after it happened, but you're a lot like me in that way-needing to get your feelings down on paper when they're still raw. I did that when my gran died, but back then I didn't have you to send it to. Thank you for confiding in me. I could tell you were quite shaken by it, and when you wrote that Marie couldn't stop crying for two days, I almost cried as well.

I guess it was a very different kind of Thanksgiving for all of you this year. It must have been a horrific time for the whole country. We followed the news of it every bit of the way. Do you think the man they arrested is really the one who did it? Now we'll never know.

Well, I won't prattle on about the Beatles or my silly day-to-day activities this time. I'll save that for next time.

Take care, chin up, from me to you,
--Maggie

T'was the night after Christmas, and Marie lay on her bed, leaning on her elbows as she read her winter vacation assignment, *Pride and Prejudice*. She didn't mind reading so much, even on vacation, but having to write an essay about it for her English class was another matter. The task became more palatable once she turned on the radio for a bit of background ambience.

Her mother knocked and entered with an armful of folded laundry to deliver to the dresser.

"I wish you'd sit at a desk properly to do your work," she said. "And without musical accompaniment. I don't know how you can concentrate like that."

"It's not *just* music. It's Cousin Brucie, too."

"Oh, pardon me. I forgot he's your study partner."

"If I have to read during vacation, I deserve a bit of company while I'm doing it. Besides, you know I get good grades this way, so why tamper with success?"

Marie's mother shrugged on her way to the door, knowing her daughter had made a fair point. And, she felt fortunate to have a daughter she didn't need to worry about, either in school or elsewhere. Marie had never caused a bit of trouble, even during these notorious teenage years, when she could have become a Tasmanian devil in penny loafers, but hadn't—so far. Likewise, Marie knew her mom was among the most easy-going of all the mothers she knew.

"Just make sure you're done with your reading before you spend the rest of the night on the phone."

Marie glanced to her night stand and the bright new pink Princess phone—a Christmas gift from Mom and Dad.

"Okay, but *The Patty Duke Show* is on soon, so I probably won't make any calls until later."

"Wow, imagine that!"

Marie returned her attention to the essay, assured that, if the going got rough, at least she could call upon Ricky and his talent with words to help her in a pinch. And, with each line she wrote, that particular option was beginning to look more necessary. She re-read the essay question, began to write again, and stopped. With a writing pace of roughly four words per minute, and New Year's approaching, she calculated that she'd be done with the essay by April Fool's Day.

Her radio, permanently set to WABC at 770 AM, had been serving as little more than background noise until Cousin Brucie's unfailingly hyperactive delivery started on a new tangent that caught her ear.

"Remember that sensational new record I promised to play for you tonight, cousins? It's by the Beatles, that group from England everyone is crazy about over there, and it's called *I Want to Hold Your Hand*. It was just released, and here it is on WABC!"

Before Marie had a chance to properly turn her attention to the song, the powerful opening guitar chords jumped out of the radio speaker and nearly propelled her backwards. Then came John's voice—then came the handclaps—then the harmonies—then...

Then, the rest of the world suddenly disappeared, including Elizabeth Bennett and the other *Pride and Prejudice* personae, leaving only Marie and that song remaining. By the end of the second verse, it was as if she had been struck by musical lightning.

"Oh, my God!" she gasped, with her smile widening to its physical limits as she continued to listen. Something about it was just so different. *Everything* about it was so different, and so...so...wonderful! With the last, drawn-out "ha-a-and" at the song's close, Cousin Brucie returned with the promise to play it again later, but Marie didn't want to wait. She frantically turned the dial from WABC at 770 AM to WINS at 1010. But all she found there was *Louie Louie*--definitely not one of her favorites, and sounding even more ridiculous following what she had just heard. She tried again, spinning the radio dial until she stopped at WMCA, 570. And there it was again: *I Want to Hold Your Hand*—although it was already more than halfway through. She strained to take in as much of the remainder of the song as she could. The DJ then reminded listeners that WMCA was the first station in New York to play the song earlier that day.

Marie didn't care who was first. She immediately grabbed her phone and dialled Ricky's number. It may have been a beautiful, shiny new Princess phone, but the rotary dial still seemed to take forever to spin around for each number.

Ricky answered, and barely reached the second syllable of "hello" before Marie erupted with a blast of Beatles-inspired insanity.

"That song! Did you hear it? That song!"

A startled Ricky held the phone a good two feet from his ear as he tried to make sense of the outburst.

"What song?"

"Did you hear it?" she repeated, somehow sounding both euphoric and desperate at the same time. "You know, it was just on--twice! Don't you have your radio on now?"

"Er….not at the moment. I'm watching Patty Duke."

"The Beatles--What's the name of that song? Something about holding your hand?"

"Oh, yeah. *I Want To Hold Your Hand*. It just came out here. But I already have the 45. Maggie sent it to me about two weeks ago. It's really good, isn't it? And the song on the B side is good too."

"You've had it and you didn't tell me?" Her voice raised an octave and sounded almost menacing.

"You never seemed that interested, so I stopped bothering trying to get you to listen."

"What the hell, Ricky! Is it in the stores yet?"

"I think so."

"I'm getting it tomorrow. Cousin Brucie just played it, and MCA just played it, too."

"You listened to MCA? Traitor."

"Missing the point, Ricky! What a great song! Gotta go. I'll see you tomorrow. Maybe someone else will play it again tonight. I have to go listen."

"But you're gonna miss Patty Du--"

Marie slammed down the phone and jumped back to the radio, spinning the dial frantically in her renewed search for the song. The phone rang seconds later. She grabbed it to answer before anyone else in the house could possibly beat her to it.

It was Kirsten. "Hey, Marie…"

"Kirsten!   I just heard something on Cousin Brucie.."

"Yeah! That song by the group Ricky is always talking about?   The Beatnicks or something?"

"The Beatles! Did you just hear it?"

"Yeah, just now. What is it, *I Want To Hold Your Hand*?"

Marie's only reply was to scream with excitement, surprising both herself and the now hearing-impaired Kirsten. The two launched into a long, rambling, high-speed dialogue—often talking over each other—about this new group they knew almost nothing about. Kirsten didn't even know what they looked like.

The next day, they hurried to the record store after school so each could secure a copy of the 45. The girl's delight repeated itself at Kirsten's house when they also played *I Saw Her Standing There* on the flip side. Ricky later provided an extra treat by bringing over the British 45 Maggie had sent him, with *She Loves You* as the B-side instead.

The girls spent the month of January catching up on the Beatles music and activities, with the help of Ricky, and, of course *16 Magazine*. They also made it a point to be in the record store on the day of the *Meet the Beatles* album release. Ricky found it amusing to watch them become so enamoured of the group he had already been listening to for months. He even wrote about them in *The Searcher*, at Marie's suggestion. As an aspiring reporter, Ricky had already—if inadvertently--written his first scoop. And, in Ricky's mind, it wouldn't have been possible without Maggie. He had a lot to write in his next letter.

Chapter 8

January 30, 1964
Dear Maggie:

*They say this is the most depressing week of the year,
because it's right smack dab in the middle of winter--
short days, cold weather, lots of snow. Is winter in
Merseyside as rough this year as it is in New Jersey?
Probably worse, huh?*

*But on to cheerier topics--
It's pretty wild how big a hit 'I Want To Hold Your
Hand' is becoming—the other Beatles songs, too. The
radio stations have been playing them constantly, but I
only listen to one of them—the stations, not the songs.*

*You would laugh at how Marie has suddenly become
such a big fan. I can't take the credit, though. She
didn't pay much attention to the records you sent me.
But now, she wants to cut school and go to the airport
in New York to see the Beatles arrive next week, on the
7th. Did you hear they'll be on the Ed Sullivan Show
here? It's a very popular variety show. So I'm looking
forward to it. But I do have to confess that I don't think I
want to go all the way to the airport just to watch their
plane land, with just a slight chance of seeing them for a
few seconds. I'll have to make Marie see sense so I can
talk her out of it...*

It was 10:30 a.m., Friday, February 7. Ricky found himself on the
bus with Marie heading towards the Port Authority bus terminal in
Manhattan. He realized how foolish he had been to think he'd be
anywhere else-including school—once Marie had made her mind up. It
was past the peak of the morning rush hour, but most of the other
passengers were businessmen making a late start for their last commute

of the week. Among the rows of men in wool overcoats, briefcases, and grey felt fedoras were the two teenagers in winter jackets and jeans. Three other teenagers huddled on the back seat; They were from another town, or else he would have recognized them. But there was no doubt that they had the same plans as he and Marie, judging by their "I Love The Beatles" pin badges, and that they were likely also heading to the airport. Ricky was surprised the bus wasn't overcrowded with the Beatles' legion of fans, all cutting school to make their pilgrimage.

Marie had her transistor radio wired to one ear in the hope that she wouldn't miss any updates on the Beatles' progress across the Atlantic on the way to the newly re-named Kennedy Airport. Ricky, in the window seat, half-gazed out the window, and half-sulked as he watched the Secaucus scenery of marshland dotted with warehouses, pig farms, and a garbage dump moved across his field of view.

"I don't know why going all the way to the airport is necessary," he grumbled. "The Plaza is one thing, but the airport too…We're lucky our parents didn't give us a hard time about going at all. Cutting school like this could lead me down the path of unrestrained juvenile delinquency."

"What?" she said, obviously paying more attention to what she was hearing in her left ear
than the right.

"And I hate taking the bus," he added.

"Huh? You ate cake on the bus?"

"No, I said I…Never mind."

Marie took the radio's earpiece out. "Oh, you hate taking the bus. Well, just be thankful this is the express. And you can't blame Kenny for being gun-shy about letting you drive his car into New York again. I think he really wants you to get your own car soon."

"So do I! I've almost saved enough to get something decent."

Marie held her earpiece tighter to receive some new piece of information.

"Their flight's still on time. It'll land just after one o'clock. We'll be there in plenty of time."

Indeed they were. By 11:30 they had entered the Pan Am International terminal, and began looking for the arrival gates. A large, newly-unveiled portrait of the late President Kennedy hung on one wall, with a plaque beneath it that the two didn't allow themselves time to read. The building was bustling with the usual crowds of travellers and those who were there either to welcome them home, or to see them off.

But also present that morning was an unusually high number of teenagers, scurrying with excitement down the concourse, changing direction together several times like a flock of pigeons before settling on one direction, hoping they were headed the right way. There was a definite sense in the air that something was happening, or about to.

"Let's follow them," Marie instructed.

They followed the crowd down the concourse, noticing other young people in small groups appearing from every direction, converging on the larger crowd to create something nothing less than a teenage swarm. The untold number of total strangers felt an immediate camaraderie with each other, exchanging bits of information, rumors, and the oft-repeated "Who's your favourite?" comparisons as they barrelled their way through the terminal. Ricky also noticed an increasing number of policemen along the way, doing their best to direct the mob of fans along the way.

Marie and Ricky instinctively held hands for safety's sake to keep from getting separated. They were caught in an ocean tide, just following the flow of energy, hoping it would lead them to where they wanted to go. Marie heard a girl in front of her say something about the observation deck.

"Is that where we can see the plane come in?"

"Yeah," said the girl a few steps ahead of her. "That's where everyone's going. Isn't this neat? I've never felt this way about a group! And they're coming all this way to be on Ed Sullivan. I'm Nancy, by the way."

"I'm Marie. This is Ricky."

"Do you live in the city?"

"New Jersey."

"We're from Brooklyn."

"That's cool," Marie countered. "Or should I say, that's fab?"

"Right! Fab!" Nancy laughed.

The crowd seemed to gain speed as the teens continued along, breaking into a trot, then a full-on run, as they followed the signs to the observation deck. Everyone climbed a flight of stairs, most taking two steps at a time, under still more watchful eyes of extra policemen, and emerged outside onto the observation deck, where a thousand other fans were already crammed, looking out onto the tarmac below. Many wore Beatles sweatshirts, others carried signs and banners. A Pan Am jet taxied toward the terminal, but it was far too early in the day for it to be the one carrying the Beatles. The crowd largely ignored it, except for some who were already in a screaming frame of mind, and chose to give their throats a lengthy warm-up.

Ricky and Marie wedged their way to a free spot against the guard railing, grasping it firmly
to keep from being pushed or pulled away by the shifting movements of the throng.

"This is incredible!" Marie yelled, fighting the volume of both the jet engines and the crowd.

"I've gotta admit, it is!" Ricky conceded. He still wasn't sure what was happening, or what exactly he was experiencing in that moment. Only two months before, most people, even avid music fans, hadn't heard much of anything about the Beatles. He wouldn't have either, if it weren't for Maggie. And now thousands of them were making a pilgrimage to the airport just to see the group's plane land.

Marie took out her radio and turned it on to follow whatever developments she needed to hear.

"Murray the K is the only one who's paying attention to this," she frowned. "And I don't even like him that much."

But Murray's on-air progress reports proved useful that day. As 1:30 approached, the fans on the deck—plus countless others on the ground—were able to properly identify Pan Am Flight 1 from London. As the plane taxied closer to the arrivals terminal, the screams of anticipation and welcome grew, and maintained a collective fever pitch as the plane came to a stop. The wheeled staircase was put in position by the front door, and, a few minutes later, the "regular" passengers appeared and made their way down the steps, no doubt enjoying the brief fantasy that the reception was for them. After a brief delay, the Beatles finally appeared and waved to the hordes. As they slowly descended the stairs, photographers and reporters insisted they stop and pose for pictures, even before the foursome could touch solid ground.

"There they are!" Marie shrieked. "Oh my God! That's really them! They're gorgeous!" She screamed the rest of her commentary, such as it was, only to be drowned out by the surrounding cacophony. Ricky had to hold his hands over his ears, but was tempted to join in, just to see how it felt to scream at the top of his lungs in public, and not have anyone take notice of him.

As soon as the Beatles entered the terminal, the onlookers above abandoned their positions and stampeded back down from the rooftop deck to catch up inside. Ricky could barely stay on his feet as Marie pulled him along and clasped their hands together again as they kept pace with their adrenaline-fueled fellow teens.

"Where are we going now?"

"Murray the K said they're having a press conference, I think at the Pan Am lounge."

"Oh, well if Murray the K said so, it's gotta be true."

She had already shifted her attention away from his sarcasm in favor of trying to catch what she could of the swirling mix of words and partial phrases in the air, which, when sorted out and arranged in some order, helped guide the herd towards the Pan Am lounge.

By the time they arrived, they found themselves at the back of a crowd twenty people deep, completely obliterating any sight or sound of the Beatles. All that was visible were the backs of fans who were lucky enough to have arrived just thirty seconds earlier. Hundreds of camera flashes bounced off the ceiling, as if a mid-summer lightning storm was passing through the Pan Am terminal.

"Oh, we'll never get to see them here," Marie groaned.

Nancy offered some reassurance. "They're going to the Plaza after this."

"I know, but we didn't drive here."

"We did. You can come with us."

"Really?"

"Sure. You and your boyfriend."

"Oh, well, Ricky's not—he's just a friend."

"His loss, huh!"

Marie smiled, unsure if Ricky heard a word of the conversation under the din of the scene.

The scene at the Plaza was perhaps even more surreal, as thousands of teens crowded the fountain square in front of the stately building to chant, yell, and exchange the latest rumors as to the Beatles' whereabouts.

Nancy had to let Ricky and Marie out of her car two blocks away, foiled by the police line keeping too many on-lookers and cars from jamming the area completely. She continued on with her friends to find whatever parking space they could, while Ricky and Marie took in the scene.

Some people claimed the Beatles had arrived a short time earlier, and sneaked into the side entrance to evade the crowd. Others claimed the group hadn't yet made it to the hotel from the airport. Ricky and Marie stood amazed at the barely-controlled mayhem. They were about to give up the notion of waiting for Nancy and her friends, when they caught sight of them working their way closer to the fountain.

But the fever-pitch excitement among the teens, and endless anticipation waiting for something to actually happen, began to drain Ricky of his energy.

"I don't think we're going to see them here," he concluded.

"I don't think *anyone's* going to see them here," she said. "And I have to confess I'm getting a little tired."

Content that they had already accomplished their goal to see the Beatles arrive in New York, they decided to take a cab back to the Port Authority and get on the bus to New Jersey. It was a thrilling day.

Sunday afternoon required stopping at the local A&P with Kenny to choose the snacks and refreshments for that evening. Ricky was never much of a party animal, and certainly didn't have much confidence in his own abilities as a host. The few times he had enough friends over for what could loosely be termed a party, he suffered from great anxiety in the hours before their arrival. Would they like his choices of snacks, drinks, and music? Would they become bored, and blame him for his ineptness at keeping his guests happy? While his parties never made front page news (or an entry on the town's police blotter), he managed to pull them off without too many hitches or complaints.

And this time, he reasoned, he wouldn't have to worry about keeping his friends entertained. They would all be there for one purpose, thus placing the entertainment duties squarely on the shoulders of the Beatles, via the 27-inch Emerson TV in the family room.

"We should have real food, too. Not just snacks," Kenny declared, as they meandered down one of the aisles. "Something we can sink our teeth into."

"What do you want me to do, hire a caterer? It's the *Ed Sullivan Show*, not a bar mitzvah. And everyone would have had dinner by eight o'clock anyway."

"How about we cook hot dogs and hamburgers?"

"Sorry, I make it a rule never to bar-be-que in February. The guests' frostbite tends to put a damper on a festive mood. I think Emily Post warned about that."

"No, not outside, we can cook them in the kitchen, or in the garage."

"We could also open a McDonald's franchise in the living room, but let's just keep it simple. And cheap."

They tossed a few bags of potato chips and pretzels into the cart, and proceeded to the rows of soda bottles further down the aisle, all lined up on the shelves like an army infantry of soft drink containers.

"So who's coming?"

"Aside from you and me, my parents and Joanne, there's Marie and Kirsten, and Dave, but I don't know if he's bringing anyone. And Elliot

Kerber is coming with Andrea-Claudia."

Kenny made a face, one he usually reserved for competing in lemon-sucking contests--which he was actually called upon to do quite often.

"Oh, who invited Elliot and Andrea-Claudia? They're such snobs. Especially Elliot. And Andrea-Claudia."

He started pushing the cart in the direction of the check-out line.

"I'm not sure. Marie told me they're coming. But I can't imagine either of them interested in watching the Beatles on TV. I would think they'd consider it beneath them."

"Hey, let's get a box of Twinkies."

"Sorry, it's not in the budget."

Kenny picked up a Twinkie box and caressed it anyway. "Ya know, they can survive for at least twenty years and can survive an atomic explosion. The army tested them in the desert during the war."

"They did not. If you want a box, buy your own."

Kenny frowned, and reluctantly put the box back on the shelf. "I bet Marie told you to say that," he muttered under his breath.

Chapter 9

It was 7:35 p.m., Sunday, February 9, 1964.

The boys went about preparing the refreshments with the help of Ricky's mom, who seemed to have an instinctive knowledge of what size and shape serving bowl best suited each snack on the evening's menu—and more importantly, in which kitchen cupboards each of those bowls could be found.

The television was already on, set to channel 2, and airing an episode of *My Favorite Martian*. Since everyone present dismissed the show as innocuous but silly nonsense for childlike minds, it served as little more than background noise as the preparations continued in the kitchen and adjoining family room. Ricky's parents had agreed to invite everyone to watch the show in that room rather than have Ricky corral his guests downstairs to watch the TV in the basement. After all, this night had all the makings of a momentous occasion.

Marie and Kirsten were the first to arrive, as expected. They could barely contain their excitement, calling dibs on their viewing positions on the end of the sofa nearest the TV. But Marie didn't approve of how the other guests were cutting it a bit fine with their arrival.

"Where *is* everybody?" she demanded. "It's almost eight. If they don't get here until after the show starts, they'll ruin everything--taking off their coats and talking, and getting in the way of the TV when the Beatles are on..."

Ricky shrugged. "I can have them wait outside in a holding pen until the first commercial break," he offered, "but I don't think that would help my reputation as a party host."

The doorbell rang, making his point moot and rescuing him from dealing further with Marie's nervous agitation. He welcomed Dave and Dave's 14-year-old sister Tracy, whose excitement had already surpassed even that of Marie and Kirsten.

"Joanne, Tracy's here!" Ricky called upstairs. His sister bounded down the stairs, creating a convincing earthquake simulation throughout the house. She sported a Beatles sweatshirt, just like the one Tracy revealed as she took off her coat. They jumped and squealed at each other, not enunciating actual words, but communicating in some mysterious manner Ricky had seen many times among excited young females, but had so far been unable to crack the code.

The girls ran into the family room and staked a claim on the carpet just feet away from the TV screen. Dave ambled in behind them, his eyes brightening as he saw the TV.

"Hey, *My Favorite Martian*! I love that show!"

Minutes later, Elliot and Andrea-Claudia arrived, remaining typically low-key as they flashed an obligatory smile and nod to the others. Elliot was known for his longish sideburns, sunglasses (which he wore even after sundown), and a turtle-neck shirt—sometimes with an accompanying sport jacket. He fancied himself a sophisticated hipster, partial to Dave Brubeck's jazz—light years from everything the Beatles represented. Most kids at school dismissed him as the height of pretension. Kirsten and Kenny couldn't help but wonder if Elliot and Andrea-Claudia were there only to heckle the Fab Four during their performance—surely the intentions only of someone with a death wish on that particular night.

Andrea-Claudia was known in school for two things. One was her stunning beauty—tall, blue-eyed and blonde, her long golden hair ironed straight and flat, covering nearly half her face, a la Veronica Lake. The boys in the school hallways often exchanged approving glances to each other as she walked by, signalling a silent wonder at such an impressive physical specimen. Unfortunately, the other thing Andrea-Claudia was known for was her insufferable snobbery, for which she had little apparent justification. She preferred classical music and, when feeling especially brazen, folk music, as long as it "meant something." Her family was no more wealthy or accomplished than anyone else in town, and she herself was not known to claim any particular personal achievement to justify her self-importance, so it must have been her appearance alone that fuelled such a strong sense of superiority. Ricky sometimes wondered if her attitude would change if, after an overnight attack of acne, she happened to awake one morning looking like a decaying zombie.

But she and Elliot were on their best behavior as they arrived and greeted the others, due mostly to the fact that Mr. and Mrs. Kramer were present, and that being surrounded by maniacal Beatles fans automatically put them in unfamiliar and potentially hostile territory. Elliot even took off his sunglasses upon entering the house.

With just minutes to go before the Sullivan show began, Ricky had the idea to get his camera out and take a few pictures of the gathering as everyone watched, and thought he might even take one or two shots of the TV screen itself and send them to Maggie.

"Dad, do we have any flash bulbs?"

"Well, about three or four, so try not to waste them."

As the seconds ticked their way to eight o'clock, everyone sat and got comfortable and chatted. The girls, however, were already too tightly wound to relax. It was not just Joanne and Tracy, who fidgeted with anticipation, as Marie and Kirsten also found their own excitement getting the best of them. Ricky's parents kept themselves in the back of the room, preferring simply to observe.

Finally, as the clock struck 8:00, the voice of the program's announcer filled the room.

"Good evening, ladies and gentlemen. Tonight, live from New York, it's The Ed Sullivan Show…"

The music swelled as Ed came out and introduced the show, Joanne and Tracy unconsciously bouncing where they sat Indian style on the floor. Ed informed the viewers that the Beatles would be on first.

"Good!" Marie said. "We won't have to watch some guy spinning plates while everyone's waiting for the Beatles."

Kenny took exception. "Ooh, I like the guys who spin plates! They're tough! Are they gonna be on tonight, too?"

Before they knew it, Ed was introducing the Beatles. The screams from the studio audience erupted as the camera cut to the group onstage, with Paul kicking off the opening line of "All My Loving." Joanne and Tracy unleashed simultaneous dual screams that jolted the others in the room. Ricky glanced across to Marie, suspecting that he heard a similar shriek coming from her direction as well. Whether she had joined the younger girls' ear-splitting duet or not, she and Kirsten were obviously overcome with—something—in a matter of seconds. But Ricky himself was not immune. He also felt himself drawn to the group whose hype in recent weeks was like nothing he'd ever known.

"There's my Paul!" Marie exclaimed. "Oh my God, he's gorgeous! Look at him!"

The others called out their own comments, observations and critiques throughout the song . Joanne and Tracy tried to caress the picture tube as each Beatle got his own close-up.

"Get away! We can't see!" Ricky ordered.

Kenny looked to Kirsten, noticing that she had a strange look on her face—mesmerized by the images on the screen, somewhat frozen, but with a distinct tear welling up in her eye. Then another. And another.

"Oh, God, they're all gorgeous!" she whimpered, before bursting into tears. This unnerved the boys a bit. "So gorgeous…" she repeated, as her voice trailed off. It quickly became apparent that she would be unable to stop crying. Mr. Kramer rolled his eyes and pulled out a handkerchief. He reached to Kirsten and tapped her shoulder with it.

"Here, you'll be needing this." She grabbed it without taking her eyes off the screen, and promptly stuffed the handkerchief into her mouth.

The Beatles continued their performance with "Till There Was You."

"Oh, I know this one!" Mrs. Kramer said. "It's from *The Music Man*." She turned to her husband. "How bad can they be if they're doing a song like that?"

Mr. Kramer remained unimpressed. "Let's hear 'em sing 'Hello Dolly,' then I'll let you know."

As Paul continued serenading the American viewing nation with the gentle show tune, the name of each Beatle appeared at the bottom of the screen as the studio cameras traded close-ups from one Beatle to the other.

"Good," Mr. Kramer sighed. "I could use some help trying to tell them apart. All I see is long hair."

John's close-up prompted another round of screams from Joanne, Tracy, and Marie. Kirsten was content to continue her crying jag, as her teeth began to rip the handkerchief to shreds. But the superimposed message at the bottom of John's close-up, *"Sorry, girls, he's married,"* triggered a mix of moans and laughter in the room.

"Oh, that's just mean for them to put that on the screen," Marie protested.

"Why, were you planning to marry John?" Dave asked.

"Stupid question! I would if I could! But I already knew he's married."

Ricky turned to Kenny. "I really doubt any of the Beatles are gonna marry an American girl," he smirked.

"How do you know? It's possible," Marie said.

"Shhh!" Joanne demanded, before letting loose with yet another scream of her own.

"They're the Beatles!" Ricky shot back at Marie. "Why would they marry American girls when they can have all the English ones they want?"

"Oh?" Marie said, "Then why do *you* have an English girlfriend when you can have an American one—as in, local—in your own town!"

"Ooh, burn!" Kenny whispered to Ricky. "Even Marie is calling your British pen pal chickie your girlfriend."

Marie returned her focus to the TV screen. Kirsten continued to cry.

"Why is Paul doing most of the singing?" Mrs. Kramer inquired softly, directed at anyone willing to answer. "Is he the lead singer?"

"Mom, shh!" Joanne repeated. "They all sing! But they probably want him to sing more cause he's the cutest." She turned her attention back to the screen and instantly let out another scream, in an almost Pavlovian response to the sight of the group.

The Beatles then broke into 'She Loves You," igniting a fresh wave of screams from the girls. As the singers reached the song's first "wooo!" Marie and Kirsten both let out a full-throated wail, raising the level of adolescent energy throughout the room.

Mr. and Mrs. Kramer could only look to each other and shrug.

Ricky took a moment to take in the Beatles' performance on its own merits, trying to shut out the extraneous distractions in the room. They were certainly living up to all expectations. He took a picture of everyone in the room watching the show, then took one of the screen, careful not to use a flash for that one, lest he create a washed-out photo of a blank screen.

The band reached the end of "She Loves You" to still more hysteria from the Sullivan show studio audience, and quite a bit more from the Kramer's family room. Ed announced that the Beatles would return later in the show, as everyone let out a collective exhale, returning to Earth ever so slowly.

Ricky tip-toed in between people, legs, and feet on his way across the room to Marie.

"Aren't they amazing!" she said.

"That was great," he concurred.

"Oh, how long do we have to wait till they're on again?" Joanne moaned, as the TV show next presented a magician, bounding to center stage to begin a card trick routine.

"I hate magicians," Ricky grumbled. "They're always so smug. 'Watch me do this trick, everyone, I can do it and you can't, and you'll never, ever get to know how I did it, nyah, nyah.' I'd love to line up every magician in the world and smack each one across the face."

"I never knew you had such a violent streak," Marie said.

"Only towards magicians. Ventriloquists are okay. Mimes, not so much."

The next forty-five minutes of *The Ed Sullivan Show* passed at too much of a snail's pace for everyone's liking. The guests took turns grabbing pretzels and potato chips from the snack bowls, pouring soda into the provided paper cups, taking bathroom breaks, and issuing instant reviews of the other acts on the variety show. British music hall singer Tessie O'Shea proved most bewildering.

"Who is she?"

"I think she's sort of like an English Ethel Merman."

"I never saw Ethel Merman play a banjo like that."

"I never saw *anyone* play a banjo like that."

The moment finally came for the Beatles to return, launching into "I Saw Her Standing There." As with "She Loves You," the song had its own built-in "woooo!" in the chorus, which, along with a vigorous head shake, again succeeded in sending the girls into delirious fits. Ricky watched Marie's behaviour degenerate into that of someone almost possessed, right before his very eyes. Joanne and Tracy continued to burn calories bouncing in place on the floor, like two yoga students suffering identical seizures. Kirsten continued to rip Mr. Kramer's handkerchief to shreds with her teeth. Even Elliot found himself nodding in time to the music, offering a random "interesting" every so often. Andrea-Claudia looked nearly catatonic, as she let the performance attack her senses, rendering her speechless, and rather motionless as well. Ricky didn't have a clue how to interpret her condition. He waved his hand in front of her eyes, but she didn't so much as blink.

All of this was merely leading up to the opening chords of "I Want To Hold Your Hand," at which point Marie totally lost whatever fragile reigns of self-control she had left at that point. She, Joanne and Tracy screamed in primal unison, as Dave danced in place, unconsciously strumming an imaginary guitar, unconcerned that he, too, felt himself strangely smitten by the group that supposedly was only for girls to love. Mr. and Mrs. Kramer took a few steps backward, a little closer to the nearest exit in case some sort of escape was necessary.

At last, the song came to an end, the Beatles shook hands with Ed, and waved to the crazed studio audience. The representatives of America's youth gathered in the Kramer house made a half-hearted attempt to compose themselves.

Joanne and Tracy lay flat on their backs beside the TV console, exhausted and dazed.

"Oh, my God," Joanne gasped. "What was *that*?"

Alas, the Sullivan show was not over. Ed next brought on one last act—acrobats, who must have drawn a short straw, because in every viewer's mind, the program was as good as over. The teens in the room continued to trade their exclamations about the Beatles with total disregard to the gymnasts tumbling across Sullivan's stage. The excitement propelled their appetites to finish the last of the munchies. Despite the fact that it was a Sunday night with school the next day, and that they had promised to be home as soon as the program ended, nobody wanted to leave just yet. They had just shared a communal feeling of having witnessed something new and exciting, even life-changing, together.

"Anyone want to watch the Judy Garland show with me?" Mr. Kramer offered, half-seriously. "It's on next." There were no takers. He considered creating a bit of Garland-mania by mock-screaming as her show began, but wisely realized that his offspring would never speak to him again if he did so.

In another twenty minutes time, the kids slowly began to get up and put their coats on to leave.

Kenny guided the blubbering Kirsten to the front door. Only about half of the handkerchief remained in her hand, while the other half could very well have been making its way through her digestive system. Elliot spied Andrea-Claudia in some secretive conference with Marie in a corner of the room.

"You're sure?" she whispered to Marie.

"Yeah, just give it back to me when you're done."

Elliot then observed Marie produce a rolled up magazine and hand it to Andrea-Claudia, who discreetly slipped it onto her coat pocket. He was certain he caught sight of the oversized white numerals "16" on the magazine cover, along with a partially-obscured Beatle face peeking out.

The next morning, Ricky interrupted his usual routine getting dressed for school by sneaking into Joanne's room, and stealthily swiping a small pocket mirror from Joanne's room. He hid it with his comb and a tube of Brylcream in his jacket pocket, and left the house for school. As soon as he came upon a familiar hedge of shrubs down the street, he ducked behind them and pulled out the mirror and comb, steadied himself, and dragged the comb from his hairline down over his forehead, stopping at his eyebrows. As he had anticipated, his hair didn't want to take to the new style, so a dab of Brylcream helped secure it in place. He combed down the rest of his hair on all sides as well, and approached the school feeling like nothing less than a rebel, presenting himself as the harbinger of a new revolution—via Liverpool, England, of course. Would people notice? How would they react? Would the girls make the connection and see him as Beatlesque, thus driving them wild, chasing him down the school hallways?

He approached a cluster of kids near one of the building entrances, recognized Kenny from behind and gently tapped his shoulder. Kenny turned around, revealing his hair also plastered down upon his forehead, but with considerably more Brylcream than Ricky would ever dare use. Their necks retracted backward like pigeons in their surprise at discovering each other's rather crude makeover. Ricky then looked past Kenny to notice that nearly every boy in sight had his hair combed similarly downward. He suddenly felt as if he was in a bad science fiction film.

"What did you do?" he asked Kenny.

"Me? What did *you* do?"

"The same thing, obviously. Except you look as if you shampooed your hair with motor oil."

"It wouldn't stay down. But once it does, we've got it made with the girls. This thing with the Beatles' hair is driving them crazy. So we'll have our pickings in no time. You'll see."

"Look around, Kenny."

Kenny, the devious mastermind, did so, and quickly caught on.

"Oh, yeah. But I have another idea. I'm going to take guitar lessons. I decided on the way home last night. Let's see every guy around here do *that!*"

"Yeah, you might have something there, except that you're definitely not a musical person."

"Yes I am."

"No you're not. You even whistle off-key. I'd feel sorry for the poor slob who would have to give you guitar lessons."

"I bet there are a lot of poor slobs who would give me guitar lessons. Especially now."

Ricky decided not to push too hard to destroy his friend's dream.

"Okay, we'll see. If it's good enough for the Beatles, right?"

"Right!"

Chapter 10

Maggie leaned against a painted cream brick wall, wondering what was taking so long. She realized that she rarely had patience for anything in life, but some things tried that patience more than others. Finally, the heavy brown painted door swung open and Claire emerged into the hallway, calling out "Thank you, Mr. Dunhill" behind her. She closed the door and met Maggie.

"Well, how did it go?"

Claire grinned. "I got it! I got the job!"

"Hey, congratulations!" Maggie gave her friend a hug. "Good on ya. I knew you'd get it."

"Although when I told Dunhill that I'm a friend of yours, he sort of made a face, like a frown."

"I don't care. This'll be great! I'll show you the ropes. It'll be a lot less dreary around here now. We're going to have so much fun working together."

"I hope so, Mags, if I don't mess up and get sacked on the first day."

"Nah, I'll take care of you. When do you start?"

"This Saturday, on your shift. Dunhill wants you to train me."

"No problem! But you know Saturday night I'm getting the phone call from Ricky. I've got to be out of here on time, not a minute later."

"Ooh, yeah, that'll be big day for you, eh?"

"It'll be a big day for you as well!"

Maggie nudged Claire, who smiled in return.

"Wonder what I'll buy with my first wage."

That Saturday, Claire began her training behind the refreshment counter, with Maggie as her guide. Since it was Maggie who put in a good word for her, she was, in Mr. Dunhill's eyes, responsible for the new employee.

It began smoothly enough as Maggie showed her around the snack counter.

"And this is the popcorn, sweet in one side, salted in the other."

"Am I allowed to eat it?"

"Officially no, but as long as Dunhill doesn't see, you can do whatever you want."

Claire grinned at the thought of free popcorn and lemonade any time she felt like it.

"Technically," Maggie continued, "you're allowed to take whatever you want, for free, on your break, so if you munch the popcorn during the day, they won't notice."

Claire nodded and pointed to the cash register. "How do I work this?"

"You just type in how much the item is, how much the customer gave you, and hit this button. You can give proper change, can't you? I mean, you can do it in your head?"

"I think so. But might take some practice."

"Let's say I wanted a large-size Coke and a packet of crisps. What would you do?"

"I'd tell you it will make your skin break out if you have too much of that stuff."

"Sorry, but you're not allowed to lecture the customers. And be careful of the drawer, it sticks sometimes." She moved away from the till and to the chiller cabinet. "This is where we keep the ice cream. Halfway through a film an usher will come with a tray and take some of this into the stalls to sell. We've got chocolates to choose from over here, and some sweets."

Claire's eyes widened. "Jelly Babies!"

Maggie laughed. "Yes, Claire, Jelly Babies. It's not like you've never been in the cinema before, you know we have Jelly Babies."

Shaking her head, Claire explained, "I never buy snacks in the cinema, it's far too expensive in here, I always go to the newsagents first and sneak pop and crisps in under my coat."

"You rebel!"

"I think I got this. Looks easy enough."

"It is, but it gets pretty busy, you have to keep moving quickly and efficiently. And remember, the customer is always right, even when they're wrong--and they're always wrong--and a smile goes a long, long way."

"Don't worry, I'm a people person. I can handle this."

"Also, today we have to get finished cleaning and sorting as soon as the film's finished because Ricky's phone me at seven o'clock sharp, and I have to be home and get prepared."

"Prepared? What, you mean do your makeup and stuff for a phone call?"

"No, I have to think about what I'm going to say, so I don't sound like a bumbling fool, and I have to make sure I have a bathroom break first. How embarrassing would it be if I had so say, 'oh, hold on, Ricky, I need the loo!'?"

As the Saturday crowd was at its thickest, Maggie and Claire, even with additional help from the other counter staff, were rushed off their feet. The queue for snacks was almost out the door. Maggie worked as fast as she could, as Claire tried her best to learn the job. She got no help from the till, which kept jamming and nearly caused her to lose a finger on its snappy drawer. Despite her swelling purple digit, she soldiered on, takin in the shouts from the customers about her not being quick enough. She also discovered, while required to give change, that her math skills were rustier than she had thought.

"Two lemonades, please, when you're ready, love," called a customer waving his money around.

Claire kept herself calm and fetched the lemonades, typing the amount into the till and taking the note from the customer. She braced herself for the till drawer to come flying open, but it didn't budge. She pressed the button again, but the drawer was stubborn.

Maggie came over to ring up her sale of three ice creams, two colas, a sarsaparilla and three small popcorns, as Claire threatened the till.

"What's wrong?"

"This piece of scrap is trying to show me up on my first day. The drawer is stuck and I'm in the middle of a sale."

"Oh, yeah, it's been getting stuck from time to time."

"I still need my change!" called the customer with the two

lemonades.

"Yes, sir, coming right up," Claire promised, turning to Maggie. "Help me!"

Maggie tried pressing the buttons but nothing happened. "What did you do?"

"Nothing!"

"I think it's jammed. This isn't good."

A few more customers from the middle of the queue could be heard complaining about their wait. Their comments, along the lines of 'at this rate, I'll be in my seat for the end credits!' weren't helping the situation.

Maggie tried pressing the buttons harder and slamming her fist on the side of the till, but the drawer still wouldn't give up.

"I'll have to get Dunhill."

Turning to the customers, as the ice-cream on the counter melted, Maggie announced, "Ladies and gentlemen, we're experiencing a small problem with the till, if you could just bear with us, the manager will be on it, and the problem should be resolved within a couple minutes. Sorry for your wait."

She turned to find Dunhill.

"Don't leave me!" Claire pleaded.

"I have to get Dunhill. I'll be right back. Just keep them entertained."

"Entertained? With what a cabaret? A tap dance on the counter? Shadow puppets against the price board?"

"Sure, but not all at the same time."

Instead, she repeated Maggie's words, letting the customers know they should only be waiting a couple minutes, then let out a meek "It's my first day."

Dunhill marched across the lobby to the snack counter and tried pressing the button on the till, as if the girls hadn't already thought to do that. The register had been acting up for a while and this looked like the final straw, but there was money inside that machine and Dunhill wasn't willing to lose it, even if he had to resort to drastic measures, short of taking a sledgehammer to it.

"Maggie, take an empty ice-cream box and use that to put the money in, there's a filled coin bag on my desk, use that as the float money. I'll get the sledgehammer."

Maggie nodded and got onto the task straight away. She quickly glanced at the oversized clock on the wall. Just a few more hours, her work day would not only be over, but she'd actually be having a phone chat across the Atlantic with Ricky. She only hoped nothing would keep her from getting on the bus no later than six p.m. It seemed like an eternity would have to pass first.

She returned with the empty box and float money, and got back to serving. Claire gave the man with the two lemonades his change out of the float.

"We can still leave at half past five, right?" she asked.

"Not if these customers aren't served and seated in the auditorium."

"But where are the people for the next shift?"

"Until they get here, the ushers take care of snacks on their trays. But we need to serve these people before we can go."

Claire started to think how working in the cinema was way more stressful than she'd anticipated, even for a people person surrounded by popcorn and Jelly Babies. "Next please," she called.

While Maggie and Claire were knee-deep in demanding customers on that hectic Saturday afternoon, Ricky's day was just beginning. He awoke that morning with the same thoughts that almost kept him from falling asleep the night before. In just a few hours, he and Maggie would finally speak to each other, for real. He was excited, but also terrified. He had never done especially well under pressure when conversing with the opposite sex. There were exceptions—Marie being the most obvious. But the idea of having his first chat with Maggie felt different. He wanted to make a good first impression. How, he wondered, was he going to get through his first talk with Maggie without making not only a monumental ass of himself, but a *transcontinental* monumental ass of himself? He was determined not to let it happen this time. Not with Maggie. He had over five hours to kill before the pre-arranged time--two o'clock Eastern time, 7 o'clock Maggie time. He spent much of the morning scribbling notes and questions to have in front of him as they chatted, to avoid any prolonged and awkward silences. He felt as if he were preparing for an appearance on a live TV talk show.

By noon, he was climbing the walls, alternating between boredom and anxiety, not knowing what to do with himself. But an impromptu visit from Kenny and Dave came as a pleasant surprise.

"Come on, we're going for lunch," Kenny announced, providing the reason for their unexpected drop-in.

"I don't know if I should go. I need to be here at exactly two o'clock, remember?"

"You haven't given us a chance to forget," Dave grumbled.

Kenny waved his hand dismissively. "No problem. We've got plenty of time. We'll just go to the diner. It won't take long."

"You don't understand. I can't be even a little late."

"Don't worry!" Kenny insisted.

"But what if…what if your car breaks down?"

"Well, should we each bring our own car?" Dave suggested with a heavy dose of sarcasm. "Then if Kenny's car breaks down, we'll get into mine, or Ricky's—oops, sorry Ricky. You still don't have a car, do you?"

Ricky relented, but even as they sat down in the diner booth, he began checking his watch with the regularity of a train conductor.

"I'm just going to have a BLT," he told the others as they scanned their menus. "It's quicker."

"For them to make, or for you to eat?" Kenny asked.

"Both."

"But it comes with fries," Dave teased. "Won't those slow you down?"

"Ricky, relax," Kenny said, giving his friend a gentle jab on the arm. "We have plenty of time. We'll get you home by two."

"*Before* two! Home *before* two! I need some prep time before I actually call her."

The idea had Dave shaking his head. "Prep time? What, you mean like take a shower, shave, and put on cologne? To make a phone call?"

"No, you guys don't understand, Ricky said.

Indeed, they didn't. Ricky wouldn't have traded them as friends for anyone else in the world, but he also knew Kenny and Dave just weren't likely to appreciate the nature of the friendship he and Maggie had been cultivating for the past year. He knew he could either try to enlighten them, or just sit back and let them make jokes about his British "girlfriend." He succumbed to the latter option.

As they sat and ate, other topics, ranging from the ridiculous to the sublime (mostly the ridiculous) peppered the conversation. Ricky wolfed down his sandwich and fries in record time, as predicted. Upon finishing a second glass of Coke to wash it all down, he sat quietly, listening to the others, shaking his foot under the table with nervous energy, and checking his watch again. The latest check revealed he was still ahead of schedule, so he allowed his buddies to shoot the breeze just a little while longer, so he wouldn't become a total nuisance to them. But he only half-listened to their chatter, as he imagined how his upcoming talk with Maggie might sound.

It didn't take long before the swiftness with which Ricky gobbled down his sandwich and drank his Cokes began to give him regrets. He felt his abdomen expanding like a party balloon.

"I feel so bloated," he moaned.

"No wonder," Kenny said. "You should be in the *Guinness Book of Records* for eating a BLT that fast."

"Do you feel sick?"

"No, just, well…gassy." He tapped his chest. "I need to burp, but I can't."

"You will," Kenny assured him. "It's easy." He cheerfully demonstrated with a resonant, self-induced belch of his own. While he and Dave found it hilarious, Ricky was not amused.

"Well, that solves *your* problem, but not mine," he said.

"Have another Coke, to help it along."

"I've just had two. That's already more gas than I can handle. I'm afraid if I get too close to someone lighting a match, I'll go up like the

Hindenburg."

A sense of panic suddenly overcame him. "Oh, no! What if I'm talking to Maggie and I accidentally let out a monster burp, right in the middle of a sentence! She'll be totally grossed out. She'll think I'm disgusting and she'll never want to speak to me again."

"Why not? Don't people burp in England?"

"I don't think they're allowed to, by law. It's too undignified for them." Dave said.

"I've gotta burp, right away, guys," Ricky moaned. "I have less than an hour. Maybe I should take some Alka-Seltzer back home."

They rose from the booth and paid at the front counter. Ricky moved slowly and heavily out the door, continuing to tap his chest and stomach as they crossed the parking lot towards Kenny's car.

"Ya want me to put you across my shoulder and tap on your back, like mothers do to burp their babies?" Kenny offered with a smirk. Dave had a suggestion for Ricky along similar, if more aggressive lines.

"If you want, I'll punch you in the stomach," he offered. "That might help."

"Dave, I just want to burp, I don't want internal bleeding."

"I'll be careful, Ricky. It could force the air out."

"It could force my lunch out, too, and I'd rather not have to deal with that right now."

At ten minutes to six, Claire served the final customer two orders of popcorn, one salted, one sweet, two colas and two ice-creams. She handed over their snacks as Maggie handed over their change.

"Enjoy your film," Maggie said with a smile, as the man and his wife took their treats and walked away. They both slumped against the counter, exhausted. "And now we're finally free! I have to catch the six o'clock bus."

Before she could escape the confines of the snack counter, a balding man with a tragic comb-over approached.

Maggie took a deep breath, "How can I help you?"

"I'll serve this customer, Mags, you run for the bus."

"I can't, it's your first day, and it's policy not to leave a new employee on their own during their first few days." She leaned over and whispered, "Don't worry, I'll get rid of him fast. Watch and learn."

"What flavour ice-cream do you have?" the man asked.

"Vanilla, chocolate and strawberry, but we're out of chocolate and strawberry."

"Do you do any with nuts?"

"Vanilla, sir. That's all we have left."

"Not with nuts?"

"What, you mean like *mocha* nut?"

"Sorry?"

"Nothing, I was thinking of another customer, far, far away. No, we don't have any with nuts. Just vanilla at the moment, no nuts." She glanced at the clock again.

"Good, because I'm allergic to nuts."

"You don't happen to have any relatives in New Jersey, do you?"

"Would you like a vanilla cone?" Claire offered. "They're wonderful. All that vanilla—and a cone. . ."

The man thought for a moment. "No thank you. What fizzy drinks do you have?"

Maggie rattled off the list. "Orange, cola, lemonade, sarsaparilla and cherry."

"I'm in more of a lime mood."

"We don't have lime. But lemon is close to lime"

"No, I don't like lemonade. Too sweet."

Four minutes to catch the bus.

"Do you do a small popcorn?" he asked.

"Yes," Claire said, as she held up the smallest size bag for popcorn, "This is small."

The man shook his head. "No, no, that's no good, I'll never eat all that. Got anything smaller?"

"This is the smallest we do," Maggie interjected. "I'm afraid we don't sell them by the kernel, sir. How about you buy the bag, and whatever you don't eat you take home and eat later?"

"It will go stale and I don't believe in wasting food."

"Do you have a pet budgie?" Claire asked.

"Why, no. I have a bulldog named Oliver, but he doesn't like popcorn."

"Well how about you just put your hand in the popcorn and carry a handful through with you?" Claire suggested with a smile. "No charge."

"Frightfully unhygienic, wouldn't you say?"

"Doesn't bother me," she shrugged.

The man thought for a moment. "No, I don't think I'd like to do that. I'd probably spill it."

Three minutes to catch the bus.

"I've got an idea," Maggie said. She collected a small plastic cup and filled it with popcorn. "How's that?"

The man smiled. "That's perfect!"

Maggie handed him the cup, "No charge, it's too small."

Feeling victorious, she prepared to leave.

The man took a taste test and grimaced. "I don't like sweet popcorn. I wanted salted."

Maggie glanced at the clock again. Two minutes to catch her bus. She grabbed the cup back, tipped the popcorn on the floor, filled it with salted, ran around the side of the counter, and handed the man the cup as she hurried past him.

"Enjoy your film," she said, and ran for the door.

Claire, impressed with her friend's the efficiency, smiled at the man as she followed Maggie out.

It was getting dangerously close to 2:00p.m., as Ricky frantically rummaged through the medicine cabinet and grabbed a bottle of Alka Seltzer, drafting two tablets into service in his race against both the clock and his own gaseous discomfort. He watched the fizz in the glass of water and quickly gulped it down. He waited. He jumped up and down a few times. Finally, he released a long, deep, bullfrog-like belch that echoed throughout the house. His abdomen compressed, then relaxed, much to his relief. But he had only minutes to spare.

Chapter 11

At last the moment had arrived. After saving money to give to his father for the cost of the call, arranging the day and time with Maggie so she'd be available to answer, everything was in place.

Ricky checked the clock one last time. It was exactly 2:00 p.m., which would be 7:00 p.m. in Liverpool. Perfect. His hand quivered a bit as he picked up the phone and called the overseas operator to give her the number. With a pounding heart, sweaty palms, and a dry mouth, he resembled a hospital emergency room patient more than a teenager making a phone call. He was glad he remembered to keep a glass of water handy to keep himself from choking on his own words.

Maggie sat on the floor against the wall in the the understairs cupboard, the only place the phone cord would stretch to that would offer her privacy. She found herself thinking how it would have been a great time to have a phone in her own bedroom – imagine that! She checked her watch. Exactly 7:00 p.m. What if he forgot to call at their pre-arranged time? How long should she wait for the phone to ring?

Ricky clasped the phone to his ear and pressed "O" for the operator. He waited to be transferred to the overseas operator, then gave her the number, and waited some more. A seemingly interminable stretch of dead air ended with several clicks and a syncopated, rhythmic, "beeeep-beep" ringing of the phone at Maggie's house, an ocean away.

The startled girl jumped at the ringing of the phone. Maggie's mum knew her instructions not to answer the phone or disturb her. Her mum was thankful enough that she wasn't paying for the call. Maggie gave herself one last reminder to sound cool, calm, and collected. In the split second before picking up the receiver, she found it peculiar how she felt more anxious awaiting this call than any call from any potential date she ever had.

Ricky glanced down at his notes, deciding on which topic to open their chat.

Maggie picked up the phone.

"Hello?" she said. The two syllables revealed to her caller a soft, delicate speaking voice, with just a touch of a Liverpudlian dialect, exactly as Ricky had imagined it.

"Maggie?"

"Yes?" A broad smile lit up her face as she struggled to keep her voice calm and dignified.

Ricky wondered why he wasn't hearing just a little hint of excitement or anticipation in her voice. Perhaps only two syllables weren't enough to go on."It is I—I mean, it's me, Ricky. Greetings From America!"
Oh, God, he thought, did I just say that?

"Hello, Ricky. All right, then?"

He wasn't exactly sure what that meant, but he assumed it was a common greeting."Er, yes! I'm all right. I'm calling at the right time, aren't I?"

"Oh, yes, we've just finished our dinner."

"Oh, good. I only just had lunch.

But I guess to you, I had it five hours
ago."

Maggie giggled, hoping his
phrasing was intentional. "You
sound good." She felt like
hitting herself in the stomach. Say
something halfway intelligent,
she demanded of herself.

"Good! So do you. I really like
your accent."

"What accent?" she said with a
smile.

Oh, no, he thought. Was it considered
an insult to tell English people that, to
Americans, they have an accent?
"Oh, I forgot," he stumbled. "You don't
really hear it, do you? I guess I don't hear
my own, either." He felt like pounding
himself in the stomach.

"Oh, it's fine. I just try not to
sound too scouser. Working class.
Makes it harder for non-scousers
to understand me, so I'd have to
repeat myself, you know?"

"I think so," he said, even though
he didn't know what she was talking
about. But he didn't dare ask her to
repeat it.

"Anyway, it's nice to hear your
voice, as well. A little strange,
maybe."

His heart sank.
"My voice is strange?"

"No, no, it's fine. Very American.
It's just strange to finally hear it
after all of our letters."

He fumbled for his notes again, while
cursing himself for having to rely on
them in the first place. But he was
determined not to embarrass himself.
Was this how Walter Cronkite felt
whenever he interviewed President
Johnson? Probably not.
"Ask-about-weather" he read to himself,
inadvertently muttering
the phrase out loud.

"Oh, right," Maggie complied.
"How's the weather?"

"What? Oh…No, I didn't mean—
I was just…The weather's fine here.
It's very…American. And yours?"

"Very fine, thanks. It was nice
today, but I had to work. We
took a walk by the river
yesterday,though."

She cringed at her own bland
words, evaluating them one by
one as they tumbed
out of her mouth, and concluded
that she must have sounded like a
crashing bore—talking and yet
not really saying anything. She
wondered if the phone cord was
long enough for her to strangle
herself with it.

Ricky again glanced at his notes.
"Ed Sullivan," he said out loud again.

"Sorry? Who?"

"Oh, er, I wanted to tell you more
About how the Beatles were on the
Ed Sullivan show."

"Oh, yes, the man you described
as very strange."

"Yeah, that's him. They've been on
three weeks in a row, the last one
was Sunday."

"Wow, that's a lot of TV gigs on
one show."

"They were great. Everyone's
going crazy over them."

"Right, just like here!"

Ricky began feeling more relaxed.
At least he knew that the Beatles were
a fool-proof conversation topic for he
and Maggie. "When they come back for
their tour later this year, I'm definitely
getting tickets."

"Oh, you definitely should!"

"Yeah, I'd probably go with Kenny,
or Marie." He froze in silence upon
Mentioning Marie, and wondered if
he should while speaking to Maggie.
Was it bad etiquette? Was he over-thinking
it? And why was Maggie not speaking?

"I hope you get to see them."
Hmm, she thought, apparently
Ricky and Marie were quite close
indeed. "Have you two been
dating?"

"Oh, no, not really. No. Dating?
No." He felt unable to control his
own inane babbling. One "no"
certainly would have sufficed.
"How about you?"

"No, I'm not dating Marie,
either," she said dryly, waiting for
a laugh, but didn't hear one.
"Oh, right. I mean, I've been
spending time with some of the
lads, like Jack. I wrote to you

about him?"

"Oh, yeah. Jack." Time to change
the subject, and fast. "How's school?
Are you taking any writing classes?"

"Just one, but it's good. Gives me
lots of practice. I think deep
down I just want to be a writer
because that's the class where I
get the best marks! The rest of my
brain isn't nearly as developed as
the part that does the writing."

"Same with me. And I like writing
for the school paper."

"Looks like Fate already has
plans for us, Ricky!"

Ricky could have taken the remark
to mean one of two things--the way he
hoped Maggie meant it, or that she
really was just talking about writing.
"Time will tell!" was all he could muster.

"Yes, indeed."

"Well, I think we're up against the clock.
I'm afraid to see how much this call will be."

"Oh, is there a way I can chip
in?"

"No, don't worry. Sorry to cut us off, but
it's all I can afford. But it's been great to
finally chat with you."

"Me, too! I hope we can chat
again sometime, maybe even in
person."

"That would be great."

"Bye, Ricky. I'll write soon!"

The phone clicked, followed by dead silence.

Ricky's anxiety about the phone chat developed into full-blown depression in the following few days. He let it all out with Marie as a sounding board, not entirely sure if that was wise.

"I sounded like a stumbling, bumbling, stuttering, inarticulate idiot who doesn't deserve to have such a cool, dignified English girl as a pen pal. She'll never want to write to me again!"

"Why not?"

"Because I'm a stumbling, bumbling, stuttering—"

"Yeah, I got that part. What did you say to her that was so bad?"

"Everything! I was boring! And when I wasn't being boring, I was being *incredibly* boring."

"Oh, I doubt it. You're never boring. You're the most interesting person I know."

"Ha!"

"I'm a good judge of people, Ricky, and you're not boring. You're interested in so many things. Besides, what did *she* say that was so fascinating?"

"Well…she…sounded so…intelligent."

"Why? Because of her accent?"

"The accent didn't hurt."

"It's just an accent. And you're intelligent."

"It got a little better when we talked about things like the Beatles, and school, but before I knew it I realized how expensive the call must have been getting, so I had to cut it short. I felt awful."

"I'm sure she understands."

"No, I blew it! She'll never write to me again. And she'll definitely never want to speak to me again."

"I've gotta say, Ricky," she said with a noticeable tinge of annoyance, "you sound pretty upset over someone you'll probably never meet. I'm right here. Do you worry that much about what someone like *me* thinks about you?"

Chapter 12

Trevor Denton, known to his friends simply as Trev, didn't have much to do that afternoon. Apart from get a haircut, which didn't take up a whole lot of time, his day was empty. And when his diary was empty, he liked to have what his mother referred to as 'larking about' time.

He headed to his most frequented bar, the Golden Oak, to see if some of his mates were hanging around there, but he didn't expect to see Maggie standing outside peering through the cloudy windows.

"Never mind, you'll be eighteen next month, they'll let you in for sure then."

Maggie turned around, startled.

"Oh, Trev, hi...I was just..."

"Inhaling the beer fumes?"

"No, I was just trying to see if Jack was in there. He told me his band plays here sometimes. Wanted to check them out."

"You know, if you're only ordering a lemonade, they'll let you inside."

"Is Jack's band on today?"

Trev looked at his watch, it was 2 p.m. "Not for another six hours."

"Oh, that's probably more lemonades than I or my bladder can handle."

"Well, it's not as if they pay *you* to drink them. And the band's only on for twenty minutes as well."

She shrugged. "Think I'll go see what Claire's up to then."

"Yeah, where is she? I do believe this is the first time I've ever seen you without her by your side."

"I don't know where she is, I thought I'd make this trip alone." She felt herself blush slightly.

"Aha. I see."

"See what?"

"Jack."

Maggie spun round fast. "Where?"

Trevor laughed. "Not here. I mean you're really here for Jack and not his band."

"Am not. I like music."

"Uh huh."

"And I'm a music journalist, so I need to keep up with all of the bands around here."

"Uh huh."

"And if Jack's in a band, I couldn't very well see the band without seeing Jack, can I? Are you going to say 'Uh huh' again?"

"Jack's band are okay, they're improving with every gig, but they're just the warm up act really. Everyone comes to see The Five Kings. *They're* good, even though there's only four of them. No idea why. Do you want me to tell Jack you were here if I see him?"

"Um, no, that's okay, I'll see his band some other time," she said, straining to sound casual.

"Well they're on at 8 p.m. If you fancy it, bring Claire."

Maggie smiled. "Yeah, I might do. Catch you later." She headed off toward the bus stop.

Trevor entered the pub, seeing Jack heading into the back room, where the landlord kept crates and broken bar stools. It was the only place where the musicians could prepare for their performances. Trevor jokingly nicknamed it "The Star Bar".

At the bar he ordered two half pints and went into the back room – the barmaid knew he was okay to go ahead. Inside the Star Bar, Jack tuned his guitar, a scratched Stratocaster that had definitely seen better days, and probably numerous owners.

"Isn't it time you laid that thing to rest and got a new one?" Trevor chuckled, placing the extra drink on a chair that had also seen better days, judging by its slashed cushion.

"I like it, it has character--like me." Jack gave a goofy smile.

"I've just seen Maggie outside."

"Oh?"

Jack didn't look up from his guitar as he turned a few keys and plucked a few strings.

"She was looking for you," Trevor continued.

Jack looked up. "Really? Why didn't she come in?"

"I didn't think you'd be here yet. She wanted to check out your band."

"Is she coming back?"

Trevor smiled. "Why? Do you want her to? You fancy her don't you?"

Jack shrugged and turned his attention back to his guitar. "She's alright."

"Wow, calm down, son, you don't want to seem too keen. Besides, it's obvious you fancy her. If you want her to come to the gig, then you should go and ask her. Or you know, ask her out properly."

"Maybe I will. After this pint. Or, rather, half pint, you cheapskate."

At 5.30 p.m. Maggie was in the midst of tackling some of her college homework. She'd neglected to do it the day it was assigned, and found herself trying to cram it all in the day before it was due. When her mother called up to tell her there was a young man at the door to see her, it came as a welcome distraction.

Mrs Carter left her daughter in private to talk with her surprise visitor.

"Jack! What are you doing here? Um, I mean, hi."

"I bumped in to Trev, he said you were interested in coming to see my band play."

"Err...yeah, I like music."

"Well we're playing tonight at 8 o'clock if you're interested. Would be good to see you and Claire in the audience, if you'd like her to come."

"Okay, yes, that sounds like fun. You want me to write an article about your band?"

"No. Well, yeah, but that's not why I want you to come tonight. I, err...is it okay if we hang out after the gig? Talk a bit?"

Maggie noticed how he seemed a little nervous, which was unlike him. "Sure. I'd like that."

Jack smiled. "Good. I guess I'll see you later then." He turned and headed down the path.

Maggie watched him walk down the street, then closed the door and ran straight for the phone and began to dial the four digits she knew by heart without even watching which buttons she was pressing.

"Claire, something amazing just happened! Jack came over! To my house!...Oh, I'm sorry, sir. Wrong number. Go back to sleep."

She tried again, this time making sure to watch what number she was dialing.

As the clock struck seven, Claire sat on Maggie's bed, watching Maggie put lipstick on, then wipe it off and re-apply it, several times over.

"Mags, promise me you'll never become a house painter."

"Don't be silly. Who paints a house with lipstick."

"So he asked you out, then?"

"Not exactly. Well, I mean, yeah he did, to watch his band play, but then he wants to hang out afterwards."

"But he invited me, too?"

"Well, just to the gig. So, when it's time for him and me to be alone, on your bike. Nothing personal."

"Well what am I supposed to do then, play in traffic?"

"Yeah, I guess. Talk to Trev. You two get on well."

"That's true. We're on the same wavelength, and he complements my addiction to sweets. I hate green sweets and he loves them...so I swap him for red ones."

"Ah, true soul mates."

"Do you have any?" Claire asked with some intensity.

"Sweet addictions, or soul mates?"

"No...just sweets in general?"

Maggie shook her head. "Nope, all out of sugary treats. Anyway, I just brushed my teeth. Can't indulge at the moment."

"I wasn't suggesting *you* eat them, I was talking about me."

"We'll get something on the way."

Claire thought for a moment. "Does your mother know you're going to a pub?"

"I go to the Cavern a lot. It's almost the same thing."

"They don't serve alcohol at the Cavern."

"As long as I'm not planning on getting blind drunk, I'm fine. What about your mum?"

"She thinks I'm at your house."

"You *are* at my house."

"Then I didn't lie."

The air in the pub was soaked in the odours of stale ale and cigarette smoke. Maggie had expected the crowd to be all middle-aged men, making her and Claire as the alien invaders to the polluted but merry meeting place. But there were plenty of young females around, some keeping company with those same middle-aged men. Maggie guessed they were secretaries, providing a bit of after-hours companionship for their bosses. She and Claire spotted Trevor at a table not far from where the band's instruments and microphones were set up. He waved them over and pulled out two chairs for them.

"Glad you two could make it. I was getting bored on my own."

"Don't you have any other friends, Trev?" Claire asked.

Trevor looked mock offended. "Of course I do. I have so many I can't even keep up with them all."

"Oh I see, so we'll make do?" Maggie joked.

"What can I get you two to drink?"

"Lime and soda please," Maggie said.

Claire nodded. "Make that two."

"Coming right up." He headed to the bar.

"I really hope his band is good," Maggie said. "I'm not very good at lying, in case they aren't."

"You lie all the time, especially to your mum," Claire said, with a glint of disapproval in her eyes.

"Not all the time. Just occasionally. Strategically. Little white lies. Jack is different."

"You don't have to lie, you just say something like 'your talent really surprised me'. It's vague enough to mean anything."

Trevor returned from the bar and placed the two soft drinks on the table in front of Maggie and Claire, as the compère came up to the microphone.

"Okay ladies and gentlemen, I hope you enjoy tonight's performance by our resident band "F Off". A few members of the audience chuckled at the name. "They'll be followed by our headline act of the night, and I hope you're going to give them a very warm welcome, The Five Kings!"

The audience applauded and cheered.

"Very good. Well, you don't need me standing here chattering all night, please welcome, F Off!"

Maggie and Claire joined in with the applause as Jack and his band came out of the Star Bar and onto the make-shift stage. Jack picked up his guitar and got into position, then scanned the room and spotted Maggie at Trevor's table. He smiled at her and started strumming along to the drum beat as the lead singer belted out the first verse of an upbeat song F Off had composed themselves.

Maggie smiled to herself. The band was off to a good start, and the audience seemed to agree.

A few songs later, and with the clash of a cymbal, F Off ended their set and took a bow to an overwhelming applause. The lead singer, Eddie Benson, pick up the microphone.

"Thank you, thank you, we've had a blast, up next is that smashing band, The Five Kings, but before we go let me leave you with this--don't forget to tell your friends to F Off."

The crowd laughed and cheered as the band left the stage, after which all four of The Five Kings, dressed in white suits, stepped onto the stage. They didn't waste time with hellos and got straight into a steady drum beat and rock n roll rhythms.

"Nice one, pal," said Trevor as he handed Jack the usual half-pint after a gig, and a cigarette.

Jack nodded his thanks and took a rewarding sip of the cool brown liquid. He glanced at Maggie and declined the offer of a smoke. She was smiling.

"That was brilliant, Jack. I can't believe I've never heard of your band before, you should have quite the reputation--or at least you will have, if I get to write about you," said Maggie.

Jack chuckled. "Thank you, we're not quite note-worthy yet though."

"Nonsense," Claire said, "I'm sure Mags will at least write a note about you in the next letter she writes to her American boyfriend."

As Maggie kicked her friend under the table, Jack took notice at the mention of Richie, or was it Ricky? Maggie shook her head. "Ignore Claire, she just likes to wind me up, she knows perfectly well that Ricky is not my boyfriend. But she's right, I will tell him about your band, let him know to watch out for you in case you make it to the big time in America."

Jack smiled. "Well I'll let the lads know we've been heard of in the States, they don't need to know that it's limited to just one person there."

"Your round," Trevor said as he drained the last of his drink.

"In a bit," Jack said. "I was hoping to show Maggie the Star Bar."

"What about me?" Claire asked, prompting Maggie to physically intervene again, with a nudge. "Oh, I know what I'm going to do, I'm going to watch the Five Kings, they seem talented. You two go ahead."

"The Star Bar, eh?" Maggie asked with a touch of scepticism.

"My idea!" claimed Trevor. "It really shows my intricate sense of humour."

"I wanted to show you how none glamorous backstage is," Jack said. "I'm not quite on the same level as the Beatles, but you bet your life that even at their level they spend a lot of time in places like the Star Bar."

He stood up and offered her his hand.

"You never offer your hand when you take *me* backstage," huffed Trevor.

"You're not as pretty," Jack replied.

Maggie blushed slightly and accepted his hand. He led her to the room at the back of the bar, as the music from The Five Kings blasted louder in their ears as they passed by the speakers.

Jack made sure he closed the door behind him to drown out some of the loud music. "Ta da!" He said as he gestured to the grimy room.

"Wow," said Maggie taking a look around. "It does have a certain earthy character."

"Oh yeah, very earthy, downright grubby."

"And dirty," said Maggie.

"And smelly."

"And..." Maggie thought for a moment. "Sorry, I've run out of synonyms."

"Good, me too. Let's just call it a shit hole and be done with it."

Maggie couldn't help but laugh. "I can see why you wanted to show it to me."

"Well, I must make a confession," said Jack, "that was just a ruse to get you in here."

"I see." She began to wonder if she should be getting a little uneasy.

"I actually wanted to talk to you, in private like."

"What about?"

He offered her the best looking stool in the room, and took the seat with only three legs, beside her.

"I guess I'm just going to blurt it out because I'm not great with big speeches, especially whilst trying to balance on a wobbly stool, so here it goes. I like you. A lot. I was just kind of wondering, or hoping, that maybe you'd like to go out with me sometime. Not here, some place nice. Decent."

Maggie looked stunned for a moment, her expression displaying what Jack had been fearing.

"Oh my God," he said, already disappointed. "it's a no, isn't it? I knew it! You're into that American lad, probably run off to America first chance you get. But hey, good luck to you, that's fair enough, you met him first. Sort of. He must write really great letters."

"Jack," she began.

"Yeah?"

"Shut up!"

She leaned over and kissed him quickly then pulled away.

He grinned, looking unusually flustered. "Letting me down gently?"

Maggie shook her head. "No, stupid, my answer is yes."

"Ricky," Mr. Kramer intoned as he stepped through the open doorway to his son's room, "I want to talk to you."

Uh oh, Ricky thought. This can't be good. Whenever a parent announces that he or she wants to talk, it's never good.

Mr. Kramer continued. "I'm in the market for a new car. I've been looking around, and I'll probably get one soon. I've got it narrowed down to a few possibilities. Maybe a Thunderbird."

"Oh, that's great, Dad! That'll be cool! So, you'll be selling your car?"

"Yes--to you, if you want it. I'll sell it to you for a reduced price--a Family Special."

Wow, Ricky thought. He loved his father's car. "Sounds great!"

"I'd ask five hundred to anyone else, but if you give me three hundred, and pay for your own gas, I'll pay for insurance, and any substantial repair bills that come along. Fair enough?"

It wasn't as if Ricky just wanted a car, he *needed* one, for the sake of his own sanity. No more relying on Kenny or others to drive him around, and it would be a definite plus for his more romantic efforts, too.

"You've got a deal!" he told his father. He promised to be a conscientious car owner, devoting part of every other Saturday to washing it in the driveway and giving the interior a proper vacuuming.

But there was an unforeseen consequence to his new status as a car owner: Kenny. Little did Ricky know upon his inaugural drive around town with Kenny and Marie, that Kenny would expect substantial compensation for the previous year of being Ricky's de facto chauffeur, during which he claimed to have driven his friend "all over creation, and then some."

As Ricky and Marie arrived at Kenny's house for the maiden

voyage, Kenny emerged with something in a paper bag. He hopped in the back seat, reached into the bag, and presented Ricky with a chauffeur's cap.

"Your turn," he said with a smirk. "Put it on, James."

Ricky grudgingly took the cap and put it on.

"Are you serious?" Marie said.

"Very."

"He never made *you* wear a cap, Kenny."

"Tough. Let's go, James."

This ritual repeated itself several times a week for the next month, with Kenny addressing Ricky only as "James"—and from the comfort of the back seat—whenever they had somewhere to go. Once they were out of the car, it was back to "Ricky," and then reverted to "James" on the road.

Even though the joke had worn thin by the second day, Kenny kept it up, and Ricky knew in good conscience that he had to take it, until Kenny deemed otherwise.

Chapter 13

7 March, 1964

Dear Ricky:

Thank you for the birthday card, it was very thoughtful of you... and thank you for the dollar bill. I'll keep it safe, and it can be the very start of my America Holiday Fund. I plan to one day be standing in Times Square deciding which shop to spend this very dollar in, maybe you could help me? I'll have to choose something very American. Maybe a piece of apple pie (though we do get that here too).

My mum organised a little party for me at our house. I'm quite amazed Claire managed to keep it secret. We had the nicest chocolate cake ever and loads of party food. And of course, we played Beatles records during the festivities. I had a great time! If I could have, I would have loved to invite you. It would have been the perfect touch for my 18th birthday.

I got lots of lovely gifts, too. Jack bought me a silver necklace with a heart shaped pendant on it. My mum got me a new record player as I seem to have worn out my last one, and Claire put the first article I had published about Gerry and the Pacemakers into a nice frame for me.

Speaking of writing, things are going quite slow with my writing career, but having said that, there's a possibility I'll have a chance to get something else published in Merseyside Music next month. I proposed to write a filler piece about new bands people need to go and see. They always mention local bands that have a good following, but I want to write about the bands that haven't made a name for themselves yet, locally or otherwise. This also means I can slip in a mention about Jack's band. And the Five Kings, though they seem to have quite the fan-base already. They are rather good, look out for them too maybe. Of course I'll have to do research on these new bands, go from place to place to listen to their music... I love the career I've chosen! I just hope it works out.

Actually, I'm thinking a lot about my future, and every day I convince myself more and more that as soon as I'm done with college, I think I want to move to London, where the real job opportunities are. It wouldn't be easy, but I should try to go.

How are things on your side of the pond?

From Me To You,
Maggie

It was the end of an uneventful March Monday for Ricky at school. The carpool ride back home had Kenny in an unusually pensive mood. With Marie already dropped off, Ricky pulled up in front of Kenny's house, expecting him to get out promptly, and with a "thank you, James," as usual.

"I've gotta tell you something," he said. "Don't laugh."

"Okay," Ricky said with some apprehension.

Kenny took a deep breath and kept his eyes focused straight ahead. "I think I like Marie."

"What, you mean you *like* her like her? No joke?"

"Yeah. I do," Kenny said, with a tone that hinted at a true longing on his part.

"Okay. That's nice."

"What should I do?"

"I fail to see the dilemma."

"What if she doesn't like me back?"

"You mean you want to ask her out?"

"Yeah, but not as friends. For real. I need to let her know how I feel."

"So, just tell her. You've known each other for years."

"I can't do that! Are you crazy? She'll think I'm weird."

"Well then how do you expect to tell her, with a secret message and a decoder ring?"

"Maybe I can tell one of her friends that I like her, and then they can tell Marie."

"I don't think that's such a good idea. And, no offense, but it sounds kinda cowardly."

"Exactly! I'm a coward!" Kenny put his head in his hands, trying to hide his over-acted shame.

"You're always flirting with her…in your own heavy-handed way."

Kenny looked up. "But now I want her to take me seriously. I like her."

"Well, I guess you could always write her a sincere note or letter, something like that. It would give her a chance to think it over without putting her on the spot. But I mean a *good* letter, not like your usual stuff, like the ones to your poor English pen pal."

"Hey, we're not all brilliant writers like you are."

"I'm not brilliant, believe me. I'm not even the best writer on *The Searcher*."

"That's it! You can write a note to Marie for me, and I'll sign it. You can be like a…a spook writer."

"You mean a ghost writer? Oh no you don't. I'm not getting involved in that sort of thing."

"Why not? It's not as if you like her that way, do you?"

Now, *there* was a question Ricky had somehow managed to suppress in his subconscious for longer than he knew. Nah, Marie was just a pal. He didn't *like* her like her…did he? What an inappropriate moment to consider the idea. Here was Kenny, pouring his heart out for the first time ever, and--

"Come on, please?" Kenny whined. "I really don't want to blow it."

Ricky suddenly felt he had a lot to sort out, but had only mere seconds in which to do it. He couldn't justify standing in Kenny's way if he himself didn't intend to ask out Marie. So, at least that was settled. But should he encourage Kenny and root him on, convinced that Marie would shoot him down?

"It's not very honest to have me write a letter to her as if it's from you," he began. "You want her to like you for *you*, right?"

"Not necessarily," Kenny replied. "I mean, I just want to get my foot in the door, if you know what I mean. I'll just screw it up if I try on my own."

"Hey, that's life. We've all got to go through this kind of thing eventually. With love and romance comes rejection, humiliation, heartbreak, all those wonderful things. Embrace it!"

"The way you put it, I'd rather embrace a porcupine. But you'll do it? Come on, please?"

"Well, maybe I can jot down a few ideas or phrases that you can include in your own letter. I'm no Cyrano, you know. I can't be there every time you want to talk to her, whispering things for you to say."

"Hey, I would *pay* you to do that," Kenny said.

"Oh, good God, man, have some dignity! Besides, you couldn't afford what I'd charge. Just don't come on too strong, or try to turn everything into a joke with her. A sense of humor is fine, but she needs to know you have a serious side—well, your version of serious, anyway."

"What, you mean, like cry when I tell her about the day my dog died?"

"You never had a dog. Honesty, remember? If you can't ask her out face to face, I'll help you with a note, but that's all."

"Great!" Kenny smiled and sat back, looking as if a huge weight had been lifted.

Ricky had too much homework that night to be bothered writing a romantic note for Kenny to deceptively pawn off as his own, but the next day he reluctantly dedicated some time to it during lunch period.

Marie emerged from the cafeteria line with her tray of food and found Ricky sitting alone at a distant corner table, concentrating on writing in his notebook. She loved watching him deep in thought, using that extra spark of insight and writing talent that most of their peers—including herself—just didn't possess. She pulled out a chair next to him, noticing how hurriedly he closed the notebook as she sat down.

"Oh, don't stop whatever you're doing just because of me," she said.

"It's nothing, just some random thoughts."

"Writing something for the school paper?"

"Okay."

"Huh?"

"Er…I mean, no, just ideas."

"Oh, I get it. Writing to your pen pal again, huh? Personal stuff? *Romantic* stuff?" she teased. But despite the joking, Marie found herself becoming more interested in learning the exact nature of Ricky and Maggie's correspondence. Was it really possible for two people living an ocean apart to be serious about each other? She didn't especially like that notion. And Ricky's reply was only moderately assuring.

"No, nothing like that. We're close, in a way, but not romantic."

"Uh huh," Marie nodded, not totally convinced. "Where's Kenny? He's usually already here, asking you for your dessert."

"I don't know where he is. I thought I saw him a few minutes ago. I'll take a look around."

He got up, careful to stack his books on top of his notebook, to put silent emphasis on how it was not to be disturbed. But as soon as he disappeared into the cafeteria crowd, Marie's insatiable curiosity had her to swiftly pulling the notebook out from the bottom of the stack, and flipping through the pages. She took a moment to look heavenward.

"I know I'm prying, but I'll pray for forgiveness before I go to bed tonight. I promise. Besides, it's not like it's a diary or anything…I'll throw in a few Hail Mary's if that will help."

She stopped at a page that looked interesting. It was filled with a lot of scribbling and cross-outs, but she could still discern a few unedited sentences:

I'm sorry I'm writing this instead of asking you in person, but it's the best way I know how. Despite how I act around you sometimes, I'm interested in knowing if you'd like to go out with me sometime, just us—on a date."

Her world-class peripheral vision helped her spot Ricky and Kenny heading back to the table. She kept her movements subtle as she slipped the notebook under the stack of books and put on her best casual, expressionless face. On the inside, however, she was beaming. "Ricky's going to ask me out!" she squealed to herself in her mind.

"He's going to ask you out?" Kirsten shouted, more as a proclamation than a question. She bounced on Marie's bed in her excitement, her legs folded under her. Marie did likewise, partially just to stave off any potential seasickness resulting from her friend's kinetic expression of joy.

"Well, I think he is."

"You think he is? You said you saw what he wrote. There's no two ways about it."

"He scratched out a lot of words. I don't know when he's going to give it to me, or what it's really going to say."

"That's kind of sweet, that he's too shy to ask you in person, but it would be nicer if he did."

"He's a writer. He always says he feels more comfortable writing things down than saying them. He doesn't have to make a speech."

"He talks just fine. He's smarter than most guys we know. He should just ask you out loud. Come on--Truth or Dare--how long have you really liked him?"

"Oh, since I was about eleven."

"Aw, he's a great guy, Marie. I'm happy for you."

"Let's not jump the gun," she warned. "But I'm happy too!"

They continued chattering as Dan Ingram's voice emanated from the radio speaker. The DJ was indulging in some chatter of his own before playing a new Four Season's song—and, as was his way, continued chattering on the air even as the song played.

Across town at that moment, Kenny studiously read the note Ricky had prepared as a guide for Kenny's actual letter to Marie. Ricky looked on, feeling increasingly awkward.

"Wow," Kenny said. "That's beautiful. I didn't know I had such a way with words."

"You don't. You have a way with *my* words. You can use a few key phrases, but you should write most of it yourself."

"Why? It's perfect."

"Because—and don't take this the wrong way—she'll know immediately that you didn't really write it."

"So? I could get a mushy greeting card from the store and give it to her, and I wouldn't have written that, either. But I'd get the message across."

"So, do that."

"Well, the only thing is that I don't think the stationery store sells any 'I'm-too-shy-to-ask-you-out-in-person cards.'"

Ricky sighed and shook his head. "Well, whatever you do, just be careful."

Kenny read through the note yet again. "So, is this how you write to your English girlfriend?"

"For the hundredth—no, *two* hundredth time—she's not my girlfriend. And I told you, we just write about what our lives are like, what we do, what music we listen to, how we feel about life…"

"How about I write my version of the note and show it to you before I give it to Marie? You can look it over, just to make sure it's okay."

"If you must," Ricky said.

The following day, Kenny used his study hall time in the school library attempting to put his own personal stamp on the note. He never used the time to actually study anyway, but at least he had something of real importance to learn on that particular day. Kirsten, sitting across the room, would have been using the study time for which it was intended, had she not been distracted by Kenny stopping to stare at her with increasing frequency--and for a longer duration each time. He finally waved to get her attention, and whispered as loud as possible without sounding like he was having an asthma attack.

"Psst—Kirsten…What's another word for pretty?"

"What?"

"What's another word for pretty?"

"What are you up to?" She wondered if he was in fact calling her pretty to her face, without having to actually *call* her pretty to her face. Could he really be that clever?

"It's nothing. Just tell me."

"What's wrong with pretty?"

"I've already used it."

"For what?"

"Nothing. Just something. Nothing." He conspicuously covered the paper, even though Kirsten was already unable to see the writing from her seat without the aid of binoculars.

"Well, how about attractive?"

"Nah."

"Cute? Gorgeous?"

"Nah. Pick another one."

"Geez, Kenny, what am I, a thesaurus?"

He furrowed his brow with confusion. "Isn't that some kind of dinosaur?"

"Are you writing to a girl?"

"Well, I'm sure as hell not writing to a guy to call him pretty."

"Who is she?"

"I can't say."

"Will I find out?" she asked coyly.

"Soon."

She smiled. She always thought Kenny was quite endearing and cute, in his own goofy way—that is, when he wasn't being infuriating with his obtuseness. She found herself assessing—and not for the first time—how she would feel if he were to ask her out. And she liked the idea.

Ricky suddenly burst into the room and ran to Kenny. "Hey, there's a fight in the boy's room. Tom Riddick flushed Cindy Miller's book report down the toilet, and she ran into the boy's room after him and punched him in the mouth. There's blood, water, soggy paper, and I think a few of his teeth all over the floor!"

Kenny jumped up to race to the scene with Ricky, leaving the note-in-progress behind. Kirsten hurried to Kenny's desk, knowing she didn't have much time. She took a quick look. It wasn't addressed to anyone in particular, yet she thought some of the wording seemed strangely familiar.

> *"I know I'm not very good at saying what I really mean, so I hope you don't mind if I write this—"*

Hmm, she thought, that sounds an awful lot like what Marie quoted from the note Ricky was writing. What was going on? Was Kenny copying Ricky's note to pass it off as his own? And who was it intended for? Kirsten? Was he just teasing her with his search for words like "pretty"? She returned to her seat a bit perplexed... but also a bit giddy.

"Kenny's going to ask me out!" she concluded. An emergency consultation with Marie was in order.

The two girls met after school at the swing set in the tot lot of their old elementary school, named for some New Jersey governor from decades before that neither of them had ever heard of. Marie was already pre-occupied with her own anxiety about Ricky.

"Why hasn't Ricky given me the note yet?" she whined. "It's been days! Do you think he changed his mind? Or maybe he was writing it for someone else all along--maybe to his girl in England."

"Or," Kirsten offered, "maybe he decided to ask you in person, and he's just waiting for the right moment. But what I want to know is why Kenny's note says almost the same thing as Ricky's."

"That's really low of Kenny," Marie scowled, "stealing ideas from Ricky's note to me—I mean, to whoever it's meant to be for."

"Yeah, well, I guess we can't blame Kenny. He's not the brightest bulb in the knife drawer...I mean, he's not the sharpest...uh..."

"No, he isn't," Marie concurred. "But would you still go out with him?"

"Sure, I guess. I like him. He means well. He's just...Kenny."

"Good. Go out with him. Then maybe he'll stop annoying *me*."

With the passing of another few days, and no sign of any kind of note appearing from either Ricky or Kenny, Marie grew increasingly depressed, irritable, and panic-stricken, rotating among those three states of mind with frightening regularity. She finally decided she just couldn't take it anymore, and demanded that the guys, and Kirsten, meet back at the playground, after school.

Her nerves frazzled, she didn't waste any time with a perfunctory "I suppose you're wondering why I've called you all here today." Instead, she had a more direct opener:

"Okay, you cowards, it's time to put up or shut up!"

The two boys looked to each other, without a clue.

"Huh?" was the joint reply.

"Ricky, do you have something to say to me or not? Even if it's written down, let's have it."

"Something to say? Er...Well, I like your new hairstyle?"

"It's not a new hairstyle. It's a new headband. A new headband is not a new hairstyle."

Marie's aggression had both boys reeling. Kenny averted his eyes as she continued.

"Don't be embarrassed, Ricky. We've all known each other for years."

"I don't know what you mean," he stammered.

The girls exchanged a look to each other, making the boys even more apprehensive.

"The note!" Marie insisted. "The letter to me!"

Ricky struggled to understand, feeling his body trembling as he worked to decipher her rant.

"The letter to *you*? Oh, that. You mean--"

"Yeah," Marie said, "The one about how you're more comfortable writing about your feelings than saying it. That one."

"How do you know about that?"

"Oh, uh…never mind. I just know."

Kirsten then turned to Kenny. "And the least *you* could do is write an original note to me instead of copying Ricky's note to Marie, almost word for word."

"A note to *you*?" Kenny asked. He turned to Ricky for help.

The more Ricky was able to figure out what was going on, the worse he felt. "Oh, yeah, well, Marie, that letter you saw was sort of for Kenny all along."

The girls both gasped in shock and confusion.

"You wrote a love letter to Kenny?"

"He wasn't writing it *to* me," Kenny offered, "he was writing it *for* me." He took a deep breath before adding, "to give to you, Marie."

Marie still hadn't caught on. "Ricky, you could at least give it to me yourself, without asking Kenny to do it."

By this point, Ricky would rather have been trapped in a Calcutta sewer than have this conversation. Kenny forged ahead with his explanation.

"No, Marie," he said quietly, "it was so I could give it to you, to ask if you'd go out with me."

The girls gasped in shock and confusion yet again. They were becoming quite proficient at such gasps.

"What…you…you mean…" Marie squeaked, "Kenny, *you* want to ask me out?"

"Now, wait a minute!" Kirsten piped up, taking a menacing step toward Kenny. "You mean you weren't going to ask *me*? And you even had the nerve to ask me for another word for pretty, to put into a note for *Marie*? You disgusting two-timer."

"But," Kenny whimpered, "I just needed a word. Another word for pretty. Then you started talking about dinosaurs and got me all confused. And I'm not a two-timer. I'm not even a one-timer."

"Wait," Marie said, turning to Kirsten, "you don't think I'm pretty?"

"Of course you are. But I didn't know *Kenny* thought so."

Marie turned angrily to Ricky. "And all this time I thought *you* were going to ask me out!"

"Well, I…I…" he stammered. "I never really gave it much thought."

"Then who came up with that stuff about me being pretty?" she demanded.

"I did," Ricky confessed, never realizing such a confession could induce so much guilt.

"So, why aren't *you* asking me out?" she said, almost daring him to ask her to be his girlfriend. Kenny tried once again, and just as unsuccessfully, to come to Ricky's defense. "He already has a girlfriend, in England."

"Kenny, shut up!" Ricky yelled. "For the three hundredth time, she's not—"

"Wait a minute," Kenny interrupted. He turned to Marie. "You mean you *want* Ricky to ask you out?"

Now it was Marie who was on the spot. "Well, yeah. I mean, that's what I thought he was going to do."

Kenny's heart sank. But Kirsten wasn't done. "So, nobody thinks *I'm* pretty? Thanks for leading me on, Kenny. And just as I was beginning to—oh, never mind."

Before the boys knew it, the girls stormed off. A chilly, lonely wind whistled through the bars of the swing set as they watched them disappear down the street.

"What just happened, Ricky?"

"Well, I think, somehow, Marie just turned *me* down because *you* asked Marie out, and Kirsten turned *you* down because you *didn't* ask Kirsten out."

"No, I think Marie turned *you* down because you *didn't* ask Marie out."

"But I wasn't *going* to ask her out, I promise! The plan was for *you* to ask her out!"

"I did! I mean, we did. I mean…"

"I don't know what's going on," Ricky sighed, sadly watching the girls disappear out of sight. "But I think we haven't heard the end of this."

He was right. Not only was he trying to understand how two girls could break up with two guys who weren't even their boyfriends, but Marie's wrath was still in full force the next night, during their shift together, with Kenny, at the ice cream shop.

Ricky found himself tiptoeing his way behind the counter as he served customers and prepared their orders. It wasn't easy performing such tasks with Marie's evil eye following his every move. He didn't dare make eye contact. And yet he still couldn't understand what he had done—or didn't do—to create such tension.

Kenny wasn't faring any better, as he continued to wonder if he had lost the girl he hadn't yet asked out to his best friend, who hadn't asked her out, either. He also wondered whether he was instead supposed to have asked out the girl who wasn't happy with the way she thought he was asking her out, even though he was doing no such thing at the time. It all gave him a headache.

Dave, cherishing the safer role of innocent bystander, somehow felt equally compelled to tread carefully that night. For once, he was happy to wash the dishes in the back room, out of the line of fire, and with Cousin Brucie on the radio to keep him company.

Marie had a good supply of techniques with which to torment Ricky. An opportune moment came when Mr. Mocha Nut arrived, squinting at the big menu of ice cream flavors as always.

"Bathroom break!" she announced, escaping to the back room.

"Me too!" Kenny said, leaving Ricky alone to deal with the man as he stepped up to the counter.

"A cup of mocha nut, please?"

The ensuing exchange failed to carry to the back room, thanks to

Cousin Brucie's mile-a-minute announcements to his millions of "cousins" in the listening area (which, on a clear night, could include forty states). Brucie read out song requests, dedications, and news of tickets on sale for a production of *The Music Man* at a Brooklyn high school.

As Mr. Mocha Nut held Ricky hostage with his ridiculous line of inquiry about his favorite flavour--which didn't exist--Dave and Kenny watched silently as Marie reached into the pocket of Ricky's jacket hanging on the wall. She then disappeared into the employee restroom.

"She's not gonna flush his keys down the toilet, is she?" Kenny wondered with dread.

"I don't want to know," Dave said.

"I don't know if I want to know or not," Kenny said. "Either way, I'd probably regret it."

Once Ricky sent Mr. Mocha Nut on his way with a cherry vanilla cone, the store was momentarily free of customers. He slumped against the wall. "I'm going to have nightmares about that guy," he moaned.

Dave had a suggestion. "Why don't you send him to a place that really does have mocha nut?"

"There is no such place, because there is no such flavor!"

Dave shrugged and resumed his dish-washing. The shop door opened. It was Kirsten.

"You serve her," Kenny whispered with palpable panic, half-shoving and half-hiding behind Ricky.

"Oh, no. I had to face the Mocha Nut nut, now you face Kirsten."

Kenny swallowed hard, and felt himself begin to tremble as he stepped forward to serve Kirsten. She appeared calm and pleasant, which was a good sign.

"Hi, Kenny."

"Hi, Kirsten."

"Can I have a chocolate cone and a glass of water?"

"Uh...yeah, sure." He cautiously packed a tennis ball-sized scoop of chocolate ice cream onto a sugar cone and, with a shaky hand, slipped it into hers.

"Thank you," she said with a smile. Uh oh, he thought, this can't be good. Her polite demeanor was messing with his already tortured mind as he handed her a glass of water. She took the glass with a smile, paid for the cone, and was about to turn away when she added, "Oh, Kenny..."

She threw the water in Kenny's face and upper torso, set down the glass and quietly walked out. Kenny slowly turned and headed to the back room and a much needed towel.

Dave took one look at his waterlogged colleague and dropped several utensils back into the dish water.

"Oh, no—don't tell me the soda fountain is broken again!"

The crew managed to get through the rest of the evening without further incident. After closing time, they cleaned the shop, re-stocked the supplies, and had everything in order in twenty minutes. Marie did a final sweep of the floor as Ricky punched the time clock and put his jacket on. He waited for Kenny to do the same, so he could drive them home. But when he reached into his pockets, it became clear something was missing.

"Hey, where are my keys? Did any of you guys see my keys?"

Kenny and Dave shared a quick glance, then looked to Marie. She calmly put the broom aside and marched past the others, straight to the walk-in ice cream freezer. The others watched in silence as she opened the door, reached in, and produced a large paper cup in her hand.

"Here they are," she said without a hint of inflection in her voice. She handed it to Ricky. He knew without even looking that his keys were frozen solid in a smoothly formed block of ice in the cup. Dave and Kenny winced at Marie's rather creative act of passive aggression.

Ricky was not amused. "Okay, Marie, I've had it with all of this! What in the world did I do to get you so angry?"

"Let's go outside," she said.

They did, leaving the others to stall before turning off the lights and waiting for a right moment to follow them out.

Once she was alone outside with Ricky, her mood changed. She wasn't angry, just sad—sad and hurt that he didn't seem to have any intention of asking her out. So, gathering a bit of courage, she went for broke and told him exactly that. It was a risk. She wouldn't want to make him feel uncomfortable around her from that point on.

"I guess it was stupid of me to think about it too much," she said, with her eyes cast downward. "Especially when you obviously haven't been thinking about it at all."

"Well, that's not totally true. I've thought about it from time to time."

That made her eyes brighten.

"But then Kenny started talking about asking you out, and I didn't want to discourage him. He was so sure about it. And anyway, girls who are friends with guys usually just want to stay friends, so…"

"Kenny, huh!" she said with a chuckle. "I definitely don't want to go out with Kenny. I'm very flattered that he likes me, and he's a good friend, but he's not my type."

"Oh," Ricky said. "You should tell him. But let him down easy." A pregnant pause followed, finally giving birth to:

"Oh, hell, do I have to do it myself?" she said with some irritation.

"Well, it's only right that you tell him."

She took a deep breath. "Ricky, will *you* go out with me? As…you know… my boyfriend?"

Wow, he thought. She really said it. Marie just asked him out. Did she? Of course she did. But girls didn't ask out boys. It just wasn't done. Was it? No. Or, maybe sometimes. Should he ask for confirmation?

"Wha…What?"

"You heard me. I won't say it again. I don't want to sound anymore pathetic than I already feel."

"But…but…" He cleared his throat as a temporary cure. "Well, aren't I supposed to do the asking?"

"Yes, you are, but sometime this century would be nice. So, if you were thinking of asking me, do it now. If you want to, that is. How about this. We give it a try, and see how it goes?"

"Well, yeah, of course we can. Okay. So, Marie…" He took the next thirty seconds to stutter some more, stammer a bit, cough, choke, and re-start the question.

"You were right all along," she sighed. "When it comes to things like this, you're better writing it down. Do you want me to go back in and get you a pencil and paper?"

"No. Marie, would you like to go out with me?"

"Really? Why, Ricky, this is so sudden!" she said with a mock dramatic flair. She could see by the confusion on his face that her sarcasm was lost on him. "Are you sure?"

He smiled. "Like you said, let's see how it goes."

"Then yes, Ricky, I'd love to."

They both broke into a laugh before embracing each other warmly and having their first real kiss—a short, awkward one, but it was a start.

Inside the shop, Dave and Kenny crouched behind a potted plant to watch it all unfold.

"Son of a bitch!" Kenny said. "They stabbed me in the back!"

"No, they didn't," Dave said. "Sorry, Kenny, but it was never going to happen with you and Marie. Now, Kirsten on the other hand—"

"Ach! That she-devil! She hates me! Look what she did to me just before. She nearly drowned me."

"Kenny, I might not be the sharpest bulb in the knife—I mean—how does that go again? Anyway, she only did that because she likes you. Everybody knows it. Just like everybody knows Ricky and Marie would probably get together eventually."

"If that's how Kirsten shows she likes me, I don't want to know what she does to people she hates."

"No, you don't. But do you like her?"

"Look at them out there--still talking, standing real close —what?"

"I said, don't you like Kirsten?"

"Well, sure I do. When she isn't yelling at me, or throwing water in my face, she's very sweet."

"Yelling at you proves that she likes you."

"I guess I've got a lot to learn about women."

"That's how I know my mom likes my dad. She yells at him a lot. And Kirsten is more your type than Marie is. Trust me, I can tell. You two are made for each other. I bet if you ask her out, she'll say yes." Dave's sudden, comforting wisdom was just what Kenny needed, but Kenny didn't want to seem like a heel.

"Yeah, but listen, Dave, I don't just turn my feelings on and off for a girl like Marie and then ask out another—what's Kristen's phone number?"

"I don't know, stupid. Look it up!"

By the next day, it was official. Ricky and Marie were a couple, as were Kenny and Kirsten.

"*And to think it only took six years*," Marie wrote in her diary that night.

Chapter 14

June 15, 1964

Dear Maggie:

Sorry I haven't written sooner since your last letter. It seemed as if every time I sat down to write to you, something would pull me away. It's been a crazy few weeks, with the school year coming to a close, and finals to study for. One thing that's certain is that I'll never be a math teacher. I think the math department has a plaque for me on its Wall of Shame. But my other grades have been good enough to make up for it.

We had our senior prom Saturday night, at a banquet hall called Livingson's. Marie looked great—I had never seen her in a formal dress before. I looked stupid in my tuxedo, but we had a great time. We went with Kenny and Kirsten, of course. My one consolation was that Kenny looked even more uncomfortable in his tux than I felt in mine. I'll send you some pictures as soon as I have them developed.

The band played a lot of Beatles songs, and nobody seemed to have a problem with it—not even Elliot and Andrea-Claudia. I think their resistance has been broken! Marie especially liked the slow dances a lot. But I have to confess, I don't know if my feelings for Marie are as strong as her feelings are for me. I do like her, but somehow I suspect that I don't feel the way I'm 'supposed' to feel. Does that make mean awful person? I feel a little bad about that. Who knows what will happen at the end of the summer. I'll be leaving for college, and she'll still be in high school. I really don't want to hurt her, or be dishonest. I'm guessing she doesn't want to think about it. Or, if she does, she doesn't want to talk about it. So, I'm glad at least the evening went well.

I have even more exciting news. The day I handed in my last article for The Searcher, the teaching advisor, Mr. McClellan, told me that my writing was good enough to get me an internship with the town newspaper, the Community Herald. Actually, it's not just for our town, but also for a few of the surrounding towns, so the circulation is about 50,000. So that's pretty good exposure! He knows the paper's editor, who agreed to it! I'll be working there three days a week during the summer. There's no pay, but it should be great experience and a good boost for me in college. I don't know much else about it yet. I'll start on July 1st. Stan asked if I still want to work at the ice cream shop on the other days, so I'll still have that income, but it might get very exhausting. I want to enjoy my last summer before college, of course...

Ricky took a deep breath before opening the door to the offices of *The Community Herald.* It had been delivered to the doorstep of the Kramer household, and just about every other house in town, for as long as he could remember, so he was familiar with it as a reader. Now he was about to experience it from the inside.

He approached the receptionist, glancing quickly to the side to get a peek of the main newsroom. From what he could see, it looked bigger than he had imagined--about twice the size of the school cafeteria. Pretty impressive for a local paper.

"Hi, is Mr. Morton in? I have an appointment. Ricky Kramer. I'm supposed to begin my summer internship today."

Before the receptionist could answer, Sid Morton appeared from a side door. He looked eerily like Ricky's long-time image of a newspaper editor: thinning hair, cigar clenched in his teeth, suspenders holding up ill-fitting pants—he seemed almost too real to be real.

"Oh, hi, kid. You're, uh, Ritchie, right?"

"Ricky. Ricky Kramer,"

"Exactly. I can see that nothing gets past you. Come this way."

Sid led Ricky through the press room, largely unnoticed by the handful of staff writers pounding away at their typewriters—although Ricky spotted one or two of them giving him the once-over as they sat awaiting inspiration. He felt both excited and extremely self-conscious.

They entered Sid's cluttered office, where he motioned for Ricky to have a seat.

"Okay, summer internship. I understand McClellan at the high school gave you the particulars. You'll be here Mondays, Wednesdays and Fridays, nine in the morning 'till three. No pay, but you get a lunch break."

"Yes, that's what he told me."

"Swell. You'll be doing a little of everything—that is, a lot of everything—running copy from the staff writers to the editors and printing department, sorting through photos, making sure everyone has enough carbon paper…"

As Sid continued the litany of office chores, Ricky kept waiting to hear something about actually writing his own stories. He waited in vain. Sid's words devolved into "blah, blah, blah" in Ricky's ears, as he began to fear that he wasn't in the right place at all.

"…And when you make the lunchtime run to the deli, remember, I like extra mustard on my baloney sandwich. Eddie just likes a little. Me, I like extra. Spicy mustard, you understand--not yellow."

Ricky's heart sank. He didn't know whether to ask about writing stories or not, for fear of Sid's response.

"Sounds like a lot," he gulped submissively.

"Yeah, well, I like mustard."

"No, I meant everything I have to—"

"Don't worry, we're *The Community Herald*, not *The New York Times*. Once we show you the ropes, you'll pick it up fine. McClellan says you're a bright kid."

"*Bright enough to write decent stories for your crappy hometown paper*," Ricky thought, *"And certainly bright enough to be a lowly office boy."*

Sid spent the next hour giving his new intern a tour of the newsroom, with further explanations of how to carry out the various tasks that would be expected of him. Ricky felt worse with each new set of instructions. Try as he might to concentrate on Sid's words, the feeling of sheer disillusionment racing through his head proved to be an awful distraction. Dare he even ask if he would get his own desk?

"Here, let me introduce you to Eddie, the Community Events editor. If there's a bake sale or Good Citizen Award ceremony going on within ten square miles of here, he knows about it. Eddie, this is our new summer intern, Rusty."

"Ricky."

Eddie shook hands with Ricky from his seat. "Ah, making corrections already, eh?"

"What? No, I was just—"

Eddie chuckled to help Ricky relax. "Only kidding. Welcome aboard. If you have any questions, just ask—someone else."

Ricky forced a smile as Sid turned him around and brought him twenty feet down the aisle to meet another employee.

"Hey, Don, drop whatever gibberish you're writing and say hello to Randy, our new summer intern. This is Don Blodgemeyer, our entertainment editor."

Don did take the trouble to stop what he was doing and rose to shake hands with Ricky.

"Hi Randy. How are ya?"

"The name's Ricky, actually. Or Rick...or Ricky."

Sid's face reflected his new-found confusion. "Get your facts straight, Blodgemeyer. I've got more to do all day than correct you when you get names wrong. Come on, Rudy, let's go back to my office. Any questions about what you'll be doing here?"

Yes, Ricky thought: What *am* I doing here? He decided to go for broke—almost.

"Er...Where do I go first when I arrive each morning? I mean, do

I have a desk, or…"

"A desk? For what?"

"I…uh…just somewhere to…never mind. It's not important."

"Oh, I get it. You thought you'd be writing stories here? Sorry, kid. Your mentor McClellan might think you're the next Hemingway, but we can't just let any high school grad come waltzing in here expecting to be given his own column to write. Maybe later in the summer, if we need one or two filler pieces, we'll give you a shot."

Wonderful. Filler pieces. Maybe. Working at the ice cream shop was suddenly looking so much better. The only possible bright spot was the chance to learn a few things from some of the writers, like Don. Of course, Ricky knew the kind of entertainment features Don usually covered were more of the local, small-time folk singers and community theatre productions than world-famous acts atop the music charts, but it was a start.

July 5, 1964

Dear Maggie:

Well, I guess I learned my lesson about being a hotshot without having much to back it up. Not that I've ever thought of myself as a hotshot, but let's just say I set my expectations a bit too high for this internship.

Truth be told, I'm not much more than an errand boy around the newspaper, following orders from a fruitcake of a boss who has a brain like scrambled eggs. But I'm glad the entertainment editor, Don, has been willing to teach me a few things about making contacts with people to get stories—press agents, managers, promoters—that would be useful if I try to get into this as a career. He's about ten years older than me, but we seem to like a lot of the same stuff. He's not a big Beatles fan, though. I guess we can't expect everyone to be! Maybe he's gotten too overwhelmed

*with all of the attention in the press they've been
getting. He seems sort of weary in general.*

*Anyway, we had our July 4th Independence Day town
fireworks last night. My family had a barbeque in the
backyard, like we usually do, with some friends and
neighbors. You know, if the colonists never won
independence from you British, I really don't know
what we'd all do with ourselves every July 4th—maybe
we'd be baking scones or steak & kidney pie (no
offense, but I don't know how you people can eat some
of the things you do). I think you'd like hotdogs much
better.*

*I'm working at the ice cream shop three days a week,
depending on when they need me to fill in for someone
who can't make it. That's fine with me. We have a lot of
laughs there, which is more fun than being at the
newspaper.*

He knew the Beatles were soon returning to America for their first
tour, and one of the stops would be in New York, naturally. And he
thought how great it would be to surprise Marie with two tickets to the
concert, as sort of one, big, last date before he had to leave for school.
But he also assumed getting tickets would be next to impossible. The
demand for them was going to be sky high.

Then he struck upon the idea of finding a way into the concert
through the *Community Herald*--perhaps with a press pass, if he were to
write an article about the concert. If Maggie could do it, so could he.
Don would probably be his best bet for help in pulling it off. But he
needed to get Don alone for a private conversation, and days could go by
before the opportunity presented itself.

Finally, one day, just before quitting time, the newsroom was quiet,
and Ricky spied Don at his typewriter, slouching and sighing in between
glances at the wall clock. He pulled up a chair next to him, and dared to
just jump in and present his case.

"So, I hear the Beatles are going to be at Forest Hills Stadium in a couple of weeks."

Don didn't seem impressed.

"Yeah, a tennis stadium. Pretty stupid place to have a pop concert, if you ask me."

"Are you going to cover it for the *Herald*?"

"No way. All that craziness, who needs it."

"Sid didn't say anything to you about doing a story? Maybe with a local angle?"

"What local angle?"

"Oh, I…uh…I don't know, really. *Local reporter covers Beatles concert*?"

"Listen, I've seen groups like them come and go. Fans are fickle. Take it from me. There's a big fuss about them now, but a year from now, nobody's even going to remember the Beatles."

"I'm not so sure about that," Ricky countered.

"You like 'em? You sound like you're jonesing to do a story about them or something."

"I'd really like to get into writing stories about music. But Sid won't let me. I do know a lot about the Beatles already. And I have a friend in England who can—"

Don's phone rang, breaking Ricky's momentum.

"Excuse me, kid. I've been waiting for an important call…Don Blodgemeyer…Oh, yeah? That's great. Okay, I'll be there to pick it up later."

He hung up, happy.

"My new bowling ball is ready. Purple and red swirl, with my name engraved in it. Can't wait to try it out. I'm in a league. Maybe the ball will bring me good luck. So, you were saying?"

"I don't suppose there's any way I could cover the Beatles concert for the paper, if you don't want to? I'd go in a professional capacity, of course, and write a very detailed and interesting piece."

"Ha! You think Sid would let you do that?"

"Well, what harm would it do if I go to the concert and write the story?"

Don thought it over, stroking his chin and taking a swig of soda as he did so. He gave Ricky a squinty eye before finally offering an answer.

"Well," he said with a long, slow breath, as if giving the word a few extra syllables, "I don't know. Maybe."

"I'd do anything!" Ricky pleaded. "My girlfriend and I want to have a big night to always remember before I leave for school."

"Oh, how sweet. So this is for your girlfriend, eh? Professional capacity, huh?"

"I can write a great story about the concert, I know I can."

"Hey, we can't always write about the stuff that interests us. I've got a couple of things coming up in the area that I'm supposed to review. One is the Community Players dong their production of *My Fair Lady* and the other is a concert by a folk duo, Wallace & Bernice, who I hate already, just for having those names. And I'd rather drown in a pickle barrel than sit through either of these guaranteed disasters and write about them afterwards."

Ricky's desperation prompted him to suggest something a tad devious. "What if I go to those shows on the sly, and ghost write a review for each one. You can still put your name on the by-line."

Don picked up on the idea. "You mean you'll do that if I get you and your little chickadee some passes to the Beatles? Hmmm…Could work."

Ricky did have a concern. "What if Sid finds out?"

"Try not to think about what Sid would do if he finds out. It'll just give you nightmares. It's bad enough for me to do this with a colleague, but with an intern…"

Ricky didn't know whether to feel ecstatic, guilty, dirty, or proud of himself for even having the nerve to approach Don in the first place.

"Okay," Don finally said, "you've got a deal."

They shook hands, after which Ricky left Don alone to finish his work for the day. Wonderful, he thought. His writing career was moving right along, from ghost-writing Kenny's love notes to ghost-writing reviews for this sleazy, two-bit newspaper writer.

"Well, gotta start somewhere," he sighed.

Chapter 15

There was a real buzz in the air throughout Liverpool; a mixture of excitement, pride and bewilderment. Maggie couldn't swear on it, but she noticed people seemed to be walking a little taller, and she was definitely one of them, all because The Beatles were returning to their home town to be honoured by the Liverpool council, before attending the premier of their new film, *A Hard Day's Night.*

Maggie and Claire had a plan to score premier tickets for the movie. After all, Maggie had sort of made connections at *Merseyside Music*, and, as always, Claire had a cousin who has a friend who knew a guy who could get tickets.

"So we have a good chance then?" Maggie asked.

"Better than most," Claire said smugly.

"We could actually get to watch The Beatles movie with the Beatles sitting right there!"

Claire nodded. "Imagine if we were sitting next to them, waving to them like at the Cavern."

Maggie giggled. "Stop it, or I'll never be able to focus on this assignment." She gestured to the homework in front of her, three pages full of her scrawled writing, the last page half full.

"You've got about two more sentences to write and then you're done."

Claire sat silently as Maggie put the finishing touches to her essay.

"Done!" she said triumphantly.

"How come you don't use your typewriter for your homework? You'd probably get extra marks for it being so neat."

"Typewriter ribbons are expensive, I'm not going to waste that on college work, that's for career building articles only."

"Okay, so back to our genius plan."

"Well we can't plan anything until we see if your cousin comes through for us."

"And *your* connections," Claire reminded her.

Maggie hesitated. "When I said I had connections, I really don't think they could get me tickets. It was probably just hype. I could try if all else fails, but right now your cousin is our best chance."

"It's a pity they're not having the premier at our cinema, then we could have served them free popcorn and reserved our seats," Claire mused, "not sure Dunhill would have allowed it though."

"What? A premier? All that free publicity for the cinema?"

"No, free popcorn."

Claire's cousin, Charlie, lived in the rough part of town, not quite the Dingle, one of the poorest sections, but not far off it. The thing about living there, if you were an insider, you were okay, you were one of them, but if the locals sensed you were from a few estates over in the nicer part of town, there was an instant sense of rivalry. Maggie always felt uneasy visiting Charlie. She liked to think she was easy-going and was a good people person, no matter where they were from, but it was an instant reflex to keep an eye on her surroundings in this area, in case there was any trouble. However, it was true all the local gangs knew not to mess with Charlie's cousin and her friends. Claire was certain they would not dare.

To get to Charlie's house, the girls had to go down a narrow back lane, as the back door was the usual way to enter his house. Only the debt collectors knocked at the front door and that was why it never got answered. Maggie always mused at the backyard walls of the neighbouring houses, a dirty brick canvas for graffiti artists to practise their skills. She wondered who 'Shrimp' was and how he managed to be in love with all the girls he claimed to love.

Claire opened the back gate and headed into Charlie's house without knocking, waving Maggie to follow her in.

"Charlie? You in?"

Charlie came into the kitchen, a comb in his hand, about to resume his ritual of slicking back his hair. "Hi Claire. I know why you're here, and I'm afraid I have bad news."

Claire and Maggie's hearts sank in unison.

"No, no, no, don't say that!"

"Sorry, Cuz, my mate didn't come through. Apparently these tickets were earmarked for other people a good while ago."

"Yeah, I bet for people who have never even bothered to go see the Beatles before they became famous!" Claire moaned.

"It's okay," Maggie said, trying to hide her disappointment. "It would have been nice but we still get to go see them at the Town Hall, it'll be great! And we'll get to see the movie another day."

The fact that they didn't have premier tickets didn't dampen their spirits. July 10th had arrived, and the Beatles were about to land in Liverpool airport. Charlie felt bad about promising premier tickets and not delivering, and he was the only one in the family who had a car, so he offered to drive Claire and Maggie to the airport to see the Beatles' plane land, and then take them to the Town Hall-- or as close to it as he could possibly get. The streets were guaranteed to be mobbed.

Maggie recalled the letter Ricky had sent to her about going to see The Beatles land at JFK airport, and, from her experience at Liverpool airport, she mused that though they were separated by three-thousand miles of ocean, they may have shared the same experience.

She had never seen so many screaming people in one place before. She and Claire could not get access to the airport rooftop, or near any windows to see the Beatles land. But they knew the boys had arrived when they heard the loudest roar of cheers in the history of roars, and, of course, both Maggie and Claire joined in the chorus. Maggie thought there was a very real chance the roof of the airport may have come flying off... cliché or not.

Though the crowd of people at the airport was impressive, it was nothing compared to the crowds lining the streets of the city leading to the Town Hall. The throngs of proud Liverpudlians were certain they were happy to show the Fab Four support for returning to their home-town as pop culture heroes.

The streets were packed out with people waiting for a glimpse of the group. The local police had a challenge to keep everyone in order. They held the crowd back as best they could, but they were outnumbered and a few crazed fans managed to sneak through and make a break for the Town Hall entrance. They didn't make it far before someone caught them and escorted them away.

"I can't see anything," Claire complained, standing behind a very tall woman. Claire thought the woman was being deliberately tall just to cheese her off.

Maggie was too caught up in the moment to notice. "This is amazing isn't it! So many people have come to support them! We have to get to the front."

"Everyone is squished tight like sardines in a tin, Mags. I don't think we'll be able to squeeze through this time. And I don't have any mince pies to put in peoples' hoods. And people aren't wearing hoods."

"Well, I need a good view so I can write a proper account of all this," Maggie said, almost willing herself to feel like a professional journalist. "Nobody wants to read about this woman's curly hair," she said, pointing to the woman in front of her. The woman turned around, put off by the comment. Maggie smiled sheepishly.

"Although it is quite lush and vibrant, ma'am. Sorry, I've been trained to notice."

She turned to Claire to explain. "I need to be able to write about the car they arrived in, who was sitting next to who, if they waved or pulled funny faces..."

"You don't have to convince me, we need to find a way through!"

Claire jumped up a couple times to see if she could see ahead of the crowd.

"Did that help?" Maggie asked sceptically.

"Well, there are first-aiders set up to the side of the building, so if one of us faints we'll be stretchered through."

Maggie thought for a moment. "Fainting to get ourselves through on a stretcher? I don't like it. It would feel fraudulent. There's got to be a regular way of getting through."

"We could ask these hundreds of people in front of us very nicely if they wouldn't mind making way for us..."

As if the crowd heard Claire's idea, the people in front stood even closer together, as if in spite, creating even less chance of them squeezing through.

Maggie looked around at her surroundings. *Merseyside Music*'s office was in the street to her left, towering directly over the bedlam. Their top floor was in direct view of the Town Hall. "Remember my connections? I have an idea!"

The secretary for *Merseyside Music* remembered Maggie from her previous visits.

"Ah, the loquacious one."

"Oh, you do remember," Maggie said, recalling her verbal slip-up. "Well, we have a big favor to ask. We noticed down on the street that you'll have a great view for when the Beatles' motorcade drives by. Could we possibly sit by a window, out of the way, and watch? I can take notes and write a bang-up article for you. And I'd love you forever if you said yes."

The receptionist wasn't prepared for such a declaration of affection. "That won't be necessary, I'm married."

She agreed, though, and led them to the upstairs storage room, which was a stark contrast to the bright, spacious room below. Cardboard boxes piled high littered the floor, while old filing cabinets lined the walls, wearing a thick layer of dust and cobwebs.

"It looks like nobody's been up here for years," Claire said.

"I know, but in fact someone comes up here every week to file away papers. Well, maybe every month."

"Well they could take a minute to dust whilst they're up here." She wrote her name in the dust on top of a cabinet.

"Stop that," Maggie said, "They're letting us up here as a favor, don't knock it."

"I'm not, it's just disgusting up here. Are we supposed to be able to see out of that window?"

The window was covered in old rain water and whatever the wind had picked up and thrown against it. It let less sunlight into the room which Claire couldn't decide if it was a good thing or not.

Maggie unclipped the latch and slid the window up. "Problem solved. Now all we gotta do is wait."

Claire looked through a box that was open, storing unsold copies of MMM and a few other things. She picked out a small booklet and flicked through it. It was clearly a mock up, something that hadn't been made available publicly, and it was all about the local pubs and clubs that offered good musical entertainment.

"Hey look at this, Mags. Maybe you could do something like this."

Maggie wandered over and looked at the booklet. "What for?"

"For all of your articles that didn't get published. Why not publish them yourself and print them in something like this?"

"No one would buy that...But!" her face lighting up, "I could leave it around local shops and things, free of charge, just to get my name out there!"

"Yes! Exactly! Give it a catchy name."

"That might work. Claire, you're brilliant!"

"Well, you're the writer. It's just an idea."

"But it's a great idea!" Maggie went back over to the window to check on the events outside. She grinned. "This day is turning out to be one of the best days ever!"

Claire chuckled and joined her friend at the window, their eyes surveying the amount of people on the pavement below.

"There must be tens of thousands of people down there," Maggie gushed.

"Yeah, at least."

"I think we have the best view of them all."

Time seemed to be ticking by slowly. The crowd started chanting song lyrics to "She Loves You" and "Love Me Do", Maggie and Claire joined in the mass sing-a-long, even though they were out of reach of everyone else. It helped to pass the time away.

After what seemed like three hours but was closer to one, the crowd went bonkers, as Maggie's eyes darted around the streets looking for the source of the hysteria. Driving slowly along the road towards the Town Hall, three black cars approached, and inside one of the cars were the four men the city had been waiting for. Maggie could see the crowd jumping up and down, hear them screaming hysterically, she could see some people crying, people with their arms reached out as if they could hug a Beatle from where they were standing. She could see one fan being stretchered away, probably having fainted.

The Beatles got out of their car, they acknowledged the crowd, gave a wave, triggering more hysteria, and were ushered inside by their security team.

"Oh my God, they're here!" Claire shrieked. "I feel so proud right now! They're coming back out, right?"

"Of course they are, they have to go to their premier later."

The two girls waited for the Beatles to come back out, as the crowd lining the streets waited too. After ten minutes, the doors to the balcony on the first floor of the Town Hall opened, and out stepped the mayor, mayoress, and John, Paul, George and Ringo. They waved to their fans. The hysteria this time somehow seemed greater, Maggie thought, if that was even possible.

They saw another couple teenagers carried away on stretchers. The police officers had a difficult time trying to keep everyone back. Maggie was sure that if the crowd had half a chance, they'd have all ran into the building.

Maggie and Claire were jumping with excitement, shouting, "There they are! There they are!"

There were no microphones, so the Beatles were unable to talk to their fans, but it seemed quite clear that they were honored by the turnout for them. Maggie wondered if it was weird for them, to come to the streets they'd lived in all their lives and have this much attention focused on them. As they waved to the fans a few more times, she could see the Mayor talking to them, probably pointing out random bits of information about the city, or the events so far that day.

It was a truly proud moment for any Liverpudlian to witness, and Maggie was thrilled she got to be a part of it. Even if she was in a dusty attic, three stories up.

Chapter 16

With the end of her college years fast approaching, it was time for Maggie to take stock of her life and strategize a strong game plan. Easier said than done. Since she didn't have much of a resume to show, and no big magazines were breaking down her door. She had only a few articles published at *Merseyside Music*, she knew her (and Claire's) idea of doing something on her own, like publishing something herself, was the best way to go. It would cost her a considerable amount of money to get the booklet of her articles put together and printed, but she did have a nice pile of money saved up from her shifts at the cinema, and she thought the whole project was indeed do-able.

She sat down with a pile of her various writing efforts—articles, essays, "Top 10" lists of what she considered to be the best bands in the city—everything she had written in the previous year. She knew a lot of the pieces were not worth the paper they were written on, but others instilled more confidence in her. She started separating her back catalogue into two piles; "to use" and "never to see the light of day". The booklet she was putting together had to show the best of her ability, there was no room for weakness.

The booklet should also have a theme, she thought, not just "Bands of Liverpool" but something more specific. Reading through her "to use" pile, Maggie tried to notice a common theme, 'Guys With Guitars' seemed to be a good one, there was no female artists amongst her reviews; not because she'd side stepped them but because there just weren't that many around setting the Liverpool music scene ablaze. Cilla Black had already made it big, so there wasn't much Maggie could write about her that hadn't already been written.

Maybe she could call her booklet "Guys With Guitars in Liverpool." It was appropriate, but did it sound too American? Too limited an audience? This whole project was beginning to seem more complicated as she piled one thought atop another. The writing was complete. but the decision- making, and switching to 'business mode' was causing Maggie's head to spin. One decision at a time, she reminded herself. At least the MM printing team were happy to print the booklets for her, for a small fee of course, but she did get a ten percent discount due to her previous work for them.

A week felt like a month, but the moment finally came where Maggie could open the cardboard box, and see all fifty copies snugly settled inside, waiting to take Liverpool by storm. She didn't know why, but she leaned over the open box and took a deep whiff. The booklets smelled good. That was the first thought that came to her mind as she reached in to pick up a few copies. Even better, they looked good! No fancy cover, just light blue, medium-weight card stock with the title and her name in the center. The smooth paper and fresh ink smell made it seem so much more tangible.

"Are you sniffing the paper?" Claire inquired.

"I'm savouring the moment."

"Well, congrats, Mags! This is brilliant! You're so clever to have done this--more clever than the rest of us."

"Even more clever than Curly Shirley?"

"Of course--far more clever than Curly Shirley! So, all you gotta do now is drop them off. And that's your name out there!"

"Well, to fifty people anyway. Actually, forty-nine. I have to save one for Ricky. Oh, and one for you. And one for me."

Claire nodded. "They look brilliant, Mags, really they do. So let's go hand them out!"

Maggie gave a huge grin. "Let's do it."

A cool, cloudy day interrupted what had been a string of more appropriate mid-July temperatures and sunshine. The girls decided to use the day to return to NEMS and listen to a few new singles fresh on the charts, but Maggie's ulterior motive was to ask permission to leave a few copies of her booklet on the counter.

They arrived to find Jack already there, busy inspecting record albums of various styles, some of which were unfamiliar to them, or just not their cup of tea.

"He was supposed to phone me this morning so we could come here together," Maggie muttered. "I just couldn't wait for him any longer. He's been doing that a lot lately, slacking me off."

Sensing trouble in paradise, Claire chose to change the subject. "Mags, I'm so happy to help my best friend spread her talent around the city."

Her choice of words prompted a frown from Maggie. "Right, well that makes me sound like a tart who rides the bus."

"Oh, right. Sorry. So after this, we'll go to the Cavern, next, and some of the other clubs?"

"Exactly," Maggie nodded, "and I'll take them around a few pubs too." They sauntered over to Jack, as he looked through the Motown releases. "You fancy helping us distribute the booklets, Jack?"

"How many?"

"I got fifty printed. That's all I can afford."

"Yeah, I think I can."

"Didn't know you were into Motown," she said, peering over his shoulder and into the bin. "Who's you're favorite?"

Jack shook his head. "This stuff's good but its seriously lacking a bit of anarchy. I'm getting into American blues, as well. But today I should be looking for something for my mum's birthday. It's next week and she loves Matt Monroe."

He continued searching through the record collection as Maggie spotted a young sales assistant walking towards her with an armful of 45s. The girl didn't look much older than Maggie, but dressed and carried herself as a person several years older.

"May I help you?" asked the assistant.

"I've just had this Liverpool music booklet printed, I was wondering if I would I be able to leave copies here for your customers?"

"How much?"

"They're free."

The assistant took a brief moment to think it over.

"Er, no."

It was not the response Maggie expected. "Er, no? They're just harmless little booklets with my own articles about the best bands in the city. Your customers would love it. Is there any chance I could convince you to turn your 'Er, no' into an 'Er, yes'?"

"Er, no."

"Well, no need to be cheeky."

"The management wouldn't approve. I've worked here for years, I'd know. They'd want a cut of the action."

"What action? There's no action—and there won't be, with the likes of you saying 'Er, no' all over the place," Maggie protested.

"Sorry."

"Right, well, I just may never return as a customer to this establishment again. . .Well, not for at least a week or two, anyway."

On that note of defiance, she marched to the door.

"Psst, Claire, come on!" she whispered both as softly and loudly as she could. "I'm trying to prove a point!"

"Just a minute, I want to get this new Cilla Black single."

"Get it tomorrow!"

Claire grumbled as she followed Maggie out.

"What about Jack?"

They looked over to Jack still carefully contemplating a Screamin' Jay Hawkins album in the Blues section.

"Oh, he doesn't care," Maggie concluded sadly.

"Are you sure?"

"Yeah, I'm sure," she sighed. "He'll always be Jack. More's the pity. I just can't figure him out."

Once outside, she felt more than a little heartsick. "Oh, no, I just told off NEMS! How could I do that? What if they ban me from the store?"

"They won't. They know you're a regular customer."

"Which should have been all the more reason to let me leave my stupid little booklet there."

"They're not the only record store in the city, you know. Let's go over to Preston's. I bet they'll let you leave a few copies there."

Claire was right.

"Yeah, just put them on the counter," the clerk at Preston's said without a moment's thought.

"Brilliant! Thank you!" Maggie said, trying not to gush in her attempt to look professional.

The assistant nodded and walked on to the back wall and started organising the records.

"That was easier than I thought," she said, producing five copies.

"See?" Claire said, putting her arm around her friend's shoulder. "Jackpot!"

They hit the jackpot at the Cavern as well, with permission to leave copies at the snack counter for the afternoon shows, and at several other venues in the area. Before she knew it, Maggie had the rest of the copies disbursed throughout the city. Now she just had to wait. What exactly it was that she was waiting for, she wasn't altogether certain. But she waited, nonetheless.

Chapter 17

August 13, 1964

Dear Maggie:

Your booklet arrived today, and it's fantastic! I'm so impressed. I don't know most of the groups you've written about, and I haven't finished reading all of the articles, but so far, so good! Maybe I can use it as motivation to write more. I'm not yet entirely sure what I want to write. But I'm glad you have such a clear idea of what you want to do.

I guess the biggest news I have for you this week is that "A Hard Day's Night" opened here yesterday. The closest theatre to us where it's playing is a few towns away. The one thing I didn't expect was that I'd be camping out overnight in front of the theatre with Marie, Kirsten, Andrea-Claudia, and dozens of other people! I've camped in the woods once or twice, but never on a sidewalk outside a movie theatre. And I think I was the only guy there.

Marie was so excited about the movie, and was so determined to see it on opening day, that she and the others brought a pup tent with them the night before, plus blankets, snacks, drinks, Beatle magazines—you name it. I would have been happy to let the girls have their little slumber party all night, right there on the sidewalk, and I would see the movie at a decent hour with Kenny the next day. But Marie wanted me to stay with them and see it for the first time together. I didn't really want to. I wanted to sleep. But I also knew I should hang around to keep an eye on the girls.

I didn't get a wink of sleep, thanks to their incessant chattering and debating about which Beatle looks the cutest in which photo, and stuff about British fashions, which Andrea-Claudia has been studying especially carefully lately. As soon as the first shot of them came on the screen, everyone started screaming like crazy, and barely stopped until after the closing credits. I couldn't hear much of the dialogue, but I think it was a fun movie.

When it was over and everyone seemed to settle down, I thought we could all finally go home and sleep, but as soon as we got outside, the girls went straight to the end of the line to see it again! I went home and waited for the ringing in my ears to go away.

But that was just an appetizer for the main course. I made a deal with a writer at the Community Herald, who is going to give me press passes to see the Beatles concert in New York in two weeks, so I can take Marie. In return, I'll ghost write a couple of stories for him that he really doesn't want to do. They don't sound like much fun, but I'm happy to do it (and put his name on it) if it means Marie and I can go to the concert. I'm going to write an article about it, and, with luck, talk the editor into printing it.

I'll write to you again after the concert, so I can tell you all about it.

Mrs. Kramer sat in the kitchen, watching Ricky gather his things as he prepared to leave for the concert.

"Are you sure you have good directions?" she asked with some anxiety. "There are so many highways going every which way in Queens. I wouldn't want you to get lost on the way, or on the way back, either."

"Yes, Mom, I have directions. It's not far from the World's Fair and

Shea Stadium, just a little ways off the highway. And I have a map. And another map."

"Can Marie read maps?"

"She got an 'A' in her Advanced Cartography class last year. She can read maps."

"Don't be fresh. I just don't want you to get lost way out there."

"Mom, it's Queens, not Outer Mongolia."

"Yeah, well, there aren't as many confusing highways in Outer Mongolia."

"We'll be surrounded by millions of people, so I think someone will be able to help us if we make a wrong turn. Don't worry. We'll make it home. Of course, Marie might be a hysterical mess by then, but we'll make it home."

"Bring some dimes with you in case you need to call."

Ricky checked himself in front of the mirror. It felt as if he was on his way to another prom with Marie. But at least he looked old enough to go to a prom. Looking old enough to have a press pass for a Beatles concert was another matter. And there wasn't much chance he could grow a moustache in the forty-five minutes it would take them to get to Forest Hills. He worried that he and Marie would look exactly like what they were: two teenagers trying to put one over on the ushers at the admission gate.

"I hope this works," he told his reflection.

Marie could barely contain herself in the car as they crossed the bridge connecting Manhattan to Queens, listening to WABC blasting through the radio speakers.

"Just try not to get too crazy," Ricky pleaded. "I'm going to be there as a journalist. And we'll be sitting with other journalists, who write for real newspapers and magazines. So if you start screaming like you did in the movie theatre, they'll know you're a phony."

"Ricky, you're worrying too much. Those guys will be watching the Beatles on the stage, they won't pay attention to us. Just let 'em try to kick us out, and I'll kick 'em where it hurts."

He winced at the thought. If nothing else, the Beatles certainly had the capability of transforming Marie into a dangerous force of nature when provoked. "I just don't want anything to ruin this night," he said. "I want you to have a perfect memory of it."

"Ricky, even if I don't hear one note of music, or just see the Beatles onstage for five minutes, I'll still have a perfect memory of this night." She clasped his hand tightly, but just for a second, so she could keep track of their route with the map on her lap.

"Here's the exit! This one! Move over!" she ordered. He took the fast-approaching exit just in time.

Twenty minutes later, with a flash of their press passes, they met with a lackadaisical nod from a bored security guard, and they were headed to the press box, located front and center of the elevated rows in the rear of the court-level seats. Under the orange-yellow sky as the sun set over the horseshoe-shaped stadium, they found themselves surrounded by 14,000 fellow fans wearing Beatles buttons, hats, carrying homemade signs and banners. The warm, humid August air was buzzing with energy, and punctuated with random screams and spontaneous sing-a-longs long before anything on stage had happened.

In the press section itself, there were a surprisingly few older men who appeared to be reporters, and most of them looked as if they'd rather be anywhere else. Some seats were empty, others quickly filled with young fans who looked as if they had no more business being in the press section than Ricky and Marie had. But nobody seemed to notice or care.

Marie was about to sit when her excitement prevented her rear end from coming in contact with the seat, as she jumped up to properly take in the scene around them.

"This is unbelievable!"

"Yeah, this is so tough!" Ricky concurred, momentarily allowing himself to lose his half-hearted attempt at professionalism. He reached into his pocket and produced several tissues. "Here, tear off a couple of pieces and stuff them in your ears. It'll muffle the screaming, but you'll still be able to hear the music. That's what I read somewhere, anyway. But at least your eardrums won't get overloaded."

The excitement in the stadium only intensified as they sky grew darker and the clock struck 8:30. The fans had almost forgotten that they were required to endure a number of opening acts before the Beatles would appear onstage. But the last two, The Righteous Brothers followed by Jackie DeShannon, got the most enthusiastic responses.

But Marie felt the delay getting to her with each passing minute. In fact, the passing minutes were about to turn into passing hours.

"What's going on? It's almost ten o'clock! Something's gotta be wrong. Are they ever going to show up?"

"I'd better go call home and let my parents know we'll be late. I'll tell them to call your parents, too."

Little did they know, until a rumor made the rounds in the stands, that the group's helicopter was delayed because the pilot hadn't cleared all of the permissions needed for the flight. Finally, the crowd saw the helicopter's lights appear on the horizon and touch down just outside the venue. Just a few minutes later and the MC's voice fought through the din of the crowd to announce, "Ladies and gentlemen, here they are, the Beatles!"

The stadium virtually exploded with ear-shattering noise. The crowd became a shaking, swirling mass of jittery movement, as an almost violent sea of jumping and arm-waving. As the Beatles hustled onto the stage, Ricky nearly dropped his notebook to join Marie—and the 14,000 other fans—in the frenzy, as the Beatles kicked off their show with the musical intro for "Twist and Shout."

A middle-aged newspaperman, already put out by the heat, leaned over to Ricky to shout if he could have an extra tissue to use as an earplug. Ricky gladly obliged.

For the next half hour, the rest of the set, including "All My Loving," "Can't Buy Me Love," "I Want to Hold your Hand," and "A Hard Day's Night," sounded like a transistor radio competing with a jet taking off at nearby LaGuardia airport. The Beatles, playing with smiles on their faces and joking in between songs, didn't seem to mind. Ricky especially enjoyed seeing the Beatles joke around on stage. He recalled Maggie's many accounts of her visits to the Cavern gigs, and how she talked of the group's antics between songs. It certainly made the band seem more endearing, and made Ricky feel just a bit like he wanted to be one of them.

By 10:30, the concert was over. The hot, tired, exhausted, but elated fans shuffled out of the stadium in search of their cars and busses.

Ricky had to pay extra attention to the road signs along the highway heading back in the direction of Manhattan. He was without Marie's help as navigator, for she couldn't focus on the map or concentrate long enough to form a cohesive sentence. But he did hear lots of "but they were just so....uhhh...guh!" from the back seat.

"Are you okay?" he asked, adjusting his rear-view mirror but still unable to see her. "Can you hear me? Take the tissue out of your ears."

"Ricky," she croaked in a voice so hoarse it hurt to speak, "did you say something? You sound so muffled. I think I still have the tissues in my ears."

"I know! Take them out!"

"Ow!" she yelped.

"You hurt yourself taking them out?"

"No, my throat hurts when I talk. And when I swallow. Ow. I should either stop talking or stop swallowing. Or both."

"Yeah, mine hurts too. But yours is probably worse. Although I must say that your screaming has improved considerably since the day we saw them arrive at Kennedy. It's more full-throated, you're exhaling from the diaphragm, your breathing is more controlled, and you've obviously got a lot more screaming stamina now. I heard an opera singer talking about that stuff on TV. I guess practice makes perfect."

"An opera singer was screaming at the Beatles?"

"No, never mind. Everyone's gonna be so jealous that we got to go to this. I hope they don't resent it too much."

"Oh, my God, we saw a Beatles concert, Ricky! They were incredible!" She grasped her throat again. "Ow. This is the best night of my—I'd better stop talking."

He knew he had achieved his goal. He actually took enough notes to construct an article about the concert, and gave Marie this night to remember, forever.

"I can't wait to tell Mag--" He quickly caught himself, hoping Marie didn't hear.

"What?"

"I said I can't wait to tell everyone about it."

Marie nodded, but she knew the sound of a sentence making an abrupt U-turn in mid-stream when she heard one.

After taking it easy on Sunday--aside from telling everyone over lunch at the diner what it was like to see a Beatles concert in person--Ricky returned to the *Community Herald* office Monday morning, looking for Don to thank him again for the press passes. He found Don—cleaning out his desk.

"Hey, Don, I just want to thank you again for…well, you know. What are you doing?"

"Packing up, kid. I got the old heave-ho."

"What?"

"Sid fired me. He looked at the reviews you wrote and he could tell they weren't mine. They were too good. He figured it out all by himself, but I confirmed it. He's not as dumb as he looks. And he hates anyone here ghost writing for another writer, especially without asking."

"Well, you could have mentioned that before!" Ricky's face turned ashen. "He really fired you?"

"More like he saved me the trouble of quitting. I was gonna get around to it sooner or later anyway."

"But it happened because of me? Oh, wow, I feel awful. I'm so sorry!"

"Nah, it was both of us, getting too clever for our own good."

"Yeah, but you're the one getting fired."

"Huh! Just you wait until he calls you into his office. Technically you're not an employee on the payroll, but he'll still kick your butt from here to California. Don't worry, nod your head a lot while he's screaming at you, look remorseful, and consider it a learning experience."

Ricky's face turned from ashen to ghostly white--rather appropriate for a ghost writer. "So, I guess he'll have no use for my concert review," he said meekly.

"Oh, he'll have a use for it, all right. Maybe to wipe chewing gum off the bottom of his shoe--or whatever else he might step in. Listen, everyone has some kind of black mark on their record. You're just getting yours while you're still in diapers, relatively speaking. But now, I get to join my cousin at his ad agency in the city. It's not who you know, kid, it's who you're related to. Or should that be, 'to whom you're related'?"

A booming voice from the far end of the newsroom left Don's query unsatisfied.

"Rudy!" Sid called. "In my office!"

"Oh, no," Ricky sighed, as he reluctantly began his shuffle to Sid's office. Once inside, Sid remained standing behind his desk, while pointing to a chair. Ricky sat, feeling every bit as submissive as he looked. He hoped Sid wouldn't notice him quivering like a cup of Jell-O atop a washing machine during its spin cycle.

"I understand you and Don had a cozy little plan all worked out, so you could have his press pass for the Beatles concert. Not one, but two press passes, for the love of –"

"Well, we were just doing each other a favour. We didn't mean any harm."

"You wrote stories for him to put his by-line on, because he couldn't be bothered to write them himself?"

Ricky felt his clothes beginning to cling to him from nervous perspiration. And, to make matters worse, once his mouth got going, he couldn't get it to stop. "Well, in his defense, Don has good instincts. The *My Fair Lady* production was awful. The only actress they had who could play Eliza Doolittle was about fifty years old, and she kept forgetting her lines. Oh, and she couldn't sing, so they tried faking it with her lip-synching to a singer hidden backstage. Didn't fool anybody, especially when the singer sneezed, but the actress didn't. And that concert with the folk singers, oh, boy. They took themselves way too seriously. All those deep, heavy songs about the meaning of life. I didn't know if I was at a concert or a philosophy seminar. I sure was looking for a pickle barrel that night, that's for sure."

"Enough of your babbling. I know your opinions, because I've already read them in the paper!"

The conversation went downhill from there, and ended with Sid's invitation for his intern to leave the premises and not return.

Ricky spent the rest of the day in shock. He wanted to feel like an innocent victim of something blown out of proportion, but he knew he had to accept most—if not all—of the blame. It was his idea, after all.

The shock softened into depression, as he explained to his parents how he made the deal with Don that would get him the press passes. Mr. and Mrs. Kramer weren't pleased at all, and made the point that Ricky could have simply asked Sid for the passes, rather than sneaking behind his back. Worst of all, he got a colleague fired for taking part. But they understood their son's good intentions. As for losing the internship, and most likely having a negative letter sent ahead to Hallenbeck University, they reminded Ricky that he'll just have to wait until he got there to learn of the consequences.

The summer certainly wasn't ending as he had hoped. And next he had to have a long talk with Marie.

"Can we go to the park?" she asked him on the phone. "I have to talk to you."

He could tell something was up by the tone of her voice. And, the phrase "I have to talk to you" is rarely a precursor to wonderful news.

It was a beautiful, hot day, one tailor-made for their favourite park, but their visit wouldn't be as carefree as the others had been. They strolled along the walking path circling the large duck pond in the middle of the park. After some stalling, he began to describe Sid's reaction to the press pass caper, how he fired Don, and cancelled the remainder of the internship. Ricky's voice, quiet and sad, almost lapsed into a monotone. It was mostly out of fear that Marie would suddenly see him as a conniving, dishonest lowlife without ethics or morals. At the very least, he imagined her reaction to be one of disappointment. But then, knowing Marie, an eruption of anger was also among the possibilities.

But that didn't happen.

"Oh, no, Ricky, that's awful. And it was really mean of him to get rid of you both."

He felt relieved by her sympathy, but only slightly. "I don't think meanness really comes into it in this case."

"You were only trying to make sure we could see the Beatles."

"He wasn't very impressed with how I carried out my act of gallantry."

"Well, it *was* gallant."

"Thanks."

She clasped his hand tighter. "At least we got to go. They can't take that away from us now!"

"Absolutely!"

She directed them to a bench along the path, facing the pond. An awkward pause followed.

"It was sort of one big last hurrah..." he said, "you know, before I leave."

"Oh, yeah, as big last hurrahs go, it was a goody. A great story to tell when we're old."

"So..." he began with considerable hesitation, "what do you want to do after I *do* leave for school?"

"What do you mean?"

"Well, we won't be able to see each other every day, like we're used to doing."

"I know that," she said. Hearing him state the obvious wasn't helping matters very much. "I've been thinking about it. You're gonna be meeting so many new people, going to parties, and staying out as late as you want, meeting girls..."

"I'm not going to the University of Sodom and Gomorrah, you know. I'll be going to classes, mostly. That's sort of the whole point of college—for some people, anyway. But I'll be home at Thanksgiving."

"That's three months away."

"Maybe I can visit before then. And we can talk on the phone once a week or so, and I'll write to you about everything."

"What if you meet someone?" she asked.

"I'm not looking to meet anyone."

"But you might. Let's face it, you'll be there, meeting new people from all over the country, and I'll still be here, in high school."

"Well, I do hope to make a few friends, but I'm not looking to meet anyone, or have a relationship, the way you mean."

"Listen, Ricky, I'm not angry, but I think we both know you already have."

"I have? Who?"

"You know. Maggie."

He let out a nervous laugh. "Oh, come on, you know she's just a friend I write to."

"And talk to," she reminded him. "But that's okay. It's your right."

"You're really jealous of Maggie?"

"Maybe jealous isn't the right word. But I can see it. I can see how she's always on your mind, probably even when you don't realize it. Everything we do together becomes something you want to tell *her* about, as if we can't have our own time together that's just ours, for us to know about. It's very clear, Ricky--not just to me, but to everyone else sees it too. We've all noticed. And it's great, really."

His knee-jerk reaction would have been to dismiss such talk as silly, and chalk it up to Marie totally misinterpreting his relationship with Maggie. But he didn't believe that argument enough to offer it as a response.

"I...I don't even...hell, she's three thousand miles away--"

"Yeah, I know. And, like I said, I'm not angry. But it's obvious. Can everyone see it but you?"

How was all of this perceptive analysis of the situation pouring out of Marie's mouth? Ricky wondered if she had seen an especially true-to-life episode of *The Patty Duke Show* that he had missed.

"Marie, I had no idea I was doing anything to hurt you, honest."

"I know. But even sitting right next to you, I sort of feel like a substitute for someone who can't be here."

"Maybe," he finally ventured, hoping to find some sort of acceptable resolution, "you and I should try to just let things happen when they happen—or *if* they happen, and not try to plan too far ahead."

She paused for a moment to gather her thoughts. "I think, since you're leaving for school, we should make a clean break of it."

Ricky wasn't totally stunned by the statement; he suspected it might be coming, but it felt so much harsher hearing the actual words. "Do you want to?" he asked.

"Do you?"

"I don't know."

"Neither do I. But we probably should anyway."

"I'm not sure I follow that logic," he said, tilting his head in confusion.

"I know how you feel about me, Ricky. You're always so sweet to me. And doing what you did to take me to the Beatles concert showed me how wonderful you are. But, call it woman's intuition, I think I should bow out."

Marie's logic and maturity brought a lump to Ricky's throat. He finally nodded in agreement. Now was the time to gently say goodbye to each other as boyfriend and girlfriend. Whatever friendship that might re-emerge between them in the coming weeks and months remained to be seen. And yet, he was beginning to miss her already.

"Okay, he said softly. "Okay."

Chapter 18

October 4, 1964

Dear Maggie:

Oh, what a crazy month it's been. I don't know if I've been adjusting to college life very well. I haven't made many friends yet, and I guess I'm a little homesick already. My roommate's name is Vance. He's from a small town in Pennsylvania. He's the first guy I've ever met named Vance, but to be honest, knowing my first Vance hasn't really made my life feel any more complete. He's a nice guy, friendly and talkative. Very talkative. What'sthat word you told me about once? Loquacious? Yeah, that's him.

Classes are okay, but some are so boring. We have to take mostly required courses this year, plus a few that are for my major, Journalism, so that doesn't leave much room for too many "fun" classes. But the Introduction to Journalism class is good. It's taught by a guy who used to be a newspaper editor (but not a crazy one like Sid). I'm enjoying it. After all, that's what I'm here for.

Anyway, about the school paper...I was terrified the day I first went there to ask if I could join the staff. I thought I might see a poster of myself on the wall with my picture on it and a caption, 'If this person asks to join the paper, turn him away. He's a menace to journalism!' But, thankfully, they hadn't caught wind of my scandalous, ghost-writing past. But I'm still the new kid on the block, so I sort of have to work on articles they assign to me. I get a few choices each week, but they don't guarantee they'll print them right away. I guess I'll have to live with that for now. It's a pretty professional-looking newsroom for a college paper, but everyone seems to take themselves so seriously. They're mostly journalism majors too--juniors and seniors- but they seem to think they're working for the New York Times.

But the campus is beautiful. I'll take some pictures and send them to you. And it's only a 3-hour drive from home—3 ½ hours if I observe the speed limit. I thought I'd be visiting home every few weeks, but I don't know if I'll be back before Thanksgiving. I haven't heard from Marie since I've been here, but then, I haven't phoned or written to her, either. I'm not sure why. I miss her, but I think if we stay in touch a lot until the next time I'm home, it might do more harm than good, and confuse the situation. But I hope she won't deliberately avoid me. Sorry, I'm probably talking about her too much. It's just strange how a relationship can change over time, or just disappear.

Write soon,
Ricky

The docks of Liverpool were a strange place to hold a date but Jack had left Maggie a message asking her to meet him there.

As they strolled along the quay, she could tell he had something on his mind that was troubling him, and it had been for the last couple of weeks.

"What's got you looking so serious?" she asked.

"I just have something I've got to say, I'm just not sure how to say it." He thought for a moment. "Thing is Mags, I really like you. A lot."

She raised an eyebrow. "So, you're either going to propose, or dump me, right?"

"No! Neither!" he replied quickly, a little alarmed. "I just--I got a new job."

"Oh, that's brilliant! Congratulations! Where?"

He stopped walking and turned to face the expanse of water. "Out there. My uncle got me in."

"In where? Or *out* where?"

"On a ship."

"But how long are you going to be away?"

"Three months, for the first trip. I come back for a week, then I leave again." He seemed surprisingly matter-of-fact about it.

"I'll never get to see you," she frowned.

"I know," he said apologetically, "which is why I think it's best if we not commit to each other right now. It's not fair on you, I know, but I leave in two weeks."

"So you *are* dumping me!"

"No I'm not!"

"Well what do you call this, then?" she demanded.

Jack shrugged his shoulders. "An amicable separation?"

"Oh, really?"

"Look, you don't want to spend three months at a time missing me, do you? You should get on with your life."

"Oh, you're just worried about *me* missing *you*? That's a bit arrogant of you, isn't it?"

"No, I didn't mean it like that. Of course I'd miss you. But I'm afraid if I don't do this now, I might never have the chance."

Taking a few steps away from Jack, as if the extra space would allow her mind to think more clearly and less emotionally, Maggie thought through her relationship with him, and the future she would have with him if she were to convince him a long-distance relationship could work. She didn't like what she could see: a miserable existence, awaiting Jack's return, then watching the clock until he had to leave again. She was upset and angry--upset at Jack for breaking up with her, and angry at herself for agreeing with him, deep down.

"I'd like it if we could still be friends, when I'm in town? You're gonna be a successful journalist one day, I wouldn't want my band to get on the wrong side of your pen," he said with a wink and a chuckle.

"That is, if I still have a band."

She kicked a few pebbles around where she stood as he moved to stand beside her again. "Yeah, well, you can bring me stuff back from your visits to America."

"Yeah, exactly! I have to take this job, Maggie, it's an opportunity to see the world. Do you understand?"

She nodded. "I'm annoyed at you so much right this second, but yeah, I understand. I guess. You have to do this. It's what you wanted to do before you met me, so I'm not going to be the one to stand in your way. I'm really not happy about it though. But I don't hate you."

Jack smiled. "Thank you. Besides, you'll still have a man in your life. Good old Yankee Ricky."

"Oh, really, Jack. He's three-thousand miles away."

"Yeah and I will be too--probably in the other direction, but still. I'll miss you, Mags, but you'll be okay."

They stood in silence as they watched the horizon, wondering what changes were heading their way.

16 November 1964

Dear Ricky:

So sorry it's been a while since my last letter. I've been hoping to have some news for you before writing. But it's been over three months since I put out copies of my booklet around the city. I got some nice responses from my friends in the beginning, but now it seems so long ago and I haven't taken the media world by storm. So much for my first real writing effort.

I've had to take extra shifts at the cinema. I've also been seeing less of Claire these days. Since we left college, she quit her job at the cinema to work full time as an assistant hairdresser in a place called "Hair Care". Claire joked that when she gets her own shop she should name it "Hair Claire".

And Jack has left the city. He decided to follow in his uncle's footsteps and joined the Merchant Navy. He said goodbye to me and sailed off to see the world like it was no big deal. I've never been able to figure him out, probably never will. I've received a few post cards from him since he left, but they're coming fewer and further between, and they'll probably just stop coming sooner or later...
I guess that's all I need to say about him. Everything good comes to an end, right? I guess you know that only too well yourself.

Write back soon, I could do with cheering up!
From me to you,
Maggie x

Maggie finished serving a customer his popcorn and lemonade and looked up to see her mum was next in the queue.

"Come to see a film have you, mum?"

"Not at these prices," replied Mrs Carter, "I've been in town, just come to tell you you've had a phone call from something called *British Music Express*. They want to talk to you."

Maggie's eyes popped out like a cartoon character's. "What? When? That's a huge magazine!"

"They said they'd come by the house and see you at half past six. Someone called Rita. 'Ere, I hope she doesn't intend to stay for dinner. We barely have enough Shepard's Pie tonight to go around as it is. I had to cut my grocery shopping time short when Mrs. Dyson sprained her ankle. She got run over by the trolley somehow. Her own trolley."

Maggie waved her arms wildly to cut off her mother's babbling. "See me about what? I never applied for a job with them. They're too big! And they're in London! They'd never hire me."

"They didn't say, but I'm sure you'll find out at six-thirty. I hope its good news, and she's not just selling subscriptions. Anyhow, I've got to get going or I'll miss my bus."

When her shift was finally over, Maggie raced home to be ready for Rita's arrival from *British Music Express.*

"This could be it!" she thought to herself.

She had just enough time to straighten up her hair, and make the living room presentable before a knock came at the door.

A tall woman with dark wavy hair, and what Maggie assumed were very expensive clothes, was standing on the doorstep.

"Rita Oswald," the woman said with a well-mannered, southern English accent, "I'm looking for Maggie Carter."

"That's me," Maggie said.

"Nice to meet you. I'm from *British Music Express*, I've come to talk to you about this."

Rita held up a rather crumpled copy of Maggie's *Guys with Guitars in Liverpool*. Maggie was caught off guard for a moment but managed to remember her manners.

"Yes, please come on in, take a seat." She led Rita through to the living room. "Would you like a cup of tea? Or stay for dinner?"

The sound of a minor crash emanated from the kitchen.

"No thank you, I have to be on the next train to London, so I can't stay long."

Mrs. Carter, eavesdropping from the kitchen and holding a newly chipped cup, sighed with relief. The Shepard's Pie was safe.

"I picked up a copy of your music reviews during my stop at the Cavern," Rita continued, "I was there doing a bit of research for a story I'm working on. I have to say I'm quite impressed with your writing."

"Really?"

"Yes, you've still got a bit to learn, but it shows potential. How old are you?"

"Eighteen, going on nineteen. Oh, that's daft, eh? Everyone who's eighteen is going on nineteen…except for people who get run over by a truck or something before their birthday."

"Our magazine is looking for fresh writers who will represent the youth of today. There's a lot going on in the music world today, as you know. You're obviously determined, a hard worker, prolific, and have initiative to get your work out there. And, of course, you're a good writer. So, you're in the running for the position, if you're interested."

"Are you serious? Of course I'm interested!"

"I'll be speaking to one or two others in town while I'm here. They're about your age, as well. The position involves doing filler stories, writing photo captions, that sort of thing, for a start. But there's always the opportunity to work your way up. Some of our best writers started out doing that, including me. Oh, and the job is at our London offices. That's sometimes a deal breaker for people so far away."

"Not for me."

"Well, before we get ahead of ourselves, I'll need to speak with a few other people."

Maggie nodded. "Of course, I understand."

"I'll be in touch. Thanks so much for seeing me."

Maggie showed Rita to the door. She tried to remember to say thank you and goodbye, but her head was swimming with images of London and interviews with the biggest names in music. This was the most exciting thing in the world.

She'd just had to wait for a decision.

"That's so huge!" Claire said, as she and Maggie headed down Liverpool high street to their favourite chip shop, Chaps Serving Chips. "A real national magazine wants you!"

Maggie grinned. "I'm in with a chance. But I don't want to jinx myself. It's not definite. She said there were a couple other people they're thinking of, but still, huge right?"

"Er... yeah!" A new thought caused Claire's smile to quickly evaporate. "But then you'd have to move to London, wouldn't you? Without me! What will I do here?"

Maggie shrugged. "You have other friends, Claire."

"Not like you!"

"Well, why not get your hair salon here?"

"Oh, just like that, eh? Snap my fingers, instant hair salon?"

Maggie nodded and shrugged again. "Or, come to London with

me?"

"Possibilities eh, Mags?" she stopped as she noticed Shirley up ahead. "Look, there's Shirley. Are you going to tell her your news?"

Shirley stood in front of a shoe shop, admiring the window display.

"I couldn't do that. That's like rubbing it in her face, and I'm not that shallow. Besides, I told you, they haven't even offered me the job."

"But nearly so!" Claire countered.

Shirley started to wander away from the shoe shop window.

"On the other hand," Maggie said, "If I get it, and leave for London, she might wonder where I disappeared to."

They caught up to Shirley, who saw them out of the corner of her eye.

"Oh, hi, Mags, hi, Claire. How are you two doing?"

"Great," Claire said. "Maggie's got some big news."

"Oh really?" asked Shirley. "Go on then."

"Well, it's not official yet, but I'm being considered for a writing job in London, for *British Music Express.*"

"No way!" Shirley seemed genuinely impressed and excited. The girl apparently didn't have an insincere bone in her body, which made Maggie feel guilty for her premature bragging. She wished Shirley wasn't being so damned nice about it.

"Yeah," Maggie continued, "an editor for the magazine saw my work, came to my house and might offer me the job."

"Oh, you mean Rita?" Shirley said, causing Maggie's jaw to drop wide open. "She talked to me as well!"

Maggie's body instantly, and visibly, deflated. "Oh, she did?"

Shirley nodded. "How weird is that? She said she's been reading MMM, and saw my article about the Beatles at the Cavern. She really liked it. She's dead nice."

"That's really…something," Maggie replied, exchanging a nervous glance with Claire. Her effort to keep her smile in place felt as if she were trying to keep a horizontal sack of flour from sagging in the middle. "They'll probably pick you."

Shirley shook her head. "What makes you think so?"

"Because you're *you*! You never put a foot wrong!"

"Oh, I don't know about that," Shirley said with a smile.

The nicer she was, the more aggravating she became.

Claire did what she could to suss out Shirley's true feelings about the job. "Their offices are in London, aren't they, Shirley? Seems a long way to go, when you could write for MM here."

"Oh, I wouldn't mind!" Shirley said, "I love London! I've got a cousin who lives there. I visit as often as I can."

Well, Maggie concluded to herself, that seals it. Curly Shirley was just too perfect not to be offered the job.

"Good luck, Mags," Shirley waved as she continued down the sidewalk to resume her window shopping.

"You too," Maggie answered reflexively. She waited until Shirley was out of earshot. "What am I saying? I don't want to wish her good luck! Her *good* luck is always my *bad* luck! Oh, I think I'm losing my appetite for fish & chips."

"Wow, you really *are* upset," Claire said. "Mind if I have yours, then?"

For the next several days, Maggie spent a good deal of time at home, pacing about the house, not knowing what to do with herself. She had no idea when Rita might announce the decision, or if she would even bother to contact Maggie in case someone else--like Shirley--had been chosen for the job. Every phone call, every knock at the door, and every piece of delivered mail received her heightened attention. She only agreed to go out when she knew her mother would be home to receive any news, be it good or bad.

Even when she agreed to return to Chaps Serving Chips, her appetite proved to be too unreliable.

"The waiting is killing me," she moaned to Claire, over a half-eaten portion of their lunch. "How long does it take for them to make up their minds?"

"It hasn't even been a week, Mags. You should just put it out of your mind for now."

"I've thought of that. In fact, I've spent every waking moment telling myself to put it out of my mind."

"Er, I don't think it works as well that way."

"I just know they'll pick Shirley, or someone else."

"But you've written a dozen articles in your booklet, and she's only written a couple for MM. You're much more productive, and you wrote those without any pay. That's dedication. They'll see that. And, you're a dead clever writer. You know words the rest of us never even heard of."

"Wanna be my agent?" Maggie sighed. "You make me sound like the greatest writer since Jane Austen."

"I bet Jane Austen couldn't write about The Five Kings the way you could."

Maggie smiled. "Hmm. I wonder what that would look like. I might give it a go: Jane Austen reviews the latest gig by The Five Kings. 'I turned to my gentleman companion during the musical performance, and queried, 'Why, Mr. Darcy, I see only four of the supposed Five Kings. Why is this, sir?'" She put her arm around Claire's shoulder. "Whatever did I do to deserve a friend like you?"

"You can repay me whenever I open my salon," Claire said. "I'll practice on you."

Thanksgiving was always one of Ricky's favorite holidays. But he didn't love the cold weather of that time of year, or the shorter days. The dead leaves on the ground and bare tree limbs looked so deathly to him, after eight months of green grass and budding flora everywhere. But he enjoyed the festive nature of the holiday, taking trips to farm stands for fresh apple cider and doughnuts helped stave off his anxiety about the even darker, colder days of the oncoming winter. And, of course, there was Thanksgiving dinner itself, complete with visiting relatives he was reasonably glad to see, as long as their presence was limited to that one day every year. And this Thanksgiving was especially exciting because he hadn't been home for three months.

Driving back through his hometown, he found himself scanning the suburban landscape for anything unexpected. Perhaps he'd notice a new supermarket suddenly occupying a previously vacant lot, or a new traffic light at an increasingly busy intersection. He didn't want to see too many changes, to make things disorienting. Luckily, everything looked the same as it had three whole months ago.

He was eager to see his parents again, and even Joanne. For all he knew, she might have really grown an inch taller since he was last home, as his mother claimed. He was also excited to see Kenny and Dave again, and the others at Never On Sundae.

Since the ice cream shop was situated between the Garden State Parkway and home, Ricky decided to stop in first to see who was working behind the counter. He entered a little cautiously, noticing two new female employees he hadn't seen before—one brunette and one blonde. There were no customers at the moment, which wasn't a surprise, since late November had never been the height of the ice cream season.

"May I help you?" asked the brunette.

Ricky was tempted to ask for a cup of mocha nut but quickly decided against it. "Is Stan here?"

The girl called to the back room. "Stan! Someone here for you."

Stan emerged, wiping his hands on a cloth. His face brightened upon seeing Ricky.

"Hey, look what the cat dragged in! How 'ya doing, Ricky? How's college?"

"Not bad."

"When did you get home?"

"I didn't. This is my first stop."

"You stopped here and you haven't even been home yet? Wow. I'm flattered."

"Is anyone else around?"

"I think I heard Dave making plans to meet Kenny here in a little while. They both got back into town earlier today. But you should go home first, and say hi to your folks. I'll tell the boys to wait for you here."

"Is Marie still working here?"

"Yeah, but not this weekend. I gave her most of the week off."

Ricky left a message for Stan to tell the guys, and arrived home for a pleasant reunion with his family. His mom was especially ecstatic to have him home again, even if it was only for a few days. After giving them his latest update on college life, he promised he'd be back for dinner, and hurriedly returned to the ice cream shop.

Dave and Kenny had arrived just moments before. It took the trio no time to fall back into their familiar groove, exchanging quips, gossip, insults, and play punching each other on the arm for no good reason.

"So…" Ricky ventured, "Have either of you seen Marie, or heard from her?"

"No, Kirsten did," Kenny said. "We're still going out, you know—that's the good part of going to college only an hour away. We go out once a week, but she said seeing me once a week is enough."

"Spoken like a true sweetheart," Ricky chuckled.

"Wait 'till you see her, Ricky. She's all styled these days, like those English models. Pattie Boyd. She's the one who's married to George Harrison, you know. Andrea-Claudia got Kirsten, Marie, and some of the other girls into all of that British style, with the clothes and the hair. But you and Marie broke up, didn't you?"

"Yeah, we did." He gazed out the window, watching a wind gust swirl some dead leaves airborne. "It got cold out pretty fast," he said, almost talking to himself. "And blustery."

Dave chuckled. "Ricky, you're the only person who uses the word 'blustery,' except for the weatherman on TV."

"But it *is* blustery."

"Yeah, it is," Kenny concurred. "It's so windy I sneezed in my own face before. Not pleasant."

Chapter 19

During that momentous train journey to London, Maggie went through the full spectrum of emotions; from excitement to nervous anxiety, from a sense of accomplishment to a question of self -doubt, from feeling independent and unstoppable to feeling insecure and very alone. A volcano of raw energy and mixed emotions bubbled the whole time she sat still in her seat.

Replaying the moment she was told the job was hers, Maggie could still feel the wave of relief and elation that initially swept over her body from head to toe. Everything she'd been hoping for was actually being offered to her. Dreams really could come true, and she was going to tell this to Ricky in her next letter; she'd have lots to write about, including how he would have to have faith that his dreams would come true too, because she fully believed they would.

With time to kill in the train carriage, and since she never went anywhere without a notebook and pencil she took them out and began to compose her next airmail letter.

Dear Ricky,

I'm writing to you from the clickety-clacking of British Rail. The man sitting opposite me is snoring away, hugging a newspaper –I've read what I can see of the headline about sixteen times something to do with financial upset. Oh well. My journey seems very long. It's only a few hours of course, in reality, but I'm so eager to get to King's Cross it feels like this train is going slow deliberately. I want to get there now! I don't know if its nerves, or excitement or the fact that my leg keeps falling asleep. It felt so strange, and sad, to say goodbye to Liverpool, and to my mum, Claire, and my other friends. Claire kept getting emotional, the dear. But we'll stay in touch always. I'll be back to

visit, of course. Mum was fine, as her sister (my auntie
Nora) will be staying for a few months. They're like
two peas in a pod, so I'm glad Mum won't be lonely.

I keep worrying that no one in London will understand
my accent, but I guess people understand The Beatles
pretty well. Right? So I should be okay too. You
understood me on the phone, right?

Anyway, listen to me talking about myself. How are
things going for you? How is college? I wish the train
had like a telephone so I could talk to you...you would
help make this journey a lot less tedious.

Well, I'm off for a walk up the carriages to get the
cramp out of my leg, so I'll say goodbye for now. Write
back soon!

From me to you,
Maggie

The anticipation remained with her for the entire journey, that when the train pulled into Kings Cross station, she was glad of the walk from there to Euston Station, to burn off some nervous energy. It wasn't far, only fifteen minutes following her map, ten minutes to a local, but Maggie desperately needed to work off some of the stored up adrenaline. So fuelled up, she hardly felt the weight of the heavy suitcase she dragged with her.

London was supposed to have been like Liverpool, she thought--a city with old, tall buildings, lots of buses going by and lots of people going in and out of lots of shops, but it was so very different. Sure there were old and tall buildings, buses and people, but it was so much more. In London, people seemed to walk faster, traffic seemed to move slower and though Maggie smiled at a few people as they walked past her, few made eye contact or even attempted to acknowledge her existence. Suddenly, she felt very vulnerable, but she held her head high and continued towards Euston tube station. She was a Londoner now!

On that first day, it took her an hour and forty-five minutes to find the accommodations she had organised. Much of the time was taken by getting on the wrong tube line, having to double back and then walk a few more blocks, before she managed to find the eighty-year-old house that had been converted into two flats. She would be living in the upstairs flat with two other people she'd never met before.

Her first day working for the magazine was bewildering. She was mentally prepared for the challenge but it was nothing like she'd been expecting. The deadlines, assigned by her new editor and boss, Sharon, came fast and furiously, and, even though Maggie was the newest member of the team, Sharon didn't go easy on her. But Maggie convinced herself she could handle it, as she'd been in training for this for the past few years.

Two months on, she travelled the now-familiar route from the offices of the *British Music Express* back to her flat, exhausted at the end of this day, but feeling good. Life wasn't luxurious by any means: before she could sit down with a cup of tea, she'd have to cook her own meal and iron her clothes for the next day.

"You're back late today," said a voice from the sofa as Maggie headed for the kitchen.

The voice belonged to Linda, a slim, blonde, twenty-one -year-old who was making a career as a model.

"There was a meeting with the chief editor. So boring. I don't even know why I had to be there."

"There's some fish and chips in the oven for you," said Linda.

"Really? Thanks!"

"No problem, my treat."

When Maggie first met her two flat-mates, she thought she wouldn't get on with Linda, who was pretty enough to be a model and she knew it. Maggie first believed Linda would have the personality and 'up herself' attitude to go with it, but those first impressions couldn't have been more wrong. Linda had a very welcoming charm, and she and

Maggie had become quite good friends.

Melissa, on the other hand, was a different kettle of fish entirely.

"Melissa is out for the night," Linda said, providing the regular update. "She came in, mumbled something about a new club in Soho, and left."

"Again?" Maggie asked with some exasperation. She returned to the living room with the fish and chips on a plate, and sat with it on her knee.

"Yep, no doubt she'll be missing work again tomorrow, burning the candle at both ends."

"And in the middle," Maggie offered. "But I guess it's none of our business really."

"True, but it will be, if she gets sacked and can't pay her share of the rent."

Linda had a point. When Maggie first met Melissa, she assumed she'd get on with her straight away. She seemed very down to Earth. But it soon became obvious that Melissa had no time for her, or Linda, or work, so it seemed.

"Oh by the way," Linda said, in a brighter tone that came with a change of subject, "a letter came for you today, has an airmail stamp on it."

Maggie smiled, knowing who had sent her the letter.

"Who do you know in America?"

"I didn't tell you about my pen-pal Ricky? We've been writing to each other for a couple of years now."

"Oh, nice! Looking for a husband all the way over there?"

"Of course not. Don't be daft."

Maggie decided not to fuel Linda's teasing by mentioning the secret fund she had been keeping for her dream trip to America. Now that she was earning a better wage than Mr Dunhill ever gave her at the cinema, she could afford to save a lot more each month for her journey. Of course, paying the rent, commuting expenses, and feeding herself took a chunk of her wages, but there was still enough left over to put a bit aside, as long as she didn't mind going without trips to the theatre or out for meals too often with her new friends.

The next day at work was "Deadline Day." All articles were to be turned in by 4 p.m., so the magazine could go to press for the new issue hitting the shops.

The assignment Maggie had been given for the new issue was a filler piece, comparing the most popular hairstyles amongst musicians. It wasn't exactly the scoop she'd been hoping for as her big break, but it gave her an opportunity to mention the Beatles. She also mentioned the Beach Boys, bringing in an American influence.

"Maggie," Sharon called as she approached from across the room, "are you finished with your article yet? It shouldn't be taking you too long."

"Yes, just checking it over now. Sorry."

"Be sure it's on my desk within the hour."

According to the over-sized white clock hanging on the back wall, it was coming up to 3 p.m., and Maggie knew she could have had the article on Sharon's desk a couple of hours earlier, but the last time she was given a filler piece to write--about a snack shop that named their sandwiches after pop stars--Sharon seemed almost disappointed that Maggie had handed it in early, as if accusing her of allowing speed to take precedent over quality. So, Maggie wasn't going to hand in her article early again, at least not until she'd earned some respect as a good writer in this office.

Whilst she pretended to be checking over her already as-good-as-it-would-ever-get article, she started composing her new and exciting letter to Ricky, in her head.

Dear Ricky,

I have some exciting news-- I'm DEFINITELY coming to America! I would like to come over in the summer, I should have enough saved up for spending money by then, I currently have enough saved to go and book my flights, I'm so excited! We'll finally get to meet in person!

*And to think it all started with that dollar bill you sent
to me ages ago. Remember? I still have it.*

"I need all articles on my desk within ten minutes," Sharon
announced to the whole office floor.

Maggie looked up to the clock--it was 3:45, the time had passed
quickly as she'd been day dreaming about her forthcoming American
adventure. She skimmed over her article one last time out of habit, and
headed over to Sharon's desk, pleased with her efforts.

Her latest assignment required her to get out of the office for a
while, which was a big welcome. There was nothing better than getting
out of the office and being paid to do so. She was to conduct an
interview with an up and coming 'next big thing' singer, at a small café
near Covent Garden. After a short ride on the tube, she was glad to see
she was the first to arrive at the designated café.

The waitress brought her a cup of tea as requested, as Maggie laid
out her notebook, pen and ID badge out on the table, ready for the
interview. The singer was already five minutes late for the meeting, but
Maggie wasn't surprised. She'd read some notes on the man in question,
Mr. Eric Sellers. She had already formed an opinion of him, as someone
who was likely to keep people waiting. She was surprised his PR
manager would allow such tardiness. They'll probably blame the delay
on London traffic, Maggie guessed.

The glass door to the café swung open and in stepped a blonde
woman looking very business-like, and a younger man, about nineteen
years old, who looked rather scruffy.

"Maggie Carter?" asked the blonde woman.

"Yes," she replied as she stood up to greet them.

"I'm Michelle O'Shea, and this is Eric--Eric Sellers, the singer you
will be interviewing."

Maggie shook Michelle's and Eric's hand. She couldn't help but
think how *Michelle O'Shea*, when said out loud, sounded as if it could

be the name of some sort of posh French pastry.

"Sorry we're a tiny bit late," Michelle said, "the traffic was simply awful."

"No problem, I know it gets very hectic out there," Maggie said, while continuing in her head: "*I managed to get here on time!*"

Eric spoke up for the first time. "Is that Scouser I hear in your voice?"

"I am from Liverpool, yes, but I've been trying to soften the accent. I tend to have to repeat myself a lot down here if I go native."

"I've played a few gigs in Liverpool before. Maybe you've seen me?"

Unsure of how to inform him that she'd never even heard of him before without sounding rude, Maggie took the wimpy way out. "Sorry, I've been living in London for quite a while now, I probably missed your shows."

Eric nodded.

The waitress approached the table. "Can I get anyone anything?"

"Two coffees please, milk and sugar in both," Michelle replied, ordering for Eric as well.

The trio made small talk about the music business, and *British Music Express*, until the coffees arrived.

"So, you have some questions for me," Eric said, more as a statement than a question. "Ask away."

Maggie shifted in her seat to get more comfortable and picked up her pen and notebook.

"Okay, so, when did you decide music is what you were destined to do? A lot of our readers would like to be musicians themselves, so I think they'd be interested in your back story and any advice you could give."

Eric shrugged. "Music consumes me. I am just a vessel for the melodies and lyrics trying to escape. There's no short cut. If you have the gift of music, you will be noticed, and if not, you should really look for a job to suit your skills."

Maggie stared at him for a moment, taking in his answer, then quickly wrote down his response word-for-word, all while thinking what a poser he was. Michelle had probably ordered him to memorize that answer.

"And who would you compare yourself to in the current music scene?"

"No one. I am a totally new kind of musical experience. There is no one out there like me."

Okay, Maggie thought to herself, as she continued to jot down Eric's bloated pronouncements, could he really have such a massive ego without any accomplishments to justify it?

"I understand you have a new record coming out soon?"

"I'm set to release an album two months from now. It's called 'Howling'. It really reflects the state of the world at the moment. I think people will like it. A lot."

Maggie nodded and continued to write. "Do you do any howling on the album?"

A startled Eric and Michelle looked at her quizzically, not getting her cheeky humor.

"I sing, dearie, I don't howl," he grumbled.

"Right," she said. She repeated "doesn't howl" aloud to herself as she scrawled it on the paper. She was beginning to enjoy this.

The more questions she asked, the more weird responses she got. Eric wasn't like anyone else she'd ever interviewed. She wondered if he truly believed what he was saying, or if it was all an act--or, if he was just plain stupid and arrogant.

After she had a few pages to work with, Maggie thanked Eric and Michelle for their time, and picked up the café bill on the magazine's expenses.

Chapter 20

One of Ricky and Kenny's weekly summer routines was to stop at Artie's drive-in hot dog stand to enjoy some gloppy "all-the-way" hot dogs, fries, and sodas, served on a tray fitted onto the edge of the driver side window. Aside from the food, Artie's had a knack for hiring gorgeous waitresses, whom the boys considered a welcome bonus.

"Now if only one of us had a convertible," Kenny said. "That would be perfection."

But on that particular day, August 11, even Ricky was too preoccupied to think much of cute waitresses and convertibles. It was the day before Maggie's visit.

"I can't believe she'll be here tomorrow! I want to do something really good for when she arrives."

"Isn't picking her up at the airport good enough?"

"No, I want to do something she'll remember."

Kenny gave it some thought. "Well, you could *not* pick her up at the airport, so she'd have to hitchhike all the way to your house. She'd remember that."

"Not helping, Kenny."

Both boys took a bite of their hot dogs as Ricky's eyes lit up with a burst of inspiration.

"Hey, I have a great idea. You know that chauffeur's cap you gave me, back when you were being obnoxious about making me drive you everywhere when I got my car?"

"Vaguely."

"So how about when we pick up Maggie, you wear the cap, and maybe a nice suit, and you can drive us back home from the airport—you know, as if I had hired a real chauffeur. That'll be hilarious!"

Kenny nodded as he analysed the scenario. "And where will *you* be the whole time? You're not going to be in the back seat with her, are you? Getting all cuddly while I'm trying to keep from getting run off the road by insane cab drivers?"

"No, nothing like that! I'll be in the front seat next to you. I'll point things out to her--you know, the skyline, the city, Palisades Amusement Park… I think we'll be a little nervous, so that'll be a way to break the ice."

"Why?"

"I don't know…it's a big deal. She's flying three thousand miles across the ocean to see me. I don't want her to be disappointed by anything--especially with me. "

"Well, it's too late to get them to repaint the George Washington Bridge for her, if that's what you mean."

"Not exactly."

"It'll be fine, Ricky."

"But that would be funny, wouldn't it--you being our chauffeur? Hey, wear sunglasses, too. And we'll make a sign that says 'Welcome, Maggie Carter' to hold up when the passengers get off the plane."

"You wanna have a marching band for her, too?"

"Good idea, too short notice. But come on, you know the chauffeur bit is a great idea."

Kenny gave it a bit more thought, then cracked a smile. "Yeah, that could be funny, all right."

"Good first impression, eh?"

"I gotta admit, not bad, pal."

"If we pull this off, I'll owe you."

Ricky could barely sleep that night. Maggie's plane wasn't due until 7:00 p.m. the following evening, but nervous energy had sent his mind racing. He eventually fell asleep but awoke early, unable to keep still throughout the morning, and into the afternoon. His mother had made sure the guest room would be neat and comfortable, but Ricky couldn't help checking and double-checking it several times throughout the day. Joanne was excited too, but she still posed a danger, in case she decided to ask Maggie embarrassing questions or make inappropriate comments. She seemed to be almost practising during the day, following her brother around with questions.

"Do you think she'll bring her own toothpaste with her? Do they even have toothpaste in England?"

"What kind of stupid question is that? Of course they do."

"I heard people in England all have rotten teeth."

"That's not true. And don't say anything like that to Maggie. She has a beautiful smile."

Joanne saw that remark as a choice opportunity. "Ooh! I get it! You want her to be your girlfriend!" she teased, in a sing-song chant.

That's all Ricky needed in his already frazzled state.

"Shut up! If you embarrass me, or her, I'll make you regret it!"

Knowing any further confrontation with his sister would only serve to raise his blood pressure, he left the house to meet with Kenny, making sure Kenny's "uniform" would be suitable for the gag.

"It's a pretty damn hot day for me to be wearing a suit," he moaned.

"We won't need to pick her up until 7 o'clock, so you don't have to put it on until we leave. It won't be so hot out by then."

"Yeah, it should drop way down to about 80 degrees."

Regardless of his grumbling, Kenny still shared Ricky's happy anticipation.

"You're sure Kirsten can't come, too?" he asked one last time.

"No, I don't want to greet Maggie with a mob behind me, even if it's a friendly mob. You're lucky you talked me into letting *you* come."

"Ah, but that was when I was going as just a person, not as a chauffeur. Now you need me."

Linda stood peering into Maggie's closet, hands on hips, as Maggie sat on the bed, quietly awaiting the verdict.

"No offense, Mags, but you need something really smashing to wear for your travel day, and you haven't got it in here."

"Well, I don't think I can afford anything smashing—if that's the standard."

"Oh, we'll find something. Trust me. I know where to look."

"Where?"

"It's my business to know where. I know a few shops on Oxford

Street, dead stylish clothes."

"Well, you're the expert. But they'd probably look a lot better on you than on me."

"Oh, give over. You're gorgeous. You just need a bit of guidance. Want to impress your American chap, don't you?"

"Well, he's just a friend."

"Sure he is," Linda nodded, unconvinced. "We'll do you up in a smart outfit, very mature, but young."

A shopping trip with Linda for new wardrobe additions proved a revelation to Maggie. Linda's modelling experience, even though she was only two years older, introduced a new world of fashion. Maggie realized how Linda had become a very caring friend. They were thrown together by chance, just as flatmates who--like Melissa--could have ignored each other more often than not, but instead came to look out for each other, and even learn from each other.

They settled on a blue jacket and skirt, white blouse, and matching hat – at Linda's insistence. They also found a shop on Carnaby Street that offered styles a bit too experimental for Maggie's tastes, but included a counter that made and sold personal name tags.

"Let's get you a name tag to wear, in case he has trouble identifying you in person."

"A name tag? What am I, a stray poodle?"

"You'll be looking a lot different wearing this outfit, walking off the plane with lots of other people. You don't want him to be embarrassed if he looks right at you and doesn't recognize you straight-away. He'll see your name, and then he'll know."

"I won't look all *that* different, will I?"

"You'll look fantastic."

"He won't recognize me if I look fantastic?"

"No, silly. He'll be nervous, and so will you. Maybe you won't even see him in the crowd. He might need some help."

"Oh, all right."

Heathrow was bigger and much busier than Maggie had imagined, and it took her a while to gather her bearings and navigate her way to the correct terminal with her luggage and her passport gripped firmly in her right hand. She had never been on-board an airplane before, let alone a Pan Am jet. In fact, she'd never been on a real holiday before; Pontin's holiday camps, a couple hours away from Liverpool, didn't really count, no matter how much fun they had been.

As she took her aisle seat on the plane, deep in the heart of Non-Smoking territory, careful not to crease her blue skirt and jacket outfit as she sat down, the excitement was almost too much to control. She wondered if the other passengers were as excited as she was or if this was all normal to them, and couldn't help but notice that some of them seemed to be looking at her oddly. Making sure her seatbelt was fastened, she sat back and nervously awaited take off.

The plane gained speed, pushing her deeply into the back of her seat. The front end of the jet tipped upward, and suddenly it was airborne. She strained to look out the nearest window to see London beneath her. She felt a little bit of envy surge through her: envy at the grey-haired man with his nose stuck in a Sherlock Holmes book, completely ignoring the view that came with a window seat. Maggie had been so excited just to be sitting on a plane flying over England and, a while later, over the Atlantic Ocean, that she hadn't even considered when choosing her seat how much better the journey would have been had she been able to admire the view without straining and contorting her body just to get a glance. On the other hand, an aisle seat did have its advantages; it made access to the loos a whole lot easier.

Later in the flight, the plane lavatory proved to be less scary than she had anticipated. Her heartbeat returned to normal shortly after overcoming her fear of getting sucked down the toilet after pressing the flush. On her way back to her seat, she noticed an older woman, dressed to impress, and calling for Maggie's attention. She stopped at the woman's seat.

"Excuse me, Miss. Can I get a coffee with milk, and two sugars?" asked the woman in a rich New York accent.

"I'm sure you can," Maggie replied, a little confused.

"I suppose it's that instant stuff?"

"I suppose it is."

"Thank you, dear. With two sugars, please."

Maggie continued down the aisle to her seat. That was odd, she thought. Did that woman just ask her to fetch a cup of coffee, or was she just making polite, if somewhat demented, conversation? Perhaps the change in cabin pressure had an effect on some passengers.

She was about to take her seat when she thought she'd quite like a hot beverage herself. She spotted a stewardess ahead in the aisle, and continued on to ask for a cup of tea—and, just to be nice, asked for a coffee--with two sugars--for the woman who flagged her down. Maggie called her the "New Yorker."

"Your coffee, Ma'am," she said, offering the steaming cup to the woman from the Big Apple.

The woman checked out Maggie's name tag. "Thank you, Maggie."

Maggie nodded and shrugged off thoughts of passengers being forward, when she was interrupted by a balding man beckoning her, wiping his nose on a handkerchief and examining it.

"Peanuts?" he said.

She couldn't figure the connection. "Up there?" she asked the man, observing the handkerchief stuffed up his nose. "That's a strange place to keep them."

"What's that you say?"

"You said peanuts."

"Yes. Can I have a packet of peanuts?"

"From where?"

"From wherever you keep them."

"Er, sorry, but I already ate my own bag of peanuts, and I didn't bring any with me from home."

"What do you mean?" asked the confused man. "I don't want *your* peanuts. Don't you keep them in some cabinet in the galley or something?"

"Oh, all right," she said, annoyed at the inconvenience. She caught a moment when the stewardesses were busy at the snack cart to take a quick look through the galley storage cabinets, and found the plane's supply of peanuts. She grabbed a bag and returned to the balding man.

"Don't shove them all up your nose at once," she said.

"Excuse me?"

"Eh...an old Liverpool expression. Don't eat them all up at once...indigestion."

Before she could sit down with her hot cup of tea, which was losing its heat by the second, she caught the eye of an elderly woman a few rows further up front. Maggie tried to ignore her, but the woman kept gesturing for her to come towards her, and since Maggie couldn't be rude to someone of the older generation--her mother had taught her better than that--she walked over to the elderly woman and asked her if she could do something to help her.

"Do you have a spare blanket, dear?"

"Not on me, no."

"Oh could you just check in the overhead bin, it's very chilly in here. There's bound to be something I could use. You wouldn't leave an old woman to sit and shiver now, would you?   After all, you're here to make me feel comfortable."

"I am?"

"Yes of course. Isn't it your job?"

Maggie felt herself losing her composure. "My job? Now wait a minute. I'm just a--oh, fine. Let's see," she sighed, opening the bin. She extracted a blanket and handed it to the woman.

"Thank you dear," she smiled sweetly.

A passing stewardess also smiled with approval of Maggie's kind gesture, adding, "Nice outfit" in an odd tone of voice as she continued on.

It suddenly occurred to Maggie to look down at her own outfit, and then back to the stewardess, and then at all the other attendants seeing to various passenger requests. Each female member of the flight crew was dressed in the Pan Am regulation blue skirt, white blouse and blue jacket. Maggie had dressed so smartly to fly, she hadn't realised she'd dressed smart enough to also work for Pan Am whilst flying. "Oh," she said as the realisation dawned on her. "Ohhh!"

She returned to her seat when the man reading the Sherlock Holmes book held up one hand to discourage her from sitting.

"Oh, miss, I was reading my book when they gave the safety instructions before take-off. Can you just give me a quick run-through of the demonstration?" He lowered his voice to a whisper. "You know, just in case we're about to crash or something."

"My tea is now cold, you know."

"Well, is that really important?"

"Was reading *Sherlock Holmes* really important during the take-off safety instructions?"

"Excuse me?"

"Fine!" she said, exasperated.

She stood at attention in the aisle, directing her speech solely at the man who had foolishly supplied her with the last straw.

"Okay, firstly, we're in the non-smoking section, so don't even think about it. Secondly, should we experience a decrease in cabin pressure, a cute little oxygen mask will drop down in front of you. And you just breathe into it normally. Not very complicated. If all of the engines go on the fritz at once and we start to nosedive toward the ocean, assume the crash position. That is, put your head down between your knees, clasp your legs firmly, and kiss your arse good-bye!"

She then sat down to take a sip of her cold tea, as an elderly man witnessing her petulant monologue from the other side of the aisle turned to his equally perplexed wife.

"The other stewardess must have forgotten that part," he said.

Chapter 21

The Grand Central Parkway was merciful with its relatively light traffic to Kennedy Airport. Ricky agreed to drive to the airport exchange for Kenny doing the honors—such as they were—on the return trip. As was their summertime custom, they drove with the windows wide open and WABC blasting on the radio. Cousin Brucie spoke excitedly (the only way he knew how to speak) about the Beatles' Shea Stadium concert, and included a bit of bragging that he was to be one of the emcees. The warm, humid August air blowing through the car as the sun baked the city didn't do much to calm Ricky this time.

"I'm nervous," he confessed. "What if...what if..." He paused, almost afraid to express his thought out loud, as if that alone would ensure his fear coming to pass.

"What if what?" Kenny prodded, again checking the chauffeur's cap on his head in the passenger visor's mirror.

"What if she realizes that she doesn't like me as much in person as she does in my letters?"

"But you're the same person in person."

"What if I can't think of anything witty to say? What if, after spending a few hours with me, she finds me hideous, and can't stand the sight of me, or thinks I'm a crashing bore, and decides she just wasted all that money and travelled all that way to be stuck in a strange family's house with a boring American jerk?"

"That's funny, that's what my pen pal called me in her very last letter to me. It sort of put the kabosh on our correspondence."

"But what if—"

"Ricky, even *I* can tell that she likes you. You've talked on the phone with her a few times, right? Didn't that go well?"

"I guess. I don't know."

"And she already knows what you look like, from all the pictures you're always sending her."

"Yeah, but the strange thing about me is that I look better in pictures than I do in person. I just happen to photograph extremely well. It's always been a blessing and a curse."

"She still wrote to you after your sister switched your good picture with the one of you snoring with drool dripping out of your mouth."

"Oh, no, I forgot about that."

"And yet she still likes you. And, you're taking her to see New York, the World's Fair, and the Beatles, playing the biggest concert ever! Hell, *I'd* date you if you took me to neat stuff like that!"

The rest of Maggie's flight became more peaceful as she was careful to keep a low profile and not to take too many trips to the rest-room, even though her plane ticket made no mention of her obligation to serve beverages and snacks for the duration of the flight.

As the sun slowly descended toward the horizon, the captain announced that they'd soon be arriving at JFK airport, and all passengers should take their seats and fasten their seatbelts. Thoughts of meeting Ricky in person within the next half hour or so were beginning to make Maggie's stomach do somersaults. This was it, the big meet-up. She thought back to their first phone call and how nervous she was back then, but that was nothing compared to this.

"Keep your composure," she told herself. "Don't look like an idiot!"

She tried all ways to keep herself calm but nothing worked, until she could glimpse through a gap in the window, catching sight of the Empire State Building and that glorious Manhattan skyline coming into view. Her nerves quickly gave way to excitement, as the amazing view before her had her speechless.

The summer's early evening sun continued to cast its brilliant orange light over the airport terminals, and against the planes taking off and landing at their rather severe angles. It was Ricky's favourite time of day—those last couple of hours before dusk, especially that time of year, when a warm breeze always seemed to kick up for a while just before giving way to a peaceful calm as the daylight dimmed.

Inside the Pan Am Arrivals terminal, through which he, Marie, and thousands of others had so madly dashed a year and a half earlier to greet the Beatles, the atmosphere this time was much less frantic. This time, his anticipation sprang from a much more personal level. And, comparing his state of mind on that cold February day to this warm, humid August evening, he was much happier to be welcoming his…dare he use the term --"soul mate"-- to his world.

He and Kenny stood before the enormous Arrivals notice board, scanning it for information on the London flight.

"There!" Ricky pointed. "Flight 03 from London, arrives 7:05, Gate 4. We've got less than ten minutes."

"Wait," Kenny warned, putting his hand on Ricky's arm to halt his forward motion. "Look over there. Flight 202 from London, arrives 7:15, Gate 12."

"No, that can't be right," Ricky said with shaky certainty. "How can there be two of them? She told me it was Flight 03. And that other one has an 'ONT' after London. She never said anything about that."

Kenny smiled at what for him qualified as an inspired thought. "Oh, I know! 'ONT' must be an abbreviation for 'On Time'."

"I don't think so. The other arriving flights say 'On Time' all fully spelled out."

"Maybe the board is broken--you know, a mechanical malfunction."

"Well, they're both going to arrive any minute. We'd better split up. I'll go to Gate 4 and you go to Gate 12. If she's on the plane arriving there, take her to me at Gate 4. If she's on my flight, I'll take her to you. But then she still has to get her luggage and go to Customs."

Kenny wasn't concerned with the particulars. "Yeah, yeah, just give me the sign with her name on it."

"Here, take this picture of her, to help you find her in the crowd."

Kenny grabbed the picture and sign and started down the concourse.

"And put your chauffeur's cap on!" Ricky admonished.

"Yeah, I gotta go!"

He ran off just as Ricky finally realized that 'London, ONT' meant London, Ontario. But he didn't have time to chase after his friend. He hurried down the concourse, dodging skycaps pushing luggage carts and random clusters of arriving passengers chatting excitedly with family members who had come to greet them.

His heart was beating fast—not from his running, but from his excitement, nervousness, and fear that the concerns he confessed to Kenny in the car might be borne out in just a few minutes.

Ricky reached Gate 4, joining an eager crowd gathered near the doorway for the arriving passengers. The plane had already rolled up to the gate. Those engines must be exhausted, he thought, but they did their job. All he could do for the next few minutes was hope that he and Maggie would recognize each other, and be happy with what they saw.

At Gate 12, Kenny maneuvered his way to a choice spot, where he'd be in the direct line of sight for the passengers departing their plane. He straightened his suit and cap, and grasped the "Welcome, Maggie Carter" sign firmly—unaware that his hand was obliterating the name "Carter" completely. A few professional limo drivers were lined up alongside him.

A female voice on the p.a. system announced, "Flight 202 from London, Ontario is now arriving at Gate 12."

"London what?" he wondered. "That woman's gotta be drunk, or she can't read English."

He remained standing, and on the look-out as the passengers disembarked. Dozens shuffled past him without giving him much notice. He repeatedly checked the photo of Maggie with each girl that even vaguely matched her features. His head bobbed up and down between checking the photo and the faces of the passengers, making him look like some mechanical toy dog.

He was about to enter the panic stage of the plan when a matronly woman in her sixties, elegantly attired and with an unmistakable air of snootiness, approached him. She carried a small carry-on suitcase and an expression on her face that announced her displeasure.

"You're my driver?"

"What?"

"I'll have you know, young man, that I go by the name Margaret, not the diminutive and overly-familiar 'Maggie,' as you've written on your flimsy little sign. Is that clear?"

"Diminu….what?"

She locked her arm with his, sweeping him along in her march away from the gate.

"Now, I have two full-sized suitcases, each with a dark green and red plaid design, like a Scottish tartan, and a matching valise, but in light blue and beige, like this carry-on."

"They sound lovely," Kenny said, nervously looking over his shoulder.

"Now, here are my luggage tags, so you don't make any mistakes. You go to the carousel while I make a phone call, and I'll meet you by that courtesy desk over there."

Kenny managed to gently pull his arm from the woman's grip. "Sorry, ma'am—Margaret--but one of us is a little mixed up. Well, maybe we both are. You really don't look like you're 19, and you don't talk like you're from England. So, I gotta go."

"What? Well, I never…"

He hurried back to the arrival gate, desperate to find Maggie—or anyone who looked like a close enough match. He waved the sign with her name too frantically for it to be readable, but finally spotted a girl who looked to be Maggie's age and general appearance, and hurried to her.

"Are you Maggie?"

"No, sorry."

"You're sure? From what I was told, you look just like her—I mean, you look just like you, in this picture."

"What?" She got only a fleeting glance at Maggie's photo. "Sorry, but that's not--"

"Do you need a driver?"

"No, not that I know of." She smiled pleasantly, but was already hoping Kenny would go away.

"Can you come with me for just a minute? We need to go to Gate 4."

"No, really, I need to wait for my suitcase. You must have me confused with—"

"Where's your accent?" he asked.

"What accent?"

"Oh, now I remember. He said you guys don't know realize you have accents."

"Who said—"

"Please come with me, just for a minute! Just to Gate 4. Everything will be explained there. Then, if I'm wrong, you can go back to being whoever you are, if you're not who you're supposed to be. 'Grab my hand, it's gonna be crazy grand!' Cousin Brucie always says that."

"Cousin who?"

"On the radio! Come on!"

At Gate 4, with the appearance of each female passenger from the plane, Ricky's heart jumped just a little bit in that split second he needed to determine if that person could possibly be Maggie. Maybe she had a new hairdo or new clothing style he wouldn't recognize. He couldn't take much more of the suspense. He realized he had been wiping his palms on his pants repeatedly.

Before his swirling thoughts could continue to torment him, he saw her. He wasn't positive, but he was pretty sure.

"That's her!" he blurted out loud, catching himself from launching into a running commentary for all to hear. He took a more careful look. No, it's not her, he realized. Just one of the stewardesses. But wait, the stewardesses wouldn't be leaving the plane before all of the passengers had disembarked. That *was* Maggie! The girl he had exchanged untold numbers of letters, and photos, was suddenly a three-dimensional person, walking carefully towards the crowd of expectant friends and relatives awaiting her fellow passengers. Ricky's mind processed a hundred observations in mere seconds. She was taller than he expected, and her hair was redder, which he liked anyway. She looked very sophisticated in her tailored suit and Pan Am travel bag. He saw how she was scanning the crowd, looking for a familiar face—his face, and no one else's. Should he yell out her name? Everyone else was yelling out names, and flapping their arms about. Oh, Lord, he thought, please let this go all right. Please don't let me do anything to make her regret ever coming here. Please—

And then she saw him. And he *saw* that she saw him. He stood almost frozen, hoping he had a smile on his face, but he couldn't tell. She seemed to smile at him, but he couldn't tell that for sure, either. He made a feeble wave at her and held his breath. Was this about to be the sweetest moment of his life, or the most awkward? Or worse?

She marched straight to him and, without saying a word, put down her travel bag at his feet and threw her arms around him, tightly. Very tightly. She didn't say a word. Following her lead, neither did he. She held the embrace longer than he would have expected, but he gladly held her just as tightly, for as long as she wanted. It was the warmest, most comforting feeling he had ever experienced with another person. Ever. It was Maggie.

"Hi, Ricky," she said softly in his ear, through the widest smile her face could manage. They loosened their hold on each other. What could he say, if anything, that would be just perfect for their long-awaited, special moment?

"Who's Ricky?" he said.

She backed away. He smiled, she laughed, and hugged him again, just as tightly as before.

"Oh, my word, it's really you!" she said. "In the flesh! It's so good to see you! You look just like your photos."

"So do you, but better. Much better."

"Oh, you don't have to say that."

"No, it's true!"

"Well, now we don't have to rely on photos anymore. Have you been waiting long?"

"Nope, just got here."

"I still need to collect my luggage and go through Customs."

"That's fine. So, how was your first airplane flight?"

"Oh…well…busy," she said cryptically.

"Busy?"

"I'll explain later."

They started a slow stroll down the concourse. "I think I mentioned that I'd be here with someone," he said. "He'll be our chauffeur for the evening."

"Really? A chauffer? How posh! You didn't have to do that."

"Don't worry, he comes cheap."

His words almost acted as a cue for Kenny to appear out of the crowd further ahead, hurrying straight at them, with the unknown girl reluctantly in tow.

"I found Maggie!" he announced triumphantly. "But she's putting up a hell of a struggle."

"I've already got one," Ricky said, indicating the authentic Maggie next to him.

"Will you let me go?" the girl said, more annoyed than frightened. She pulled her arm from Kenny's grasp.

"Sorry," Ricky said sheepishly, "A slight misunderstanding."

The girl made an about-face and raced away from them as quickly as possible.

"Maggie," Ricky said with a sigh, "this is Kenny--our chauffeur."

"Ah, Kenny! Ricky's told me a lot about you...and I think I see what he means."

The Manhattan skyline loomed before them as Kenny managed to avoid an anxiety attack behind the steering wheel. Ricky kept a close eye on Maggie's expression as the city's steel and concrete landscape drew closer.

"Pretty amazing, eh?" he said proudly, as if he could take any credit for it.

"Yes, it's fantastic. It looked great from the plane, as well."

"Oh, yeah, I bet that was a great sight."

"It was an amazing view!"

"How are you feeling?" he asked. "I guess the jet lag will be hitting you pretty soon, right?"

"I'm not sure. Let's see." Her head suddenly fell back against the seat, her eyes closed shut. She started to snore.

Ricky laughed as Kenny caught a glimpse in the rear view mirror.

"You bored her to sleep *already*?" the faux chauffer said. "And she hasn't even seen Jersey yet!"

She opened her eyes and joined his laughter. "Don't worry, Kenny," she said. "I'll wait until we're in New Jersey before I fall asleep."

Ricky shrugged. "Yeah, that's what the rest of us do. Jersey has that effect on people."

He turned somewhat more serious again. "No, really, you're still on London time, right?"

"Well, my flight left London at 6:00 p.m., but we arrived here at about 7:00p.m. New York time—but it's past midnight London time. So, for me, it's quite late, yes.

"Wow," Kenny said, "that's so tough! So it's like you went back in time to get here."

Maggie wrinkled her forehead. "Did I? I guess I did, in a way."

Kenny continued his headlong dive into his own convoluted thinking. "So, if something really big happened in London, we wouldn't know about it for five hours?"

Ricky felt he just had to intervene. "It doesn't work that way, Kenny! Maggie went back five hours, but the flight took six hours."

"So," she ventured, "I'm missing an hour, then?"

"I don't know—it's probably still hanging over the Atlantic somewhere."

"And, my flight back to London leaves at 8:00 p.m. here, which is 1:00 a.m. there. But it will take a little more than six hours to get there, so I won't arrive until after 7:00 a.m., and then there will be the whole day to go through after I land. So, that day will be about 36 hours long for me…I think."

"See?" Kenny said, "That's why I don't do that kind of long distance traveling."

"Never mind, driver," Ricky said mockingly. "Just keep your eye on the road."

Maggie complicated the already exhausting mental exercise still further. "I read that the Earth rotates at a thousand miles an hour, from west to east. But jets fly at less than 600 miles an hour, so how will my plane ever catch up to London?"

The question brought a sudden silence to the car—except for Cousin Brucie.

Chapter 22

"We're home!" Ricky bellowed as he opened the front door. Maggie followed him in, almost tip-toeing, with Kenny lugging her suitcases behind her. Mr. and Mrs. Kramer appeared from the kitchen and greeted Maggie warmly and with lots of chatter, although they had agreed not to bombard her with too many questions at once. No sense in making her visit feel like a police interrogation.

"It's so nice to meet you, Maggie," Mrs. Kramer said, "after everything Ricky has told us about you. You're lovely!"

"Oh, ta," Maggie said, with a blush.

"Was your flight okay?"

"Oh, yes, I met a lot of the other passengers."

"Are you hungry?"

"We ate on the plane, but it already seems so long ago."

"We have some snacks if you're not too jet lagged," Mr. Kramer offered.

"Oh, that would be nice."

"I love your accent," Mrs. Kramer gushed. "Sorry, I don't mean to make you self-conscious."

Joanne bounded down the staircase.

"Joanne, this is Ricky's friend Maggie, from England."

"Hi," was Joanne's only greeting.

"Hi, Joanne, pleased to meet you."

Joanne had a tendency to stare at visitors to the Kramer home, rather than interact much with them via speech. She sat on the stairs, peering through the bannister to give Maggie the once-over.

"Let me give you a quick tour of the house," Ricky said, "and show you the guest room before we eat."

Kenny chose the moment to pipe up. "This is where my chauffeur duties end, as of now. I'm back to being a civilian."

"Okay, thanks Kenny," Ricky said.

"Yeah, thanks ever so much, Kenny!" Maggie echoed, with

considerably more sincerity.

Joanne then decided to actually join the conversation. "You guys are going to the Beatles concert?"

Ricky glared menacingly at his sister with his familiar "don't-say-anything-embarrassing-or-else" look on his face. "Yes, you *know* we are!" he said.

"Wish I could go."

"Well, you can't."

Joanne all but ignored Ricky's retorts, keeping her attention on Maggie. "I've got more Beatles stuff in my room than Ricky does," she bragged.

"Oh, I'd love to see it!" Maggie said.

"Well, we'll leave you to it," Mrs. Kramer said. "Ricky's a very good tour guide."

And so the tour of the Kramer residence began. Ricky needed to pinch himself in case he was dreaming that Maggie was actually right beside him, in his house. They headed up the stairs, with Joanne on their heels, refusing to leave them alone.

"Show her my room first!" she demanded.

"What are you, seven years old?" Ricky growled.

"No, I'm fourteen!"

"Fine," Ricky sighed.

Joanne's room did indeed live up to her promise of being the most elaborate Beatles shrine in the house. Pictures of the Beatles plastered the walls, Beatles magazines lay strewn about her bed. Maggie didn't need to exaggerate her wonder simply to placate Joanne. She was genuinely impressed.

"This is the best Beatles room I've ever seen--including mine!"

Joanne beamed with pride.

"Well," Ricky conceded, "it's to be expected. She's a typical 14-year-old American girl."

"I am not!"

"It wasn't meant as an insult. I'll save that for later."

They continued across the hall to Ricky's room, where he abruptly closed the door in his sister's face.

He watched Maggie as she looked around, identifying various knick-knacks, photos, and books that he had either told her about in his letters, or appeared in the background of pictures he sent her.

"*Pride and Prejudice!*"

"Huh?"

She reached for his copy of the Austen classic on the bookshelf. "My favorite book of all time!"

"Really? Mine too."

"Fancy that. Not too many chaps take to it, do they? You know, a romance novel, from a hundred and fifty years ago."

"I just love her use of the English language. It's so brilliant and um...loquacious."

Maggie giggled and nudged Ricky on the arm. "I can't believe I'm here, in your room, Ricky."

"If I had a dime for every girl who said that...Just kidding!"

She gave him another warm embrace, just as unexpected, but also just as welcome, as the one in the airport.

Once the tour concluded, Mrs. Kramer stood over the dining room table of sandwiches and soft drinks almost apologetically.

"Sorry, Maggie, you deserve a proper meal, but Ricky insisted on this kind of stuff for tonight. I don't know why I listened to him."

"Oh, it's fine, really! A snack now is all I need."

"I wanted to serve you something like—what is it, steak and kidney pie? But that's not so easy to find here."

"Mom!" Ricky jumped in. "She just came across the ocean to experience a bit of America, and have some American food. Why serve something she has all the time in England?"

"Oh, yeah, I didn't think of that. So, Maggie, are you looking forward to the concert?"

"Oh, too right, Mrs. Kramer."

"I understand you've been a Beatles fan before anyone in America heard of them? Ricky said you've seen them lots of times."

"I think it's thirty-three, mostly when they were playing clubs in

Liverpool, like the Cavern."

That tidbit of information greatly impressed the others.

"Wow!" Joanne said. "Do you know them personally? Do you have their autographs?"

"Sorry, 'no' to both questions. But they'd probably recognize me by now, if we passed on the street – or at least they might have done a few years ago."

In Joanne's eyes, Maggie had instantly become a celebrity in her own right--someone to fawn over. And, even better, she was staying with them for four nights!

The doorbell rang.

"I'll get it," Ricky said, as he sprang into action. "Must be Kenny again."

He discovered Dave and Tracy at the door.

"Hi," Dave said. "Is she here?"

"What are you doing here now?"

"It's only 9:30." He strained to look past Ricky. "Is she here? Your English girlfriend?"

"You mean Maggie, who isn't my girlfriend? Yeah, but we're having a snack with my parents."

"Can we see her?"

"You mean *look* at her, don't you? She's not some alien who just arrived by spaceship."

"Of course not. She came by plane, didn't she?"

Dave ignored Ricky's attempted obstruction and swiftly stepped past him on his way through the living room, with Tracy in tow. Mr. and Mrs. Kramer greeted them, as they casually had done a thousand times before, offering them some sandwiches and soda. Tracy hurried to whisper in Joanne's ear, as an exasperated Ricky looked on. He felt powerless to prevent such shameless and poorly disguised gawking at Maggie. After a few minutes of small talk among everyone—designed primarily to hear more of Maggie's accent—he delicately took her aside.

"I'm sorry, I didn't know they were coming."

"Oh, that's all right."

"I didn't want you to feel overwhelmed by so many—"

The doorbell rang again.

"Bloody hell!" he shrieked, almost unaware that he was borrowing a phrase from Maggie's side of the pond. She smiled as he again hurried to the door. He found Elliot and Andrea-Claudia at the doorstep, dressed in suspiciously sophisticated summer wear, standing in a casual manner that looked oddly forced.

"Hello, Ricky," Elliot said. "Beautiful night, eh? We were out for a drive in the convertible and wondered if your friend from London had arrived yet, and might like to join us."

Ricky turned anxiously to the gathering in the dining room. "Well, yeah, but I'm sure she's tired."

"What's her name? Margie?"

"Maggie, but—"

"Ricky," Andrea-Claudia began, with a newly-acquired British accent, "I've just got to ask her about the new London fashions I've been seeing in the magazines. I bet it's going to be all the rage here within days. Days! And, you know, since I've been told I look so much like Pattie Boyd—you know, George Harrison's wife--so Margie's bound to relate."

"Now? You want to talk to her about fashion *now*? She just got here a little while ago. And her name's Maggie, not Mar—"

"Is that Dave I hear?" Elliot said, peering into the house.

"Dave who?"

"Ooh, I can hear her accent from here," Andrea-Claudia gushed. "So elegant."

"Yes, just like yours, but she's had hers all her life. I've never noticed yours before."   "Really, Ricky, you needn't keep her hidden away. She came here to meet Americans, didn't she?"

"Actually, she came here to meet me. And the Beatles. I mean—"

"You don't want her to think someone like Dave is representative of young America, do you?"

"Well," Ricky said defensively, "Dave's okay, and besides, I like to think that *I'm* sort of representative—"

Andrea-Claudia wasn't interested in his reply. "You need us to balance the picture for her, Ricky. Dave and Kenny occupy one unfortunate end of the spectrum, and we occupy the other."

Elliot piped in with a newly-rehearsed accent of his own. "You'll thank us later, old chap."

They brushed past him to follow the sounds of conversation in the increasingly crowded dining room. Along the way, Andrea-Claudia turned to Ricky.

"Oh, and Marie says hi."

"What?"

Ricky let Maggie sleep as long as she needed the following morning, so she could feel refreshed after her long travel day and the spontaneous social gathering that night. They took their time getting ready to go out, but when the doorbell rang during breakfast, Ricky got the feeling they had taken perhaps a little too much time.

Joanne reached the front door first this time, to reveal Kirsten's arrival. She held a wicker basket covered with a cloth napkin that closely resembled a Union Jack flag.

"Hi, guys," she said to the Kramer siblings with a big smile. "A little bird told me that you have a visitor from jolly old England staying with you for a few days."

Ricky rolled his eyes. "A little bird, huh? Well, there were enough little birds here last night to make a Hitchcock movie."

"I thought you would like a little breakfast of tea and scones," Kirsten said, joining the newest trend of inviting oneself into the Kramer house before Ricky could thwart her plan. "Is she here? She's not still asleep, is she? Does she have a cool accent? Kenny says you almost brought home an old woman with you from the airport last night. I didn't know what he was talking about. But your girlfriend's our age, isn't she?"

Maggie entered, allowing Ricky to introduce the two. Kirsten presented her with the basket, repeating the "jolly old England" phrase. Ricky cringed.

"Oh, that's so sweet!" Maggie said of the gift. "I feel like a star, but I haven't even done anything."

"Yes, Kirsten, that is nice," he conceded. "We just finished breakfast, but I guess we can have them tomorrow."

Kirsten was interested only in hearing what Maggie had to say—while also studying the kind of clothes she was wearing, what she thought of America, and what it was like to speak with that neat accent. Ricky turned various shades of red with the embarrassment he felt for both himself and Maggie. But Maggie took it all in her stride, finding each of his friends entertaining in ways he had never considered.

After a good fifteen minutes, he gently nudged Kirsten away so he could begin the day out with Maggie.

"I don't really have a lot planned for today, to be honest. I can give you a little driving tour of the area, and we can make a few stops at my usual hangouts."

"That's fine! Remember, everything will be new to me. So, carry on."

She especially appreciated a stop at the record store, just to compare it with her favourite music shops at home. And rumors were rampant throughout the Kramer household that a backyard bar-be-que might be on the cards for dinner.

Later that evening, with everyone in the house well-fed and asleep, Ricky had too many things running through his head to rest. He got up and went downstairs to find Maggie watching TV, with the sound very low, barely audible. She looked fascinated with everything that flashed on the screen, including the most mundane of commercials.

"Oh, I hope the telly didn't wake you," she said softly.

"No, I can barely hear it, even now. Are you lip reading or something?"

He sat next to her on the sofa.

"I didn't want to make it too loud. I thought I'd be knackered, but I must have some sort of reverse jet lag, or second wind. Just goes to show that I don't know much about how that works after all."

"So, if I can repeat Kirsten's question from earlier, any impressions of America so far? Apart from my friends being very nosey and overbearing?"

"Oh, your friends are dead nice. Everyone made me feel very welcome."

She thought for a moment. "Let's see…Your cars are bigger than ours. Much bigger."

"Really? Is that good or bad?"

"Good for Americans, I suppose, but they'd probably be too expensive for most Brits.   Everything's bigger here, it seems."

"But you're living in London now, and I'm sure London has big…stuff."

"Oh, yeah, London's brilliant. I love it. But some things between here and there are just different. I see you've got more TV channels for a start, but more adverts as well."

"Oh, you mean commercials? Yeah, they're a drag."

"But you don't have a TV license here, right? We have to pay to watch."

"No way!"

"And I love your dollars. I like buying things with dollars and quarters."

They chatted a bit further, then a silence followed, as they watched the opening titles for 'The Late, Late Show'. The black & white movie that night was an oldie that neither of them had ever heard of. For the first time, Ricky didn't feel a sense of panic during the silence between them. It suddenly felt okay, perhaps because the TV was there to fill the gaps in the conversation. But he had a question for Maggie that, for reasons he didn't fully understand, he felt brave enough to ask out loud.

"So…is there any special person waiting for you back in London?"

"Special person?" she echoed a bit coyly. "Well, Claire's rather special. I don't tell her that enough, but I should. She's such a loyal friend, ever since we were tots. Is that what you mean?"

She knew perfectly well that wasn't what he meant, but she couldn't resist teasing him just a bit.

"*Yeah, yeah,* Ricky wanted to say, *"that's not what I meant and you know it."*

At the same time, she felt bad for her answer. *"Don't toy with him,"* she scolded herself. *"He's wonderful. Let him know it."*

"What about a…guy?" he ventured.

"Hmmm," she pondered, teasingly. "What have you heard?"

"Nothing!"

"I can't think of any guys. I'm usually too knackered at the end of the day to go out on dates. In other words, no guys." Well, she thought, in for a penny, in for a pound. Go on and ask him. "And you?"

"No, I don't date guys, either. I mean, I do--date, that is. Girls. But I don't. I mean, not lately. Not for a very long lately."

Aside from being pleased that he had no rivals for Maggie's affections, Ricky was impressed with how seriously she had been taking her job--treating it like a career, and not just a pay check. Her ambition was beginning to make him feel almost like a goof-off in comparison, being a mere college student when she was already out in the world, doing what she loved to do—and getting paid for it.

"Linda sometimes drags me out, though," Maggie continued. "London's great at night. There's always something to do, even if it's not with a date. I've been on a few here and there, but nothing worth pursuing. Hardly worth calling them dates at all."

"Uh huh," he said, masking his relief at her answer. "I don't have a very good track record. Did I write to you about Cindy?"

"Maybe. Was she the one with the laugh?"

"Yes! She seemed very sweet and demure, but when she laughed, it was the loudest, most obnoxious sound I ever heard. More like a scream than a laugh. You could use a recording of it as a burglar alarm. It was embarrassing in public. So, I deliberately tried to *avoid* making her laugh. No jokes. But after a few more dates, she dumped me because she said I had lost my sense of humor!"

"Poor, confused Cindy," Maggie said, shaking her head. "Do you not see Marie anymore, when you're both home from college?"

"Well, we got together once--a few weeks ago, in fact. I didn't mention it to you because it didn't go very well. I did all of the talking—and I mean *all* of the talking. I don't know what came over me. Nerves, maybe. But I just kept yapping away. Her eyes started to glaze over. Eventually, I think I actually bored her to tears. Either that, or she has nasty hay fever in the summer."

"I'm sorry," Maggie said.

But she wasn't *that* sorry.

"I don't think she's in any hurry to see me again," he concluded. Neither he nor Maggie was sure how much further to take that aspect of the conversation, but they had each found the information they were seeking. Ricky decided to change the subject.

"So…big day tomorrow!"

"Oh, too right. Maybe that's why I can't sleep."

"You should try. It's going to be very exhausting."

"For you as well! I feel bad about all of the driving you'll be doing, between here and the Fair, and then again when you take me back to the airport…"

"Oh, that's no bother. I planned it that way all along, and I saved money just for all of this."

"You must let me help pay for expenses, like tolls and petrol."

"Petrol? You mean gas? No, that's not necessary."

"Ricky, you've done so much for me already. Collecting me at the airport, getting the concert tickets, letting me stay here with your family…I saved money for this as well, you know. Don't make me feel like a cheap fool, you silly Yank."

She gave him a cheeky wink.

"Oh, okay, we'll see. I'm sure we'll find something for you to pay for tomorrow, if that will make you happy."

"Yes, it will!"

"You can buy me a hotdog at the Beatles concert," he said.

"More hotdogs for you? You just had a few for dinner."

"One thing you have to learn about Americans--we love our hotdogs. We don't want to know what's in them, or how they're made, but we love them."

"Well, it's your stomach," she relented, before giving herself a moment to find the right, careful way of phrasing her next thought. "I've never met any chaps back home quite like you. Most of them are either footballers, or musicians, or hooligans. Some of them are all three at once."

"That must be quite a sight to see. I thought you like musicians."

"Well, yeah, but sometimes I like the music more than the musicians, if you know what I mean. But you're not like them. You can bet none of them have ever read *Pride and Prejudice*."

"After the Beatles were on Ed Sullivan, Kenny tried to take guitar lessons to get girls."

"How did that work out?"

"He quit after two lessons. Not a big shock, knowing Kenny."

"You don't need to learn the guitar," she said. She felt so comfortable, that she did something that didn't require any thought, analysing, or second-guessing on her part. She wrapped her arms around his arm, and lay her head on his shoulder as the movie on the TV screen continued to softly illuminate the room. Ricky felt himself almost melt into the sofa. *Oh, lord*, he thought, *this feels good*.

Chapter 23

"Now, *this* is big!" Maggie marvelled, as she stood in the shadow of the twelve-story high Unisphere, the World's Fair's most identifiable symbol, with its stainless steel silver continents casting broken shadows across the reflecting pool and fountains encircling it. Ricky stood a good fifty feet back, tilting his camera vertically to take a picture that would include both Maggie and the entire world.

"That looks great!" he said, taking the picture and then dodging the masses of fellow visitors as he returned to her. "Let's get one with the both of us. You ask someone to take it."

"Why me?"

"Trust me. Ask a guy. Any guy."

He handed her the camera and sent her back into the flow of the crowd, where she randomly picked out a young man to ask.

"Excuse me, will you take a photo of me and my friend in front of this?" she said, indicating the sphere.

The man was glad to do so, thanks in no small part to Maggie's smiling face and accent. He handed the camera back with a smile as she thanked him and turned to Ricky.

"You're exploiting me, you are," she said. "I might have to unionize."

They surveyed the scene before them, teeming with thousands of people meandering their way along the concourse. Flags of every country waved in the breeze, meticulously tended flower gardens provided countless dots of color along the walkways, and the dozens of corporate pavilions and exhibit centers beckoned people to come in and see the present and future wonders awaiting them--courtesy of Sinclair, General Motors, Coca-Cola, Eastman Kodak, and others. And, of course, to the far left and a few hundred yards away stood Shea Stadium, built along with the Fair, and both completed just the previous year. The stadium's circular facade, adorned with large, confetti-like sheets of multi-colored, wavy metal squares, sparkled in the sun.

"Just a few hours to go," Ricky said.

"I know. It's going to be tremendous. I can't believe so many people will be there."

They continued their day-long stroll across the grounds. "Sorry we only have time to see a fraction of this," he said with a sweep of his arm, across the wide span of the grounds. "It's way too much to see in one day."

"No worries. This is fantastic, just walking about is enough. You Americans can really put on a show when you want to."

"Yeah, I've been here about a dozen times since it opened, and I never get tired of it. After going to the Mets games, we usually need cheering up, because they usually lose. So, we come here and eat, and see some of the exhibits. I think I've seen all of them by now. I'll show you a few, if you don't mind waiting on the lines. Oh, and speaking of eating, ever have a Belgian waffle?"

"No, I doubt it."

"Oh, we've got to have some! It's the best thing here to eat! Too bad it's all gonna close for good in the fall."

"Sorry?" she asked.

"In the fall. October, I think."

"You mean autumn?"

"Huh? Oh, yeah, in the autumn. You Brits don't say "fall"?

"Usually only when we fall. We say autumn. Do you have two names for every season in America? Like, fall, trip, stumble and crash?"

"Yes, we're a very clumsy people."

Maggie laughed. "Silly Yank."

They continued on through the sprawling grounds, stopping to indulge in a Belgian waffle, which had become the talk of the Fair. And, at one point during their stroll, Ricky realized that they were holding hands. He didn't say anything about it. Neither did Maggie. It felt like the most natural thing in the world to both of them.

They chose 7:00p.m. as their time to start their walk to Shea. The setting sun triggered the illumination of brilliant lights of the Fair, as well as the lights resting atop the stadium's giant structure.

The concert wasn't due to begin for another hour, but as they got closer to the stadium, the periodic screams from within had already begun to fill the warm, humid, evening air.

"What in the world could they be cheering and screaming at already?" Ricky wondered aloud, "the guy setting up the microphones?"

"From the sound of it, he must be doing a *very* good job!" she surmised.

"Well, remember, most of the people here aren't old pros like you. They haven't seen the Beatles fifty times already."

"It's only thirty-three. And believe me, I'm just as excited as everyone else!   How many people did you say this place seats?"

"About 55,000, but I bet they'll squeeze in a few thousand more, somehow."

"That's bigger than the Roman Colosseum—but I guess there won't be any lions eating slaves during the show."

"Not tonight, anyway--hope that won't disappoint you."

They giddily handed their tickets to the men at the turnstile entrance, received the stubs in return, and continued on to the escalators.

"We're on the Mezzanine level, the blue seats."

"Is that good?"

"Shoot, yeah! We're not as high up as the Upper level, but we're out from under the overhang, so we'll be in the open, under the sky."

"And that's good as well?"

"That's the way I love it. Trust me."

"I do trust you."

They marvelled at their thousands of fellow fans, who were generating an electric excitement among themselves even in the stadium's interior concourse, dotted with snack stands and souvenir counters. A cluster of girls compared their buttons and homemade signs declaring their love of one or more of the Beatles. Another group posed for pictures with a boy who, either foolishly or brilliantly, came dressed as a Beatle, complete with collarless suit and shaggy wig.

Ricky and Maggie bought their souvenir programs and lingered for a few moments at each gathering of fans, absorbing as many facets of the experience as they could. Maggie turned to a blonde girl about her age who was carrying an 'I LOVE YOU, PAUL' sign.

"You love them all, I hope!" she said with a smile.

"Oh, yeah," the girl said, "but Paul's my favourite."

"I can't decide myself," Maggie said, at which point the girl noticed her accent.

"That's not your real accent, is it?"

"I'm visiting, from London. But I'm originally from Liverpool."

"Really? That's so neat! You've come all that way to see them here?"

"I'm visiting my friend," she said, indicating Ricky.

"That's me," he said. "But I'm from Jersey."

"Me too," the girl said. "I'm Meryl."

"I'm Maggie, this is Ricky."

"Did you ever see the Beatles before?" Meryl asked.

"Oh, I saw them a lot in Liverpool."

"No way!" Meryl gasped. "That's so cool!"

"But it was nothing like this!" Maggie was quick to add. She didn't want to come off sounding jaded.

"Come on," Ricky said, "let's get to our seats. See ya, Meryl."

Passing through the cinder block archway, they stepped out to see the whole of the packed stadium before them. Flashbulbs popped with specks of light, banners hung from the railings of each level of seating, and the buzz of the crowd frequently escalated into full-throated screams, for reasons not immediately apparent. On the ball field itself stood the stage, set squarely over second base. There wasn't much else--no backdrop, no frills-- just a lot of cables and cameras.

Once in their seats, Ricky reached into his pocket.

"I have something for you," he said quietly. He produced a small package of tissues.

"For our ears. I've learned from experience. We don't want to go deaf. We'd never be able to hear the Beatles again! That would be a cruel twist of fate, wouldn't it?"

Maggie took a tissue and ripped off a piece for each ear. "Ooh, perish the thought. Good thinking!" She then chuckled to herself. "But if that twist of fate were to happen, I guess we'd have to call it 'Twist and Shout'."

Ricky made a sour face. "That's the worst pun I've ever heard."

"Why, thank you, Ricky!"

The hour of 8:00 p.m. arrived, as Cousin Brucie introduced his radio friend/rival Murray the K, who in turn got the evening's musical program underway, but not before he allowed himself to soak in a bit of glory for himself, shouting his trademark, "Ahh-bay!" to get the hysteria level of the crowd amped up considerably. He went on to introduce a line-up of go-go dancers prancing about the stage to the instrumental versions of contemporary hits. Blues sax player King Curtis led the band, perhaps discovering for himself that he had just taken on the entertainment industry's Ultimate Thankless Job.

More musical acts followed, going largely unnoticed by the crowd. The screams of anticipation had already begun to reach a deafening volume, and Maggie appreciated having the tissues in her ears. She looked at Ricky as his attention was drawn elsewhere, and thought of how he really was taking such good care of her.

After an hour of the opening acts, Ed Sullivan finally took to the stage to introduce the Beatles, who promptly trotted to the stage from the third base dugout to the expected, ear-piercing screams. The group kicked off the concert with "Twist and Shout," but the songs themselves were of little importance to the crowd, since most of the singing and playing was virtually inaudible. The jets soaring over the stadium on take-off from neighboring LaGuardia airport were virtually inaudible, too.

But it didn't matter. Ricky and Maggie weren't in the midst of a concert so much as an *experience.* They knew it was hopeless to try to carry on any kind of conversation, so they relied on a few hand gestures, facial expressions, and pointing to the various momentary distractions in the stands--such as fainting girls being carried away by policemen—all as the Beatles played on. Maggie had the presence of mind to write down each song on the back of her ticket stub as soon as she was able to recognize a few notes in a row, figuring it might come in handy if she were allowed to write a piece on the concert for the magazine.

She found it difficult to believe how her life had changed so much in such a short time. It seemed like only yesterday when she and Claire were regulars in the front row of the modest Cavern, to watch the Beatles storm through a set of classic rockers and original songs, with the thunderous chords of their guitars and Ringo's, or even Pete's, drums reverberating against the stone walls of that dank, stinky cellar. Back then, the music drowned out the noise of the crowd, but here she was witnessing the opposite effect, sitting among more than 55,000 fans—Americans, no less!—who didn't have a clue about the Beatles back then, but, to their credit, were now screaming themselves to exhaustion for them just the same—and drowning out the music as they did so.

After barely more than a half hour onstage, Paul announced that the next song would be the last of the evening—at least that's what Maggie *thought* he was saying. He then suddenly screeched the opening line of "I'm Down," and the other Beatles jumped in, singing, playing, and having a ball. John amused himself by running his elbow up and down the electric keyboard for his "solo," no doubt knowing they had scored a triumph that night as no other group ever had before.

Even after the Beatles disappeared into the night, the fans in the stands were in no hurry to leave. Ricky and Maggie followed the slow-moving crowd in front of them back through to the inner concourse of the stadium, surrounded by crying, laughing, screaming girls as the thousands shuffled down the exit ramps.

The following afternoon, there was one more car ride the two needed to make – the one back to JFK airport for Maggie's flight back home. As they drove, they crammed their conversation with any and all references to things they had been telling each other in their letters, adding new details that came to mind. Ricky occasionally interrupted to point out something he wanted her to see along the skyline, before the opportunity was lost. Mostly, they talked about the events they had shared together in the past few days.

"It's been wonderful, Ricky. I can't thank you enough for everything."

"It's been my pleasure! But you'll have to come back someday to see everything else we didn't have time for."

"Absolutely. And I hope you'll come to see me sometime as well. I think you'd love London."

"I'm sure I would too. I promise to visit as soon as I can."

The boarding announcement for the London flight sent the passengers reaching for their belongings as they lined up to have their boarding passes checked.

"Well," Maggie sighed, "here I go."

She turned to him. They slowly leaned in to give each other a goodbye kiss. But it became a long, long kiss--certainly not a kiss just between friends. They surprised themselves, and each other, but continued with a tight embrace, slowly rocking from side to side, and finally, but reluctantly, separated. Neither one knew what to say, because neither was quite sure what had just happened.

"Well…well…" Ricky sputtered.

"Yeah," Maggie said, in agreement, even though she wasn't sure what she was agreeing with. "Well, well."

And yet, they were in agreement about something: at this moment of their parting, they had taken their friendship to another level.

"I'll write as soon as I get back," she said, and turned to move up in line. He watched her continue through the door and, with a final wave a moment later, onto the plane.

The next day, at the diner, Ricky sat at the table with his chin resting on his hand, and the weight of the world seemingly resting on his shoulder. He had barely touched his cheeseburger, which he usually downed in mere minutes, and barely noticed a trio of beautiful girls entering the diner--a sure sign that all was not right with him. The straw in his glass of Coke slowly bobbed along the rim with each vibration of the table, thanks to Kenny's and Dave's heavy elbows. They were thankful for the brief break in Ricky's latest round of insecure ramblings.

"I don't see what you're worried about," Dave said. "It sounds as if everything went perfectly the whole time she was here. You took her to see New York, and the World's Fair, and the Beatles concert, and she gave you a big kiss good-bye. I should be so lucky to have a weekend like that with a girl."

"Bingo," Ricky said sadly. "What if she meant the kiss to say, 'had a great time, and you're a swell guy, but we'll probably never see each other again, so here's a big, long kiss to remember me by.'"

Kenny and Dave exchanged a confused look. "Then it worked," Kenny grumbled, "cause you haven't stopped talking about her for a minute all day. We still don't see the problem."

Dave tried to maintain a more sympathetic approach, but he was finding it increasingly difficult. "Maybe you two kissed like that because you really, *really* like each other."

"But I don't want it to be the last time we ever see each other," Ricky moaned.

"So go visit *her* next time, in England. Maybe next summer. And you can still write to each other until then."

"Next summer is too long to wait."

"Wow," Kenny said, "that must have been some kiss."

"It wasn't just that. I think we were beginning to feel like more than just friends or pen pals. We had long talks, told each other a lot about ourselves. We told each other a lot of secrets. I mean, I told her things about me even you guys don't know about."

"Like what?" Kenny asked with his first dose of genuine curiosity.

"I think you're missing the point," Ricky said. "We even held hands—just naturally. It felt great."

Dave shook his head. "Well, I can certainly see why you're so miserable! Good God, pull yourself together, man! Or I'll have to beat you about the head and face with a blunt instrument."

"I'm sorry, I'm all mixed up," Ricky conceded. "I just know I'm going to miss her a lot. What if she's—you know, the one?"

"The one what?" Kenny asked blankly.

"The *one*! The one for me, as in, forever."

"But she lives in England. And you only spent a few days together."

"Ah, but we've known each other for almost three years."

Dave attempted one last offer of rational thought before giving up. "You've had girlfriends during that time, though."

"That was before."

"Before what?"

"Before what I've just been telling you about! And, look, Marie even broke up with me because of Maggie. Now it feels different. I don't think I want a girl other than Maggie."

"In other words," Dave said with considerable exhaustion, "we all knew you were in love with Maggie before you did."

Hearing it phrased that way sounded so strange to Ricky, but he also couldn't argue the point. "But what if she starts dating guys over there, and falls in love with someone? What if I'll always be just a friend?"

"Did she say she has a boyfriend?" Dave asked.

"No. I asked her, and she said she doesn't."

"Well then, shut up already! You've got it made!"

"She does live across the ocean, you know," Ricky mumbled.

"Ah, but where there's a will, there's a way."

As they rose from their table and headed out, Kenny took Dave aside and leaned towards his ear. "I'll say it again—that must have been some kiss!"

Chapter 24

The first day back to work after a vacation was always difficult for Maggie. She had to get her brain back into gear after having had the biggest adventure of her life. Even though she loved her job, she wasn't quite ready to return to the daily grind.

As she slowly strode towards her desk, as though the extra seconds before she sat down all counted towards extending her vacation time to the last possible moment, she spotted a bouquet of flowers waiting for her. She briefly looked around the office to make sure everyone was sitting at their regular desks, just to make sure the staff hadn't been switching places on her whilst she'd been away--which would mean the flowers might not actually be for her. But no, everyone was where they should be, and the flowers were undoubtedly placed on her own desk.

A thought dawned on her; they were probably from Ricky. He was sweet like that, always going the extra step to make someone else feel good. She smiled to herself and picked up the bouquet, looking for a card to read, but was unable to find one, when a delivery man approached her.

"Are you Maggie Carter?"

"Born and raised," she said, noting the bunch of flowers in his hand. "Are you a flower delivery man?"

"Seems rather likely. Yes I am. These are for you."

He handed her the second bouquet of flowers, smiled and headed back out of the office. She stood looking uneasily at both bouquets.

"Did I die, and nobody told me?" she queried out loud.

"Someone's got an admirer," Mary, a fellow staff writer, said with a wink, as she walked passed Maggie's desk and to her own.

"It must be the delivery guy," Maggie guessed half-jokingly. "And he's got the perfect cover. Who would suspect him?"

"Well, you, for a start," Mary pointed out.

Maggie picked up the card from the second bunch of flowers. It read:

'Maggie, missed you more than I could have imagined, will be in town soon. X'

"What? Ricky's coming to London?" she wondered. "No, couldn't be. I just got back. Then who's this bouquet off?"

She found the card from the first bouquet of flowers by her foot. She picked it up and it read *"From your secret admirer. X"*

Well, that was no help. But she laughed to herself when her next thought was of Kenny, and how he might have sent the flowers to wind Ricky up. But she quickly realised that Kenny probably wouldn't go to such measures for a joke. Although, he did seem quite taken with her accent. But then, so was everyone else she had met on her visit. So, the mystery remained, who could they be off?

"Did anyone see who left this first bunch on my desk?" she called out to the rest of the staff.

"No, love," replied Mary, "But I wouldn't worry about it, just enjoy it."

"Enjoy it? Some mysterious person—or *two* mysterious people--sent me flowers, and I'm supposed to enjoy it? I'm a journalist. I need to get to the bottom of this."

The over-sized clock on the wall struck eight-thirty and she was no longer on her own time, but belonged to the magazine again. She'd have to write a thank-you note to Ricky later and figure out who the other flowers were from after she'd finished her work. Maybe she wouldn't mention the secret admirer to Ricky.

Later that day when she finally got home, she checked the post to see if there was an accompanying letter from Ricky. There wasn't, and realistically there wouldn't have been enough time for a letter to arrive from America, unless Ricky had sneakily sent it whilst she was still with him in New Jersey. However, there *was* a letter, with an English stamp in the corner of the envelope, for her. The handwriting on the envelope looked like Claire's. Maggie tore it open and began to read.

"Hi Mags,

How's life in the big city?

I have some mixed news. You know my great-aunt Mavis? The one who always carries mints on her? She passed away a few days ago. I was very sad when I was told but she was eighty-five and had been quite poorly these past few months. Turns out she was allergic to those mints, and died from a reaction after she accidently overdosed on them. So, her favourite sweets cost her her life. There might be a lesson there somewhere, but I'm not sure. Anyway, I feel guilty writing this sentence within the same paragraph of bereavement, perhaps I should have started a new paragraph, but aunt Mavis left me some money! They won't tell me how much, but it's enough for me to come visit you and spend a few days in London. When do you want me to come down? I've missed you.

Write back, or phone me,
                              Claire"

Maggie remembered Claire's great-aunt Mavis, and her unlimited supply of fresh-mint sweets, very well. She often wondered if the older woman's reliance on a particular brand of sweets was somehow the source of Claire's obsession for Jelly Babies. She'd need to phone Claire later to tell her how sorry she was to hear of her family's loss, and to arrange a good weekend for her to come visit London.

The next day Maggie was no further forward with finding out her secret admirer's identity, and she still hadn't written her letter to Ricky to thank him for his flowers. She'd meant to do it straight away, as she didn't want to seem bad mannered in delaying a response, especially after their awkward kiss. Ricky might think she was avoiding him if she didn't write back straight away, but the night before she'd spent a good deal of time talking to Claire on the phone, and chatting with Linda about the new change in their living situation .

Melissa, their third flat-mate, had given them notice that she was moving out of the flat within a week; something about moving in with a boyfriend whom neither Maggie nor Linda had heard Melissa speak of before. But to be fair, they hadn't really heard Melissa speak much about *anything* before, considering she was never around. The living dynamics wouldn't really change with her gone, but the prospect of two girls sharing the rent instead of three was worrying. They decided to advertise for another flat-mate but had no idea how long it would take for someone to respond, or if it would be someone they'd even want living with them.

But that was out of hours stuff, and the large office clock was about to reach eight-thirty again to remind Maggie she had an article due in. She had managed to push the flower mystery to the back of her mind as she worked on her latest article for the magazine, an article about a battle-of-the-bands competition being held in a popular club in Soho. But what she really wanted to write was a story about the Shea Stadium concert. Predictably, Sharon dismissed it as old news. The magazine, as she quoted the publisher, did not print last week's news. Whenever possible, they wanted to print *next* week's news. Even so, Maggie wrote the article in her spare time for her own enjoyment, much like a diary entry, and with as many details as she could remember. It almost felt as if she were writing it as a letter to Ricky--but for once, she didn't need to send it to him.

At the end of the working day, Maggie tidied her desk and said goodbye to the couple of staffers working overtime, and headed for the building exit, hoping that when she arrived at the tube platform it wouldn't be too crowded. It was usually heaving with commuters and she really couldn't be bothered to fight her way onto an underground train car today.

Before she could get three steps away from her magazine building, she was stopped by a familiar male voice with a scouser accent.

"Please, miss, can I have your autograph?"

Maggie spun on her heels to find herself standing face to face with Jack. He was holding the latest issue of *British Music Express* up to his face, peeking out from behind it.

"Jack! How?-What?-What are you doing here? How did you get here?"

"By boat. Via India. Long journey."

They gave each other a somewhat awkward embrace, but it seemed a necessary gesture.

"You're looking good," she said.

"You're looking great! I read your latest article about that Eric Sellers joker. Very good, though he comes off as a bit of a fool. Was he coached to give those quotes?"

"No. I don't know. Probably. I asked, he answered, with his manager's help. Or whoever she was. That's it really."

"Well, you did a good job with it."

She smiled. "Thanks. So, what are you doing here?"

They started down the street, away from Maggie's tube station. Neither knew where they were going. She couldn't think very straight with the surprise of suddenly being face-to-face with Jack again.

"Didn't you get my flowers?"

"They were from *you*?"

"Yeah, didn't you get the meaning of the card?"

Feeling her cheeks blush slightly, she looked away. "Well, you didn't sign your name and I don't like to presume things. You weren't half extravagant sending two bunches of flowers, though."

"Two bunches? I only sent you the one."

"Oh. I got another one on the same day. Wondered who they were off."

Jack fell quiet for a moment. "Oh right. I didn't think. So you're seeing someone now then? What am I talking about? You're living in the big city, you're a real looker, you've got a good job, of course you'll be dating."

"No," she said, perhaps a little too quickly. "I mean, I'm not seeing anyone right now. I guess the other bunch was from some sort of secret admirer. Probably a wind-up from the lads in the office."

"I imagine you have loads of admirers," he said smoothly, "secret and otherwise."

An awkward silence passed between the two of them. It was Jack who broke it.

"So listen, I'm in town for a few days, staying with a mate. I was wondering if maybe you'd like to meet up with me. Maybe go for some food, get a drink? Tomorrow night maybe? Or tonight even, if you're not busy."

"I can't make tonight, or tomorrow, but I am free the next night—Friday night--if you're still going to be here then."

He smiled. "Yeah, I don't leave 'til Sunday. And I'm only going back to Liverpool, not the other end of the world again. I've got two months off."

"Two months off? Cushy job."

"Believe me, it's not all that."

Maggie wondered why he was asking her out. There was no future for them, not if Jack was always going to be sailing off to distant countries, and they'd both have grown into their own lives now. And there were other things to consider, other people to consider. So, a drink and something to eat was fine, but the flowers--what did they mean? Was Jack just being...Jack?

"You know, we're actually walking in the wrong direction for me to get home," she informed him.

"Oh, sorry, I have no idea where I'm going to tell you the truth. I wasn't paying attention."

Maggie chuckled and led him back in the opposite direction. "I'll put you on the right tube, where do you want to be?"

"Euston," he said. "I have to catch a different train from there."

"No problem."

She walked him to the tube station platform and told him how many stops he needed to wait before he arrived at Euston station.

"Right," he said, "See you Friday. There's a nice place near Covent Garden, Emilio's Grill. Meet you there at 8:00?"

Maggie had heard good things about the restaurant, but couldn't remember who had told her about it. Now she had two days to over think what meeting Jack for dinner would mean for the two of them.

It was the next day during lunch when things got even more interesting for Maggie. Waiting for her in the building canteen was none other than Eric Sellers. He stood to greet her as she entered the lunch room.

"Hi, Maggie," he said. "I'm Eric Sellers, we met a few weeks ago for the interview. Not sure if you remember me."

"Hi, yes, of course I remember. The soon-to-be-famous Eric Sellers!"

He looked the same, but was acting differently from how she remembered him.

A blur of thoughts rushed through her head in a split second as to why this rising star was waiting for her on her lunch hour. The strongest of those thoughts were *'Oh my God! He hated the article! He's going to sue me!'*

Smiling, she asked "What can I do for you?"

"Well, this is a bit embarrassing actually." He looked around to ensure they weren't being overheard. "But I was wondering if you'd like to maybe go out with me sometime. I really feel we had a good connection when we did the interview."

Maggie was stunned. A good connection? She remembered it quite differently. "Me? You want to go out with me?"

"Yeah, if you'd like to. Sorry if I was a bit of a crab that day. Had a row with my manager on our way to meet you. But you seemed dead nice. Did you like the flowers I sent you?"

Her eyes widened. "They were from *you?*"

Eric nodded. "Yeah, I guess I should have been more brave and actually signed my name on the card, but I'm here now. In person."

"Yes, you are," was all she could think to say.

"So how about it? A date? Are you free on Friday?"

"Friday? Well, actually—"

"Oh. I hope I'm not stepping on any toes here. You don't have another man in your life or anything, do you?"

"Not really—but…It's just that—"

"Great. Friday it is. About 8:00? Maybe closer to 8:30. I'd rather be on time for 8:30 than late for 8:00. Hey, that could be a song. I'll work on it. There's a nice restaurant I know called Emilio's Grill. Have you heard of it? It's a very 'now' place. Very happening."

"Oh, I really don't—"

"Now, now, don't worry. No agents or managers, just us."

He took a pen out of his pocket and asked Maggie to write her number on his hand. It seemed like a rock star-ish thing to do. He must have been taking lessons.

He left her sitting alone at the table, slowly eating a cheese and pickle sandwich, wondering how that whole conversation had just happened. Since she'd returned from America, things had gotten freakishly weird in her life. She was not accustomed to finding herself with two dates for the same night, at the same place. And it didn't seem likely that she would be able to get out of either one.

And then there was Ricky.

Chapter 25

Friday evening was fast approaching, and Maggie was feeling more than a little anxious, just as she had done for her very first date with Jack. Her nerves weren't only due to dining with him--perhaps he might have had something up his sleeve--but also to the prospect of Eric showing up for *his* date with her—and perhaps having to wait his turn! Maybe he wouldn't show up. That would still leave her face-to-face with Jack. What if, after all this time, they had nothing to talk about, or she might have changed too much for him to the point where he wouldn't like her as much? What if she had the opposite problem and talked too much? What if Jack talked too much about his life as a sailor, visiting disease-infested ports in uncivilized lands? What would she say... and why in the world couldn't she rid herself of worries about what Ricky would think?

Out of the questions rotating in her mind, the first one she had to answer was what should she wear. After much deliberation, and a mini catwalk show for Linda, Maggie decided to go with an over-priced, white blouse with black polka dots she'd bought but never had an opportunity to show-off yet. She hoped Jack would like it...but the appropriate amount for what she was comfortable with, whatever that was.

Jack was right, and so was Eric, about Emilio's Grill. It was a nice little restaurant that seemed to be extremely popular on Friday nights. The décor was superbly modern, the music was to Maggie's taste, and the waiting staff had the manners of royal butlers, with uniforms to match: black and white suits for the men, black and white polka dotted dresses for—

"Bloody hell," Maggie sighed.

Jack had booked them a table by the window, much to her relief. Dining by the window was great for when conversation slowed, allowing them to make fun of the passers-by for walking too fast, or too slow, or anything silly to make them giggle. No, better be mature, she thought to herself, as the host showed her to the window table and removed the reserved sign. You're a London girl now. You've seen it all.

Jack stood up to greet her. He looked very handsome in his grey suit and tie. A far cry from his Teddy Boy look in Liverpool--and he certainly didn't look like a sailor-- but then, this was a Friday night, in a busy part of London.

"You look very nice," he said.

"Oh, ta, so do you."

"Yeah, I bought this suit especially for tonight."

Maggie smiled and took her seat. Why was Jack buying suits especially for a night out with her? What did that mean?

"I haven't—" he started, when she blurted out:

"Is this a date?"

The sudden question actually left Jack's jaw open.

"Huh? Er…well…"

Maggie's cheeks turned a subtle shade of crimson under her pink blusher. She hadn't meant to sound so accusatory.

"I mean, is this a date?" she said again. "Sorry. I'm just not sure of the situation."

Jack chuckled uneasily. "Well, it's not a cricket match as far as I can tell. I like that you haven't lost your need for answers."

"It comes with the job."

"Well, I'd *like* it to be sort of a date. I mean, dinner's on me. That is, I'm not suggesting we pick up exactly where we left off in Liddypool, I know we can't do that." He paused for an instant to give her room to correct him. She didn't. "But maybe see where we stand? I have missed you a lot."

He seemed unusually awkward, which wasn't like him. The Jack she remembered was always so cool, calm, and a bit aloof. And, not knowing how she felt herself, or how to respond, she said the only thing that came to mind. "I'd better say for starters that I went to New York and met with Ricky."

A pause, pregnant enough to need a maternity ward, hung in the air.

"That's...nice. New York, huh? What did you think?"

"Loved it. I didn't get to see it all, but I did go to the big Beatles concert at the stadium. Ricky bought us tickets. It was amazing! Did you hear about it?"

"Well, well, now you're going all the way to New York to see Beatles concerts, eh? So how many times is it that you've seen them now?"

"I've really lost count. If Claire were here she could tell you."

Knowing the nature of Maggie and Claire's friendship, Jack wouldn't have been surprised to find Claire hiding under the next table, listening in and announcing the correct number.

"I think it's about the thirty-four or thirty five mark," Maggie continued.

As they talked, she noticed how Jack was avoiding mentioning Ricky's name. Was that deliberate?

"I've been to New York as well," he said. "It was one of the ship's stops, I had half a day to walk around. My first thought when we docked was of you."

Maggie smiled. "Perhaps I was there the same time as you. How ironic that would have been."

The waiter brought over wine, that Jack had pre-ordered, and said he'd return to take their food order in a few minutes. The wine helped. Their conversation was kept in the safe zone, not talking about dating or their past relationship—such as it was--but when they began to run out of safe topics, the silences in between became longer and uncomfortably so for Maggie. Not like her long silences with Ricky. The arrival of the main course came as a relief.

Jack broke the silence first, using the pedestrian traffic outside as a convenient distraction. "See that geezer out there trying to get the chewing gum off his shoe?"

They observed a middle-aged man across the street shuffling along the pavement, looking rather comical.

Maggie laughed. "He looks like a robot. Well, a robot with chewing gum on its shoe."

They continued to laugh at other passers-by, who weren't necessarily deserving of such mockery, but Maggie and Jack seemed to find humour in it, and the rest of the evening began to move along more smoothly. Their repartee eased into the groove they had when they were in Liverpool, where they'd spend time strolling along the Albert Docks planning their futures. In fact, with the food and wine to help fuel their chat, they both started to enjoy the evening in earnest.

Then Maggie spotted someone across the room. Her face turned ashen. It was Eric Sellers, striding in and shaking hands with staff and customers alike. She panicked.

"What is it?" asked Jack, noticing the sudden change in Maggie's relaxed attitude, and loss of color in her face.

"No, nothing."

"What? Did the Beatles just walk in or something?" He looked around the room, not recognising anyone especially noteworthy.

"It's nothing, I thought I saw someone I knew but I don't. I mean, I didn't. I still didn't. So, now, what were you saying? Something about the Marie Celeste?"

"Titanic," he corrected. "We sailed the same path as the Titanic, I'm not superstitious but at night, in the middle of the cold Atlantic, it did get a bit spooky. The older blokes telling their stories of near misses and all. I kept a keen lookout for icebergs."

She barely heard a word he said as she kept her eyes on Eric as he made his way to the bar. He carefully looked around the restaurant as he found an unoccupied stool.

"I wouldn't like that," she said, trying to sink low enough for her nose to rub the edge of the table. "There could be sharks."

"I'm not sure about sharks in cold water," said Jack, "but…what? What is it? Did you drop your napkin?"

He looked on curiously as Maggie twisted her torso at a contorted, 45-degree angle to keep an eye on Eric over her shoulder. There he sat at the bar, starting on a pint of lager, presumably waiting for her to meet him for their date.

"Who?" she asked.

"What?"

"Huh? Who what?

Jack shook his head. "Are you okay? Or have you started speaking Korean? 'Cause I don't know Korean."

"Yeah fine, I just have to go to the ladies room. Be right back. Then you can tell me more about the Lusitania."

She struggled to pull herself upright in her seat, not realizing that her legs had wrapped around the table post. She tumbled to the floor as Jack leapt up to help her.

"Are you okay?"

"Fine. I guess that Chardonnay really packs a punch." She regained her composure and headed to the rest-room, picking up a menu from an occupied table to hide her face as she passed by Eric.

She nearly made it to safety when a customer approached her, waving for her attention.

"Excuse me, miss, can we have a plate of the Swedish meatball appetizers for our table? That table in the corner."

Oh, Maggie, realized, the damn outfit. "Er, that's not my section, sir, but I'll see what I can do."

Once in the rest-room, with the menu dumped on the sink counter, she looked at herself in the mirror and tried to pull herself together. She gave herself a good talking-to.

"Why are you freaking out? So Eric Sellers is in the same restaurant as you when you're on a sort-of date with someone else. What's so bad about that? You're single. But then it could be awkward if he spots me and I have to introduce him to Jack. Eric might think I only agreed to go on a date with him because he's a musician, to further my own career. He could tell my boss. I could get a name for myself—a very impolite name. Oh my God, he could tell the world about me in interviews. And then there's Jack, he could really get hurt if he thinks I'm dating other people too, and not being honest about it. But is this a *date* with Jack? He's interested in dating me again, but does tonight count? And oh my God, how long has that piece of broccoli been in my teeth?"

She set about removing the offending piece of broccoli whilst trying to calm herself.

"So what if Eric sees me here, I've not even been on a date with him yet, I don't owe him anything. And Jack will understand. Probably. I know Ricky would back me up. Oh God why am I bringing Ricky into this? What would he think?"

She took a deep breath, checked her teeth and eye make-up once more, and straightened herself up, accompanied by the sound of a toilet flushing.

A woman in her sixties stepped out of the stall and approached the sink next to Maggie.

"I'm glad I'm not in your shoes, dearie. But that's the price you pay for being such a loose woman."

It was then that Maggie realized she had been expressing her concerns out loud. The woman left the ladies' room with a sneer, leaving Maggie alone and mortified.

"I've got to stop doing that," she thought—out loud. "If I stay in here any longer Jack will be wondering what I'm doing. I'm just going to go out there and act normal. I have nothing to hide. Confidence is key."

Back in the restaurant, she looked back and forth between Jack and Eric; good thing they were both oblivious to each other. Striding across the restaurant, Maggie tried to keep her head held high, which was hard to do whilst also trying to keep an eye on two different men at opposite ends of the room. She was going for 'normal' but was certain she was hitting wide of the mark.

Eric took another sip and looked up to scan the room again, at which point Maggie ducked down behind a couple seated at a table. They looked at her curiously. She wasn't sure how to explain what she was doing on all fours, so she tried the first excuse that came to her. "Um, I think you dropped a mushroom, ma'am."

She picked up a cold, dusty mushroom she'd spotted from under the table and offered it to the woman, who turned away in disgust. "That's not my mushroom."

"Oh, must be someone else's. I'll just put it back where I found it."

The seated man and his wife looked to each other incredulously.

"Is the management in the habit of having the employees offer food off the floor to the patrons?" he asked brusquely.

Maggie put the mushroom back under the table, then peered over the table to see what Eric was doing. He hadn't seen her, making it safe for her to stand up. "Well, waste not, want not, my gran always says."

The bewildered couple watched her as she strolled away from their table.

She picked up a small round serving tray to once again shield her from Eric's gaze, when another customer inadvertently blocked her path back to her table. Before she knew it, her alternate route brought her face-to-face with Eric.

"Oh, there you are, Maggie! I was beginning to wonder."

"Eric...there you are, yourself!" she stammered, putting the tray down on the bar. "Listen, I...uh...I'm afraid I don't think tonight is going to work out."

"Why not?"

Before she could answer, the bartender placed a set of drinks on the tray—and, without bothering to look up, announced, "Two Cokes and a scotch & soda for table 8."

Maggie stood frozen, her eyes darting between the tray and Eric's confusion. He responded with a knowing smile.

"Oh, I get it," he said, lowering his voice. "You're moonlighting here but you didn't want to say. That's okay, love. No need to be embarrassed. They must pay you slave wages at that magazine."

Miracle of miracles, he had just supplied Maggie with her own perfect excuse.

"Too right," she sighed, picking up the tray of drinks. "I'm sorry, Eric. It's very busy tonight. They had to call me in on short notice. Perhaps another time?"

"Of course. Oh, and mum's the word about this."

"Yes, please!"

Feeling obligated to serve the drinks to table 8, she did so before finally returning to her own table and Jack.

"Are you okay? Where have you been?"

"Oh, Jack, a lady never tells. But I'm sorry."

As Jack settled the bill with their waiter, Maggie stepped outside, taking a long needed breath of fresh air after her stressful night. Her head was spinning and she wasn't sure if it was because of the wine, or the pretense of moonlighting as a waitress whilst trying to instantly figure out her feelings for her ex, whilst also failing to avoid an awkward encounter with a rising rock and roll star.

Jack joined her outside and offered her his arm, she happily took it and they strolled towards the tube station on the next block.

"The food was dead nice in there, think I'll go there again one day," he said.

"Atmosphere was rather hectic though."

"You think so?"

She shrugged. "Maybe it was just me."

"Well I had a great time," he replied with almost too much enthusiasm, "hope you did too."

But Maggie was already lost in thought.

"Come on, Mags, at least lie and say you did," he said, giving her a cheeky grin.

"What? Oh yeah, I had a nice evening."

"But…?"

"But nothing."

He shook his head. "I know you too well, Maggie Carter, I can see a 'but' coming a mile off."

"Must be my cousin Wanda," she giggled. "Immaturity aside, there's no buts."

As they approached the steps to the underground station, she slowed down, then stopped altogether and looked at him. "Where do we go from here?"

"Well, where do you fancy?" He then realized the different intent of her question, and looked her square in the eye. "I think, or I hope, you know where my feelings lie. All I thought about whilst I was away was you. I really surprised myself. And how stupid I was to break up with you. I know I have to work away, and that's by choice, granted. I thought seeing other parts of the world would make it easier to be away from you. But I think we could make things work. Plenty of men in my crew are married, their relationships survive."

"Yeah, well, I've also heard the expression 'one in every port'."

"Not with me. But long-distance relationships are possible. I didn't think so before, but I've seen them work. I love you, Maggie. What do you think? Can we try again?"

She stood silent by her surprise. Jack had never told her he loved her before. The words sounded lovely, and yet strangely out of place for that moment—perhaps because she knew she couldn't, in all honesty, tell Jack that she loved him too.

"Say something," he said. "You're speechless. A bit unsettling."

"I've missed you a lot, too. But you spend half of your time at sea, and half of your time in Liverpool, and I obviously live in London now."

"I can spend my leave in London, with you."

"What about your family?"

"It's my life. But, honestly, Mags, it's sounding a bit like you're finding obstacles."

"Pretty obvious obstacles, you can't deny that."

He didn't respond. He began to see that he was fast losing his already-shaky hold on Maggie.

"When you left Liverpool, you told me not to wait around for you, and I didn't, I got on with my life. Jack I--"

"No, it's okay. I knew deep down I couldn't just walk back into your life and expect you to be waiting with open arms. Just a fantasy of mine, I reckon. Can't blame a bloke for trying, eh?"

"Not at all," she said. "But I guess this clears the air a little. I still want to be friends. You mean a lot to me."

"Right, that's what people say before they go their separate ways and never speak to each other again."

"No, I don't want that to happen! You're the man who taught me four chords on a guitar, the man who pulled Beatles tickets out of his pocket when all was lost, the man who encouraged me to get this far in my writing career, so you have a place in my heart for life."

Smiling, Jack nodded. "I'll take you home, then I'll get a taxi. Oh, and if you and that Ricky lad ever get married, I'd like an invite to the wedding."

She looked at him quizzically. "Huh? What wedding?"

"Oh, I'm not saying I'll definitely attend, but it's nice to be asked."

"This has nothing to do with Ricky."

"Doesn't it? Come on, I can tell, as much as I hate to admit it. You're in love with him. Fair enough, I understand. People can't help how they feel. But if you do love him, remember what I said. Long distance relationships can work. I just want you to be happy."

"You're too good for me, you are."

"Nobody is too good for you."

The two headed down the steps to the station, still arm in arm.

Arriving home, Maggie closed the door on the chilled night air, and with it, on her relationship with Jack. Chucking her keys on the stairs, she headed straight for the kettle in the kitchen, but she stopped in her tracks before she could flick the switch.

"How did *you* get there?"

There was someone unexpected sitting at the kitchen table, sipping a cup of hot chocolate with Linda. It was Claire.

"Well, it's about time you got home!" Claire said with a smile. She hurried to Maggie for an embrace. "Where you been? Linda said you had a date. Anyone nice?"

"Jack."

"Jack? *Jack* Jack? Or another Jack?"

"My Jack," replied Maggie. "Well, not *my* Jack but--wait, why are you here?"

"I'm your new flate-mate!" she beamed.

"What? Seriously? How?"

"The inheritance I got from Auntie Mavis. Lots, Mags, lots! I've moved to London! Rented a shop to cut hair. 'Hair by Claire'!"

"Wahhhh!" Maggie screamed with excitement. "Oh my Gosh, this is huge!"

They hugged and jumped up and down as if they were ten years old again.

"Tell me all about it!"

"Well, turns out she was allergic to--"

"No, I know about that. How can you just up and move? How—how did you do all this? And without telling me along the way?"

"Why not? You did it! And it's not like I don't have connections down here."

"Who?" Maggie wondered.

"You, silly. I can be clever when I want to be. I'll give you the details later. I was trying to be careful not to spill the beans in case it didn't work out. But it did! I hope you don't mind."

"Mind? Don't be daft! This is fabulous, Claire!"

"So, getting back to the subject at hand, what's going on with Jack?"

"Oh," Maggie hesitated, "We just went out for a meal. He's in the city for a few days."

"Aha. And?"

"Well, he kinda wanted me back, but I sort of said no. It wouldn't work."

"But...but we *like* Jack! You like Jack!"

"Of course I do, but it won't work. He lives at sea."

"He's not an octopus, Mags. He does come home sometimes."

"Yeah, sometimes," Maggie nodded, "I don't think I can work with sometimes."

Claire looked at her suspiciously. "Ooh! Let me guess--is this about Ricky?"

"No! Why does everyone keep saying that?"

"Why do you think?" Claire shrugged.

Maggie shook her head. "So you're really here to live?"

"Well, I'm not here to do your laundry twice a week. Yep! I'm a Londoner now."

Linda, silently entertained by the exchange, stood up and placed her empty mug in the sink. "So, you two know each other, then?"

"Oh, yeah, Linda, this is my best friend Claire, who I may have mentioned a couple of hundred times. Claire, this is Linda."

Claire giggled. "Yes, thanks, Mags--we've been chatting for the past hour you know. We didn't sit in silence with our hot chocolates. You're the one who's late to the party."

Chapter 26

Ricky's junior year at Hollenbeck University was only a few weeks old in October of 1966 when he found himself falling into the routine of unwinding from his afternoon classes by stopping at the student union building. It was the aroma of French fries wafting through the air in the lobby that usually lured him into the snack shop. He'd always stop in front of the lobby's massive bulletin board along the way, to see if any of the notices, leaflets, and announcements--all printed on papers of various colors and thumbtacked on top of each other to create a haphazard collage--might be of interest.

One afternoon, as he tried to shake off the dizzying boredom still lingering from his Sociology class, one of the notices on the board caught his eye.

New Work-Study Programs—
Home and Abroad
Get practical job experience as you
earn college credits!
Ask your guidance counsellor or
department head.

Ricky didn't really know what it meant, but it sounded intriguing. Work abroad, and get credit for it? That's pure genius! Could "abroad" possibly include somewhere like England, or would such a thing just be too good to be true?

He sacrificed his French fry snack in order to make a bee-line to the Dean's office in the Journalism school. He wasn't sure if he'd be able to personally see the dean, but anyone who could answer the mounting number of questions in his head would suffice. He'd even be satisfied if some disinterested secretary silently handed him an information sheet, without looking up from her typing.

Lucky for him, Ricky got to meet both the disinterested secretary *and* the dean. Dean Pennington was stepping out of his office just as Ricky had turned to leave with the information packet.

"Oh, here he is," the secretary announced, waving to get Ricky's attention. She leaned toward her boss. "He's asking about the work-study program."

"Sure," he said, turning to Ricky. "What would you like to know?"

"Everything," Ricky said.

Dean Pennington checked his watch. "Come on in. I have a few minutes."

Ten minutes later, Ricky could barely contain his excitement on his way out.

"Pretty dress!" he chirped to the secretary as he skipped out the door.

October 7, 1966

Dear Maggie:

You won't believe this—I have a real chance of spending an entire semester in London this year, working for one of the tabloid newspapers! It's part of a new type of program that colleges here are beginning.
I can use a semester working in the "real world" while I get academic credit! I just need a good grade point average, which I have, a few recommendations, which I'm sure I can get, and a well-written essay— and money. But if I can arrange all of that, I could do it next semester, beginning in January. I talked with my parents about it and they're all for it. So, I'm really excited, but nervous. I've never done anything like this before, but I remember when you told me to take more risks in my life. And so I am.

How about that? I'd have to find a cheap place to live,

but they'll provide me with some information.   And I think the tabloid is the "New London News." Do you ever read it?

I'm so excited to know what you think about this. I wouldn't be getting in your way—I'd love to see you a lot, but I wouldn't want to disrupt your life while I'm there or anything like that..."

He wrote so fast, he almost didn't know what he was writing. His mind raced. How would Maggie respond to this news? Would she even welcome the idea of the two of them living in the same city for half a year? Could he really handle living on his own, so far from home, for six months?

As Maggie finished reading the letter, she rushed off to the living-room to find Claire practising hair styling on a very trusting Linda.

"Guess what!" she said, as she hopped in place.

"You seem excited," Claire mused. "Either the Beatles have asked you to dinner, or you've heard Curly Shirley got banned from writing forever."

"Who's Curly Shirley?" Linda asked.

"No, neither of those," Maggie said. "I just read the letter I got from Ricky. He's coming to London!"

"London, England?"

"No, London, Ontario. Of course London, England! Here!"

Claire broke into a huge smile. "Wow, Mags, that's amazing! Is he coming for a visit, or to whisk you away in his arms back to America?"

"Really, Claire."

Claire laughed. "Right, I won't get ahead of myself. Oh, but where will we put him? There isn't any space."

Maggie shook her head. "No, he's coming here to work for a newspaper. They found a flat for him. He'll be here for a whole semester, getting university credit. Six months! We'll get to hang out every day, how brilliant is that?"

"That's really exciting, Mags!" Claire said, "I can't wait to judge him--I mean, err...to meet him!"

"Yeah," Linda sighed, "I've heard so much about him, I feel like I know him already."

"I've been feeling that way for years," Claire said.

Linda sighed again. "...*So* much about him."

On any other day, Maggie would have had a snappy retort for Linda, but instead preferred to beam from ear to ear. "I'm sending a letter back saying I'll help him settle in. He's bound to be nervous. I know I was. I can't wait!"

She skipped out of the room on Cloud Nine, leaving Claire and Linda to exchange a look.

"I told you about them," Claire said.

Linda nodded. "No need to. I know."

Dear Ricky,

This is the most exciting news I've heard since I got the job in London. Now you're going to be joining me! It's like destiny or something, if you think about it, we met in a letter and now we're going to be living in the same city!

If you don't like the accommodations they'll be giving you, I will help you out with suggestions for places to live (you need a nice area for the lowest price... London isn't cheap). Just think, we will get to see each other every day (if you don't get sick of me...) Maybe phone me and we can make arrangements?

All my love,
Maggie

A brief, mid-January thaw helped get 1967 off to a tolerable start, but relief from winter's usual meteorological cruelty was not foremost on Ricky's mind. As he and Mr. Kramer stepped up to the BOAC ticket counter, Mrs. Kramer and Joanne kept off to the side. Kenny and Dave completed the entourage, as they weren't due to return for their spring semester for another few days. And neither wanted to miss the chance of offering Ricky a hearty *bon voyage*, knowing they wouldn't see him for six months—the longest any of them would be absent from the others in all the years they had been friends.

The ticket agent, a cute brunette with a charming English accent, checked in each of his three bulging suitcases in exchange for his boarding pass.

"Your flight departs at Gate 17, sir. Have an enjoyable flight. Travelling on your own, are you?"

"Spending six months in London," Ricky said, still struggling to believe his own words.

"It's a lovely city. I'm sure you'll enjoy it."

With business concluded, the group shuffled out of the way from the others in line.

"Gate 17," Ricky announced, as the others followed in a small herd. Mrs. Kramer produced a tissue from her purse and dabbed her eyes. Joanne took one out of her pocket and tended to a sniffle of her own. She was almost sixteen and growing fast, maturing from the bratty kid who enjoyed giving Ricky grief, to becoming more his contemporary, even a friend. With each passing year, their 4-year age difference seemed to shrink. But now big brother would be away for a long time, and as excited as Joanne was for him, her tears wouldn't be denied.

"My baby's going away!" Mrs. Kramer sniffled.

"Mom," he reminded her, "I've been away for two years at school, remember."

"That's not the same thing. At school you're only a few hours away, and you come home to visit a lot, and were home all summer. "

"But I've been away for long stretches," he said, knowing he was fighting a losing battle.

"Seventy-three days," she shot back. "That's the longest you've ever been away at one time."

"Are you serious? You've literally counted the days I was away?"

"Well, maybe just for the first year. It's a mother's prerogative. But this will be six months. I'll worry about you."

The group arrived at Gate 17 and found some empty seats in the departure lounge.

"Maggie will be there to help me get settled, and I have a list of phone numbers to call the school gave me if I need something important. And there will be people at the newspaper to help, too. I hope." He began to struggle believing his own words of reassurance. "I'll write to you, and maybe we can even talk on the phone once in a while."

"Write to us too, will ya?" Dave implored. "Then I'll finally be able to say I have a pen pal in England, too—even though you're not English."

Kenny wasn't having it. "That's why it wouldn't count--because he's not English."

"Who says it wouldn't count?"

"If you go to England for a vacation and send me a postcard, does that make you my pen pal? Of course not. Ricky's just going on a long vacation, so it doesn't count."

"It's not a vacation," Dave countered. "He'll be living there, in a real apartment, not a hotel. That's different. And who made you an expert? You managed to get your own pen pal to hate you without ever meeting you."

And so their bickering continued, inadvertently providing Ricky with some familiar, and comforting, background noise as his departure time approached.

A half-hour later, as the line for boarding the plane formed near the door to the tarmac, the group said their final good-byes to their solo traveller. Ricky felt the lump in his throat grow with each hug and handshake. He also felt an increasingly queasy feeling in his stomach as he turned to hand his boarding pass to the ticket agent. This was really happening. In about six hours, he was going to be on his own, in a strange city, in a foreign country--English-speaking, which helped, but still foreign. His mother was right. This was nothing like leaving for college. This was a big deal. This was life-changing. This was terrifying.

He followed the line of passengers onto the tarmac, in the shadow of the 707, waiting to take him across the Atlantic. His face grew pale, his heart seemed to beat double-time. What was he getting himself into? Work experience was all well and good, and getting to see London was an exciting idea, but he didn't really *need* to do this. He'd have to learn so much about living on his own there. He'd be homesick. So why was he doing it?

He found his seat on the plane and did his best to settle in. As a thousand thoughts swirled through his head, the most important one managed to stand out from the others. It answered the question of why he was doing it. Yes, he would be frightened, and he would be homesick...

But he would be with Maggie.

Chapter 27

All of the sardines were packed into their Underground tin and heading for Heathrow Airport, Maggie mused, as she found herself yet again squashing into a tube train car, and having absolutely no personal space. Her head was far too close to a business man's armpit as she clung to the yellow pole in the centre of the car.

As she clung onto the metal pole, she couldn't help but remember her last journey to Heathrow--on her way to America, and her first time meeting Ricky in person. Now the roles were being reversed, and even though she was excited to show him her stomping grounds, she was also a little nervous at the prospect of seeing him again.

She also wondered if Ricky would be at all anxious about seeing *her* again. She expected him to have some apprehension about living in a different country without his family for half the year, but what was he thinking about her? She didn't want to presume too much. Where did she fit in with his plans? Did he think of her the same as he thought of his friends from back home--as just a pal? A long-distance pal, or something more? It was exciting to think that Ricky would willingly leave his home to essentially spend his time with her--when he wasn't working, of course. But what if their second meeting somehow just didn't feel as special—as magical—as the first?

She didn't want to question his motives too much. Perhaps it would all remain purely platonic, and just an adventure for him. She was already proud of him for having the courage to do it at all. But she could not quiet the nagging voice in her mind—as well as the memory of their good-bye kiss--that something magical just might happen again.

Such thoughts consuming Maggie's mind were interrupted when the crowded carriage came to an abrupt halt in the enveloping darkness of the underground tunnel. People were thrown a little and Maggie was thrust further into the business man's arm-pit. She steadied herself and tried to maintain her composure.

"Attention please, passengers," came a tinny voice from the

speakers, "this is your driver speaking."

The passengers all looked to the speaker grill in the carriage, as if it were rude not to, when it was addressing them.

"Due to unforeseen circumstances, that we, er, did not foresee, there will be a slight delay, whilst the London Zoo-keepers collect a ten-foot python that seems to have slithered its way down into the tunnel. Apologies for any inconvenience."

The passengers, visible to each other only by the clinical glow of the strip lighting overhead, looked to each other, confused and bewildered. A few became agitated, anxious to get to whatever meeting they were now running late for.

"Pythons! They eat people don't they?" came a woman's voice from the crowd.

"Given half a chance," said another.

Maggie shook her head, and checked her watch, straining to see in the limited emergency light. This was awful. She couldn't be late to meet Ricky. She somehow didn't think he'd believe her excuse of a python on the train tracks.

"What's if there's more than one?" the woman continued, sounding increasingly anxious. "Could be a nest, they could surround us and start picking us off one by one."

Just as Maggie was trying to think of something reassuring and/or patronizing to say in response, the tinny voice from the speaker grill came through again.

"Attention please, this is your train driver speaking, again. There seems to have been a mistake due to miscommunication. There are no zoo-keepers coming for an eleven-foot python in the tunnels. My mate Bob was trying to tell me he's got no goal keepers for the eleven-aside tonight, for his team, the Pythons. We can move on with our journey…This is your driver speaking."

A collective groan came from the crowd as the train slowly started to move forward.

Great, Maggie thought--now she'll likely be late, thanks to poor reception on the train conductor's radio set--and a rather dim-witted train conductor.

Heathrow Airport, as she remembered from her previous visit, was, in a way, an example of organized chaos. People scurried in all directions with large collections of luggage and trolleys; a few had wheels that seemed to think for themselves, and head straight for Maggie's ankles. But none of that bothered her as she strode straight for the Arrivals board to find the latest information for Ricky's plane. Making a mental note, she headed straight for terminal three, her nerves building with every step, seemingly propelling her faster. There were still ten minutes until Ricky's plane was due to land, but that didn't seem like much, and she had to be waiting at the gate for him.

By the time she reached the gate, she could see the BOAC plane slowly being taxied to the arrivals building. The large glass wall gave her a good view of the entire tarmac.

She stood amongst the other people waiting and watching for their loved ones to descend the mobile staircase from the plane. She hoped Ricky's appearance hadn't changed too much, so she'd be able to recognise him straight away. It could be embarrassing if she let him walk right past her, but she also realized such a concern was probably just her nerves getting the best of her.

As the passengers began to emerge from the plane, she checked the faces of each, and when they were starting to bottleneck, she hoped Ricky wouldn't get lost in the crowd. She started searching more furiously, determined to find him before he was the last one standing, and obvious to spot. There were a few passengers who looked a bit like him, which didn't help matters.

To make things worse, an unintentional bump from someone behind Maggie caused her to drop her handbag. As she reached down for it, a foot belonging to another stranger inadvertently gave it a kick, sending it sliding another few feet. Maggie awkwardly hunched down to chase it, but accidentally kicked it herself as she reached to grab it. By the time she snatched it up from the floor and looked up again, she had missed several passengers entering the Arrivals lounge from the plane. Panic began to set in as she looked around frantically for Ricky.

She felt a tap on her shoulder and spun around. And there was Ricky's smiling face.

"Glad you could make it," he said.

"Ricky!" She threw her arms around his neck and gave him a huge, tight hug which he eagerly returned. They held their embrace as if to continue right where they left off in New York.

"Oh, Ricky, I missed you," she said.

"I missed you, too."

They kissed.

"You're here, you're really here!" she said, with the look in her eye she had when they parted in New York. His fears that he might not see that same look again quickly vanished.

"You look a little different! But you still look like you! Very Beatle-esque!"

"Yeah well, I haven't had a hair cut in a while. Everyone's growing it longer, and my folks don't seem to mind. It's so good to see you!"

"I can't believe you're actually here. I can't wait to show you around. There's so much I want you to see."

"I'm sure I'll get to do everything. I do have six months."

He followed Maggie to the baggage carousel and waited for his suitcases to come around.   "How was the flight?"

"Long. But worth it. And I didn't get mistaken for a steward."

"Ha, ha, well you wouldn't, with hair like that."

They found a cart and loaded the suitcases on.

"Let's get you to Customs. You're not smuggling any contraband, are you?"

"I don't know…Let's find out!"

"Once you're done with that, brace yourself for the cold. English weather and all. We can take a specialty coach back to the city."

Ricky nodded. "I'll follow your lead."

During the bus journey into London, he told her all about his flight, about his recent semester in college, and how his mom had cried at the airport when he left. Maggie offered her latest news about her progress at the magazine, the positive reviews from readers and colleagues alike, and how fun it had been living with Claire and Linda.

The two didn't stop talking for the entire trip, equally as excited to be in each other's company again.

Ricky didn't know whether to look out the window to take in the unfamiliar scenery, or to gaze upon Maggie's smiling, animated face as they chatted away. He did his best to alternate between the two.

"It's hard to believe it's only been a year and a half since we've seen each other. Seems longer!" he said.

"A lot's happened in that time," she nodded. "I like your paisley shirt. Very hip!"

"It is? I'm not exactly a fashion maven."

"Linda's taught me a lot about the latest looks. She really knows her stuff, as she would, being a model, after all."

"What I meant was," Ricky said with a touch more intensity, "is that a lot has happened to us, especially to you. Moving to London, working at the magazine, winning awards."

"Oh, right. Well, they're not *real* awards. Nothing to put on my CV, if I'm being honest. The magazine arranges it so everyone wins something or other, like giving out goody bags at a kid's birthday party."

"Hey, don't sell yourself short! I've read your stories. You're really beginning to mix with the big shots."

"Well, what about you? Coming across the ocean on your own, working at a major tabloid right off the bat. That's a very courageous thing to do. I'm so proud of you, Ricky."

"I haven't really done much yet. But I don't think I would have gone through with this if you weren't here."

"Somehow I think you would have anyway."

"You're the one who encouraged me to take more chances in my life. So, here I am!"

"You'll be fine. I'll help any way I can.

Sitting across from them was a man in his sixties, who couldn't help but overhear their conversation.

"You two have a real mutual admiration society going on," he said. Ricky and Maggie responded with smiles. "And it's making me right nauseous. Excuse me." He abruptly rose and left his seat for a quieter section of the bus.

"I hope that wasn't my welcoming committee," Ricky said with a frown.

"No, *I'm* your welcoming committee. And the others will be too, when you meet them."

"Maggie, I hope you're not worried that I'll be clinging to you all the time. I don't want to get in the way of your usual routine."

"Nonsense!" She put her hand on his. "For the next six months, you'll be a big part of my routine, and I've been looking forward to it, more than I can say. So don't worry, silly Yank."

The bus pulled into Waterloo Station and Maggie took Ricky's back-pack while he manoeuvred his suitcases onto the platform.

"Taxi from here?" she asked.

"Sure, whatever you say." He checked a slip of paper. "It says here 15 Bedford Place, near Russel Square."

"That's near me!"

"But I have to go fill out some forms first, and get the key."

Even the cab made a big impression. "Wow, a real life black cab, just like the ones in *A Hard Day's Night.* I always thought they looked cool, and now I'm in one!"

Maggie had never really thought about it like that before. The cabs had been a part of everyday life since she moved to London. She smiled. "It's our version of a yellow taxi in New York."

Ricky laughed. She could tell how excited he was to be in London, and if he was anxious at all, he was doing a good job hiding it.

After a stop at the letting agency to sign some papers and pick up Ricky's new house keys, the black cab pulled up outside a terraced house, it had a blue door and a brass number '15' screwed to the wall.

He found his flat down the second floor corridor, opened the door, and excitedly went to explore his new home. His bedroom was roughly the size of his bedroom at home, and contained a bed, a wardrobe and a set of drawers. Marvelling at the high ceilings of the old building, he hoped he wouldn't have to change a light bulb.

The next door he opened revealed a bathroom. It seemed clean enough for his standards, and didn't need that much inspection—the bath tub, toilet and sink all seemed in order. He was about to close the door when something alien caught his eye. There was a box with what looked like a coin slot next to the boiler. He walked over to give it closer inspection. Maggie followed, amused at his curiosity.

"What's this? Looks like some kind of money box screwed to the wall?"

Maggie chuckled. "That's the meter."

"The meter? What for?"

"For the hot water, silly. They don't give you it for free. Every time you take a bath you put a coin in the slot and you'll get a bath tub amount of hot water."

His jaw hung open a little. "Every time I want to have a bath? I've never heard of that."

"Welcome to England. I have one in my bathroom too. Saves on bills, you pay for what you use and not what your house mates use."

Ricky tore his eyes away from the shocking money box. "This is *very* different from home. I'll have to make sure I keep lots of change in the house then. And I'll have to make sure I learn what the coins are...a shilling is like a nickel, right? Or more like a quarter?"

"Um," started Maggie, "that's sort of like saying a sock is a shoe. They both go on your feet, but one won't get you through a puddle."

"I'm not sure we're having the same conversation," he said.

"Oh, right, I'll help you learn about our money."

"I tried reading about it in one of my guide books but it got very confusing."

"Well, you know what a pound is, right? There are twenty shillings to a pound, and twelve pennies to a shilling. So, a pound is 240 pennies, or pence. And a penny is divided into two halfpennies, or four farthings, or-"

"I think I need to write this down--slowly."

"We can go over it again later. But there's a lot more, I'm

afraid--guineas, florins, and Crowns…"

"Wonderful."

"But the farthing coins are what you'll need for the meter."

Ricky knew he'd experience some culture shock, but didn't expect it so early into his stay--and concerning matters involving his bathroom habits. And he soon realized he was seeing just the tip of the iceberg.

"I also notice there's no TV here. I hadn't thought of that. I'll have to buy or rent one? I don't think I could live without it. Can't wait to see the shows you have here."

"Yes, we'll have to sort one out for you. You'll need to register and pay your fee."

"A fee? For watching TV?"

"Afraid so. Like I said, welcome to England!"

They spent the next few hours getting Ricky unpacked and settled in. Maggie liked his house and considered him lucky he didn't get lumbered with a hovel. It was getting quite late into the evening when Maggie felt her stomach rumble and she realised neither of them had eaten.

"I'm hungry," she announced.

"Yeah, I could eat right about now. The meal on the plane seems forever ago."

"No problem, we'll go out for food, and do a bit of grocery shopping for you later. What do you fancy for dinner?"

He shrugged. "Well, you might think I'm giving in to a cliché, but I sort of promised myself that my first meal in England would be fish and chips."

Maggie smiled. "Fish and chips it is then. There's bound to be a chippie nearby, there always is, no matter where you are. We can walk it."

Twenty minutes later they returned to his flat with their fish and chips wrapped in newspapers. They sat at the little kitchen table and opened out their meals, the aroma spurring Ricky's stomach rumbles even more.

"Did you put plenty salt and vinegar on?" Maggie asked.

He nodded. "I heard about them putting food in newspapers, I never quite believed it."

He stared at the now greasy, crumpled tabloid that held his traditional English takeaway.

"It's okay," she said, "won't harm you. They use edible newsprint and paper for the fish & chips.

"Cool."

"I'm only having you on!" she laughed. "But try not to eat the newspaper, really! And remember, call them chips, not fries, if you want to sound more like a local."

He took a closer look at the newspaper holding the meal. "Hey, wait a minute. This is the *New London News*—my new employer! That could be a bad omen."

"Or a good one, you never know."

"How can it be a good omen if they're using it to wrap greasy fish & chips?"

"Don't take it personally, Ricky. The *New London News* is known to be the most absorbent paper in England."

"Some comfort." He took a few bites. "So, when do I get to see your place?"

"You can stop by tomorrow after work. Maybe the others will be home, as well. Hey, we still get you some groceries and what-not."

"Oh, good," he said eagerly. "I like what-not!"

Maggie smiled, thinking that's just the kind of retort she would have made, too.

It wasn't just the jet lag that began to affect Ricky by the evening hours of his first day in London, it was the many surprises he had confronted throughout the day that had him exhausted.

So much to take in, like a stimulus overload--not the least of which was Maggie.

He was just finishing unpacking and placing his folded shirts in the wobbly dresser drawers when he heard a bit of commotion from just down the hall. It sounded like someone stumbling and falling onto a trash heap in the room next door. His curiosity won out over his exhaustion. He arrived and stood at the open doorway to the next-door living quarters to witness a young lad, seemingly Ricky's age, seated in the middle of the room, virtually surrounded on all sides by sets of reel-to-reel tape recorders, microphones, unknown electronic gadgets, and miles of twisted wires forming a spider web around him. The young man, with short blond hair and wearing thick eyeglasses, was busy connecting plugs leading from a central mixing board into one of the recorders. Just by chance, he glanced up and noticed Ricky at the doorway, observing him at work.

"Oh, hi. Sorry about the noise."

"Are you okay?"

"Oh, yeah, fine. You just moving in next door then?"

"Yeah. I'm Ricky."

"I'm Clark. Are you here for the semester?"

"Yeah, but I've got a job as part of a work-study program back home."

"Full time job, eh? Dinner's on you tomorrow, then. You're American?"

"Yeah, New Jersey, right across the river from New York."

"Oh, right."

The conversation was briefly interrupted by Clark electrocuting himself with one of the live wires.

"Ouch!" he yelped, shaking his hand to free it from pain. "Happens all the time, those shocks. That's why I wear rubber-soled shoes. Well, that's one reason. I also find them very comfortable, especially on cobblestones."

"That's good to know," Ricky said. "This is quite a set-up you've got. Very impressive."

"Come in! I'll show you."

Ricky ventured halfway into the room, almost feeling lured into the lab of a half-mad scientist.

"I've been working on my imaginary radio show."

"Imaginary...?"

Maybe Clark really was a half-mad scientist.

"Well, not really. I'm doing an internship as well, at BBC Radio. But they said one day, if I hand in a good demo reel, they might think about finding a spot for me on the air."

"Wow, that's great, to work for the BBC!"

"Sometimes it is. I go out on stories with a producer and sound recordist. But I'm just an extra pair of hands. And when I'm not there, or in class, I'm usually here, working on these tapes."

Ricky was genuinely impressed. "You've got to start somewhere, I guess. I'm going to be at the *New London News*."

"Oh, right. I read that sometimes, usually after I've finished with my fish & chips. That's a very absorbent newspaper."

Ricky's smile dropped. "Well, I'm sure they aim to please."

"Hey," Clark said with a fresh burst of energy, "I know what we can do. Sit down."

Ricky carefully tip-toed through the wires on the floor, as Clark spun around in his seat to re-set his tape recorder. He then placed a microphone atop its stand inches from Ricky's face, and slipped on a pair of headphones.

"Right, welcome to my studio. I'll interview you, all right?"

"Well, I guess…"

Clark took off his glasses, cleared his throat, switched on the tape recorder, and suddenly adopted the well-heeled tone and cadence of a professional BBC radio presenter, as if his body had become possessed by the spirit of some British version of Edward R. Murrow.

"And now we're talking with our special guest, Ricky…er…"

"Kramer."

"Ricky Kramer, from America. So, Ricky, what brings you to London?"

"Eh, BOAC Flight 22 from New York," he quipped with a smirk.

"Ah, very droll, Ricky. I understand from my copious research that you're a new employee of the *New London News*?"

"Well, I haven't started yet. My first day is Wednesday."

"No doubt you're itching to blow the lid off the latest scandal involving, say, members of Parliament and local prostitutes?"

"Well, not really, I'm just going to be a lowly assist—"

"Ricky, you're an American. So tell us, what's going on in Vietnam? You're sending more and more troops there, but the situation just keeps getting worse. Thousands are getting killed, and for what reason?"

Ricky found himself breaking out in a cold sweat. "I, uh, I wasn't the one who sent them there, you know."

Clark leaned in. "Well, I mean you, as a representative of the United States of America…"

"Oh, I'm not really a rep—"

"--And a student, no less. We keep hearing a lot about student protests on college campuses and elsewhere, against the war. Have you and your contemporaries been protesting the war?"

"I really have to finish unpacking now."

He leaned in, nose-to-nose with Clark. "You're not going to play this to anyone at the BBC are you?"

Clark laughed, seemingly transforming himself back to his natural state. "No, of course not. It's just a practice tape. Hang on--have you written home yet?"

"Well, my plane landed just a few hours ago, so—"

"Because instead of writing home, I can help you record messages on tape to your family, and you can send those to them--that is, if they have a tape recorder as well. They can hear you in your own voice tell them about your time here, instead of just reading letters."

"Hey, that's a great idea! But I'm probably a better writer than performer."

"It just takes a bit of practice. We can do little skits, put on sound effects, you name it, like a real broadcast, and you'd be the star."

"Yeah," Ricky said, "Maybe I can give it a try next week sometime?"

"I'll be here. I don't have a girlfriend, so I'll be here. Do you have a girlfriend?"

"Er, not really. Or, maybe. I'll let you know. As soon as I know."

"Right. Nice meeting you, Ricky."

Ricky made a hasty exit from the room, not really sure what had just happened. One thing he did know was to never let himself be interviewed about world affairs on the radio.

Chapter 28

It was Ricky's first day at the *New London News.*

The grey stone building on a narrow side street just off Fleet Street looked respectable enough for a tabloid newspaper, he thought, as he stood at the entrance, ignoring the chill of the morning to consider the significance of the moment. He was about to join the ranks of real-world journalists at a London newspaper. He tried not to let his nervousness overwhelm his excitement, because he didn't really know what to expect—hopefully not a British version of the noodnicks at the *Community Herald*, or the snobs on the college paper.

The lobby receptionist directed him to the second floor (her instructions for him to "take the lift" left him momentarily puzzled), and, standing in the hall by the double doors marked *New London News*, he took a deep breath.

"Try to remember everything they tell you when they show you around," he instructed himself. *"These are dignified British newspapermen, with the highest of standards. It's bad enough already, having an American accent to make yourself sound so...American, without coming across as some dope who never saw the inside of a newsroom before."*

With the pep talk in his head concluding on that optimistic note, he knocked on the door and waited. A commotion seeped through from the other side—a lot of shouting, as if some mass panic was going on. He timidly opened the door and stepped in, witnessing a flurry of activity. He heard more shouting, with the sounds of things slamming and agitated paper rustling mixed in. There weren't as many employees present as the commotion had indicated. But those who were there scurried about like ants on an anthill. It couldn't *always* be like this, he thought. Maybe it was some kind of emergency.

After a few seconds, the shouting voices became a little more distinct, as they emanated from a smoky side office, presumably belonging to the editor.

"Fenton! Where'd he go?"

"I'm coming!" another disembodied voice yelled back, but nobody appeared.

"Reg, where's Bixby?"

"Don't know."

"Damn it! We need him, fast!"

"He's not here."

"Haversham?"

"Nope."

Two men hurried out of the side office. The first was somewhat stocky, in his early thirties, wearing a tight-fitting grey suit, porkpie hat, and camera around his neck. The man behind him, older, taller, and grasping several papers in one hand and a cigarette in the other, seemed to be the boss—a very aggravated boss.

"We don't have time to wait, Reg!" he said to the man with the camera. "He won't be there all day. Grab anybody to go with you. Anyone who can take notes."

Ricky, standing there mute and confused, caught the editor's eye.

"Who are you?"

"Uh…Ricky Kramer, student intern." He realized how his answer sounded like the title of a hopelessly boring TV drama.

"Oh, the American kid?"

"Yes. It's my first day—"

"Go with Reg. He'll explain everything. Hurry!"

"You mean right now?"

"Not bloody tomorrow! Yes, right now!"

"Come on, kid," Reg gestured as he grabbed his coat, heading for a side door. "We'll take the stairs. The lift's too slow."

Without much obvious choice, Ricky hurried to catch up. The two bounded down a cinder block stairwell, taking two steps at a time.

"I'm Reg, one of the photographers. That other bloke is the boss, Derek. More about him later. We've got to get to Harrod's. You've heard of it?"

"Uhh…big department store?"

"Right. We'll take my transportation. Taxis are too slow."

They nearly burst through the stairwell door at street level, where a Vespa scooter stood chained to a NO PARKING sign. Reg hurried to free the scooter as he explained.

"We got a tip that Lord Bradbury is secretly shopping in Harrod's, wearing a dress."

"What? Who's Lord...wearing a ...are we going on *that*?"

"The only way to beat the traffic. Hop on."

Reg got on the scooter and started it up, as Ricky stood slack-jawed.

"Well, come on! Hold on tight."

"Hold onto what?"

"To me!"

Ricky clumsily mounted the few inches of the seat Reg had allotted to him, and reluctantly wrapped his arms around the photographer's pudgy midsection. In an instant, they were accelerating down the side street, the cold January air feeling ten times colder as it swirled around Ricky's head.

"I'll get pneumonia!" he protested.

"Nah, you'll be fine. We'll be there soon."

Reg's idea of "soon" was nothing like Ricky's. The trip through the city felt like a nightmarish amusement park ride that felt as if it would never end.

"Lord Bradbury is 38th in line to the throne," Reg continued, turning his head slightly to the side to shout the rest of the story to his freezing and terrified passenger. "He's a useless prat, but fancies himself a celebrity, so he thinks he needs to go out in public with a disguise. Lately he's taken to going out in drag to avoid detection. But he just looks like Lord Bradbury in drag. *Everyone* knows it's him. He'd have a fighting chance to pass as a bird if he thought to shave his moustache."

"A b-b-b-bird?" Ricky asked through chattering teeth. "Wait, is he d-d-dressed as a bird or a woman?"

"Same thing, mate!"

"So, you want to get a picture of him shopping in Harrod's wearing women's c-c-clothes?"

"Oi, this is a big story, son. He usually shops at Marks & Spencer!"

"What do you need m-m-me for?"

"I'm a photographer. You're a writer, aren't you?"

"Well—"

"Got a notebook on you?"

"I think."

"When we find him, I'll take the pictures, you get a written description. Hold on tight--big turn here…"

The scooter leaned into a turn at a 45-degree angle, giving Ricky yet another thrill he could have lived without that morning. He didn't know which felt worse, his frostbite or his nausea.

Upon arriving at a Harrod's maintenance entrance, Reg parked the scooter and knocked on the door, in code. A few seconds later, the door opened as a maintenance worker stepped out, shaking his head.

"Sorry, Reg, you just missed him. Left a few minutes ago. He bought a few scarves and a handbag, but made a quick getaway. He's gettin' clever."

"I was afraid of that, Dan," Reg sighed.

"But he's got good taste in handbags, I'll give him that."

Dan looked past Reg to the shivering Ricky on the scooter. "Who's that?"

"Don't know, really. New kid on the paper. American."

"He looks a bit green."

"Yeah, not much experience yet, I reckon."

"No, I mean his face looks green, like he's about to lose his breakfast. But his lips are definitely blue."

"Thanks for the tip anyway, mate. That's all right. We'll go on to Plan B. Here's a fiver for your trouble, as agreed." He handed Dan a bill and returned to the scooter. "Keep your eyes open for next time, eh? All right, kid, let's go warm you up."

Ricky soon found himself seated at a tiny table in a noisy pub, watching Reg light a cigarette and start on a pint.

"Feeling warmer?"

"Yeah, a little, thanks," Ricky said. "Isn't it a little early to be drinking in a pub?"

"You wanted to warm up, didn't you? Really, you Americans can't take a bit of cold, can you?"

"Well, a bit of cold, yes. A frigid wind tunnel, along with motion sickness, well…I just wasn't prepared, that's all."

"Fag?"

The bluntness and personal nature of the question had Ricky taken aback. "Uh…no, I like girls, thank you."

"I mean a ciggie. Do you want a cigarette?"

"No thanks, I don't smoke."

"Why not?"

"Huh? Oh, well, it's not healthy. Bad for your lungs."

"Oh, you're one of those."

"One of what?"

"Those health freaks I've been hearing a lot about lately, from California or who-knows-where, eating rabbit food and wheat germ, thinking it will help 'em live to be a hundred."

"I'm not a health freak, exactly. I just don't smoke. Or drink."

"You eat meat?"

"Yeah, sometimes. Fairly often."

"Oh, right. Good. You had me worried there for a minute."

Ricky felt his head reeling, even without the benefit of ales, lagers, or whatever the Brits called beer. There he was with a total stranger, having spent most of the morning holding on for dear life on the back of a scooter racing through central London, failing to get a picture of some lord who dabbled as a transvestite, and now he was struggling to breathe in a smoke-filled pub, clumsily attempting to justify the fact that he didn't smoke.

And it wasn't even lunchtime.

Reg began to fill in some of the many details of what Ricky had gotten himself into.

"You wouldn't know it to look at me," he began, "but I'm one of the most famous people in London who most people have never heard of."

"Excuse me? I don't understand."

"Every doorman, concierge, chauffeur, cab driver, and maître d' in the city knows me. They tell me who's doing what, and when, and I'm there to get the pictures for the next edition. Film stars, singers, members of Parliament, you name it. They don't make a move anywhere in this city without me hearing about it. I know where they're going to be before *they* know themselves."

"Oh, you're a—what's the word…a paparazzi?"

Reg shrugged. "I've been called worse, especially by the paparazzi."

"Sounds glamorous, to be rubbing shoulders with so many celebrities."

"Glamorous? Oh, but you haven't heard the rest of it, son. I'm also one of the most *hated* famous people in London most people have never heard of. I've been spit on, threatened, assaulted, arrested, hospitalized…but I don't take any of it personally. All part of the job. Remember, getting the story is the goal. And selling papers is the most important goal of all."

"You mean you'll do *anything* for a story?"

"Now you're catching on."

Ricky wasn't sure how that philosophy sat with him, but he didn't feel to be in any position to debate the point on his first day.

"Well, I hope I didn't slow you down in trying to get that story about Lord Bradbury."

Reg dismissed the idea with a wave of his hand. "Ah, no problem. That's what Plan B is for. We can go either of two ways. We crop his face onto a picture of some bird shopping in Harrod's. Or, we go to our trusty Lord Bradbury lookalike and set up a photo shoot with him."

Ricky was shocked by the idea. "You're just going to fake the whole thing? Can you do that? Aren't there aren't any laws or…or ethical rules—"

Reg's boisterous laugh interrupted Ricky's flow of thought. "You've got a lot to learn, son!" he chuckled. "We know he was there and how he was dressed, it would just be a re-enactment."

Eight hours later, and with his mind-boggling first day over, Ricky could have easily slumped onto his sofa and fallen fast asleep, but instead he gladly accepted Maggie's dinner invitation at an Indian restaurant she enjoyed.

Exotic aromas wafted from the restaurant as the couple approached the entrance to The Spice of Bengal. Ricky had never eaten Indian cuisine before, and, as an introduction to the various styles of restaurants in the city, Maggie decided to treat him to one of her favourites.

"You're going to love it," said Maggie. "And it's cheap."

"I like Chinese food, is it anything like Chinese food?"

"Yeah, totally," she said. "Except not at all."

"Well, that clears things up."

"There's rice, but it's cooked differently. And there's spices in the sauces, but different spices than you probably know. Trust me, you will want to eat here every day of the week once you've tasted it."

"Well, if it's cheap like you say, you're probably right."

They entered the restaurant, met by a waiter who showed them straight to their reserved table and took their drink order of two large colas.

Sitar music gently played through the speakers and Ricky took note of the portraits hanging on the walls, showing scenes from what he assumed was Indian history and culture. He was embarrassed to admit he did not know a great deal about life in India, but Maggie seemed to know enough to point out what the different portraits represented and what the different dishes in the menu contained.

There was one dish in the menu that Ricky had heard of.

"Vindaloo. I think I know that one. That's a popular dish, right?"

"Oh yes, but I really don't think you should start with that one. It's very hot."

"What are you going to order?"

Maggie had the menu practically memorized, but gave it a cursory glance anyway. "Mmmmm," she began, "I think I'll have chicken tikka masala with egg pilau rice and a garlic naan bread and an onion bahji for starters, I think. How does that sound?"

"Like another language."

"Yes, well, it is."

"Is that what I should have? What is pilau rice? And naan bread??"

"The rice is like a boiled long grain rice with pieces of boiled egg mixed in. And naan bread is a flat bread that's great for dipping in the sauce."

Ricky nodded. "That sounds nice. I think I'll have that too."

They nibbled on popadoms and dips while waiting for the starters to arrive. Ricky liked them.

"They're like a big chip...I mean, err, crisp."

When the onion bahjis arrived, he wasn't quite sure what he was expecting, maybe something like an onion ring, but it was more like a ball. He tried it and liked it. Everything so far was delicious and, as Maggie predicted, he imagined he could eat there often.

Their conversation flowed well, in between bites.

"Tell me more about your first day at work," she coaxed. "Other than your unexpected scooter ride through the city. Sounds like a real rite of passage for you."

"I thought it was going to be *last* rites for me a couple of times," Ricky recalled with a nervous chuckle. "And I'm not even Catholic. It's not exactly how I imagined the paper to be like."

"But do you like it?"

"I'm not sure. It seems very...sly. That's the only word I can think of. I mean, they keep me busy, and I'm never bored, and the people treat me reasonably well. They showed me how to find stock photos in their big filing cabinets, and they had me doing a lot of basic research for some stories. So, I'm learning, but some of their methods shock me. I swear I heard the editor, Derek, practically make up a story out of thin air about a sex scandal involving a member of Parliament."

Maggie nodded, thinking how Ricky's innocence was so cute. "Ah, yes, well, the story could be true. There was a big scandal like that here a few years ago. I guess we'll all find out if this one's true soon enough. I think someone at your college should have warned you when you signed up for this about the differences between the tabloids and the broadsheets. Tabloids like juicy gossip, if you want to be a serious reporter, you'll have to head for the broadsheets. The stuff the middle-class and business men like to read."

"*Now* you tell me. But that's more financial stuff isn't it?"

"Well, there's the *Financial Times*, but also the *Times of London, the Guardian*... I don't read them much myself. I like the tabloids, even though I don't believe everything they print. They have more stuff about musicians and stars and I kind of need that in my business."

"So, in other words, they print lies?"

"Well, what's a lie, when you think about it?"

"Er...something made up that isn't the truth. See? I thought about it."

"What the tabloids do is find a seed of something, and they stretch it out. A little truth goes a long way with them. Just take what they print with a grain of salt. Thing is, you're just an apprentice now, really. If you actually got a full time job there, you could write the truth and the facts if that's what you wanted, and if your editor allowed it to be printed. But right now, you're just learning the industry, so I say, see it through, if you don't lose sleep over it. If it bothers you that much, find something else before you jump ship, or you might have to go back to America and lose out on those college credits. And we don't want that! I mean, I'd hate to see you go back early."

Ricky thought over Maggie's advice. She seemed so worldly wise at that moment, having had more experience in the world than he had. "Well, I don't have much choice, so I'm hoping I'll get to see some good to it, but at the minute it's not really what I thought I signed up for."

"Give it time, Ricky. It's only your first day."

"Maybe I should buy my own scooter, so I wouldn't have to cling onto Reg's backside on the way to a scoop!"

"There, now that's positive thinking!"

The waiter approached their table with their main courses. It smelled good and was making Ricky hungry, even though he'd just stuffed his onion bahji and giant crisp into his mouth.

The waiter placed an empty plate in front of Ricky and Maggie, and put the dishes of egg pilau rice and chicken tika masala in the middle of the table. He put the naan breads alongside the empty plates.

"Is there anything else I can get you?" he asked. The two both declined the offer. "Enjoy your meal," he said.

Dishing up the rice and chicken tika masala onto the plates, Maggie waited and watched as Ricky took his first bite.

The spices and other new flavours hit his taste buds in abundance.

"Nice," he grinned.

Maggie beamed and tucked into her own meal. She showed Ricky how to dip his naan bread into the rice and sauce. He enjoyed the exotic bread but hoped his breath wouldn't reek too much like garlic.

But despite his regular sips of his fizzy beverage, she worried that Ricky might be finding the meal a bit spicy. One tell-tale sign was how his eyes were beginning to water a little.

"The spice tends to build with the more you eat," she said.

He nodded. "I'm getting that."

"Don't eat so fast, really. Take your time."

"But I'm hungry!"

"To me, this is quite a mild dish," she said, "but to a beginner, the spices are quite strong. I went through this, too."

Ricky took another sip of his cola, bravely attempting to downplay the troubling new side effects of his repast. "It's tasty. It's just starting to...burn a little."

Maggie tried to hold back a giggle. "They say a cup of tea will put the fire out of your mouth faster than a cold glass of pop."

"I hope they're right, whoever they are."

She caught the attention of the waiter and asked for two cups of tea.

"I'm okay, really," Ricky said, as he took a mouthful of rice that hadn't touched the spicy sauce. "I'm not sure how adding hot liquid to the heat already in my mouth will put out the fire. But a bucket of ice, might help."

"You don't have to eat any more if you don't like it."

"I do like it," he said, as a few beads of sweat formed on his forehead, "I think I just need to build up my level of spice tolerance."

Enunciating words was beginning to hurt, so he took one last bite of chicken covered in masala sauce and swallowed. He blew out a deep breath, worried that it might set the tablecloth on fire. He wafted his hand in front of his mouth and took a sip of Coke.

"Not helpful!" The odd and intensifying sensation in his mouth had him in a near panic. He grabbed the steaming cup of tea and took a drink, then promptly spat it over his plate. "Hot hot hot! I think I burned my tongue!"

Maggie looked on helplessly, remembering her own trial by fire, years before. "But has the spice gone?" she asked.

"No! I think my teeth are melting."

"Is everything okay, miss?" asked the concerned waiter.

"Yes," said Maggie, "He's just not used to the spices."

"Can I get you another drink?" asked the waiter.

"Water, please?" replied Ricky. "A few gallons should do it. Or two."

The waiter left to get a pitcher of water.

"Are you okay?" she asked.

Ricky nodded, his eyes streaming with tears, his cheeks red, and his speech reduced to a lisping, slurring stream of nonsense syllables, as if he had a handful of marbles in his mouth. "Yeth, I'll be okay. Wow. Juth wawant ethpecting it to be tha haa--"

"Sorry?"

"Nothing."

Maggie paid the bill as Ricky guzzled his last glass of water.

They stepped outside into the refreshing night air.

"I weally enjoyed the foo...I better thop talking for a few mimutes..." he conceded. "I think I'll be better at it next time."

She gave him one of her raised eyebrows. "You mean you want to go back?"

"Well, maybe not thraight away, but shuure." He was beginning to drool again. "I'm not returning to America until I've reached vindaloo level, if it doethn't kill me firth."

She laughed. "Silly Yank. Well, I don't mind helping you train for the vindaloo Olympics."

"Of courth you don't," he slurped, trying to find easier words to pronounce. "No pain for you."

"Well, fancy a stroll before you walk me home? It's a beautiful night."

Ricky nodded to spare himself further oral discomfort, as well as further humiliation. Maggie softly giggled to herself again as they started down the street, clasping his hand in hers.

Chapter 29

Even after only one date with Maggie, Ricky relished the idea of seeing her again, as often as she could stand him. He wasn't sure if "date" was the right word, but the previous night certainly felt like one, and knew he wanted more of them with Maggie--just not at Indian restaurants too often.

Their date the following night didn't begin as he expected. In fact, it didn't begin at all.

As he approached the front door to her flat, he noticed a piece of paper folded over with 'RICKY' in capital letters, pinned to the door. With his smile fading, he picked up the note and began to read.

> *"Ricky, sorry I'm not here though we agreed to meet at this time. I got called into work. I should be back soon but in the mean-time, go to Claire's salon, it's not far, and she will give you the key to let yourself in. So sorry!*
> *Maggie x"*

A list of directions to Claire's salon followed.

Ricky sighed with disappointment as he turned to follow the directions.

"Can I help you, son?" a voice called out of nowhere. He saw the face of a middle-aged woman sticking out her front window. A kerchief wrapped around her head and a mop nearly obscuring her face told him she had interrupted some housecleaning just to snoop. "You a gentleman caller for someone here?"

"Oh, yes, for Maggie. She's not in. But she left a note, thank you."

"I do like to keep my eye on who comes and goes, you know."

"Are you the landlady?" he asked, restraining himself from adding, "or just nosy?"

"Mrs. Beckersley. Oh, that Maggie's a doll. You her boyfriend?"

"Well, I--"

"You don't sound like you're from around here."

"I'm visiting, from America."

"Oh, fancy that! Maggie's got an American boyfriend."

"I don't know if--"

"Right, well, you just watch your p's and q's with her, young man, and we'll get on fine."

With that, she disappeared from the window. Ricky shook his head and proceeded to follow the directions on the note, turning left out of Doughty Street.

"Hair By Claire" was hard to miss. The large sign, with the words "GRAND OPENING" temporarily affixed to it, and the partially-deflated balloons still waving outside the window from opening day, drew in lots of attention. Ricky could smell peroxide and hairspray as he approached, checking the sign above the shop against what Maggie had written. Just then, Claire stepped outside to remove a bit of litter from the sidewalk in front of the doorway.

"Hi, welcome to Hair By Claire, do you have an appointment?" she said.

"Err, no, I-"

"Well don't worry, you don't really need one today. And we're unisex. The first in the neighbourhood. That means we serve both sexes."

"I know, but—"

"I'm sure I can squeeze you in."

Before Ricky could say a word, Claire ushered him into a black swivel chair and draped a protective gown over his shoulders.

"Are you Claire?"

She began running her fingers through his hair.

"That's me. So what can I do for you?" She pulled out a black comb and started back-combing Ricky's locks. "A cut and re-style perhaps? You have fabulous hair. So dark and lush. You just need to update the style a bit."

"Err, thank-you. But I actually just came in for-"

She turned her attention to the two ladies sitting under the large, egg-shaped overhead hair-dryers, which reminded Ricky of the alien pods he'd seen in an old sci-fi movie.

"What do you think, girls? He could pull off the John Lennon look, couldn't he?"

Ricky's eyes widened. This was definitely Maggie's Claire. She managed to fit a Beatles reference into a conversation without even needing to have the conversation itself.

"Well what I was saying was-"

"Hmm, sounds like you're from America," Claire surmised. "Am I right? You're American?"

"Yes."

"Where abouts?"

"New Jersey. I'm from New Jersey, America. So, as I was saying-"

"Gosh, I've been open only a few days and I've already gone international. My first American customer. How fab is that!"

Claire picked up a spray bottle and began to dampen Ricky's hair. He hoped it was just water. Then she produced her scissors.

"My best mate has a friend in America."

"I know. I'm--"

"So what are we going for? I can give you a trim of say, an inch, to tidy things up a bit, and then how about we shape the sides around your face? A bit of John Lennon, eh? Give you a fringe?"

"A fringe?"

He shifted to sit forward but Claire eased him back down. "I definitely think you want to keep some length to it. It's all the fashion. You're too young for the same old short back & sides. You don't want to look like a soldier."

"Yeah, I do want to keep it this length but-"

"So, just a trim then, yeah? Neaten it up a bit?"

"Okay yeah," he gave in, "just half an inch…or an inch."

"My, aren't we adventurous," she teased. "No worries."

She began to measure his hair between her fingers and cut along her guide line.

There was a moment of silence, as she concentrated on the task at hand, when Ricky saw his opportunity.

"So, as I was trying to say, I'm really just here for your house keys."

Claire stopped in mid-snip. "Pardon?"

"Your house keys. To let myself in."

"Into my house? Well, really!" she said, amused. "I mean we do want to be accommodating to our customers, but there are limits, mate. That might be how you do things back in New Guernsey, America, but in Liverpool, we don't go around swapping house keys. And yes, I know we're in London, but sense my accent."

"Wait, no, I didn't explain myself properly," he said, mindful that he seemed to have agitated a girl who was holding a pair of scissors against his neck. "Maggie told me to come here and you would give me a key because she's at work."

Claire's eyes opened wide. "Oh my God, are you Ricky?"

"Y-yes…If that's okay."

She burst out laughing. "Oh my Gosh, Ricky! I should have recognised you from your photos! And your accent!   And being from--"

"New Jersey."

"Yes! I must be stupid as mud!"

She put her scissors down and gave him a hug—somewhat awkwardly, as he was still seated in the chair. "Welcome, Ricky!"

"Thanks!"

"Your hair is so much longer now than in your pictures."

"A lot of guys are wearing it like this now."

"But you're Ricky!"

"That's me."

Claire laughed again, then stopped an allowed herself a lingering gaze. She slowly shook her head. "Maggie's Ricky."

"Well, I don't know if I'm exactly Maggie's—"

"Oh, you are," she nodded with a vague smile. "You are."

He was unable to interpret that. It was as if Claire knew something he didn't, but had no intention of sharing it with him.

"I thought you were a nutter asking for my house key! Yes, Maggie told me to give you the key. It slipped my mind, being so busy here. But you'll have to wait 'til I finish cutting your hair. I've started it now."

"Yeah okay, no problem."

She turned to the shop of customers and hair stylists. "Everyone, this is Ricky. He's all the way from New Jersey, America—next to New York-- to visit my best friend Maggie, for six months!"

The announcement spurred a mix of exclamations and shouts of "Welcome, Ricky," from the ladies.

A woman under one of the hair dryers strained to hear from under the noisy machine. "He's going to do *what* to your friend for six months?"

Claire turned her attention back to Ricky. They spoke to each other's reflection in the mirror, which was easier for her as she worked, but awkward for him.

"Anyway, Ricky, it's so lovely to finally meet you. I've heard so much about you. And America. And your friends and family. I feel like I know you already."

"I know what you mean. Maggie has told me a lot of your adventures together in Liverpool, especially all of your Beatles stories."

"Oh, right! We've got a million of them. So, what's it like living in America?"

What a Kenny-like question, he thought. But it somehow seemed more forgivable coming from Claire.

"Pretty much the same as here," he said. "Except everyone there has an American accent."

Claire laughed.

"And we have dollars," he added. "But I've no idea what *your* coins are, they make no sense."

"No, it's pence, not cents."

"Er, I meant--"

"You'll get used to it. I hear they're talking about changing the currency anyway. I hope they don't, that would be far too confusing."

"Also, I've never walked so much in my life! I've come to realise how much I use my car back home. Over here, I've been walking everywhere! Although I do like the Underground. But even to get from one platform to another is a decent walk."

"Oh you got your car then? I remember reading your letter about wanting a car. But that was a few years ago, right?"

"You read my letters?"

"Yep, lovely hand-writing you have. Looks just like my sister's."

He wasn't sure how to respond to either of those revelations, but then, he did share some portions of Maggie's letters with Kenny, so he was in no position to object.

"Whatever happened to Marie?" Claire asked, as if trying to catch up with a soap opera plotline. Each comment or question out of her mouth was more surprising--even intimidating-- than the one before. "You *do* like Maggie more than you like Marie, right? Because I must warn you, if you mess Maggie about, you'll have me to answer to."

Ricky shrank back a bit in his chair. Claire's scissors suddenly seemed to have grown as large as pruning shears. "I don't see Marie anymore. I haven't for ages. She has a new boyfriend I think, according to a friend of hers."

"Who, Andrea-Claudia?"

"Well, as a matter of--"

"How is she?"

On top of everything else, it was the strangest sensation for Ricky to be asked about his friends by someone he had just met--in a hair salon--three thousand miles from home.

"She's fine."

"And Elliot? Still a toffee-nosed git?"

"He's fine, too. I'm not sure if he's really a...whatever you just called him...but with Maggie and me, I don't know if we're really a couple--but I would never hurt her anyway."

Claire gave him another knowing smile. "That's good to hear," she said. Her mood seemed to lighten again, giving Ricky the chance to exhale.

Switching back to light conversation , she asked, "So, I've always wanted to ask an American-- why do you all say things differently than we do, if you're supposed to be speaking English? I mean, you don't say *al-you-min-ee-um*, you say *al-loom-in-um*. And it's *lift*, not *elevator*. And *crisps*, not *chips*...chips are chips, ya know?"

"I'll be sure to take that information back with me," he said, as she began combing through his hair again, checking that the lengths matched on both sides of his face. As she put the scissors on the counter, he felt bold enough to offer a rebuttal. "But then, why do *you* say "*lef*tenant" instead of "lieutenant"? Where's the f? Do you see an f? I don't see an f. And why do you say "clark" when the word is spelled "clerk"? Where's the a? Do you see an a? I don't see an a. Why not? Because there's no a! So, if anything, I think we Americans have made some improvements."

"Good point," she said, "But I'm only pulling your leg. Call things whatever you want to call them."

"Oh, okay. But I'll follow the rules here. As they say, 'when in Rome...'"

"And I'm fluent in American, I've seen all the good movies. Used to work in a cinema you know."

"Oh yeah, with Maggie."

"Yep. Right, you're almost done. Unless you'd like a perm. You could join Mrs Stubbs and Mrs Olsen under the dryers, if you want a perm."

"Er, no thanks, I'm good with just a trim."

"No problem, and since you're Maggie's Ricky and didn't actually come in here for a haircut anyway, I'll give you it half price." Ricky stood up and brushed his shoulders of loose hair clippings. As he began to reach into his pockets for money, she added. "Only joking, Ricky, it's on the house! But don't forget to tell your friends, 'At Hair By Claire, the prices are fair!'"

"I will tell everyone I meet! And I'll tell them back home in New Jersey, too."

"Oh, I'm loving you already."

She collected her purse and took out her front door key.

"Now then, just retrace your steps to get back, right? Let yourself in. Make yourself comfortable. Eat and drink whatever you can find, except the Jelly Babies. They're mine. Okay, you can have one. But not a red one. Help yourself to the green ones. Maggie should be back soon. I know she's really sorry she's late."

He nodded and took the key.

"Thanks for the haircut. It was nice to meet you after all this time."

He left the shop and started to retrace his steps. So, he thought, that was Claire. Meeting her left him nearly as exhausted as meeting Reg had.

He arrived at the flat, let himself in, and took a look around the living room. Without its tenants present, the quiet and stillness felt a little odd. As he poked around the room, side-stepping a few articles of clothing on the floor, and felt inspired to think of a surprise for Maggie when she arrived--something silly. But just exactly what he wanted to do wasn't clear yet.

He continued to look around, now with more purpose. Let's see, he thought, it would be hilarious to put on some things of Maggie's and strike a pose for her as she entered.

He stood at the doorway to the bedroom and peered in. A girl's bedroom was sacrosanct, he learned long ago, not to be entered under any circumstances without permission. But if he could just reach for something from the doorway without actually entering, surely that wouldn't count, would it? And he wouldn't feel like some sort of weirdo creeping around her bedroom.

He reached in to grab a few things hanging on a hat rack just inside the bedroom doorway, stretching his body like a gymnast to avoid stepping into the forbidden zone. He managed to grab a multi-colored scarf, a hat, and frilly coat. His next idea was to practice an impersonation of Maggie's busybody neighbour, Mrs. Beckersley.

Within the twenty minutes after entering Maggie's flat, Ricky had made a pot of tea, found some scones that hadn't turned totally rock hard yet, and was in his improvised costume awaiting Maggie's arrival. The instant he heard the key slip into the lock, he positioned himself in a pose, and began to pour the tea into a cup, as he launched into his Mrs.

Beckersley imitation.

"Fancy some tea, dear?"

A scream pierced through the air from the direction of the door, causing his head to snap upwards to see a tall, blonde girl standing there in terror. Within the same millisecond, the startled Ricky dropped the tea-pot and screamed back in shock. The girl was Linda, and, as far as she was concerned, Ricky was an intruder—possibly dangerous, and in drag. She'd seen *Psycho*.

Linda grabbed for any handy object she could to brandish as a weapon. A feather duster would have to do. She pointed it squarely at Ricky.

"Who are you? What are you doing?" she shrieked, not awaiting an answer to either question.

In his panic, he sought safety in the bathroom, dashing across the living room as Linda advanced, waving the feather duster like a Samurai sword. He slammed the door behind him and locked it just in time.

"Don't shoot!" he pleaded.

She banged on the door and jiggled the doorknob.

"What are you doing here?" she demanded. "I'm calling the police."

"No, please don't."

"What are you, some sort of transvestite burglar? And having the cheek to make a pot of tea for yourself?"

"No! I'm not a transvestite, *or* a burglar! I can explain."

"You're not gonna tell me you're that Lord Bradbury prat, are you?"

"No, I'm Maggie's friend Ricky."

He suddenly wondered if he was even in the right flat. Maybe this girl had no idea who Maggie was.

"Prove it! Let's see some identification."

"Okay, okay. I have my student ID card, from New Jersey, America, on me. It has my picture on it. I'll slide it under the door."

With shaking hands, he pulled the card from his wallet, slid it under the door, and waited.

"This picture doesn't look much like you," Linda said.

"Well, because in the picture I'm not wearing women's clothes and looking terrified."

"Fair enough." She slid it back under the door, but she wasn't done with her interrogation.

"What are you doing in our flat on your own?"

"Maggie left a note saying she was going to be late, and sent me to get a key from Claire at the hair salon, so I could let myself in and wait for her."

"Oh, yeah? Well, if that's true, then how many fingers does Claire have?"

As if he weren't stressed enough, he was totally thrown by the question.

"Uhh...Ten?"

"Okay, that's correct. Well, then, open the door, slowly."

"Only if you put down the feather duster. I have allergies."

"Okay."

She backed away from the door as he slowly opened it. "Come out."

Ricky cautiously stepped out of the bathroom, feeling humiliated, as Linda assessed his odd choice of apparel. "Do you usually prance around empty flats wearing women's clothes?"

"Er, no, this is my first time. And last. And they're not really women's clothes, they're Maggie's."

"Well, what's Maggie then, a kangaroo? And those aren't her clothes, anyway. They're mine."

"What? Yours? I got them from that bedroom."

"Yeah, that's *my* bedroom."

"Ooooh! I thought it was Maggie's room. No wonder these fit me so well. You're quite tall. But then, so is she. But you must be about five foot nine or--"

"You're a weirdo!" She raised the feather duster again with renewed aggression.

"No, please! I'm not! It was a gag. I just wanted to make her laugh when she walked in, imitating your neighbour downstairs, Mrs.

Beckersley."

"Maggie doesn't imitate Mrs. Beckersley."

"No, I meant *I* was imitating Mrs. Beckersley. Just a little joke."

Linda took another moment to stare at Ricky. "You're a terrible practical joker."

"No kidding," he said, defeated.

"Well, then, as long as you're Maggie's Ricky, you might as well make yourself comfy."

"I guess you must be Linda?"

"Oh, right, forgot to introduce myself. Where are my manners? Yes, I'm Linda."

"You're a model, right?"

"Yes."

"You certainly do look like a model."

"Do I? Which one?"

"No, I mean you're pretty enough to be a model. Am I allowed to say that? I don't mean that in a lecherous way. Maggie thinks you're pretty, too, so I hope it's safe for me to say so. Not that I don't find Maggie attractive. But you look more like a model--please don't reach for the feather duster again."

"Cheers. But there's more to it than just looking a certain way. It takes hard work, you know."

"I'm sure."

Just then, Maggie arrived outside the door, and, hearing voices, took a moment to listen in.

"Ricky, you'd better hurry and get those clothes off. Maggie might be here soon."

"Yeah, you're right. Good thing they're easier to take off than put on."

Curious, and a little concerned, Maggie hurried to unlock the door and swung it open, to see Linda removing her own coat from Ricky's frame.

"What the...?" Maggie sputtered.

"Oh, hey, Mags," Linda said casually. "This is your Ricky, is it?"

"Uh, yeah…only…are those Linda's clothes you're wearing, Ricky?"

He struggled hopelessly to retain a shred of dignity. "Yes, they are, Maggie. They are indeed Linda's clothes I'm wearing. But in my defense, I thought they were yours when I put them on."

"Oh, really?"

"He must *really* like you, Mags!" Linda said with a smirk. "That's what I call devotion--or perversion."

"Ricky," Maggie began with a frown, "is there something you need to talk to me about?"

"Can I explain over a cup of tea? Oh, and please don't tell Mrs. Beckersley about this."

Chapter 30

February 9th was a big night on television for Beatles fans in Britain. The music show *Top of the Pops* had announced that it would show not one, but two promotional videos that night for the new songs "Penny Lane" and "Strawberry Fields Forever." Of course, Maggie and Claire planned their evening around the show.

With only minutes before the program was to begin, the buzzer at the door sent Maggie up and running, like a Pavlovian-trained dog. She swung open the door and pulled in Ricky by his arm.

"Hurry, it's about to start! You're cutting it quite fine."

"Sorry. Hi, Claire."

"All right, Ricky?"

They hurried to the sofa in time for the program's opening titles, but then had to exercise a bit of patience until the films were actually presented to viewers.

"Have either of you heard the songs yet?" he asked the girls.

"I think I heard part of 'Strawberry Fields,'" Claire said. "It sounded a bit odd. Probably John's song, then."

"I haven't heard either of them," Maggie confessed.

"That's a surprise," Ricky said. "I thought you had the inside information and stuff, and got to hear new songs at the magazine before they're released."

"Nah, not Beatles songs. They keep things pretty close to the vest until they're good and ready."

"Hey, Mags," Claire pondered, "Strawberry Fields is somewhere in Liverpool, right?"

"Yeah, not far from John's house. I walked past the gates to it on Beaconsfield Road a few times with—"

She stopped herself as she was about to mention Jack's name. "—someone whose name I forget."

She exchanged a quick, uncomfortable glance with Claire. She knew it was an unconvincing way to end the sentence, and she didn't know why she stopped. Ricky certainly knew about Jack, and that Jack was not going to re-enter Maggie's life, but at that instant, she realized she didn't want to bring that part of her past to the evening's activities—even as just a quick mention. She hoped Ricky hadn't noticed.

The three of them paid only half attention to the show until the first clip, "Penny Lane," was introduced. The scenes of the street, intercut with shots of the Beatles and accompanying Paul's jaunty song about one of Liverpool's shopping districts, excited the girls to no end.

"Claire look! The number 46 bus! Ricky, we've taken that bus I don't know how many times."

"Really? Cool!" His eyes stayed transfixed to the TV screen.

"Shh, listen!" Claire ordered. The girls delighted in hearing the song's lyrics dedicated to their hometown. Maggie found herself getting teary-eyed; her boys hadn't forgotten their stomping grounds after all.

"Look at those moustaches!" Claire said. "They all have 'em! They look so different."

"They're just moustaches," Maggie countered. "They look more adult with them. I like them."

The film ended as Maggie wiped her eyes. "Oh, that was great! Bring on the next one!"

"Did you ever kiss someone with a moustache?" Claire queried.

"No, I don't think so."

Claire glanced at Ricky, who volunteered, "Neither have I."

"Well," Claire advised, "avoid one, is all I can say."

As they watched the "Strawberry Fields" film, each viewer had a different reaction. Maggie loved the surreal images, Ricky concentrated, trying to figure out what it all meant, and Claire made a face as if she had been sucking on a lemon. "Well," she said, "this song looks just as odd as it sounds. Why is there a piano under the tree? I don't get it."

"Well, it's different," Maggie conceded, "but it's cool! It's so surreal! And psychedelic. It's just great seeing them in something new again. What's the matter Claire? Don't you fancy them anymore?"

"Don't be daft, of course I do. It's just that they've come a long way since *A Hard Day's Night."*

As *Top of the Pops* continued, their interest waned.

"Hey," Ricky said, "today's the 9th, right?"

"For the next few hours, yes," Maggie said.

"I just realized--it was exactly three years ago today that I was home watching the Beatles' first time on *The Ed Sullivan Show*."

"Really? Exactly three years?"

"Yep, I'll never forget the date. And now look, here I am *in London* watching their new songs on TV again. Who would have ever thought? Not me."

"I do remember you told me about having your friends over to watch it."

"Oh, yeah, that was a great night. Everyone came over—Kenny, Dave, Elliot, Andrea-Claudia…and, uh…someone whose name I forget."

He shot Maggie a knowing wink and a grin. Oops, she thought, Ricky was on the ball tonight.

Ricky wasn't sure which kind of work day he enjoyed more at the *New London News*—the kind with a lot of hustle-bustle, when everyone seemed to be running in several directions at once (including himself), or the quiet days when half the staff seemed to be out somewhere, leaving him and a handful of co-workers holding the fort, and manning the phones.

It was on one of those quieter days, with the receptionist away from her desk on an errand, and the newsroom momentarily deserted, when Ricky was left to answer the ringing phone. He never really liked to answer calls, but tried to do so in as professional manner as possible.

"*New London News*, may I help you?"

"I have an anonymous tip for you," said a male voice on the other end. "Eric Sellers, the pop singer."

"*You're* Eric Sellers, the pop singer?"

"No! My anonymous tip is about Eric Sellers. You've heard of him, haven't you?"

"Well, he's a…pop singer. And your tip is…?"

"Anonymous."

"Yeah, I've got that. So, now that we've come full circle…" Ricky was getting the feeling that the mysterious person was just as new at passing along a tip as Ricky was at receiving one.

"I know for a fact," the voice continued, "that he's having an affair with a married woman," the voice said.

"Is Eric Sellers married?"

"No."

"Well, then technically, she's the one having an affair."

"But she's having it with *him*, that's my point. Do you want to know who it is?"

"You just said it's Eric Sellers."

"No, the *woman*!"

"You're not going to say that she's anonymous too, are you?"

"No, no, only my tip is anonymous. It's Bootsy Rogers."

"What, you mean *you're* Bootsy Rogers?" Ricky asked.

"No! He's having an affair with Bootsy Rogers! Why would I say I'm Bootsy Rogers if I'm giving you an anonymous tip? I'm not even a woman, anyway. I don't even *sound* like Bootsy Rogers. People are always telling me that I don't sound anything like her."

Ricky, having never heard of Bootsy Rogers before, could only offer a shrug in response to the information, with a simple "Okay."

"What do you mean, okay? Are you sure you really work there? You know who Bootsy Rogers is, don't you?"

It sounded like a good name for a go-go dancer, Ricky thought, but since his answers had thus far only succeeded in irritating the informant, he treated it as a rhetorical question.

The voice continued. "I happen to know that she's going to spend the night with him at his house in St. John's Wood. She's going to sneak in the back way, around ten o'clock, to avoid being seen by the press. But you'll know to hide in the backyard. There's a row of hedges right behind the house."

"How do you know all this?" Ricky quizzed the caller, figuring the best defense is a good offense. "Are you her husband, hoping she'll get caught or something? And why are you telling me this?"

"Oi, Sunshine, someone with an anonymous tip is *supposed* to know more than everyone else. That's what makes it a tip. And, to answer your second question, you're the *New London News*. It's your job to spy on people like that and put it in the paper, isn't it?"

"Did you call any other newspapers about this?"

"No. Your paper happens to be my favourite. It's very absorbent."

"How sweet."

"I'm running out of coins. Gotta dash."

"Wait, I didn't catch your name."

"Bert Weckerley—oh, damn! Forget I said that! I'm supposed to be anonymous!"

"So you said."

"Promise you'll forget my name!"

"I promise."

The phone clicked as the line went dead.

As a few co-workers began to meander back into the newsroom, Ricky stood at the desk, perplexed—not just by the nature of the phone conversation, but from being unsure of what to do next. Should he tell anyone? Did he really want to be a part of uncovering some private matter as a big scandal? He reasoned that he should tell Derek, and let the boss decide what to do with the information. After all, he merely answered the phone, so his conscience could still be clear.

He knocked on Derek's half-open office door.

"Yes, Ricky?"

"I think I just got an anonymous tip about something."

"Oh?"

"Someone just called and said Eric Sellers, the pop singer, is having a secret affair."

Derek sat up with considerable interest. "Is that so. Did they say anymore?"

"He said the woman he's with is someone named Bootsy Rogers.

He said she'll be sneaking into Sellers' house tonight around ten, and the informant suggested we hide in the bushes to get pictures or something."

A beaming smile spread across Derek's face. "Oh, really! Well, well! Good ol' naughty Bootsy."

"Pardon my ignorance, but who's Bootsy Rogers?"

"To put it kindly, Mavis Rogers--affectionately known to one and all as Bootsy, and probably a few other nicknames as well--is a two-bit actress of severely limited talent."

"That's putting it kindly?"

Derek picked up one of several copies of the *New London News* spread across his desk and searched through its pages. "Our television columnist, Dan Waters, wrote about her just last week. Ah, here it is. He says, 'She's not so much an actress as she is a blonde, smiling mannequin whose services are usually called upon whenever a sitcom producer deep within the bowels of the BBC shakes his head and says, 'This show needs a bit of crumpet, get me Bootsy Rogers.'"

He smirked as he put down the paper. "She's played the wacky next-door-neighbour type in four or five sitcoms over the past few years, was terrible in all of them."

Ricky decided to be brave and challenge the idea of exposing her newly-detailed private activities. "So, that's a good enough reason to print a rumour based on a tip?"

"Of course not," Derek said. "We're not cold-blooded monsters, Ricky. We wouldn't do that."

"Good."

"So you and Reg will have to provide confirmation."

"What?"

"We know where Sellers lives in St. John's Wood. So, you two need to be there by ten o'clock tonight, and wait for Bootsy to arrive."

"But—"

"Good job, Ricky. Looks like you're fitting in quite well here!"

Ricky decided immediately that this was one assignment he was never going to tell Maggie about, if he could help it.

As the last of the daylight faded from the sky that evening, a single lit bulb faintly illuminated the back door of the Sellers residence, leaving the rest of the back yard in almost total darkness.

Ricky and Reg crouched behind the row of tall, thick hedges stretching across the width of the yard, near a low stone wall separating the yard from the adjacent property. There the two felt confident they could observe Bootsy's clandestine arrival without being discovered.

Ricky hated being there at all, but he knew he might as well concentrate on the mission at hand, and kick himself for it later.

"How can you take any pictures when it's so dark out?" he whispered to Reg.

"High speed film, plus a long shutter exposure, plus the proper aperture setting, equal a great shot. I've done this a thousand times, Sunshine, trust me. Just take notes of whatever you see."

Ricky peered through the shrubs at the back of the house. "At the moment, I only see a few trash cans, doing nothing at all. And it's too dark to write what I'm seeing, or to see what I'm writing."

"Didn't you bring your torch?"

Ricky recoiled, aghast at the idea.

"Torch? My God, isn't that be a little excessive? I wouldn't want to set the whole yard ablaze."

"No, no, you dunce. I mean a…what do you call it…a flashlight?"

"Oh, right."

"You're still speaking American," Reg reminded him with considerable annoyance.

"I forgot to bring it."

"I thought you might." He reached into his pocket. "Lucky for you, I didn't."

He handed Ricky a small flashlight. "Don't wave it about and attract attention."

"But what if—"

A sudden rustling in the hedge twenty feet further along caused them both to freeze.

"What was that?" Ricky whispered, even more softly than he had been to that point.

"Maybe a bird, or a rodent," Reg whispered back.

"What do you mean, a rodent?"

"I don't know...squirrel, rat, wombat..."

They heard the sound again. Ricky nervously pointed the flashlight in that direction. He saw the backside of a woman protruding from the hedge, as she attempted to wedge herself between a gap in the shrubs and a man alongside her.

"Give me more room! Move over!" she said in a strained whisper, nudging her companion to the side.

Ricky steadied the light beam on her.

"Wait a minute--Maggie?"

The female backside jolted and fell backwards into the clearing, like a squirted watermelon seed, revealing that it did indeed belong to Maggie. She sat startled on the ground. She squinted and held her hand up to shield the light beam from her eyes.

"Ricky?"

"What are you doing here?"

"Well, I...err...Oh, hell, what's the use. I can't even think of a good lie. Okay, we got a tip about Bootsy Rogers having an affair with Eric Sellers, and..." Her speech slowed down to reflect her increasing humiliation. "And...we're waiting for her," she mumbled. "This is Ken, my photographer."

Ken poked his head out from the lush greenery. "Oi, put out that torch! Oh, hello, Reg, is that you back there? How are ya?"

"Cheers, Ken. How's things?"

Maggie tried to turn the tables on Ricky. "And what are *you* doing here?"

Ricky shrugged. "I work for the *New London News*, remember? But I thought you guys at the *Express* were above this sort of thing."

"I am—I mean, we are—but we got this anonymous tip, you see, and my editor thought that, since I've already written a few pieces on Eric Sellers, and his less-than-skyrocketing rise to fame..."

"Wait," Ricky interrupted, "you got the same tip we did? That guy on the phone told me he was giving us an exclusive."

"And you believed him? Oh, really, Ricky."

Reg interrupted with a prolonged "Shush! Sellers might hear you and call the coppers."

Another noise, this time from the opposite end of the hedge, revealed a cluster of still more reporters clumsily making their way along in the dark, searching for a choice observation spot. Ricky could hear them only marginally better than he could see them.

"Oops, excuse me…Oh, hello, Clive."

"Evening, Reg. 'Ere, is that Ken down there?"

"Yeah, it's me. Evening, Clive. Waiting for good ol' Bootsy's arrival, eh? You bring the sandwich I asked you for?"

Before he knew it, Ricky felt a procession of bodies squeezing their way past him, as they tried to cram into whatever gaps in the shrubbery were still available.

"What time is it?" someone whispered.

"Just after ten," another answered.

"Oh, good. If she's coming, she'll be along any minute now."

"What if she knows we're all back here waiting," Ricky pondered, "and decides just to use the front door after all?"

"She's not that clever."

The gathering of reporters and photographers stayed silent for a moment, crouching and waiting, before a voice let out an emphatic, "Come on, Bootsy baby, time's a wasting."

"Let's see ya, Bootsy," another voice chimed in, "You're about to make history! I've got a tenner on you as well!"

"Oh, for goodness sake," Ricky sighed. He scrambled along the back of the hedge, careful not to trip over random feet and camera bags, and crawled to reach Maggie. There was just enough light to see the frown on her face. He imagined that his own frown was just as visible for her to see.

"Let's get out of here?" he suggested.

"Yes, let's."

They asked their respective colleagues to report back to them in the morning, in case Bootsy and Eric did indeed make history that night.

A short while later, they sat in Maggie's favourite snack shop. It was about to close, but the owner knew and liked Maggie, so he took some extra time tidying the shop to let them share a few moments over a cup of tea.

Ricky tiredly rubbed his eyes with the palms of his hands. The harsh florescent lighting overhead made him look even more ragged than he felt.

"What a night," he said.

"A bloody palaver."

"A what?"

"Oh, that's lot of bother over nothing."

"I guess all of the tabloids, including mine, will have screaming headlines tomorrow about Bootsy Rogers sneaking into Eric Sellers' back door, complete with photos—as if it were actually newsworthy."

He looked out the shop window and into the distance. "Back home, and in school, I was so excited about learning to be a good journalist. But this stuff is a joke. And *you're* definitely too good to be sent on an assignment like that. You've won awards!"

"Goody bags, remember? Anyway, this was just a one-off. I hope," she said, a little meekly.

"Not for me. Derek's been sending me out on all sorts of ridiculous stories like this." He shifted a little uncomfortably, avoiding looking her in the eye. "I just…I just don't want you to be ashamed of me."

Maggie sat up straight. "Ashamed of you? Ricky, I'm the opposite of ashamed. I'm so proud of you!"

"Why?"

"Oh, let me count the ways…Generally, I'm proud of you because you've been settling in so well here, so far from home, which I know isn't easy. But more importantly, I'm proud of you because you have enough personal integrity to *know* the difference between real journalism, and what they make you do at the *New London News*. And you obviously don't have much say in the matter now, of course, but it's just for a few months. Once you're back home, you can re-join the world of real journalism again."

Her unfailing words of encouragement were, for the first time, beginning to fail.

"I don't know," he sighed. "I feel as if I'll have the scarlet letter 'T' for 'Tabloid' sewn into my soul forever--or at the very least on my resume."

"That's a bit dramatic, no?"

"Maybe Clark has the right idea. Broadcasting. Radio, maybe even TV. We're having a ball playing around with his little homemade recording studio. And he's got his foot in the door at the BBC—well, maybe just a toe—but it seems really exciting. I don't know if I could get into anything like that back home, but I think I'd like to try."

A tap on the shop window drew their attention to some of the reporters and photographers they had left behind in the thickets of Eric Sellers' back yard. The scruffy crew all looked quite happy and pleased with themselves. Maggie guessed they were probably drunk, or well on the way. Ken the photographer opened the door and stuck his head in.

"Hey, you two left too early. You missed the best part!"

"Did Bootsy show up?" Maggie asked.

"Read about it tomorrow!"

The others laughed as Ken closed the door, joining them on their way down the street.

"Prat," Maggie grumbled. "Ricky, don't worry. You'll find your true calling. From what you just said, maybe you already have."

"Maybe. But I wish it would call a little louder, and faster. It's been easy for you. Everything seemed to fall right into place for you."

Maggie suddenly recognized those words--she used them to tell Curly Shirley the same thing once. "Oh, not even. I did work hard, remember, putting together my little booklet, trying to get anyone in Liverpool to notice…but I had no idea someone from the magazine would read it and offer me the job. That's just pure luck." She flashed her familiar warm smile at him again and reached across the table to take his hands in hers. "But I'm even luckier that you're here."

For the first time that evening, Ricky smiled back.

Chapter 31

Maggie often received mail addressed to her care of her magazine office, so the pile of envelopes that had just been dropped on her desk one early May morning was no surprise. The letters were usually responses to her articles--not fan mail exactly, she didn't want to feel too conceited by calling it that, but half the pile was usually from readers complimenting her on an article well done, and the other half of the pile was from readers trying to correct her regarding a date she'd gotten wrong, or the middle name of a rock star, if she'd only used the initial. Of course, half of the people complaining were wrong themselves. Maggie wondered if they really had nothing better to do than write her notes of nit-picks in her work. Still, it was their stamp, and it gave her a break from working hard on her current assignment.

Rifling through the envelopes, one in particular caught her attention. It was unlike the others, as her address was printed on the envelope, not hand-written, and there was a stamp with the sender's address in the corner. It looked important.

Using her steel letter opener to slice along the envelope, she found a couple sheets of paper. She began to read:

> *"Dear Maggie Carter,*
>
> *We are pleased to inform you that you have been nominated for Entertainment Journalist of the Year award at the National Media Awards. We hope you are able to attend our awards*
> *Banquet on the 20th of May, please RSVP for yourself and a guest of your choice. Tickets and venue information are overleaf.*
> *Congratulations,*
>
> > *Yours Sincerely,*
> > *Albert Monroe*
> > *(Head of Nominations Committee)"*

Maggie had to read it twice to be sure she wasn't seeing things. This was the first time she'd been officially recognised for her work.

"What's that then?" Tina asked, sitting at the next desk.

"I think I've been nominated for a National Media Award."

"Really? Oh my, that's huge! Congratulations, Mags! Let me see!" She took the invitation to give it a closer look. "The magazine won one of these last year. It's very prestigious. Go tell Sharon!"

"I can't believe it. Me! Nominated!" Maggie beamed. "I'm going to an awards dinner!"

The conversation was beginning to draw attention, as the other journalists in the office began to crowd around Maggie, so she could tell them all, including Sharon, her good news. She could hardly take in all the offers of congratulations, she was so excited.

Tina spoke up from reading the letter. "Says here you can take a guest. Who are you going to take?"

Maggie didn't need to think about it. "I'm going to take Ricky."

The Empire Room in the Dorchester Hotel was a fitting venue for the National Media Awards. It was a grand ballroom, with high ceilings, chandeliers and hardwood floors. A dais for distinguished speakers on the stage took up one end of the hall, whilst the rest was filled with large tables, forty or so, seating about ten people each. Name cards were placed at each table, with a centre piece indicating which publication or company belonged there. A few bottles of bubbly and champagne glasses rested on the white table cloth.

The attendees arrived and gathered at the hotel entrance amid considerable attention from press photographers and onlookers. Maggie, Ricky (in his rented tuxedo), and the other invited colleagues from the *British Music Express* found their table and took their seats—but not for long. The custom at an event like this was to mingle with fellow guests, collect gossip, wheel & deal, and, for some of the veteran journalists, reminisce about the good old days.

"This certainly seems like a big deal," Ricky said, looking around at the other guests in their evening dresses and tuxedos. "I feel like I'm crashing someone's wedding reception or something."

"I'm even more nervous now," Maggie said. "Part of me hopes I don't win. I don't want to have to get up on stage in front of all these people."

"Even if you're not hoping you'll win, I am."

She smiled at him. "You look so smart in your tux. Thanks for coming, Ricky. I need you here. It helps my nerves calm down--a little."

"Wouldn't miss it for the world. But you have everyone else at the table to support you, too."

Sharon leaned in towards Maggie. "You should really use your time here to mingle. Make connections. Meet the competition and editors from bigger magazines. That's what this business is all about, if you want to progress, anyway."

"Are you saying you want me to look for another job?"

"No, but you never know who could help you at some point down the line. Everyone here is looking to get ahead, whether they admit it or not. Go on, then. Tina can introduce you to a few of them."

Maggie looked around the room at the clusters of people standing chatting together whilst sipping from their champagne flutes. She leaned over to Ricky.

"I think I'm going to have to introduce myself to a few people."

"Yeah, that's fine, I'll do what I can to help you," he said.

As the evening went on, several courses of the meal were served, and the odd speech was made, explaining that the awards would be given out after the last course and coffee. With each passing minute, Maggie felt her nerves twinge a little more, but speaking to the various other people who were up for awards made her feel slightly better. She wasn't exactly on her own.

Tina, speaking with an older gentleman with a comb over consisting of only the dozen strands of hair he had left, broke off the conversation and dashed over to Maggie.

"I've just been talking to Oswald Osborne. He's the chief editor of *Much Music*, and there's an opening for a music journalist at one of his other publications. We were talking about you. He really likes your work."

"What? But I already have a job that I like. And I don't know if I could work for anyone named Oswald Osbourne—not with a straight face, anyway."

"No, you haven't heard the best part yet! The job is in New York! As in America. He's starting up a new magazine there. A dream job!"

Maggie's eyes widened, as did Ricky's. They stared at each other for a moment, letting themselves imagine the possibilities, then Maggie shook herself out of the fog. "I can't afford to move to New York. I have things, people, and responsibilities here. I wouldn't move all the way there just for a job. Unless it paid a fortune. Maybe *you* should try for it."

"If you win the award tonight," said Tina, "you will probably get offered jobs from a lot of rival magazines. Trust me, New York would be the best opportunity for your career. Just go introduce yourself, you don't have to accept a marriage proposal, just go over there and open some doors, as it were. Besides, he wants to wish you luck on your nomination."

"Can't hurt just talking to the guy," Ricky said with a shrug.

"Okay, I can do that. I'll introduce myself. I'll be a few minutes."

Maggie, did her best to be the picture of confidence as she approached Osbourne.

At the table, Tina took a moment to look Ricky up and down. "So you're Maggie's American 'friend'? I bet *you* would like her to get a job in New York."

Ricky shrugged. "Sure, but that's got to be something she'd want."

"Hmm, that's very modern of you, Ricky."

"It is?"

"But you don't fool me. So what do you do?"

He had been dreading that question since the moment Maggie invited him to the event. "Oh, I, uh, I work for thenewlondonnews," he mumbled quickly, looking down at his rented shoes.

"The what?" she strained to understand.

"*The New London News.*" He hated hearing himself say the words out loud.

"Oh yeah, I don't read that. Do you like working there?"

"Well, I'm learning from it, I guess. It goes towards my college credits back home."

"I'm sensing you don't really like it then."

He paused for a moment, and shook his head. "It's not what I thought I was signing up for. They have me doing all kinds of crazy assignments. It doesn't feel like proper journalism, if you know what I mean."

"Listen, Ricky, as long as the paper sells, and you do what they tell you, you're doing okay. It's all about sales at the end of the day. Don't let it put you off. You're just, well, sort of a journalistic tart at the moment, that's all."

Ricky took a sip of his drink--more like a gulp. "Wow. But I'm just not sure I'm cut out for it. I really thought I was, but working there... The people are okay, don't get me wrong, but I wouldn't want to do that kind of job for the rest of my life."

"So what would you *want* to do for the rest of your life?"

Ricky shrugged again. "I don't know. I have this friend, Clark, and he's doing some really cool stuff with broadcasting. I was thinking I might enjoy that. Radio, or TV. But it's probably really difficult to get into. And I think I'm more of a writer than a talker."

Tina grabbed his hand and dragged him across the room. "Nonsense. You're smart, good looking, you speak well, and you can read and write. That's all there is to it."

"It is?"

"That's more than ninety percent of your colleagues can say about themselves. It's mainly *who* you know, not *what* you know. You just have to get talking to the right people." Still grasping his hand, she approached a man who had quite the crowd around him, and elbowed her way through. "Ainsley! It's been such a long time!"

"Tina! My favorite crush!" Ainsley said with a twinkle in his eye. "How are you, darling? Nice to see you again. How's Tom?"

"Oh, I dumped him last year. Caught him with his pants down, so to speak. And he wasn't alone. You'd have to ask his new bit of stuff how he is."

"Aw, the man's a fool to himself, doing that to you. But now that you're free of him, I know I wouldn't mind doing--"

"Ainsley, this is my friend Ricky, he's from America, and he's looking to get into broadcasting. What do you reckon? Ricky, this is Ainsley Wallace, he does a lot of the hiring and firing at ATV."

Ainsley reached out for Ricky's hand and shook it vigorously. "Nice to meet you Ricky. Tell me, have you been working in broadcasting long?"

"No, I'm working as a journalistic tar--er, as a newspaper journalist at the moment."

"Oh really, which paper?"

"The, err...thenewlondonnews," Ricky mumbled.

"The what?"

"*The New London News*," he repeated with greater clarity, and accompanying shame.

"Oh, I thought you said you're a *journalist*!" Ainsley chuckled with considerable gusto, as Tina playfully poked him in the side. "Sorry, old joke in the business. Yes, my brother's friend's cousin, Geoffrey, used to work there."

"Small world," Ricky replied with a weak smile.   He felt about two inches tall.

"Tell me, are they still making up half of their stories?"

For a moment Ricky didn't know what to say. He tried to be as diplomatic as possible. "Well, let's just say if it's a slow news day, they'll find something to print, no matter what it is."

Ainsley let out a hearty laugh, as did the people gathered around him.

"Yes, that sounds like them. Very good answer. Geoffrey got into trouble trying to break into Princess Margaret's boudoir for an exclusive interview. Can you imagine? I don't know what he thought he was going to do—interview her on the loo or something. The security guards made quick work of him. Poor bloke, can only breathe out of one nostril now.

Listen, get yourself some broadcasting experience, then come and see me at ATV in a few years. Tina's got my number."

"Do I ever," Tina said, rolling her eyes.

Ricky smiled and shook his hand again. "Thank you, I will."

Ainsley nodded and turned back to his audience, as Tina guided Ricky back to their table.

"A few years?" he said incredulously, "I'll only be here until June. But he seems like a nice guy. He's the first Ainsley I've ever met, anyway. We don't have any in the States."

"He's a lech, but a harmless one. He's not joking about the experience though. He won't give you a job if you don't prove yourself first."

"How do I do that?"

"I don't know. But it's something for you to think about."

The guests enjoyed their dinner, even as they interrupted it with visits to each other's tables for more hellos and back-slapping. Ricky sat at the table watching Maggie wolf down her food before she resumed her hobnobbing from one group of people to the next. What was that she had said earlier, about needing him there with her? She'd only managed to speak two words to him, which were "having fun?" She didn't even stick around to hear the answer--which was okay, he guessed. She was bound to be caught up in all the work related stuff and socializing, but boredom began to dominate his thoughts-- and yet he felt overwhelmed by the event at the same time.

A bit of feedback from the dais microphone sent the speakers squeaking, as everyone turned their attention to the evening's host, a former BBC presenter named Darren Hull, dressed in a rather snazzy white and powder blue suit—perfect for someone not at all shy in the spotlight.

"Can I have your attention please, we're ready to present this evening's awards. Would everyone like to take their seats?"

The hall quieted down as people returned to their tables. Maggie reclaimed her seat next to Ricky, her nerves seemingly all gone. "You won't believe the people I've been talking to," she whispered. "I'll tell you about them later."

Darren Hull gave a short speech, dropping names of celebrities he had interviewed and played tennis with through the years, and then reminded the audience of his own professional accomplishments (not that anyone had asked), before getting around to the meaning of these annual awards. He assured everyone that just to be nominated made them winners—something not even the nominees believed. Then he began to read out the categories, the nominations and the winners. The recipient of each award was invited on stage to collect their oval-shaped, engraved plaque, whilst the audience applauded and a photographer took each winner's photograph. It was all going pretty much as Maggie expected, then it came to her category.

"And the nominees for the 1967 Entertainment Journalist of the Year are: Richard Banks – *Much Music Magazine*; Dennis Maitland - *Our Planet*; Cyril Splevak - *The Radio Times*; and Maggie Carter – *British Music Express*."

Maggie held her breath.

"And the winner is...Maggie Carter, from the *British Music Express*!"

Maggie's table gave the biggest cheer so far that evening as the rest of the room applauded. Shocked, Maggie rose as Tina and Sharon each gave her a big hug, beating Ricky to the punch. The others reached to give her pats on the back as she walked over to the dais. She was aware of the applause but it was drowned out by the beating of her own heart. Her legs felt like jelly.

Up on stage she shook Hull's hand and received her plaque. She was determined to keep her speech short and simple—and she succeeded.

"Thanks so much to everyone at the National Media Association who voted for me, and to my wonderful colleagues at the magazine, who taught me so much. I hope to use this as inspiration as I continue on with my career."

She held up the plaque and smiled for the photographer, then as quickly as all that, she returned to her table as Hull went on to announce the nominees for best magazine cover.

Everyone at Maggie's table congratulated her and admired the plaque.

"That was smashing, Mags!" Tina gushed.

"I can't believe it," Maggie said, still stunned. "My mum will be over the moon!"

Ricky gave her a warm hug, without competing with the arms of others. "I knew you'd do it," he said. "I'm so proud of you!"

"I can't believe it," she said again.

The *British Music Express* magazine won an award for best Christmas issue, which Sharon collected on behalf of the entire magazine staff, and once the final award was given out--the big one, for Best Entertainment Publication, which went to *Much Music* magazine--Darren Hull thanked everyone for attending and congratulated all those who won. The evening would last as long as the last people standing, so the band kept playing.

"Whenever you're ready to leave, I've got a little surprise for you," Ricky said.

"What surprise?"

He shrugged his shoulders. "Oh, just a little something, to say congratulations. It's back at my place."

"Oh that's so sweet of you," she beamed, "we'll go soon. But I don't want to look like I'm grabbing my award and running."

Spotting Oswald Osbourne again, this time as he approached their table, Ricky groaned a little to himself. What more could this guy have to say to quash Ricky's self-esteem?

"Maggie," Oswald said, with a whiff of alcohol on his breath, "Congratulations on your win tonight. I was hoping you'd be victorious."

"Oh thank you."

"As you might know, every year after these awards I throw a little after party back at my club, Hampstead House. I keep it very exclusive, but you're most welcome to come."

"Oh I--um-thank you."

Oswald then turned to Tina. "Tina, you're coming as well, I trust?" he asked eagerly.

"Of course, wouldn't miss it," she said.

"Jolly good. See you all soon." He left with a little extra spring in his step.

"You're coming Maggie, aren't you?" Tina asked. "He really does know how to throw a good party. Come for an hour or two, I'll look after you. It's the place to make contacts on a real one-to-one level, much better than here. And last year they de-bagged some of the guys from the *New London News*—oh, sorry, Ricky."

"Is Ricky invited as well?" Maggie asked a bit anxiously.

The question caused Tina's speech to suddenly take on a halting, unsure rhythm. "Oh, I guess so. Er, didn't Oswald just invite the both of you?"

"Not technically," Maggie said. "But Ricky is my date for the evening."

Tina leaned in closer. "It's really quite exclusive, Maggie. Oswald does all of the inviting personally, so…"

"Maybe I should go catch up to him and ask him?"

"Ooh, I don't know if that's a good idea. A bit forward."

Ricky assumed--Maggie being Maggie--that she would indeed hurry to find Oswald and ask anyway, protocol or no protocol. But he saw her hesitating as she looked to him with a look of helplessness in her eyes. He got the picture.

"You go ahead," he said, trying to put an end to the growing discomfort--both Maggie's and his own. "I don't think I'm invited."

Tina was not being helpful. "Oswald didn't even invite his brother's friend's cousin Geoffrey when *he* was working for the *New London News*," she said. "Although, come to think of it, Geoffrey never got invited to any of the parties I've been to."

"I'm tired anyway," Ricky said. "You go, Maggie. You've got contacts to make."

"I'm sorry, Ricky…but I don't…" she stammered.

"That's okay. I'll see you tomorrow, though?"

"Yes, definitely, one o'clock, my place."

She gave him a hug and kiss, and he left, feeling awful.

What a lousy night, he thought.

The next day, at one o'clock sharp, Ricky arrived at Maggie's with the little surprise he had for her. He knocked on the door and waited eagerly, with the wrapped gift behind his back. Surely Maggie's appreciation for the gift would wipe away the memories of last night.

Linda answered the door.

"Oh hi, Ricky. Come on in. Didn't you get Maggie's message?"

With a familiar, sinking feeling, he asked, "What message? Is she hungover, and can't get up?"

"She had to go into work--something about a big meeting, but she asked if you can come back later, at about 6 o'clock?"

Okay, he thought, trying to remain calm--technically it's not another cancellation, like last time, it's only a postponement. "Yeah, okay, 6 p.m."

He headed back to his flat, clutching the gift. The wrapping paper was beginning to crease—a lot.

He wasn't sure what to do with all of this unexpected free time, but he knew he was feeling frustrated, and restless. Maybe Clark would be around, or Mitchell, the guy upstairs, who seemed like an okay guy; he was an American, too, and they had talked a few times about school, music, and seemed to have the same likes and dislikes. But Mitchell was a bit odd, calling everyone "man," and usually had some sickly sweet aroma wafting from his flat. His eyes were often bloodshot, too. Probably allergies, Ricky concluded. He decided to convince Clark to get some fresh air, and accompany him to get lunch at a local snack stand.

The sign poised above the stand claimed to offer "authentic American-style hot dogs." That could be a nice bit of home after so many months away. Ricky, being a hotdog connoisseur, proved to be a harsh judge, and was not impressed. Clark had nothing to compare his hotdog with, so he gobbled it down without complaint.

"You should visit my neck of the woods someday," Ricky suggested, "and you'll see what a real American hotdog tastes like."

"Maybe I will," Clark said. "I'd like to see New York someday as well."

"Oh, it's the greatest city in the world. London comes a close second, but there's nothing like New York."

"Right, you buy me the plane ticket and I'll be there before you know it."

Ricky laughed at the suggestion. "Sorry, but that's not gonna happen."

Clark had a new idea in between bites. "Fancy we do a bit with the recording equipment later?"

"Sure, sounds like fun, if I don't get home too late after seeing Maggie."

He was just returning home from his disappointing hot dog lunch when the phone rang.

"Hello, Ricky?"

"Maggie?"

"Yeah, it's me. Listen, I know we're supposed to meet at six, but I'm still in the city, I'm not going to make it home in time. But can you meet me at Annie's cafe, say in an hour, for a quick meal?"

"But that's a half-hour tube ride just to get there."

"Yeah, I know, but we can still get a bite to eat together."

Stifling a burp from his imposter of a hotdog, he wasn't thrilled with the suggestion, but he didn't want to disappoint Maggie. And at least it was a chance to see her and give her the gift. "Yeah, okay, I'll leave for the station now."

Annie's Café was an artsy hot spot for young people. Its new décor featured a kaleidoscope of bright colors, with flowers painted on the walls, and a partition of beads hanging from the doorway. Ricky and Maggie often met there when they were given the same lunch hour.

She arrived first, and sat at her favourite table by the window, sipping at a cup of tea, watching for him, half-listening to the Hollies' latest song, "Carrie Ann," playing on the shop's sound system.

Before she got to her last sip, she saw Ricky waving at her from across the street. She asked a waitress for another cup of tea.

The waitress brought Ricky a fresh cup of tea as he sat down.

"I've never drank so much tea in my life back home," he said. "I'm getting quite fond of it. Well, I'm used to it, anyway."

"How was your day?"

"Not much going on today, really. How was the party?"

"Oh, it was okay. Nothing Earth-shaking. But I talked with a lot of people, don't even remember half of them now. And I doubt they'll remember me, either."

"But you're an award-winner now."

"Yeah, that's cool, gotta admit it! So, what did you do today?"

"When Linda told me you had to work, I just went back home, went out with Clark for a hotdog. You Brits have a lot to learn about hotdogs."

"Sorry about earlier, I couldn't get out of the staff meeting. It's for the big Sgt. Pepper issue I was telling you about."

"It's okay. You have to go to work." It wasn't really okay, he thought, but again, he had no say in the matter.

Maggie smiled. "Let's order some food, I'm starving."

She ordered the egg, chips and beans while Ricky went for a lighter option of tomato soup and a bread roll. As they waited for the waitress to clear their plates, Ricky reached down for the bag between his feet. "I still have to give you your surprise."

He brought out a wrapped gift, small enough to fit in his palm. "This is for you. Congratulations."

"For me? Wow! Thank you, Ricky, that's so lovely of you. You shouldn't have got me anything, how did you know I was going to win?"

"There was no doubt in my mind. Besides, if you hadn't of won, I would have called it your consolation prize."

She giggled as she unwrapped the gift, revealing a small perfume bottle. "Oh, thank you, so much. That's really lovely, and it's Sophisticated Lady, my favourite kind."

Ricky blushed a little. "I know, I saw it on your dresser when I was trying your clothes on."

That comment caught the attention of the waitress collecting their plates. She gave Ricky a look, complete with raised eyebrow.

"Oh, I didn't really try on her clothes," he explained with a pained smile. "They were, uh, her roommate's clothes. Her roommate is...very...tall." He decided to quit while he was behind, as the waitress silently left to attend to the other tables.

Maggie checked her watch. "Oh, damn, I'm really sorry, but I've got to get going in a few minutes."

"Already? But we practically just got here. You asked me to come meet you. What about your food?"

"I know, I wanted to catch up with you after yesterday. I feel like I ditched you to go to the party. But I didn't want to put a foot wrong in front of all those big shots. I'm sorry."

"Well, I guess it's not your fault that I was called a journalistic tart the same night you won a major award--and I was called that by the same guy who didn't invite me to that party."

"Yes, like you just said, it's not my fault. And thank you for this, really, but I do have to get going."

Ricky felt like expressing a bit more of his frustration, even as Maggie was getting ready to leave. "Okay, but it did take me almost forty-five minutes to get here. For soup. I wasn't even that hungry."

"Then why did you order it?"

"So you wouldn't have to eat alone. You said you were starving."

"I was only trying to find some time for us to spend together, Ricky."

"Yeah, but twenty minutes here, ten minutes there...I don't think it's too much to ask for us to have a proper, leisurely meal together, without you constantly looking at your watch."

"Sorry."

"You've been cancelling on me a lot lately. Is that a subtle way of telling me you're bored with me or something?"

"No, that's not true at all! It's just my job, I have to be where they say and *when* they say."

"But you've already had your meeting. Where do you have to be now?"

"I said I'd go with Tina to Mr. Osbourne's office. He wants to tell us about his New York project."

"I thought you weren't interested in moving to New York," he sulked.

"Doesn't mean I don't want to hear him out. He hasn't even offered it to me, or anyone else. Now, please, I really have to go."

"Yeah, okay, I don't want to make you late."

"Don't be like that, Ricky."

"Like what? You're the one who seems to be avoiding me."

"I'm not." She checked her watch again. "But if you keep *accusing* me of avoiding you, I just might begin to!"

"Yeah, well, I'd hardly notice the difference," he mumbled.

"I don't want to argue. Even if I did, I don't have time."

"Well, we could make an appointment to argue, but you'd probably break it."

"You know, the way you're acting, I'm tempted to break your nose instead! I'm leaving."

"Go on then, I'm not stopping you."

Maggie hurried out of the café, feeling hurt, and leaving the perfume on the table.

Chapter 32

It was Sunday morning—the cloudiest, greyest, gloomiest Sunday morning ever, or so Ricky estimated. His fight with Maggie left him feeling angry, heartsick, even disoriented. He got dressed and took a walk, only because sitting in his flat, not knowing whether to phone her, or hope that she might phone him, was driving him crazy.

London suddenly felt like a very big, very lonely city. He had long gotten over the novelty and excitement of his first days there--seeing a red double-decker bus go by, or walking in the neon glow of Piccadilly Circus at night. He wasn't a tourist, anyway, he was a resident—albeit a temporary one. But the one person who made his time in London such a joy now seemed to be gone. True, she was still living only a few blocks away, but it felt as if Maggie had simply disappeared.

Two days passed, with no word from her. Then another day. No more late-night "cuddle" phone calls. They stopped coming, as did all other forms of communication from her.

Four days passed. Then five. Ricky continued to go through the motions of working on still more nonsense stories for the *New London News*, but he did so under a cloud of misery. Why not just call Maggie to apologize? It made sense; he knew he had acted like a petulant child. But maybe she didn't want to hear from him. Was he really wrong to say what he said? Shouldn't he have the right to speak up if he thought he was being taken for granted?

He hated spending time in the flat, but also worried that he might miss a call from her if he went out. At times he wanted to jump out of his skin. He found temporary distractions, knowing they were just temporary distractions sapped him of any interest. He just didn't feel comfortable being *anywhere*--unless it was with Maggie.

A full week went by, and Maggie hadn't heard a thing from Ricky. She felt awful about storming out on him, and wanted to go over to his place to put things right--but, she figured, he'd probably just slam the door in her face. She felt sympathetic for him, in a way. There he was, thousands of miles away from home, living by himself, and she had allowed work to consume her free time with him. But then, he knew that she had worked hard to get where she was, and that she'd have to continue working hard to move up in the world. He knew her career was important to her, so why was he being so stroppy about staff meetings? Why did everything have to go his way?

But it didn't matter whose fault the argument was. All Maggie could think about was missing him.

"Claire..." she said, entering the living room.

Claire was on the sofa reading the *New London News*. "This paper is rubbish. What a joke. To think trees had to die for this. You can see this photo was faked. Sean Connery would never wear a bib at the Savoy."

"Claire..."

"Aha?"

"Do you think I should be the one to go first, and speak to Ricky?"

"No way. He blew his top just because you had obligations. He doesn't own you, Mags."

"But I did ask him to come see me, and then I hurried out."

"Well, yes, there is that. But you were short on time, weren't you?"

"So, I should go see him?"

"Do you *want* to go see him?"

"Yes, I miss him terribly!"

"Oh, gee, we hadn't noticed, except for all of the times you've been moaning, 'I miss Ricky!'"

"Well, I *do* miss him, and I want to see him. But I'm afraid he'll tell me where to go."

Claire shook her head. "He wouldn't do that. But if you're worried, then don't give him the opportunity."

"So what should I do?"

"I'll tell you what my cousin Shelley once told me about relationships: Don't ever give in, even when you're wrong, because then they'll expect it all the time."

"That's hideous advice. Besides, didn't Shelley's husband leave her for the lady who ran that chip shop? They moved to a farm in Wales, didn't they?"

"That's beside the point," Claire grumbled. "I'm not saying I agree with the advice, I'm just relaying it to you."

"I think I'm going to go see Ricky. Or phone him. No, I'll go round there in person."

"Good for you. You tell him what's what. He really upset you, don't forget, and that's not on."

"But I want him back."

"Good. You'll get him back…after you tell him off."

Ricky knocked on Clark's hallway door, which always seemed to be half-open.

"Got a minute?" he said, poking his head in.

"Sure, mate. You're always welcome to enter my lair."

"I need you to interview me."

"Eh?"

"On your tape recorder. Interview me, you know, the way you do. I want you to ask me about Maggie."

Clark responded with a puzzled look. "Why?"

"I need to work out what happened, and if you ask me objective questions about it, maybe I can see things more clearly."

"You want me to ask you questions about your relationship with your girlfriend? Oh, I'm not sure. Sounds risky. I don't know much about that sort of thing, with girls. I'd be embarrassed."

"You have my permission to ask me anything. Talk to me like you did when we first did this, when you first interviewed me."

"What do you want me to ask you?"

"Tough questions."

"Well, if you say so. I'm willing to help."

Clark set up the microphones and switched on the tape recorder. As soon as he did so, he again became instantly possessed by the same aggressive spirit that took over his body each time he assumed the role of a no-nonsense BBC radio interviewer. He was the Jeckyll & Hyde of aspiring broadcasters.

"Right, well today we're talking with Ricky Kramer, who, I understand, has had a bit of a to-do with his beautiful, sweet, talented, award-winning girlfriend, Maggie. Is that right?"

"Yes."

"Oh, my, what have you done, Ricky?"

"Well, I guess I got impatient when she began to cancel several of our dates, due to her work."

"It put you off?"

"Yeah, it put me off."

"And when did this start to happen?"

"Over a period of the past month or two. It really became noticeable after she won her award."

"Oh, I see, so her winning the award and the praise she received from her peers afterwards triggered your feelings of jealousy, inadequacy, and selfishness?"

"Oh, I wouldn't say-"

"And her success has come right at a time when you've been unhappy with your own job working at that two-bit scandal rag, the *New London News*, yes?" Clark pressed.

"But I'm very happy for Maggie's success!" Ricky insisted.

"Sure, as long as she doesn't dare postpone a date with you in favour of working on her assignments, using her highly professional, award-winning journalistic skills, is that it?"

"It's okay with me if she's busy with her work--within reason. But sometimes I wonder if she's begun to use it as an excuse not to see me."

Clark leaned into the microphone. "Ladies and gentlemen, if you've tuned in late, you are listening to our guest, the self-absorbed American, Ricky Kramer, who is fast becoming a snivelling, whiny, insecure toad--but who, by his own admission, still claims to be happy with Maggie's success."

"I *am* happy for her success!"

"You just accused her of using her job to avoid being with you.

Now why would she do that?"

"You're right, I shouldn't have said that."

"Is she happy with you?"

"I think so…or I thought so. We were very happy until this."

"You mean, she was happy until *you* started giving her a hard time?"

"Oh, I don't know. Wow, now I feel like a terrible person. I guess I really am a snivelling—whatever you said."

"I believe it was 'a snivelling, whiny, insecure toad'."

"Yeah, that's me."

Clark suddenly reached forward and slapped Ricky across the face. "Good God, pull yourself together man! She's a wonderful girl, and she wants to be with you, but she has responsibilities! This is the real world. She'll get sacked if she doesn't do her assignments. Apologize to her and give her some space, and you two will be fine."

Ricky slumped in his chair. "You're right," he conceded, rubbing the sting from his cheek.

"The tape is about to run out."

"That's okay, I think I've got it now."

Clark switched off the recorder and, with it, his intimidating alter-ego.

"Oh, I'm so sorry I slapped you! Really! I'm so sorry! I don't know what came over me. Here, slap me back, right across the face, hard. It's all right."

"No, that's okay," Ricky said, getting up to leave. "I deserved it. You know more about relationships than you give yourself credit for, Clark. And you're cheaper than a shrink! I'm going to go apologize to Maggie, right now. I feel better already!"

A rejuvenated Ricky stood at Maggie's door, apprehensive but still hopeful. He took a deep breath, pressed the bell, and as he waited, ran through his apology in his mind one more time.

The door opened. It was Claire, greeting him with a scowl.

"Well, look who's here—someone with a lot of cheek. And it's quite red, as well. What do you want?"

"I'm here to grovel, please—if Maggie will allow me to."

"First of all, you can grovel, but only if I'm allowed to watch, because you've really made her unhappy, and she didn't do anything wrong."

"I know."

"And I want to see you beg for her forgiveness. Beg like a dog."

"Yes, you can watch."

"Second of all, she's not here now. I don't know where she is."

Linda's voice called from within the flat, getting louder as she approached.

"Who is it, Claire...Oh, it's you, the cross-dressing prowler. Are you here to beg Maggie's forgiveness, or do you just need to borrow my miniskirt for the evening?"

"Definitely the first one," Ricky said, still aching with embarrassment. "Claire and I were just discussing the terms of my surrender. I guess you want to watch me grovel, too?"

"I've got nothing planned for today. All right."

"If it's humiliation you want to see, I'll wear the miniskirt, too."

"The hell you will!" Linda objected. "You'd stretch it beyond all recognition."

"But," Claire added, "for what it's worth, we did tell Maggie that it wasn't right for her to muck you about by cancelling dates with you. We know how she feels about you, Ricky, but she shouldn't give you the idea that she's taking you for granted."

"Oh, well...thanks."

"We know you're a good chap."

"Thanks again. But I still want to apologize to her."

"Too right, you will!" Linda snapped. "We'll let her know you were here."

At the same moment Ricky was trying to fend off Claire and Linda, Maggie had ventured into his building and tip-toed down the hall, stopping at his door. She knocked, waited, and knocked again. There was no sound from inside. Discouraged, she turned and slowly walked back the way she had come, stopping at Clark's open door. He was, as usual, busy tinkering with some recording equipment.

"Hi Clark," she said sadly.

"Oh, hi, Maggie. Ricky's not in, then?"

"No."

"It's, uh, good to see you."

"Thanks."

"Come in," he offered with a gesture of his hand.

"You're sure? You don't hate me?"

"Nah. Just watch your step."

"Oh, you don't have to tell me. I know I've been awful. I don't want to do anything to lose Ricky."

"No, I mean watch your step on those wires. Don't trip."

She stepped carefully around the wires and equipment scattered across the floor.

"Sit here," he said, patting the seat of the chair facing him. "I don't often get visitors of the fairer sex."

"Oh, haven't you heard? We're not called the fairer sex anymore."

"You're not?"

"Well, I mean, we *are* the fairer sex, but we're equal."

"Equal to what?"

"To men!"

"Oh, right."

"That's what the feminists are saying, anyway. It's been in all the magazines. Not that I need them to tell me I'm an equal, right?"

"I'm not even sure what a feminist is," he conceded.

"You really need to get out more, Clark. Meet some girls." Her voice went soft, and sad. "Who knows, maybe that's what Ricky's doing right now."

"Oh, I don't think so."

"I got awful cross with him."

Clark sat for a moment, wrestling with a thought. "Maybe I shouldn't do this, but I'd like to play this for you."

"What is it?"

"It's Ricky."

"Oh, just mucking about on your tapes?"

"No, not mucking about. He might kill me for letting you hear this, but I'll risk it, if it helps you two. Take a listen. I'll be back in a moment."

He switched on the tape recorder and eased himself out of the room as it played, to give Maggie privacy.

She listened to the interview, amused by it at first, especially by Clark's rabid interrogation technique, but quickly found herself hanging onto Ricky's every word of contrition for their falling out, and for his behaviour. By the time Clark's recorded voice announced, "The tape is about to run out," Maggie had tears welling up in her eyes, and a lump in her throat.

The flesh and blood Clark returned to the room. "I just talked the landlord into giving me an extra week to pay my rent! Not bad, eh!"

Maggie got up and gave Clark a hug. "You're a good friend, Clark."

She said nothing else as she continued out the door and down the hall, to the exit.

Ricky kept a quick pace on his way back home, lost in thought, and more determined than ever to offer Maggie a soaring, impassioned, no-holds-barred apology. He recognized the irony of how, during this week apart from her, he missed her even more than he had for those long months—even years—when they were separated by an entire ocean. This time was different. They were a real couple now—weren't they? He didn't care what label would best apply to them. All he knew was that he felt he had endangered what they had, due to his whiny selfishness--or however Clark had so eloquently phrased it.

Maggie continued her march from Ricky's building to her own, finally knowing for certain what she had suspected--that he had been just as unhappy as she was during their time apart and that they needed to end the silence and patch things up. They needed to be together again.

They both turned the corner at the same time, narrowly missing a head-on collision.

"Oh, hi," she said, startled, but with the slightest trace of a grin.

"Hi," he returned.

"I just stopped by your flat."

"I just stopped by yours, too."

"I'm not home," she said.

"I know. I'm not home, either."

"I know."

"Oh, yeah…me too," he said, shifting his weight from one foot to the other.

Maggie scrambled for a phony explanation for her visit to Ricky's flat. "I, uh, I just thought you might need reminding that *Sgt. Pepper* comes out on Thursday."

"Oh, yeah! I haven't forgotten. I guess you've been hearing a lot of things about it, huh?"

"Just a little."

"Have you heard any of the songs yet?"

"No, I didn't want to spoil it for myself. I think the BBC played them the other day, but I'd rather sit down and listen to the whole album at once, at home."

"Yeah, me too."

An awkward pause followed, but Maggie had no intention of letting it last long enough for things to get too uncomfortable. It wouldn't be helpful to stop the modest momentum of their exchange. "I'm planning to buy my copy at the HMV store on Oxford Street on Thursday morning, after I call in sick. Do you want to go with me?"

The invitation sounded to Ricky as if it had been personally delivered by an angel from heaven—an angel who happened to be a serious Beatles fan.

"Of course I want to go with you," he said, almost choking on his words.

"Good."

He couldn't keep it in any longer. He had to tell Maggie how sorry he was for everything. Go for broke, he thought. Just let it all out.

He took a deep breath. "Maggie, I am *so* sorry for-"

She quickly put her fingers to his lips, catching him in mid-syllable. "Shh," she said softly. "So am I."

She gently put her arms around him and pulled him tight against her—something she was so good at, he had always thought. Was she sniffling? He thought he heard it, but he wasn't sure.

"Never again, eh?" she whispered in his ear.

"Never again," he said.

Chapter 33

Thursday arrived and, almost like a sixth sense, Maggie could feel the excitement emanating from every Beatles fan in the city. Today was the day every music stockist from HMV in Oxford Street, to NEMS in Liverpool, to the independent music stores in the highlands of Scotland, would be displaying the latest Beatles record in their display windows and on their shelves. As far as Maggie was concerned, *Sgt. Pepper's Lonely Hearts Club Band* was the most exciting thing to hit the music world since, well, *Revolver,* the last Beatles album.

She and Claire met Ricky outside his building that morning and the three of them headed in the direction of Oxford Street. They were going to get there before the shop opened; Maggie imagined there would be long queues and she didn't want to be disappointed by having to wait another week for more stock to arrive. Ricky followed her lead by calling in sick to work. Claire, being her own boss, wouldn't have believed her own illness excuse, so she allowed herself only the morning off.

Ricky and Maggie walked hand-in-hand on the way, as Claire kept a quicker pace a few steps ahead.

"Come on, you two, they're almost open!"

"All right, Claire," Maggie said with a tad of annoyance, "give them a chance to switch the lights on!"

They approached the store and, as Maggie had guessed, found a queue. It wasn't as long as the queues for the first few Beatles album releases, but the fans seemed just as excited.

"Do you think they're all here for *Sgt. Pepper*?" Ricky asked.

"Well, let's be honest, I'll bet they're not here for a new Freddie and the Dreamers record. But our chances look good. I think they'll have enough copies for us."

The trio joined the end of the queue of about thirty young people, all of them buzzing about the Beatles. But they still had twenty minutes before the shop was due to open.

The shop-front display windows were enough to both keep Maggie and Claire excited and impatient. Huge posters of the Sgt. Pepper album cover decorated the glass front. Maggie had seen photos of it for *British Music Express*, but it was so much more exciting seeing them ten times the size of her magazine.

A woman from EMI records was present, to hand out special Beatles promotional buttons for only the first hundred people waiting in line. Maggie took hers and proudly positioned it right under her collar. Claire did likewise, while Ricky discreetly slipped his into his pocket for the time being.

A few people down the line started singing Beatles hits, choosing them randomly, starting with "Can't Buy Me Love," followed by "Help". Claire, Maggie and Ricky joined in. The crowd seemed to focus mainly on the chorus, and were catching Maggie and Claire out every time they went to sing a verse.

Finally, a cheer from the front of the line sent a stir all the way down to the back. The store manager had finally come to unlock the doors. He and the HMV staff were all sporting the same buttons the EMI lady handed out to the early customers. As soon as the doors were opened, the crowd rushed inside, heading straight for the large Beatles display holding hundreds of copies of *Sgt. Pepper*. Maggie, Ricky and Claire came within reach of the long-awaited album--another minute and they would have the fresh vinyl in their hands.

"Over here!" Claire waved in her excitement, picking up her copy. Ricky followed close behind, turning to Maggie behind him. "When did I ever think I'd be buying a Beatles album on release day, in England, with you?"

Maggie smiled. "Guess we've come a long way since the days when I sent you their first 45s."

But before she knew it, she was several steps behind him on the way to the display, somehow finding herself face to face with a man in his seventies, glancing down at her Beatles button.

"Excuse me, miss, I'm looking for the complete set of Beethoven's symphonies, recorded in 1963 by the Berlin Philharmonic, conducted by

Herbert von Karajan."

"Well, I hope you find it," Maggie said, trying to squeeze past him, with her eyes fixed on the Sgt. Pepper display less than ten feet away.

"Can you show me to the classical music section? This store is so big, I don't think I'd know where to find it."

This was the last thing on Earth Maggie wanted to do at that moment. She was tempted to inform him that he could find the classical music section by looking for the large, impossible-to-miss 'CLASSICAL MUSIC' sign hanging from the ceiling. But, with an eerie feeling of déjà vu, she sighed and said, "Oh…right, this way."

She reluctantly led the man to the impressive classical music department, home to nearly every recording of every piece of music written in the past several hundred years. They headed to the "B" section, by which time Maggie had already forgotten what the customer had asked for. Now, what did he say—Beethoven, played by Irving Berlin? No... Herbert Berlin?

Much to her own surprise, she found the box set in plain view, on a nearby display wall. "Ah, here it is, sir."

"Oh, wonderful. I imagine this has been a steady seller through the years. It's considered to be the definitive version of the Nine Symphonies."

"Oh, yes, it's been flying off the shelves."

"I must compliment your manager on hiring such an astute and helpful staff."

"Oh, no need, really. All in a day's work."

She managed to make her way back to Ricky without further interruption. They stood looking over the album's unique cover photo, and marvelled at how the song lyrics were actually printed on the back. No rock group had ever done that before. They exchanged a lingering smile.

"Don't just stand there getting all gooey-eyed," Claire called to them, pointing at the cash register. "Have you seen the queue?" There were three clerks ready and waiting to take the customers' money, and the trio happily joined the line.

Claire understood that Maggie and Ricky had planned to listen to the album on their own at his place, and she was okay with that. She had to get back to the hair salon anyway, and would need to wait until that evening before experiencing *Sgt. Pepper* for herself.

Back in Ricky's flat, he closed the curtains and kept most of the lights off, as Maggie carefully took the record from the fold-out sleeve.

"I hardly ever listen to a new record this early in the day," he explained. "It seems more of a late-afternoon or evening thing to do."

"Well, we can turn the clock around if it will help you lose track of time. Or do you want to wait until later to hear it?"

"No, now is fine!"

He put the disk on the turntable platter, switched it on, and in a few seconds, he and Maggie heard the fade in sounds of an orchestra tuning up.

From that point on, they were swept up in an amazing musical experience, filled with strange sound effects, instruments they had rarely, if ever, heard before, and lyrics bursting with imagery, puns, and even simple narratives—some happy, some sad, some just odd—but all fascinating.

They lay on the rug, holding hands, occasionally following along to the lyrics on the album cover, but mostly keeping on their backs, gazing at the ceiling as they absorbed the new Beatles creation.

After George's exotic, moody, sitar-inspired "Within You, Without You," the jaunty strains of Paul's "When I'm Sixty-Four" eased them further into their happy mood. They listened to Paul singing to his unnamed partner, asking if he could rely on being taken care of at the ripe old age of sixty-four. Ricky and Maggie looked into each other's eyes as the "cute" Beatle sang, *"Will you still need me, will you still feed me, when I'm sixty-four?"*

"Yes, I will," she quietly murmured with a warm smile, as if Ricky himself had asked her the question.

"What?"

"I will."

It took him an instant to make the connection, before taking in her meaning. He smiled back.

"Of course. And beyond."

They rolled toward each other, clutched each other tightly, and began a kiss that lasted well into the first half of "Lovely Rita, Meter Maid."

Ricky lay on his back again, stroking Maggie's hair as she rested her head on his chest. She began to speak, but kept her eyes fixed on the record player, rather than looking him in the eye.

"Ricky..." she began.

"Yeah?"

There was a pause. She didn't say anything else right away, as he expected. Was something wrong that she was hesitating to tell him? He waited a bit longer. Had she fallen asleep? Was she upset about something?

"I love you, Ricky."

He wasn't expecting that. But at that moment, the surprise was the greatest of his life.

"I love you too, Maggie."

Neither of them moved. They just stayed as they were at first, each replaying those words in their own heads, over and over again.

Twenty minutes later, he needed to take the phonograph needle and replay the remainder of the album, because neither he nor Maggie had heard a single note of the last three songs on side two.

The next day, Maggie and Claire sat facing each other on the sofa, their feet up and crossed beneath them, a bowl of crisps on the middle cushion to share. Maggie had a faraway look in her eye.

"It was just so...special," she said dreamily. "You know, I fell in love with the Beatles five years ago, and I fell in love *to* the Beatles last night."

"Last night? Hardly, girl. You've been in love with him for years. But tell me everything!"   Claire reached for a salted flavoured snack and waited intently.

"It was one of the new songs, 'When I'm Sixty-Four'-"

"Oh, yeah, that old-timey sounding one. I love that song."

"Well, listening to those words, I decided, I want to do all those things for Ricky when *I'm* sixty-four. I don't want to ever be without him."

"Mags, do you know what you're saying?"

"Of course I do."

"Aw, that's so sweet. No, it's fantastic! Then what happened?"

"Well, we kissed--among other things."

"Other things?"

Maggie nodded with a big smile.

"Did fireworks explode?"

"You could say that," Maggie giggled. "Unless that was his furnace. But this was different, because of what we said to each other."

"And the rest?"

Maggie just smiled again, quite coyly.

"Mags!" Claire repeated, this time with more of a gasp. "You didn't! You did? Really? Well, to be honest, I thought you two were already…I mean…and you just haven't been very talkative about it."

"No, I would have told you."

"I thought you were holding out on me."

"No--I mean, we've been *feeling* like a couple, anyway."

"Well, yeah, holding hands and kissing each other all the time was a bit of a giveaway. And that's just in public."

"Really, Claire. I don't know, it just sort of evolved over time."

Claire took a handful of crisps from the bowl and crunched them appreciatively.

"I love him," Maggie continued. "I just had to be a hundred percent sure. And I am. Now, it actually hurts that he has to leave soon. I don't think I can say goodbye."

Claire nodded. "It will be hard I guess, but it won't be goodbye. You'll see him again. It'll be your turn to visit him next."

"But it will be months. A year maybe. He might forget about me, or his feelings will fade."

Claire huffed. "I doubt it. He's besotted with you. Besotted, I say!"

"Three thousand miles is a long way."

Claire shrugged. "But it's do-able. You remember jet planes? You've already been on one. And he loves you! And you know that can't be bad...Hmmm, that sounds familiar."

Maggie smiled. "He does. And I love him." She shook her head. "Those Beatles. They're to blame for this!"

Ricky sat almost nose-to-nose with Clark.

"I have something to tell you."

"Uh oh," Clark said, leaning back, "the last time anyone said that to me, I was six, and my father was explaining why my pet turtle hadn't moved for three days."

"No, no, nothing like that. I think I'm engaged."

"What? You're engaged?"

"I said I *think* I'm engaged."

"You *think* you're engaged? Don't you know?"

"I think I know. But I don't know."

"Did you propose to Maggie?"

"Not really."

"Well, then, did she propose to you?"

"I don't know. Maybe. But girls don't propose to guys, do they?"

"I don't know, either. I haven't even had a date in...Well, anyway, what did she say?"

"She said, 'Will you still need me, will you still feed me, when I'm sixty-four?'"

"What does that mean?" Clark asked, bewildered. "You'll be engaged when you're sixty-four?"

"It's a song, on the new Beatles album, *Sgt. Pepper.*"

"So?"

"It's about people promising to still take care of each other even after they get old."

"I don't get it. Did she sing it to you or something?"

"Well, we sort of sang it to each other, as we were listening to the record. They printed all of the lyrics on the back cover, ya know. Isn't that cool?"

"And because you sang a song to each other, you think that means you're engaged? Man, I may not be very experienced, but I'm afraid to hear where you think babies come from."

"You had to be there. We had just made up after our big fight. But we were so happy to be back together, it was magical. And when that song came on, we were sort of looking into each other's eyes, and sang it as if we were promising to take care of each other, when we're sixty-four—or older, presumably."

"Well, that sounds nice, I guess. But did either of you actually get on one knee and say, something like 'Will you marry me'?"

"We were already on the floor, so technically that would have required getting *up* on one knee. But no, neither of us did that. It was more subtle than that."

"So, then, I would conclude that if neither of you asked the other, then you're not engaged."

"But I *think* we are," Ricky insisted.

"Right, this conversation has come full circle—a couple of times. Let me know when you've put a ring on her finger. Until then, you can sing to each other all you want to, but I'd say you're not engaged."

"But we're committed to each other exclusively."

"Well, that is a good first step, I'll give you that."

Ricky awoke on the morning of June 14 with a sinking feeling. This was his last day in London. In another 24 hours, he would be on his way to Heathrow, leaving the fabulous city, and the fabulous girl, he had grown to love.

One last day. Maggie had already told him they could do anything and everything he wished for the entire day. He gave it some thought, and decided he really just wanted to take one last, grand sweep through the city, stopping at their favorite sites, and then finish with dinner at The Spice of Bengal, the same Indian restaurant they dined in on his first evening in London.

"Let's walk 'til we drop," was his simple directive. And so they did, with some occasional help of a cab or the tube. Hyde Park, Trafalgar Square, a walk along the Thames in the shadow of the Parliament buildings--and, of course, EMI studios on Abbey Road, just to be within reach of the Beatles, who just might have been recording a new classic as their fans kept vigil on the sidewalk outside.

As the low rays of the sun began to give way to dusk, it was on to Piccadilly Circus and Leicester Square for some free entertainment from the buskers and street performers.

They watched a limbo dancer contort his slender body under a bar only inches from the ground, to the accompaniment of a flute and tambourine. "I'm envious of you," Ricky said to Maggie. "You'll still get to see all of this any time you want to."

"Maybe," she said. "You really think it would be the same without you?"

Finally, they returned to the restaurant, where neither of them needed more than a quick glance at the menu.

"I'll have the birhiani and egg pilau rice," Maggie told the waiter.

"And I'll have the onion bahjis, and chicken madrass," Ricky said.

"Very good, sir," the waiter nodded.

"Ooh, look at you," Maggie said proudly, "So well-versed in the cuisine of the sub-continent!"

"You've taught me well."

"Maybe, but I get the feeling you've been here a few times without me."

"I plead guilty. But Clark isn't as pretty a date as you are."

They held hands, allowing the moment to linger. She finally broke the silence.

"What are you thinking about?"

"Besides how tired my feet are? Oh, I'm just looking back on the past six months. I had no idea the time would fly by like this. I can't believe I'm leaving tomorrow."

"You came here as a newspaper intern…" she began, as he nodded.

"…And I'm *leaving* here as a newspaper intern."

"Not so!" she protested. "Well, technically, yes, but I think you've found your calling. Consider yourself an aspiring broadcast journalist now. Give radio a go, or something like it."

"I will, thanks to Clark. I just have to inform the dean at school. But look at you. When I got here, you were just a lowly staff writer, and now you're an award-winning journalist."

"I'm also the girl who's head-over-heels for--"

"Bahjis?" the waiter interrupted with a jolt, setting the dish down.

"Yes, bahjis..." Maggie said--and, once the waiter headed back to the kitchen, "I think a toast is in order."

She raised her glass and Ricky followed, "To Ricky, who flew three-thousand miles to pursue his dream of journalism, only to discover dreams aren't always what they seem--but it led him to his true passion, his true love."

She paused for a moment. Over the past few weeks, knowing Ricky's time in London was coming to an end, she had tried to stay positive with reassurances like, 'we still have two whole weeks together', 'we still have two whole days together',   But now they had only a matter of hours and Maggie couldn't put a positive spin on that.

"I did find my true love, Mags."

"So did I."

She felt a tear sliding down her cheek. He reached over and wiped it away with his thumb.

"We still have about twelve hours until we have to say goodbye," he said.

"We're not going to say goodbye though, right? Just more of a 'see you later'?"

"Yeah, because we'll definitely see each other again. Even if I have to swim the Atlantic."

She chuckled. "Silly Yank."

The day had arrived. It was Ricky's departure day. He looked out the window—again—straining to see down the street as far as he could, in each direction. Still no sign of the taxi.

"He's late! He's already ten minutes late!"

"No," Maggie said calmly, "he's only five minutes late."

"No, he was five minutes late five minutes ago. Now he's ten minutes late."

"Shall I phone the dispatcher and find out where the cab is?"

"We know where he is – he's ten minutes late, that's where he is."

"Don't panic, Ricky. You've still got plenty of time. Anyway, you don't have to seem so eager to get out of here."

"Of course I'm not. But missing an overseas flight isn't the same as missing a cab or a train. Or a bus, or a boat."

"You left out rickshaw," she said. "Ricky, calm down. We can just hail a cab out on the street. They pass by all the time."

He began to pace. "Too hit-or-miss. It could be twenty minutes before one comes by, and that one could be occupied." He checked his watch again. "Eleven minutes. How can we get there fast?" He froze as a burst of inspiration caught him in mid-step. "I know! Reg! He can take us!"

Maggie wasn't impressed. "You mean, if he's not already busy. He might not even be home now."

"But if he is home, I'll offer to pay him. He's an absolute maniac on the road. He'd be perfect."

"A maniac? That's your idea of perfect?"

"What I mean is that he goes to Heathrow all the time to take pictures of celebrities getting off planes. He knows all of the shortcuts to get there."

Maggie knew of Reg's preferred mode of transportation. "On his Vesper? That little scooter?"

"No, he has a car—his wife's car. He can use that."

"If she's not already driving it around somewhere."

"Only one way to find out." He fumbled through his address book, dialed Reg's number, and waited.

"Reg? It's Ricky...Yes, I'm still here, that's why I'm calling. We need to get to Heathrow right away. Can you take us?...No, in your car.

Maggie's, coming, and so is all of my luggage, so the Vespa just won't do...Oh? How hungover?...Well, can you walk straight, and drive?...No, just one at a time...You're sure? Good enough. Can you get to my flat right away? I'll pay you...Oh, I don't know, double the regular cab fare to Heathrow. That's all the money I can spare...Yeah, I thought so. Please hurry!"

He hung up with a big sigh of relief. "He'll be here soon."

"Quite a friend, I must say."

"Friend? He's only doing it for the money. Although he did add that it would be a pleasure for him to escort me out of the country."

"Are you sure he's sober?" she asked with suspicion.

"He probably is by now. They had a farewell party for me after work yesterday at the pub around the corner from the office."

"But you were with me after work."

"Yeah, I wasn't invited. It leads me to suspect that it wasn't really a party for me. They were using it as an excuse to get smashed--as if they ever needed an excuse. Come on, let's wait outside."

As they sat with Ricky's luggage on the front steps of the building, Claire and Linda arrived, as did Clark and Mitchell a few minutes later. Ricky's emotions prompted him to address his friends with a heartfelt good-bye.

"I'm going to miss you all so much," he began, just as Reg's car appeared from out of nowhere and came to a screeching halt alongside the curb in front of them.

Leaving the engine running, Reg jumped out, and in his finest, no-nonsense mode, tossed the luggage into the trunk, adjusting his hat and unlit cigarette (in deference to Ricky's sensitive respiratory system), and hustled his passengers into the car.

"We'll miss you, Ricky!" Claire called out, her eyes getting moist.

Reg turned to Ricky and Maggie in the back seat. "Hang on."

The car peeled out down the street before any more sentimental good-byes could be exchanged. True to form, Reg expertly weaved in and out of the London traffic like a veteran Hollywood stunt driver. Ricky was certain he saw his own entire life flash before his eyes--with repeats. Maggie experienced the same phenomenon, having shut her eyes completely for most of the first twenty minutes, out of some primal self-preservation reflex.

It wasn't until they were on the motorway headed toward the airport when Reg bothered with proper conversation.

"'Ere, are *both* of you going to America?"

"Why, would you charge us extra if we were?" Maggie snapped.

"No, Reg, I'm the only one going," Ricky said, exasperated.

Maggie wrapped her arms around Ricky. "But I might visit him at Christmas," she informed Reg.

"Oh, so will I have to drive you to Heathrow then as well?"

"No, please don't!" she implored. "I'll make other arrangements."

At the airport, Reg parked his car swiftly, to the sound of screeching tires, leaving it somewhat slanted in its space. He didn't care. They had made it to the airport in good time. As they pulled the suitcases out, Ricky and Maggie knew they only had moments left before they would have to say goodbye.

The trio made their way through the terminal entrance, where they were nearly consumed by the activity of people hustling in all directions and families saying goodbye to loved ones. Ricky turned to face Maggie, and took a deep breath.

"I guess this is it. I had a brilliant time."

"Me too," she said.

"It was okay," Reg shrugged apathetically. His attention quickly turned to some mystery person causing quite a stir on the main concourse. He saw a small crowd of people taking pictures of the unseen individual. He sniffed the air like a predator in the wild detecting its prey. "I smell a celebrity. See you in a bit!"

He hurried off in the direction of the crowd.

"Good ol' Reg, always the sentimental one," Ricky said.

"He *will* drive me back home, won't he?"

"Oh, sure. He's like a dog chasing a squirrel. He always comes back, eventually. As I was saying, I've loved every minute of it. Well, maybe not working for the *New London News*, but I guess I learned things. A lot of things."

"I'm going to miss you, Ricky. So much."

They pulled each other into a hug. No words were needed, just a few appreciative moments.

A voice came over the speakers. "Flight 005 to New York is now ready to board. Can all passengers please make their way to the gate."

"That's me," said Ricky.

"Don't forget me?" she said, with a wisp of desperation in her voice.

He felt almost insulted by the question. "How could I forget about you? I'm in love with you."

"I'm in love with you too. We'll write to each other, and phone?"

"Every day."

She smiled. "Well, perhaps not *every* day. We'll get writer's cramp. And only phone if you're sure you can afford it! I will, as well. But I'll miss you. The second I get enough money, I'm coming to see you."

"I'll help with the air fare."

He leaned in and kissed her. They both savoured the moment. Tears began streaming down her cheeks.

"I have to go now," he said, his voice beginning to quiver. "Take care of yourself. Be good."

"Have a safe trip--from me to you!"

He nodded and smiled, then turned and headed for the gate, wondering whether a new phase of his life was ending, or just beginning. Perhaps both.

Maggie watched him recede into the crowd as Reg returned to her side. She didn't notice him.

"It was only Roger Moore struttin' around like he owns the place," he said with disappointment.

Maggie still didn't hear him. "That's the man I'm going to marry," she said, watching Ricky disappear down the concourse.

"Roger Moore? Good luck with that, love."

Epilogue

Maggie Kramer
55 East 9th Street
New York, NY 10003

10 April 1970

Dear Claire:

I've taken the morning off, partly to write to you, and partly because it's a   beautiful day in the city and I'm skivving off work, which has been hectic, as always, but I've decided to skip the office and work from home, maybe go to Washington Square Park and sing along with the hippies. But the first thing I do when I'm supposed to be working is write to you whilst I wait for Ricky's radio show to come on. He sends his love. His show is doing well, he gets a five minute slot now a few times a day. Doesn't sound like much, but it's popular, and his boss thinks he might get more air time when they move around the schedule. We'll see.

I found a spent roll of film you left behind on your last visit, so I went and got the photos developed. I've enclosed them with this letter, they're fab! I'll send them to you next week.

I hope you and Clark are well. You must be crazy busy opening the new salon. Three in as many years, eh? You've got your own empire!   I'm so proud of you.

Ricky sat at his desk preparing his notes for his mini-program, as he called it. His ten o'clock segment would include an interview with a record producer about where music might be headed in the 1970s. Later in the day he would introduce his "Where are they now?" segment, catching up on fading pop stars who had enjoyed only brief success in the '60s. His first installment was to feature the one and only Eric Sellers, and his latest attempt at a comeback. At last, Ricky was able to combine his journalistic skills with broadcasting, while becoming somewhat of a minor celebrity himself. His listenership may have been modest, but he was being heard on FM radio in New York several times a day, and was rubbing shoulders with some big names in music, broadcasting, and TV. With Maggie working for Oswald Osbourne, overseeing the growth of a trendy magazine for young people, life was good.

Ricky gave his notes one last glance as he got up from his desk, and started toward the studio, just minutes before he had to be on-air. He heard a buzz of commotion. His producer, Ted, called out from the newsroom.

"Hey, Ricky, over here. Take a look at this."

There wasn't much time to spare, but it sounded important. He poked his head in the newsroom and saw Ted standing by the teletypes, holding a few sheets of paper freshly ripped from one of the machines. A few colleagues stood close, straining to read it.

"What is it, Ted? I'm on in a few minutes."

"Reuters is saying the Beatles have broken up."

"What?"

"Doesn't seem to be a rumor, like the other times. Paul released an official statement today, saying that he's leaving."

Ricky's first thought was that it must be some kind of joke by his co-workers—and a cruel one, considering he was due on the air in about two minutes. But the proof was on the teletype sheets Ted handed to him.

"Read it fast," Ted instructed, "and open your segment with it. Hell, just scrap what you had planned and stay with this. We might be the first station in the city to air it."

"With no confirmation?"

"We'll start making calls and watch for more on the wires, but for now, read it. Take it with you into the booth."

Ricky couldn't believe it. But he had no time to process the information for himself before announcing it to his listeners.

"Good morning, New York, This is Ricky Kramer with you, with a bulletin of sorts we've just received over the news wires. According to a press release put out by Paul McCartney through the Beatles' Apple label, Paul has announced his departure from the Beatles, and it seems the other group members have also decided to go their separate ways. They had been working on various side projects in the past year or so, but no Beatle has come out and said publicly that the group will no longer continue—until now. The group, who had their first hit in England back in 1963, changed the world of music in the years since, and touched the hearts of millions of fans--but now, from the looks of things, no more."

Listening at home, Maggie sat on the sofa, wiping away a small tear escaping from the corner of her eye. This was it. It was all over. She hoped it wasn't true, like the morbid rumor the year before, about Paul supposedly being dead. But she knew this was for real. No more Beatles. The idea left her numb, as she continued listening to Ricky doing his best to speak without notes and still try to make some sense of the news he was imparting to his listeners. The past ten years of his and Maggie's life had been anchored in their love of the Beatles. And now the Beatles were over. What, if anything, could fill that void?

Ricky needed to wrap up his on-air segment. "I can almost hear the hearts of Beatles fans breaking right now, and one fan in particular," he said.

As soon as he was off the air, he phoned Maggie.

"Were you listening?"

"Yes! Is it true?"

"It seems to be," he said.

"Maybe they're just taking a break?"

He sighed. "I don't think so. The signs have been there for a while, if you think about it."

"I don't want to think about it. I can't believe it's true."

"Me either. I'm sorry, Mags, but I guess it had to happen someday."

"When can you be home? I suddenly feel very lonely. I want to be with you."

"I can't get home any earlier than usual, I'm sorry. It's gonna be a long day."

"When you get here, I want to listen to Beatles records all night tonight, until we pass out."

"Okay.'

"Ricky, I'm glad I heard it from you."

By the time he got home, they had both had several hours to absorb the news, but they both felt exhausted as well. They kept their promise to skip watching TV that night, and spend it curled up listening to the music that had served as the soundtrack to their relationship, virtually from the beginning.

"Ya know," Ricky said at one point, "I was just thinking--it's almost fitting, in a weird way, that I first heard about the Beatles from you, and you first heard about their break-up from me."

"That's true!" she said. "Something cosmic about that. But I think you got the best out of that deal."

"Sorry."

"Remember the time when we tried having a conversation using only their song titles?"

"Yeah, after a few turns, we weren't making much sense."

She smiled as the song "From Me To You" began. "After this first came out, I signed my letters to you that way."

"Then I started signing mine that way, too."

"My idea first!"

"It didn't seem as romantic when I signed one of mine *I am the walrus!*"

"Silly Yank," she said, holding him tighter--as they listened...and remembered.

The End